LUV UNDER STARLIGHT

LUV SHUV

N M PATEL

Editor: Librum Artis Editorial Services

Proofreader: Editing4Indies

❀ Created with Vellum

DEDICATION

To all the eldest daughters who bear the weight of the world on their shoulders, who make endless sacrifices for their families, you are the unsung heroes of countless households.
You deserve happiness.
You deserve to choose yourself.
You deserve the greatest love.

AUTHOR'S NOTE

Trigger Warning

Mention of the suicide of a family member in the past, mention of suicide of two farmers.

1

Song: Mere Sapno Ki Rani
  - Kishore Kumar

Meera

L*axminagar*

FIVE YEARS AGO, my father killed himself.

He left behind a mother, a daughter, a son, a never-ending debt, and constant, gut-wrenching pain. I still wasn't used to living with that pain—the constant itchy stab to my heart. Maa was struggling. My little brother was growing up without feeling the love of a father and not even realizing the loss of his presence. And if it were up to me, he never would.

The quick, unmistakable footsteps that could rival the stomping of a herd of elephants alerted me of the arrival of my baby brother, Hari, pulling me out of melancholy and bringing a smile to my face. A moment later, Hari ran into my room, jumped on my tidy bed, and shouted in our native language, Gujarati, "Didi! Maa is calling you downstairs!" Didi is a respectful term to address an elder sister.

"I'm right here, Hari. You don't have to shout." I tried to clutch his hand to get him down, but he was an expert in escaping my grip. He giggled at my failed attempts to get him off the bed and continued bouncing randomly across the now-rumpled bed.

"Hari... Hari! Stop jumping." I got on the bed and scooped him into my arms. His skinny little body twisted to get out of my grip, but as soon as I lightly tickled under his neck, he shrieked and burrowed into my arms.

"Didi! Stop! I pee. I pee." I released him at once, and he ran off across the room.

Some of my hair had come out of my bun. I undid my hair and ran my fingers through the curly, unruly mess. I got the entire thing in control, and as I twisted them into a top bun, I said to Hari, "Go tell Maa that I'll be there in a few minutes."

He ran off, already screaming my message for Maa. I shouted right behind him, "Careful, Hari!"

That did nothing. I could hear him running downstairs.

I shook my head and got back to packing the last of my things in boxes. Not that I was going anywhere. Just moving most of my stuff from my room upstairs to the living room downstairs.

We had a tenant coming to live with us for the next three months.

From *America*.

The man would pay us five hundred dollars a month for rent. That was equal to about 41,000 Indian rupees. I would gladly sleep in our bathroom for that much money. My life was stuck in paying off the endless debt my father had taken on to make ends meet as a farmer, and I was tired.

Tired of constantly putting aside most of the salary I earned from teaching in the local government school.

Tired of asking for the compensation the government promised to give to the families of the farmers who committed suicide.

Tired of begging Maa to sell off everything and move to a city, where I could care for them better.

Tired of dealing with the cruelty of money-hungry sharks.

Tired of saying no to Hari every time he wanted a toy that I couldn't afford because I bore the cost of my father's helplessness.

Tired of seeing the sadness in our house.

Just. So. Tired.

I opened my cupboard, grabbed a pile of salwar and kameez—the traditional Indian outfit of loose pleated trousers worn with a tunic—and dumped them in the cardboard box.

To get over one lakh rupees in three months, I would happily kiss the man's feet in gratitude for wanting to stay with us. Moving out of my room was no big deal to me.

It helped that I knew the man.

Luke.

I didn't even realize I'd stopped packing as his face flashed behind my eyes, followed by his joyful laughs and his intense gaze.

He visited the village last year with Sam and Akira. Akira's family used to live in this village years ago, before they moved to the city of Ahmedabad. Akira's father and my father were childhood friends.

I still remember playing with Akira and her cousin Ria as a child. They would bring me toys from the city. But as time passed, their visits to the village became fewer. They had their own life in the city. And we were all but forgotten.

Last year, Akira told her family that she had fallen in love with her American classmate, whom she met while studying in

America. Her family brought Sam and Luke to show them their village, and Akira and Ria invited me to join them as they roamed the landmarks.

That was where I met Luke.

"*Hi, Meera.*"

"*Hi.*"

Two words from him and one word from me. Throughout his trip, we'd exchanged three words in total. His eyes on me had burned, making me feel as if he could look into me and know all my secrets. Two days. That was all I had been able to handle. Their fortune, their lack of burdens in life, and their easy laughter were too much to bear.

I think Luke saw it.

When others had laughed too much, he had always looked at me. He looked at me when they bought things from the local market without thought. As if he could read my mind and see my envy...and my despair. I did not meet his eyes. Not once.

And now, he was coming back.

Not for a day or two.

For three long months.

To live with me. With my family. He would see the life we lived.

My life had no place for people's judgments or pity, yet the thought of Luke seeing my living situation burned my insides.

One lakh rupees. One lakh rupees. One lakh rupees.

Those were the only three words I had to keep repeating in my mind. The faster I got the money, the closer I would be to paying off all the debt.

With those three words in mind, I grabbed my cassette player and collection of cassettes and gently placed them in another empty box.

With those three words in mind, I packed up the last of my belongings and left the room for the person who would lead me one step closer to freedom.

Luke

A blast of hot air pushed me back inside the air-conditioned airport of Ahmedabad. The same thing happened to me last year when I came to this boiling hot city with my best friend Sam and his girlfriend, Akira.

Our trip was too short for me then, so I returned this year. The only struggle was tolerating the sweltering heat of summer. Just yesterday, I was home in my tiny apartment in New York City, enjoying the cool spring breeze. I took a deep, cool breath of the air-conditioned air and braved the outside once more.

I pushed the baggage cart in front of me, hoping it would protect me, and braced myself for the full impact of the hot air. I squinted my eyes in the bright sun and spotted the laughing faces of Aakar and Abhi, Akira's brothers. Before I could roll my cart to them, I stopped and got my shades and cap out of the front pocket of my carry-on bag. I learned my lesson the last time I had to face this cruel heat. By the time I put them on, Aakar and Abhi had made their way to me.

"Welcome back, Luke," Aakar said, pulling me in a hug.

"Hey, man. Good to be back." I slapped him on the back and turned to Abhi.

"I see you came prepared," Abhi said with a laugh and handed me a cool metal bottle.

"What's this?" I shook the bottle. I would've opened it if my other hand wasn't holding the baggage cart.

Aakar noticed and took over the cart. "Let's get you in an air-conditioned car."

He walked ahead as Abhi and I walked behind him.

I opened the cold metal bottle and looked inside.

Abhi shook his head, eyes shining in laughter. "Just drink it. You'll thank me."

I took a sip, and cold, orange-flavored water slid down my throat. My feet stopped walking, and all I could do was groan at the sheer relief that flowed through my body.

Abhi chuckled. "It's Glucon-D, our very own energy drink. If you plan to survive this summer, we'll have to stock you up."

I had no words. I squeezed Abhi's shoulder as I gulped down half the bottle. The drink cooled my body and pumped me with life. It was magic.

Once I had my little moment, we joined Aakar, who was nearly done putting my luggage in the car.

Aakar got into the driver's seat, Abhi got into the back seat, and I sat in the passenger seat. The car seat was hot enough to burn my skin where I touched it, but I had the elixir of life in my hand. When Aakar turned on the car, hot air blasted from the vents. By the time we were out of the parking lot and on the main road, the car had started to cool down.

Aakar was Akira's older brother and Abhi was younger. We had stayed with Akira's family for about two weeks last year when Sam came to meet her family to gain their approval for their relationship. Sam had brought me along for moral support. After some initial tough conversations between Sam and Akira's family, everything went well. We had a blast visiting the amazing historical monuments and architectural marvels.

We had even seen Akira's house in their ancestral village.

That tiny village is what drew me back to India today.

I had fallen in love with stepwells, an Indian architectural form. I had never seen anything like that in my life. And as an architecture student in his last year of grad school, I had the perfect opportunity to study them more for my final year thesis.

I planned to visit and study as many stepwells as possible during the three months of my summer break.

"So how is Akira?" Abhi asked.

I turned around to face him. "She's great. Happy. I'm glad she took an internship at Wilson & White Construction. Since I won't be there this summer, it will really help Sam out."

Sam's and my father jointly own Wilson & White Construction. Since we would soon take over the company, we also decided to provide architectural services. Hence, the post-grad degree in architecture.

Aakar nodded while Abhi asked, "Did she send me an iPad?"

I chuckled. "Yes. Hold on."

Opening my carry-on bag, I got the iPad out. The moment I handed it over, Abhi was lost to us.

Aakar shook his head. "You should've waited until we reached home."

"Nah, let him enjoy it, man."

"How come you decided to stay in Laxminagar and not our place here?" Aakar asked as he turned at a crossroad.

I fiddled with the AC vent as I thought out the answer. "Well, when we visited your village house last year, I loved the stepwell we saw there. Before coming here, I researched their history, and to be honest, the stepwell of your village is a perfect size for me to measure and document. I would love to observe and be a part of the culture and life revolving around the structure. I'm more interested in studying the utilitarian, cultural, and architectural aspects."

Well, that's what I said and what I made myself believe. I did not mention the somber-eyed woman I met in their village last year—the woman who tugged at something in my chest despite exchanging only three words with her. And no matter how many logical arguments I laid down for choosing that particular place to study the stepwells, my heart knew *she* was a good part of the reason I returned to the small village.

Aakar nodded. "Makes sense. And are you sure about

staying at Meera's place? We can open up our house in the village for you."

My heart jumped at her name.

Meera.

And yes, I had offered to rent a room at Meera's.

Hoping that Aakar would think I had gone red because of the summer heat, I nodded without meeting his eyes. "I'm sure. Akira mentioned that Meera's family had been struggling for a few years. I thought the rent money would help them out. I know you guys won't accept any rent if I choose to stay at your place. That's all."

"I still have to say, Luke. Their house is a bit small. And I'm not sure if you would be comfortable. At least you would have more privacy in our village house."

"Thanks for the offer, man. I appreciate it. And it's no inconvenience. If you think about it, I won't have to worry about food and other day-to-day shit by staying at Meera's place. I'm hoping they'll help me get settled and navigate the village."

Aakar nodded, his eyes focused on navigating the crazy traffic on the road. Once we stopped at the red light, he turned to me. "They're good people, Luke. I hope your living there helps them."

I nodded. "Yeah. When do we leave for Laxminagar?"

Abhi piped up. "How about you stay with us for a day or two? Mom has cooked a feast."

"Oh man, I love your mom's cooking."

"We'll have to shop for a few essential things before we leave for the village."

"Cool. I'm ready."

I still remember seeing Meera with Akira and her cousin Ria for the first time. She seemed to carry a million heartbreaks in her eyes. Her gaze lingered on other people's laughs while her own smiles were few and far between. She was with us but felt so far out of reach.

I recognized those stages of grief and anger and acceptance.

The pain and the helplessness in them compelled me to choose her village for my thesis.

Her family had been thrilled to let me rent a room at their place, and I'd let Akira handle everything with Meera.

Staying at Meera's place for three months would give me shelter, food, and help with managing all my site visits and different travels in India. In return, Meera would get the financial support she needed.

Simple.

And if I could make her smile a few times in the next three months, this trip would be worth it.

2

Song: *Leke Pehla Pehla Pyaar*
   - Asha Bhosle, Shamshed Begum and Mohammed Rafi

Meera

Laxminagar

The moment I turned onto the narrow dirt road leading to my house and the field, I saw it: a big car parked right at the entrance gate, leaving no space for my two-wheeler vehicle to enter the small compound of the house. I parked my Activa near the car and removed my helmet, hand gloves, and the dupatta—long scarf— covering my face for protection from the summer heat.

He was here. I'd had plenty of days to prepare myself, yet my heart pounded in my chest. I took a few breaths to get it under control before stepping into the house. I was barely two steps in when Hari ran at full speed and crashed into my hip.

"Didi! Didi! Look what I got!" he crowed, showing me a brand-new cricket bat in his hand and a ball in his other.

I lightly pinched his cheek, trying to capture his smile in my palm. "Oh wow, Hari. Who got you this?"

"Abhi bhai and Aakar bhai and Luke bhai. I got even more gifts, Didi. Come inside. I will show you." Hari clutched my wrist and pulled me with his entire body.

The moment I stepped inside, my mother's laughter greeted me. When did I last hear that sound? She was laughing at something Aakar bhai had said. Aakar bhai was about four years older than me, so it was natural to address him as bhai, meaning older brother. I looked around our small living room and the stairs leading up, searching for signs of others.

My eyes met Aakar bhai, and I smiled at him. "Was the drive okay?"

Aakar bhai's eyes softened, and a genuine smile lit up his face. "It was good. How are you, Meera? How is work?"

I moved into the small room and sat on the sofa adjacent to Aakar bhai. I kept my purse in my lap and clutched its strap. "I enjoy teaching, so work is good."

We talked in our native language, Gujarati, for the next few minutes.

Maa stood from her spot on the bed in the corner of our living room. "Meera, why don't you freshen up, and I'll reheat lunch?"

I nodded at Maa and Aakar bhai and got up. I was about to climb the steps when I remembered I didn't have my stuff in my room. I shook my head and went to the end of the hallway, where we had a big cupboard. I had stuffed all my clothes in there with Hari and Maa's clothes. I got a change of clothes and went to the bathroom in the small hallway.

I was out of the bathroom in five minutes. Maa would need some help in the kitchen since double the number of people were having lunch. I was rushing to the living room when I crashed into *him*.

Luke.

I instantly backed off a bit and hit the wall behind me.

"Uh... hey, Meera," he said.

A thrill went down my spine at hearing my name on his lips.

He ran a hand through his hair as he held a box in his other hand.

I looked at him, and my heart started to beat faster. His eyes were a warm brown, his gaze friendly and inviting. His lips curved up into a polite smile.

I tried to smile back. What came out was just a rough exhale.

"Hi. All settled?" I asked. My fingers automatically went to the dupatta and clutched the tiny ornaments lining its edge.

He looked at my hand clutching the dupatta and dragged his gaze at me. His cheeks were a little pink. "Ah... almost settled. A few things left."

"Good. Umm...if you'll excuse me, I have to go help Maa."

I ran off into the kitchen without waiting for a response. Maa was heating up the paneer sabzi and dal. "Meera, beta, please start preparing the roti while I set up the rest of the food."

I nodded and began kneading the rolled dough to soften it. By the time everyone sat on the floor in the living room, I'd prepared about thirty rotis. I bet Luke, Aakar, and Abhi never had to eat while sitting on the floor.

"Oh, what's all this?" Luke asked in English as everyone filled their stainless steel dishes and bowls. We didn't have fancy glass plates to serve food for our wealthy guests. Maa and Hari didn't understand what Luke said. Hari had just finished his fifth grade in school and had barely learned his English alphabet.

I looked at him, expecting perhaps wariness in his demeanor, but genuine curiosity shone in his eyes. Before I could answer, Abhi pointed at the dal and said, "This is lentil curry. Don't ask me the English name of this lentil."

"Split red gram," I blurted out.

My eyes widened in shock. So did Luke's.

But a big smile came over his face.

Before he could say anything, Abhi interrupted. "Wow, Meera Didi. That's cool. I have no idea what all our Gujarati dals are called in English."

Luke nodded his head in thanks, and I nodded back.

I absolutely did not focus on Aakar bhai looking at Luke and me.

Abhi kept the conversation going as we ate, and I listened. I felt my dupatta getting pulled. I looked down at Hari and raised my brows. He called me closer with his small hand.

I couldn't help but smile. I looked around, and my eyes met Luke's. He watched our interaction with a quiet smile as he kept eating. I bent down to get closer to Hari. He put his hand at my ear and brought his mouth closer.

He cleared his throat and whispered, "What are they talking about?"

My curious little brother. He didn't enjoy not understanding the grown-ups. I turned his face to whisper in his ear. "Abhi bhai is explaining the food to Luke bhai. He is from America. He doesn't know our food."

Hari rolled his eyes at me as if saying that grown-ups could do better.

I lightly poked my elbow at him and pointed at his dish. He quietly got back to eating his food without any more questions. I looked up to see Luke busy eating his food, totally eating it the wrong way. He took a bite of roti and ate the paneer sabzi with a spoon. I shook my head and continued eating everything with my hand, just like everyone else.

~

Luke

She smiled for her brother. When I ran into Meera, I'd almost dropped my box full of expensive pencils. She wore traditional Indian attire that I'd seen plenty of women wear on the streets. Abhi called it *salwar kameez*. She'd played with the scarf-like thing she wore around her neck when we talked.

And for the first time, *we talked*. Her slightly breathy voice made my heart clench. Little Hari was a bundle of excitement and energy. When we arrived at Meera's place, he had run out to greet us. He helped us carry small things from the car to my room on the second floor. The moment Abhi handed him the cricket bat and ball as a present, he had shrieked in delight.

How could Meera not smile at her brother?

Meera sat on the sofa, teaching something to Hari as he kept flopping around to get away. I tried not to laugh every time I passed the living room.

It was early evening when Aakar, Abhi, and I finished setting up everything. When Abhi went to get some chai, Aakar said, "You keep looking at Meera."

I swallowed the wrong way and hacked for a minute straight. I had not expected that from him. With a deep breath, I said, "No. No. I'm not. I'm just taking it all in, you know. I'll be living with them for the next few months. Just getting to know them."

Aakar didn't look convinced, but he nodded. "Sure. Anyway, Abhi and I will be leaving after chai. We're hoping to be back home by dinnertime. You all set? Need anything?"

I looked around my room. We had finished installing the air conditioner and making the queen-sized bed with new bedsheets and comforter. The room already had an empty cupboard, a desk, and a chair. One window opened to fields beyond, and the other window was right beside the door, which opened to a big terrace. A narrow flight of steps at the corner of the terrace led to the living room downstairs.

"Everything's perfect. Thanks for everything, Aakar. I really appreciate it. I think I'll manage from here on."

Aakar peered into my room from the window and nodded. "Yeah. And if you need anything else, you can ask Meera. I've talked to her about getting you a vehicle or something. She said she'd set you up tomorrow. So you can travel wherever and whenever you want."

"That's great. Thanks, man."

Abhi got three cups of chai from downstairs. Hari followed him quietly, sneaking glances at me. I gave him a big smile and a wave.

He gave me a big smile in return and showed me his yellow truck.

During lunch, I realized he didn't understand English. So I gave him an exaggerated thumbs-up and said, "Very good."

At his even bigger smile, I crouched down and extended my hand. "Luke," I said and pointed at myself.

He looked at Abhi and, at his nod of approval, placed his tiny hand in mine. "Hari."

"Hari," I said back, and he laughed. He had two gaps where he might've lost his baby teeth and a few new teeth popping up. Just adorable.

He offered me his yellow truck and played it back and forth on his hand.

Assuming he asked me to play, I shook my head and turned my finger, indicating, "Later, kiddo."

Abhi said something to him, and he ran off downstairs. We had our chai in silence.

I could see the barren farmland beyond.

"They stopped farming on this land five years ago," Aakar said, taking a sip of his chai.

"So Meera is the sole provider of the house?" I asked.

Aakar nodded, looking at the bright orange light reflected on the clouds. The sky was starting to turn a cool blue, and even the barren land looked a little golden. The air didn't burn as much as it did during the day.

The sun hadn't even set when Aakar gulped the last of his chai and said, "Okay, Luke. We need to leave if we want to reach home by dinner."

"Sure thing. I'll see you off."

We got down the stairs to find Meera's mom knitting on the double bed in the corner, her needles moving in a quick rhythm. I could hear the clangs of the pot, the sizzle of something cooking on the stove, and the aroma of stir-fried onions. We'd just had chai, yet my mouth watered.

Aakar went to where Meera's mom sat and talked to her in their native language. Abhi and I went outside, where Hari played near Aakar's car. In no time, Aakar was out. We exchanged hugs, and I promised to call soon. I called Hari near me when he crept too close, wanting to watch the car.

The moment the car disappeared, Hari turned to me, his hand clutching his little yellow truck, and waved in front of my face. His eyes bubbled with expectation and hope, so for the life of me, I couldn't deny him.

We played for what felt like hours, running his truck back and forth between us, him zooming the truck every which way. Every time I had to dive to get the car, he laughed. So I did it more. And he laughed more.

No words were needed.

Only laughter.

Not that my words would hold any meaning here for most of the family members.

Only one person understood my language.

Meera.

If I had any hope of having a regular conversation around here, I needed to befriend Meera and get her to talk to me. Fast.

3

Song: Ek Ajnabee Haseena Se
  - Kishore Kumar

Meera

I climbed the stairs leading to the second-floor terrace as I clutched a pillow and a blanket in one hand and my cassette player in the other. Soft sounds of a person's presence and movement carried from the partially closed door of my former room. I turned on the light in the hallway, placed all my things on the charpai—a traditional bed made of wooden posts and interwoven ropes stretching between the four sides of the bed— on the open terrace, and closed the door to the steps downstairs.

I planned to sleep on the terrace. I'd already prepared my bed by laying a mattress on the charpai. It was summer, and the living room had only one double bed where Maa and Hari slept. I didn't need a room to sleep in at night. What I needed was a moment of peace, some solitude, and a place where I could breathe out the day. What better place for that than under the stars?

I placed my cassette player at the foot of the bed and plugged it in to the outlet extender that went into the only available socket, which was outside Luke's bedroom wall. As I was laying down my blanket, I heard a cough behind me, causing me to startle and drop the pillow.

Luke had his hands outstretched, his posture in surrender. "I'm so sorry. I didn't mean to scare you. I was just trying to get your attention."

My body relaxed. I breathed out and tried to act calm, even though my heart was racing. "It's okay. Next time, use my name. I respond to that better."

He smiled. His easy, broad smile that made me want to smile back.

"Noted. So, Meera, how have you been?" he asked.

My name sounded different on his lips. Gentler. Smoother.

How does someone answer that question without lying? Did he really want to know that I was struggling, tired, living one day at a time, going through the motions, trying to put food on our plates every day?

No, he didn't. No one wanted to hear that.

"I've been good. Are you all set? Please do let me know if you need anything."

The light from the hallway fell on Luke, highlighting his broad shoulders as he leaned against the column.

He chuckled lightly and, with a sheepish look on his face, said, "Uh... Aakar told me you'd help me get a vehicle to use while I'm here. Just let me know when it's convenient for you. There's no rush."

"Oh, yes. Sorry, I forgot to bring it up. How about tomorrow morning? We can drop Hari off at school, and then I have some time before I have to teach my class. Would that work?"

"Yeah. That works great. Thank you so much."

Luke walked out into the terrace and looked up at the sky. He stood at the parapet, staring off at a distance, where land and sky met in the darkness. The rustle of the trees and the chirping of the crickets broke the silence of the night.

Luke took a deep breath, his back expanding, which for some insane reason caused butterflies to swoop low in my stomach. Wind ruffled his hair, his white T-shirt clinging to his body, making him look like an angel. Time stood still.

"It's so peaceful out here."

"Magic of the night," I murmured, my eyes riveted on his back.

He turned to me, and I quickly averted my eyes. He gave me a small smile. "Magic indeed."

His eyes drifted to my bed, and small lines appeared between his eyebrows as if my bed broke the spell of his magical night. "Okay, then. I'll be off to sleep."

I nodded.

He walked across the terrace and passed me, his head turned down. I shook my head and opened the folded blanket, my eyes on his retreating back.

All of a sudden, he turned around, and said, "Oh, what time do we leave tomorrow morning?"

"Seven thirty. Hari's classes start at eight."

"Cool," he said, taking a few steps backward.

As he turned around with a smile, he nearly collided with the column. He yipped and took a step back, and I couldn't help but chuckle at the sight.

He grinned back at me and shook his head, clearly knowing he looked like a fool. "You could have warned me," he said.

I tipped my head back and forth in a "maybe" motion. "Seven thirty sharp."

He saluted me quickly then retreated into his room, closing the door behind him.

Luke

I closed the door of my bedroom and moved over to the window that looks out to the terrace. Meera lay on the bed, looking up at the sky. I shouldn't be watching her. I held the window shutters and pulled them in to close them, but a soft, soulful melody stopped me. I opened the window shutters a little to look outside.

In the quiet of the night, a singer's sweet voice crooned in the background. Meera's fingers glided over her cassette player while she gazed up at the midnight sky, lost in her thoughts. As a gentle breeze blew through the air, it caused Meera's blanket to flutter, and she paused in her movements to feel the coolness of the night. The same breeze that touched her also ruffled my hair. The soft music and the singer's soulful voice made my stomach clench. The stillness of the night, with Meera gazing up at the sky and me watching her, felt oddly intimate.

I shook my head and closed the window gently to avoid making any noise. I could still hear the soft music that felt more like a lullaby.

I went to the other window, where we had installed the air conditioner. I turned it on, and the ceiling fan, and switched off the light and lay on my bed. I could see the fan's blades rotating steadily, making my eyes droop. My thoughts drifted to the image of Meera lying on her bed just on the other side of the wall.

A part of my mind was filled with questions. Was she cold? Was she hot? Did the mosquitos bother her? Was she comfortable? She did give up her room for me. I was struggling with guilt about that, but another part of my mind kept trying not to be concerned. She wouldn't have agreed to let me stay if she was uncomfortable.

I succumbed to sleep with the sounds of the sweet melody drifting into my room, the low creaking of the fan above, and the memory of Meera's chuckle that ended too soon.

INSISTENT KNOCKING JOLTED me out of my sleep. I waved my hand to shut it up, but the stupid, loud noise of the knocking was like a drumbeat to my brain. I pushed my head under the pillow, and it still didn't stop.

"What?" I groaned.

"Uh... Luke?" That soft sound traveled through the door and sent a surprising jolt of wakefulness in me.

My body automatically jumped out of bed and, without any mind of its own, walked to the door.

I opened the door to find Meera's hand raised to knock on the door again.

I squinted as the early morning light touched my eyes. "Hey, morning."

A pause as Meera looked at me. No expression whatsoever on her face. This girl could easily beat an experienced poker player.

I raised my brows in question, breaking her gaze. She cleared her throat and said, "We leave in an hour. I thought I'd wake you in case you forgot."

"Uh...yeah. Thank you. I'll get ready." I ran my hands through my hair and yawned.

She was still here. Our eyes met, and finally, a reaction. Light blush coated her cheeks, and she stumbled upon her words. "Uh... Would you like some chai and breakfast?"

I had brought a coffee machine with me. Abhi and Aakar had taken me shopping in Ahmedabad. "Oh no, it's okay. I don't want to trouble you."

Her cool stare met my eyes. "It's no trouble. I'm making

some chai for myself and Maa. And I'm already preparing breakfast for Hari. You're paying plenty of money, you might as well reap the benefits of home-cooked, traditional food."

Not a single smile this morning. She delivered everything in her no-nonsense tone. I couldn't help but smile at that. "Well, if you put it like that, I'd love some chai and breakfast."

She nodded, pushed some of her curly hair behind her ear, and left.

I went back into the room, got my toiletries bag, and went to the bathroom on my floor. Aakar had warned me about the toilet situation. And upon observation, yep, no toilet paper here. There was a water tap near the water closet with a small bucket under it. There was an even smaller container hanging off the bucket. Aakar's bathroom in the city also had a bucket. But they had a bidet. I won't lie—I did try that bidet at Aakar's place, where I had spent two days before coming here, and the force of the water was like a power washer. My poor asshole felt like it had been sandblasted.

So when we went shopping in Ahmedabad, I bought three giant packages of toilet paper. It was the only thing that reminded me of home, damn it, and I was keeping my toilet paper. Period. I finished my business, freshened up, took a quick shower, and was out the door in a few minutes.

I walked to my room to find Meera setting breakfast on the terrace. I put my old clothes on my bed, slung my wet towel on my shoulder, and walked to the terrace. "Where should I put my towel to dry?" There was no washer or dryer here.

With a chai in her hand, Meera pointed at the drying rack in the far corner of the terrace. "Thanks," I said, and hung the towel.

The sun wasn't out yet, and the gentle pinks and blues of the dawn bathed the field around the house. Cool, humid air blew Meera's stray hair that had come off her tight bun on top of her head. I walked closer and sat on the bed across from the one Meera sat on. I leaned forward and took my cup of chai. The moment I leaned back with my chai, Meera gulped down her cup and got up.

"I'll wake Hari up and get him ready. I'll call up when it's time to leave."

"Sure."

I took a few sips of the chai. The sweet, dense flavor of the tea and a slight spice that hit my tongue fired up my mind. The sky transformed from dawn to brighter orange, and I just had to get up to look at the fields around the house. I placed my chai on the wide parapet and got my camera from the room.

Arranging the camera atop the parapet, I tried to capture the approaching sunrise. The barren, rugged land appeared softer. The leaves of the trees seemed to have just woken up. The golden-orange light blanketed everything in its warmth. I even took a photo of the cup of chai with the beautiful sunrise in the background.

Before long, I'd finished the chai and was going through the pictures in the camera when a light flurry of footsteps had me turning behind. Little Hari stood at the stairs, his small face scrunched in concentration.

I turned to him. "Good morning, Hari."

He met my eyes and said the words carefully, as if reciting from memory. "Didi call you down."

Before I could respond, he ran off.

I chuckled and took the tea tray with me downstairs.

Meera rushed from the kitchen to the living room as she packed Hari's lunch in his bag, gave breakfast to her mom, who sat on the bed, brought a water bottle, and put the water bottle strap around Hari's neck. I quietly approached her, and her laser-focused eyes met me. She looked at the empty cup and tray in my hand, nodded, and hustled to the kitchen with it. I sat beside Hari, who seemed unfazed by his sister's movements. Meera shouted something, and her mom yelled back. She shouted something again, this time at Hari, but Hari was busy playing with the strap of his water bottle.

Another sharp shout. "Hari!"

Wow. Meera had some solid vocal cords. Afraid she'd shout again, I touched my elbow to Hari. The moment he looked up, I pointed my finger toward the kitchen, where another louder, sharp shout came from Meera.

Hari rushed into the kitchen, where they bickered back and forth in Gujarati.

Soon, they rushed out. Meera got her purse and scarf, and Hari grabbed his bag.

As if she wasn't shouting just a minute ago, Meera looked at me with an utterly calm face and said, "Let's go."

Outside, Meera got on her scooter and tucked Hari's bag at the foot of the vehicle. Hari climbed behind her, then both of them looked at me expectantly. I looked at the tiny space they'd left for me and bit my lip.

She frowned, her eyes sharp, and jerked her head, telling me to climb behind Hari. Thank God we were getting my vehicle today.

"There's not much space here," I said.

Meera rolled her eyes and shifted a little forward. Hari went forward with her, and an extra inch of space cleared for me. Cowed by Meera's glare and the recent demonstration of her shouting skills, I quickly climbed behind Hari and clutched the small handle at the back, rested my feet on the leg-rest on one side, and let the other leg just swing in the air.

Before I could say a word of prayer, we were off. A little squeak might have escaped me, causing Hari to shake with laughter. I pressed my lips together, not wanting any movement that might affect Meera's balance. But I didn't need to worry. She drove us like a pro, zigzagging along the narrow dirt streets. The constant bumps slid me forward on the seat, pushing Hari into Meera. Every now and then, she slid herself back, pushing Hari into me and me into the small handle at the back.

The moment we turned to the main road, she gunned it hard, making me scream. Hari laughed, his little head falling to my shoulder. Meera shouted, "Don't move!"

I instantly clamped down and clutched the handle tighter. Other two-wheeler vehicles flew past us. Some, we flew past. Warm wind blew my hair back, and water rolled out of my eyes and flew behind, never even reaching my cheeks. They just flew away. After what felt like the longest roller-coaster ride of my life, we slowed down after a turn and stopped at the gate of a building.

Before I could even get down for Hari to climb down, the little guy slid down from between us, leaving nothing but air between Meera and me. Meera helped him get his bag on his shoulder and said something to him as she arranged his hair. He laughed and ran off into the gates.

A small silence ensued as Meera realized the human shield had run off to school, leaving behind just a few inches separating us. Slowly, Meera slid back a little but kept some space between us. I tightened my hold on the back handle, and we were off.

Soon, we reached a shop with several vehicles parked in the parking lot. After parking, we walked to the entrance of the shop.

A short, bald man with a mustache approached us.

Meera said something to him in Gujarati, and he nodded along. She turned to me and asked, "Would you rather have a car or a two-wheeler like mine? Remember, the car's driving seat is on the other side. Not like in America."

Fuck. I did not want to risk driving on the opposite side of the road. And, a two-wheeler on Indian roads was out of the question after the hair-raising ride this morning. Meera must have seen the dread on my face because she turned to the man and asked something in Gujarati. They talked a bit before Meera turned to me and said, "So they have a service of drivers too. You can rent a car with a driver. Anytime you want to go out, you can call the driver, and he will come and take you wherever you want. We can keep the car with us. He'll come to the house, take you, and drop you off at home."

With every word Meera spoke, relief spread through my veins, and words like *Perfect, Yes, That's it* flew out of my mouth. Meera's lips curved slightly upward in a smirk, and I couldn't help but smile back.

She talked to the man, and we discussed the prices. And lo and behold, I had a car and a driver. Once everything was signed and paid for, and I'd exchanged numbers with the driver, Meera turned to me. "Okay, the driver is going to drop you home. The car is already thoroughly cleaned and washed. I'm going to the school directly from here."

I wish I could have dropped her in the car. The sun was starting to burn. All I could do was nod. She had just turned around when I remembered.

I called out to her, and as she turned, I asked, "Can you give me your phone number?"

Her eyes widened, but she quickly recovered. "Sure."

I pulled out my phone to note her number as she recited them, saved it and sent her a quick text.

After a pause, she said, "It gets too hot between ten and four. Try to get your work done from home at that time. Go to the stepwell and other places before ten or in the evening once the sun has begun to set."

I nodded in thanks, and she was off to her vehicle. She wrapped her scarf around her face, then slipped on her hand gloves and a helmet. She drove off into the traffic, back where we came from. I watched until my new driver tapped me on the shoulder to let me know he was ready to leave.

I got into my new car, and we rode back to the house. The

driver attempted to point out different things in his broken English. I smiled and leaned forward in my seat, ready to explore more. Getting a driver and a vehicle made me feel better—more independent.

My phone vibrated with a text.

Meera: Message me if there's any issue with the driver.

Me: I will. Thank you.

I smiled the entire way home.

4

Song: Gori Tera Gaon Bada Pyara
  - K. J. Yesudas

Meera

S oft murmurs and chatter in the staff room muted the loud thoughts in my mind. After two periods of constant talking, my throat needed a break. I wish the students engaged more in class, but I couldn't really expect too much from fourth graders. All they wanted to do was play with their friends during recess.

I had just finished checking a few copies of homework when my best friend and coworker, Kriti, dropped on her chair beside mine. "I hate ninth graders."

I couldn't help but smile at her. "At least they're more interested in learning than fourth graders."

Kriti dropped the homework copies of students on her desk and dramatically rolled her eyes. "You're delusional if you think that. The girls constantly giggle while some boys keep making googly eyes at the girls, and other boys think they're kings of the jungle. All the while thinking I'm dumb enough not to understand them."

I turned on the table fan between us since the staff room was never cool enough. "You have a point. At least my students know I'm the smartest in the class."

The steady flow of air from the fan caused the pages of the homework books to flutter. She pressed the switch to oscillate the fan and turned to me with a mischievous look in her eyes. "Well," she teased, waggling her eyebrows like a lunatic.

I raised my eyebrows in question. "Well, what?"

Again, she rolled her eyes as if I was torturing her. I kinda was. She lightly smacked her palm on her desk. "Stop being so cruel and difficult, and tell me about your new tenant."

Luke's face, when I'd woken him up this morning, flashed in my mind. His eyes were bleary in the early morning light, a faint line of a pillow's impression ran along one of his cheeks, and several lines appeared between his eyebrows. And his complete transformation into a striking beauty after his shower had unnerved me so much that I had to run off on him while drinking tea. His skin was so white, his hair a rich, dark brown, and his voice a deep rumble that gave me goose bumps.

I shook off the memory and, without meeting Kriti's eyes, said, "There's nothing much to tell. He arrived yesterday with tons of stuff and now lives in my room. We went this morning to get him a car and a driver to roam around."

She chuckled at that. "So is he really fair and handsome?" Her play of words of *Fair and Handsome,* also a name of the beauty cream, wasn't lost on me.

Her eyes brimmed with excitement and curiosity. I understood. Nothing new or exciting ever happened in our lives or in the village. An American man living in my home for three months might be the most out-of-the-ordinary experience we will ever have.

In answer to her question, I nodded. "Yeah. He's very, very *fair*."

We Indians came in all shades of brown, from fairly light skin to very dark skin. But we can always tell when a person is not an Indian. They just look exotic and *foreign*, which is why in places that don't get many foreign tourists, locals would straight up ask to take a picture with them.

I was pretty sure my face had gone red just by thinking about Luke.

As if my answer wasn't enough, Kriti bumped her shoulder into mine. "And handsome?"

Her teasing smile almost broke my serious facade. "Why does it matter?"

She pouted. "It would be more fun to look at him if he was. Does he have green eyes? Golden hair? Big muscled body? Is he really tall?"

With every question, her voice dropped lower. She kept coming closer to my face, her expressions hopeful. She was crazy. Chuckling at her antics, I said, "He's not like the guys from your romance books."

"How would you know? You never read them."

I rolled my eyes and reminded myself of the fact that Luke was my tenant. "Whatever. I'm just glad his rent money will help me pay the loan."

Kriti turned from joking to serious in an instant. She was good at that. Her ability to know when to lighten things up when I got too somber yet turn serious when I needed it has been a godsend for years. She always knew what I needed.

After my father passed away, many of my friends stopped talking to me. Maybe they didn't know what to talk to me about, or maybe they couldn't handle my grief. Whatever it was, many turned their backs on me and moved on with their lives. Not Kriti. She was always there. She helped me get a teaching job and helped me make sense of my life when I was lost.

In a serious tone, she asked, "Has that asshole come to collect the debt?"

I shook my head. "Not yet. But he will. He always does."

Before she could say anything, the bell rang for my next class.

I squeezed her shoulder in thanks and headed to teach social science to my fourth graders.

THE DAY PASSED QUICKLY, and around two o'clock, Hari and I were back home. No sooner did we enter the house than Hari ran upstairs to check on our guest. Not that they could talk to each other, but my little brother was very intrigued by the newest member of the house. My instinct was to go upstairs to my room, too. It would take some time to get used to the new living arrangement.

Maa sat up from where she rested on the bed in the living room, thanks to Hari's loud steps thundering down the stairs. I grabbed his arm as he raced past me to get his toys from a shelf. "Go clean up, Hari. No games or toys before lunch and homework."

"Please, Didi. One game," he begged in Gujarati.

"No. Wash your hands and face two times, and then start your homework."

Once he shuffled off to the bathroom, grumbling under his breath, I made my way to the kitchen. Maa had already started reheating the sabzi and dal. I got the prepared dough out and kneaded it again. The aroma of the spices from the potato and onion sabzi infused the tiny kitchen. Maa stirred the dal with a ladle, mixing the spices that had floated up.

"Did you see the big car outside?" she asked, pouring a tiny amount of dal into a small bowl.

"Yeah. Luke rented it. He also hired a driver to take him around."

I took some dough and started rolling it out on a patli with my mother's velan. The wooden rolling pin was worn smooth from her hands, as was the rolling pin board. I wiped the sweat gathering on my forehead against the sleeve of my top.

"Do you think he will let Hari ride in his car?" she asked. I understood why she asked. Neither she nor Hari had ever ridden in a car in their life. I'd gotten the chance with some friends during my college years in Junagadh city. But Hari has never stepped out of the village.

"Maa, I don't know."

"Could you ask him? Hari will enjoy it."

I'd long ago stopped feeling sorry for myself. You live the life dealt to you. One day at a time. But sometimes, it hurt. With the weight of a rock on my heart, I said, "You know I can't ask that, Maa. But in a few years, I'll buy a car for us and take you and Hari wherever you want."

She made a noise and turned her attention to the stove, taking off the heated sabzi and dal. Maybe she thought I couldn't do it. Maybe it was too much to hope for. I let it go and heated the iron pan to cook the rotis.

Once the food was ready, Maa and I carried everything to the living room. Hari rolled out the mat. I asked him to call Luke for lunch. He ran off upstairs while I sat down on the mat to set up the plates and serve the food.

As quick as he left, Hari was back, his footsteps once again more like an elephant than a small boy. In contrast, Luke followed him nearly silently. Our eyes met, and for a second, I forgot what I was doing. His steps faltered.

"How was your day?" he asked, his voice low, a soft smile directed at me.

My mouth went dry, and my heart kicked up a beat. "Good," I said.

He wore a light green shirt, its sleeve stopping at his bicep, and loose black pants. He looked relaxed yet energetic. Not many people smiled at me like that. Like I was interesting, like I was noticeable. The moment was broken when Hari's squeaky voice said in Gujarati, "I don't like potato onion. I want *only* potatoes."

His face scrunched up, preparing for a tantrum. Maa told him to eat what was served, and their argument somehow broke the silence between Luke and me. He shook his head and sat beside Hari. Maa and I sat across them with food in between.

"Everything okay?" he asked, tipping his head slightly at Hari's grumpy face and Maa's occasional glares in return.

I rolled my eyes at them and said, "Yeah. Just a little tantrum."

He chuckled and started eating food in his typical fashion: taking a bite of the roti, scooping the sabzi in a spoon, and eating dal with a spoon. We, too, eat dal with a spoon, but we scoop the sabzi into the piece of roti. It didn't bother me. I was sure if I ever went to America that I would make a total mess of everything.

Once we had finished, Luke insisted on doing the dishes, which horrified my mother and shocked me. "Absolutely not. You're a guest of ours. You do not wash the dishes."

"But—" he said.

"No." Before he could argue further, I quickly gathered the dirty dishes and went to the kitchen.

As I came out to the living room to gather the remaining utensils, I shouted to Hari in Gujarati, "Play something with Luke bhai for a while, and then we'll do homework."

Instantly, Hari forgot all about the onion injustice and grabbed Luke's hand, tugging him toward the door.

Shock lined Luke's face and then he shot me a suspicious

look. He knew what I'd done. Little brothers are the best weapon to wield against big men sometimes.

Giving Luke a small smile in return, I went back into the kitchen to clean up everything.

I opened the window of the kitchen to let the fresh air in as I washed the utensils while Maa put the leftovers in the fridge. Hari dashed into the kitchen to get a drink of water. After having half a glass, he said, "We're playing cricket. Luke bhai doesn't know how to play. He cannot hit the ball with the bat."

His words turned into laughter at the end, and once more, he disappeared, his laughter and joy soothing something inside me. I washed the utensils faster. I wanted to watch them play. Specifically, I wanted to watch Luke play.

Filling up a water bottle with cold water, I went outside the house and sat on the cot outside the main door. Luke and Hari played a few feet away in the open space in front of our house.

The moment Luke saw me, he entirely missed the shot. Hari laughed and ran off to get the ball. Luke straightened from his crouch and laughed in embarrassment. Something light fluttered in my chest, and I realized I was smiling. It felt foreign, like wearing a new kurti.

Hari returned to Luke, held Luke's hands, and showed him how to bat. He acted out the movement of his legs, his face serious, his small hands moving Luke's legs in the proper position. Luke humored him, nodding along to Hari's demonstrations, then getting into different positions and intentionally messing up, making Hari groan in frustration and riling him up even more.

I couldn't help but chuckle at them. When Hari got fed up and took away the bat from Luke to show him the batting technique, Luke looked at me with a sly smile. I shook my head at him, smiling at his antics, and he winked at me. In an instant I was obliterated, blushing like Kriti's ninth-grade girls.

Before I could do anything else, Hari pulled on Luke's shirt, handed him the bat, and asked him to repeat his movements. Luke turned his full attention to Hari, pretending to be serious, and breaking out in full-wattage grins every time Hari turned his head away from him.

Before I could stop myself, I blurted, "Did you go to the stepwell?"

He glanced at me quickly in surprise before returning his attention to Hari, then said, "No. I've called my driver to come at five this evening to pick me up."

I nodded. Before I could say anything, he asked, "Would you like to join me?"

Did I want to? Yes.

Should I? Not really.

"Yes," I said, before I could convince myself it was a bad idea.

This time, Luke's shock made him turn to me and stand straighter, missing the ball Hari threw, causing him to groan.

Luke quickly turned to Hari, apologizing profusely.

Once Hari ran off to get the ball, he turned to me and said, "Great. Uh...it'll be fun."

When I nodded, he said, "So we leave in an hour."

Again, I nodded, not knowing what else to say.

Before long, Hari returned with the ball, and they went back to their training session, communicating in groans and actions and wild gestures and connecting through smiles, encouragement, and cheers. Words rarely helped convey true feelings anyway.

~

Luke

Ramesh, my driver, arrived right on time. I was all ready for my site visit to the stepwell. My letter-sized sketchbook, pencils, and markers were in my bag, and my DSLR camera was around my neck. I was busy adjusting the settings of the camera in the passenger seat of the car when the back door opened.

Little Hari jumped into the car and poked his head between the front seats to look at my camera. Meera was right behind Hari; she quickly got in and gently closed the door.

"Ready?" asked Ramesh. He looked at me for approval.

I looked at Meera, and asked, "Hari is joining us?"

She adjusted her scarf thing on her shoulder and, without meeting my eyes, said, "Yes, if it's not a problem. Maa insisted on taking him along."

"Not a problem." I looked at the driver and said, "Let's go."

The moment we were off, Hari's entire focus was on the road. He sat in the back, his tiny body leaning forward between the front seats, his hands clutching the seats, mouth agape in wonder.

As my eyes met Meera's, she explained, "It's his first time in a car."

Her words punched through my chest. Affection and protectiveness for the kid instantly took root in my heart. It made me want to give more to Hari. Take him for *all* the car rides. Give him everything he desired.

Meera's joy at the expression on Hari's face squeezed my heart. Her dark brown gaze met mine, catching me staring. Just to say something, I asked her, "Could you ask Hari if he's having fun?"

I wish I could ask him myself, but I'd take what I could. Meera asked the question to Hari. He turned to look at her, his wide smile nearly reaching both ears. He said something to Meera that seemed to have caught her off guard and made my driver chuckle.

"What? What?" Curiosity had me looking back and forth between Meera and Ramesh.

Meera shook her head and said, "Hari loves the car ride, but according to him, he's also here for my protection."

A chuckle escaped me at the now serious expression on little Hari's face. "Protection from whom?" I asked.

With a smirk, Meera answered, "You."

"Me?" I squawked. "I'm harmless."

Meera mumbled something as she looked outside the window.

"What?" I asked.

She rolled her eyes at me and, with a small, almost self-deprecating smile, said, "It's pretty normal for mothers to send someone along if her single daughter is going somewhere with a single man."

"Ahh. So why would you go out with someone who you don't trust? And how would little Hari protect you?"

"First, this little Hari could scream like a lunatic, run and get help if something happens. But he's also here as a...umm... how do I call it? A watchman. Keeping an eye on the single man so that he doesn't touch me. I don't touch him. If something happens between a man and a woman, they wouldn't be able to do anything publicly in front of a kid."

Understanding dawned on me. A big cockblocker in a tiny body. That's little Hari.

With a tiny smile, Meera said, "I see you now understand."

She shook her head, a small smile playing on her lips, as she ran her hand through Hari's hair, who was now watching the trees passing by. I was getting addicted to her small smiles. The way her eyes would light up even when her lips didn't curve into a smile had me achingly desperate to see her full, genuine smile even more.

I had yet to see her laugh. Or smile in utter joy. But I was resolved to make it happen.

I turned to face the road and looked at the passing trees, occasional houses, shops, and people walking along the side of the road. There weren't any sidewalks. People were just walking on the dirt road on the edge of the main road.

Soon, Ramesh parked the car on a dirt road beneath a tree. "We walk. Car with tree. Not hot." I understood what Ramesh meant. He just wanted to park the car under the shade so it doesn't get hot later on. I'd talked to him briefly on my way back from the car shop yesterday. His broken English was good enough for basic communication.

The evening heat turned the dirt road golden, the sunlight gleaming from between the trees and turning them into various shades of orange and brown. Ramesh walked ahead of us, and Meera beside me, clutching Hari's hand.

We climbed up the steps at the gate of a temple complex. The complex had a large courtyard in the center with a temple on one side and a series of steps descending into the stepwell on the other. Ramesh parted ways to visit the temple, whereas Meera and Hari decided to join me.

As the three of us climbed down the steps of the stepwell, I was struck by the stunning and elaborate architecture. The intricate carvings and incredibly detailed designs on the stone walls showcased the skilled craftsmanship of the builders from thousands of years ago.

As we continued our descension, I felt awe at walking within a structure constructed so long ago that continued to be an important site in the community. This was why architecture was my calling—what other job can you do that you're ensured of contributing something to, that would be used and admired for generations?

Our footsteps echoed through the structure, adding to the sense of mystery and wonder.

I turned on my camera and started taking pictures of everything I noticed. The walls on either side at the underground level were made of large stone blocks dirtied and stained over time. However, the farther down we climbed, we found the stone walls covered in green moss at certain locations due to its exposure to the water in the well.

The steps opened into a small court with six massive, intricately carved columns holding the decorative structure above us. Moving farther, more steps led us down toward the open well in the center that was filled with water.

All along the walls, carved niches and ornamented columns made my fingers twitch with the need to sketch them and capture their beauty on paper. According to my research, this stepwell was built in the thirteenth century CE, somewhere around the 1240s. It was mind-boggling that an eight-hundred-year-old structure remained in sound condition.

Hari and Meera's murmured conversations were a steady stream of background noise. They sat on one of the steps, protected from the sun by the shadow cast from the structure above. When my gaze met Meera's, I grinned, unable to mask my joy at experiencing the beauty of an architectural masterpiece.

"How many times have you been here before?"

Her eyes roamed around the structure, her fingers wandering and feeling the cool, coarse stone steps she sat on. "Twice before. We came here as a family to visit the temple when I was really young, and I think my father was curious about what else was here. We saw these steps going down and down, but Maa was scared, so my father and I went down until we reached the water."

Her eyes had glazed over, and her face turned toward the water a few steps down, as if reliving those memories. Silence stretched around us. Hari had gone near the water, touching the stone carvings on the columns and chattering as he recognized some of the gods and symbols portrayed.

Before I could say anything, she continued, "The second time was last year when you guys came to visit the village."

"That must've been difficult," I said. To visit a place for the first time where you've had beautiful memories of the past. A past you couldn't bring back.

She looked at me, her face a veneer of strength and steel. With a slight nod, she conveyed her acknowledgment, a confession that appeared to have required great effort. "It was," she murmured.

Two words, and they held such vulnerability they compelled me to sit down beside her. A sign of support. A hint of friendship.

She instantly turned rigid—like an impenetrable fortress.

We sat in silence for a while, hers wary and mine cautious. Soon, she relaxed and released a deep exhale.

While I sat, I took in the beauty of my surroundings. Countless numbers of people must've sat on these steps, pondering their lives while feeding their animals and quenching their own thirst from the well. After days of travel, they would've enjoyed a moment of shade from the constant heat and a moment of reprieve from the grind of survival.

And here we sat, side by side, facing this body of water, living beside the shadows of history.

Not to disturb the stillness, I murmured, "To think that the architects and builders constructed these structures with such precision and knowledge to survive and function through centuries... It makes me so proud to be an architect— not that I am in any way as knowledgeable as them. They created something necessary to the survival of their people and also made it a work of art."

"Makes our little lives feel insignificant," commented Meera, still looking at the water.

"So it does. But it puts our own struggles in perspective, does it not?"

"That it does," she murmured, her gaze stuck on Hari.

I caught a few shots of Hari playing, tracing the carvings

with his hands, and showed the picture to Meera. "An insignificant moment in history."

Looking at Hari's smiling face in the camera, she said, "Pretty significant to me."

A smile graced her lips as she looked at the photo, and I wish I could capture it on my camera, too.

"You ready to leave?" she asked.

I looked around. I'd clicked some pictures and seen the place. I would need to come here a few times to measure everything and document the details and history. But today was good.

Very good.

"Ready," I said.

We reached home late in the evening. I gave some money to Ramesh when he dropped us off and parked the car. Meera went inside while I collected my stuff from the car.

Hari and I played cricket outside while Meera and her mom prepared dinner. The meal itself went by quickly. Hari talked his mother's ear off in a language I didn't understand, though the excitement in his gestures and the change in his pitch made me glad we brought him along. Meera smiled at me in gratitude as Hari regaled his mother with his adventure.

Soon, I retired to my room, tired but oddly satisfied. The low sounds from Meera's cassette player lulled me to sleep.

I RAN. Sweat soaked my shirt, yet I ran. My mom screamed my name. My sister shrieked my name. My feet slipped downward. Everywhere around me, dunes of sand sprawled for miles. Screams and shouts surrounded me, yet I kept slipping into the hot sand. The heat suffocated me.

I woke up with a start, sweat running down my forehead, neck, and chest.

I looked around the dark, still panting with the exertion of my dreams. It was dead silent—no whirr of the AC, no squeaking from the old fan. I grabbed my bottle of water and took a few sips. My heart pounded as the horrible dream lingered behind my eyes.

I stretched over and flipped the fan switch back and forth. Nothing. The AC had stopped, and the heat was intolerable, especially after the dream. Must be some problem with the electricity. It was just my second night here, and the challenges didn't stop at night. Just great.

I got up and opened the window that faced the field beyond. Then I opened the window facing the terrace near my bedroom door to get some cross ventilation.

Meera slept soundly on the open terrace, her head facing me. She slept in a blanket cocoon, the fabric covering her up to her ears. Soft wind ruffled her dark brown curls. The open sky and light breeze called to me and compelled me to go outside.

There was an empty cot a few feet away from Meera, so I picked up my pillow and blanket from the bed and opened my bedroom door. Sleeping in the stifling hot bedroom was out of the question tonight.

The gentle melodies continued to play from her cassette player, providing a sense of calm for my racing heart, and the cool breeze brushed against my sweat-soaked T-shirt, relieving my overheated body. Carefully, I placed the pillow on the cot and nestled myself beneath the blanket.

The stars twinkled above, the stillness of the night enveloped me, and the combination of the peaceful music and Meera's sleeping face all worked together to ease my mind. As I drifted to sleep, images of Meera's curly hair, gentle breezes, and small, comforting smiles filled my dreams.

5

Song: Aapki Aankhon Mein Kuch
  - Lata Mangeshkar and Kishore Kumar

Meera

A sudden gust of wind and the chirping of birds startled me awake. I blinked a few times, clearing away the sleep, and froze when I saw Luke's sleeping form in the cot beside mine.

What was he doing out here? Why was he asleep beside me?

And why was I staring?

He slept with his body turned toward me, his blanket draped around his waist. His face was all sharp angles, yet his lips rested in a soft smile. His longish hair was splayed across the pillow, some covering his eyes. My fingers twitched, wanting to brush it off his beautiful face. I clenched my hand into fists but did not—could not—stop staring.

The chirping of a bird pulled me out of my musings.

What a sight to wake up to!

I closed my eyes, said a small morning prayer, and got up as quietly as possible to avoid waking him.

The approaching dawn cast streaks of pink and orange light across the horizon. Inhaling deeply, I filled my lungs with the crisp morning air, which carried a faint scent of dew, dried grass, and the earthy aroma of our barren farm.

The beauty of the early morning wrapped around me, and my eyes were drawn back to the foreign beauty sleeping on the cot. His flawless complexion, ivory-toned skin, and well-built physique made him almost otherworldly.

I hated that he was so captivating. So polite. And that he was also such a nice person.

And I hated it even more that I thought about him so much.

Determined not to think any more about Luke, I went into the restroom upstairs.

Entering, I turned on the light. And nothing happened.

Realization dawned on me. That was why Luke was outside.

Poor guy must've had the shock of his life. It wasn't uncommon for the power to go out, and it could get suffocating inside the house. He didn't even have a mattress over the cot. I'd have to keep that cot prepared in case this happened again. His back would kill him today.

It hadn't been three full days, and already, I had warring emotions for him. I hated that my mind kept returning to thoughts of him, yet I couldn't stop myself.

The moment I stepped out of the restroom, my eyes met Luke's. He leaned against the parapet, and the door opening had him turn around to look at me.

"Good morning," he rasped. His rough morning voice did something to the pit of my stomach, not to mention his sleepy eyes and unkempt hair.

It took everything in me to appear unaffected, to meet his eyes and not soften, to give him just a nod as I said, "Good morning. Chai?"

His smile widened, his body turning to face me. "Yes, please."

I quickly nodded, tried for a smile, and walked toward the steps leading downstairs, keeping my pace unaffected when all I wanted to do was run. Run away from his soft gaze and his lazy smiles.

Plucking some mint leaves from the small mint plant I kept on my kitchen window ledge, I let the chai simmer in the pot before adding some freshly washed leaves. Mom and Hari slept in the living room. Our house wasn't really that big: just the living room, kitchen, and restroom downstairs, and one bedroom, a restroom, and the terrace over the living room upstairs.

I took the two cups of chai and some tea biscuits upstairs to the terrace. I had just put the tray on Luke's cot when he appeared, his hair a little wet and his eyes bright.

"Thanks, Meera," he said as he sat on his cot near the tray and picked up a cup.

I picked up the remaining cup and settled on my cot across from him.

We sat in companionable silence as the world around us woke up. For a few minutes, I basked in the changing colors of the sky with the cool breeze against my skin as every sip of hot chai awakened my body.

Mornings like this made me grateful that our house was away from the congested part of the village. Our village was situated a few kilometers from a bustling city, and the houses closer to the city were much more compact. Our house was a little farther from the city and deeper into the farms. It was a lot more peaceful around here.

"Does this ever get old?" Luke asked.

I looked at him, his eyes staring off at the distant farms. "Never," I said.

This was my second favorite time of the day.

Luke extended the plate of biscuits, and I plucked three from it.

"When do you leave for school?" asked Luke, dipping his biscuit in the chai.

"Around seven thirty. I have about forty-five minutes before I have to wake Hari up and get him ready."

Luke nodded and continued his biscuit dipping.

His mannerisms, the way he held himself, seemed so sophisticated—as if he could handle any difficulty the world threw his way. As if living wasn't a struggle. As if keeping his family well-fed wasn't his burden to bear. As if he could do whatever he wanted, be wherever his heart desired.

And he was.

In this middle-of-nowhere town where he knew nothing and no one.

I couldn't stop myself from asking the question that had plagued me since Akira called to make arrangements for his visit. "Why did you choose this village for your study?" I'd been trying to escape this place for five years now, and Luke had deliberately walked into it.

His smile widened in excitement. He clutched his cup tighter, leaned forward, and said, "When I came here with Sam and Akira, I was fascinated by everything and kept thinking about it after we returned. It was the first stepwell that I'd seen in my life."

His eyes glimmered with awe and respect for that piece of architecture. His passion for it poured from him in his energy and his wide smile.

Yet I frowned. "Thousands of stepwells exist in India, and most are better than the small one in this village."

He nodded, took a sip of the chai, and ran his hand along the rim of the cup as he said, "You're right. But this was located in the heart of the village. It still has water in the well and the typical temple near it. And it is the perfect size for me to measure and draw the entire thing. There might be other smaller stepwells, but I'd already *seen* this one. I knew Akira's family could help me find a place to live for a few months while I worked."

And with a soft whisper, he added, "Everything fit."

Everything fit. Words I'd never felt in my life.

Two little words, an ocean-wide gap between us.

Our worlds, too far apart.

I nodded and looked away at the barren brown fields of ours. Weeds crept up in multiple places, dried grass turning gold in the early sunrise. We finished our chai in silence for the next few minutes before I got up to face the chaos awaiting me.

Luke

I reached the stepwell with Ramesh right around eight in the morning. We left right after Meera and Hari left for school. Per Meera's advice, I decided to go for the visit early in the morning. However, I brought a few packets of the energy drink Abhi had gotten for me at the airport.

Ramesh and I walked toward the entrance leading to the open court between the temple and the stepwell.

"Ramesh, you coming?" I asked, pointing toward the direction of the stepwell. Yesterday, he decided to go to the temple.

Ramesh ran his fingers over his mustache, his eyes deep in thought, looking back and forth between the temple and the stepwell.

I was about to tell him not to worry about it, but he huffed in mild exasperation and said, "I come. You need me. I sit nearby."

I couldn't stop the chuckle at his lack of confidence in my

ability to handle myself. I humored him and said, "Thank you. I do need you."

He gave me a sincere nod. "I know."

Even in the early morning, plenty of people were everywhere. The temple was crowded, with countless devotees coming and going out of the complex. As we neared the stepwell, we saw a few people sitting in the stone niches and corners of the structure.

Beside me, Ramesh murmured, as if telling me a secret, "Couples. Meet in secret before work."

I grinned. "Is that a normal thing?" I whispered back.

My smile spurred him on. He was clearly pleased with my interest.

He proceeded to tell me stories about all the types of people I'd find here. According to him, the place bustled with young people during the weekdays and families on Sundays, while the temple was a frequent haunt for the elderly, particularly on weekdays. With its hundreds of steps and steep inclines, the stepwell was a no-go for the elderly.

As Ramesh regaled me with his stories and anecdotes, I pulled out my sketchbook and pencil from my bag and climbed down the steps until I reached the first landing. Ramesh followed and sat down, leaning against one of the huge columns.

I sketched while he talked.

The air began to heat, and the humidity rose, the sunlight washing across most steps leading from the ground floor to the landing underground. Soon, the heat was unbearable for most couples, and they left.

I got lost in sketching the details and ornamentation of the columns, the slab above it, their joinery, and the intricate details of the niches.

I was so intensely focused that I jumped several inches off the ground when a throat cleared loudly right by my ear.

"Damn it, Ramesh," I said, putting my hand on my wildly beating heart. "You scared me, man."

With an apologetic shrug, he said, "I bring tour guide."

Wasn't he the best?

I slapped him on his shoulders in thanks and said, "Oh man, you are great."

And I emphasized *great* since I felt kinda bad about getting loud when he scared the shit out of me.

However, Ramesh seemed to have already forgotten and touched the collar of his shirt in pride.

He introduced me to the tour guide. We discussed prices, and Ramesh quickly jumped to my aid and started bargaining. The argument escalated to the point where I had to put my hand on Ramesh's shoulder and hand a little extra money to the tour guide.

The disappointing glare that Ramesh threw my way had me burying my face in my sketchbook. He shook his head at me and said something to the tour guide, apparently resolving the conflict.

Soon, the tour guide, Mohan, led us back to the entrance of the court, right where we had begun in the morning. He spoke English well, pointing at different structures, explaining the tiny details I might've missed, and shared various stories—some believable, some not—of the history of the hallowed grounds.

An hour passed as we toured the temple and the area around it, examined the stepwells from all directions, and shared some dubious expressions every time the guide was adamant about the accuracy of his outlandish stories. Mohan called his other tour guide friends to validate his stories when Ramesh and I couldn't stop laughing.

I recorded everything, mostly so I could refer to the tour later, but I didn't even stop recording during our friendly arguments.

By the time we finished the tour, the heat was high, and I'd already finished my glucose drink. We said our goodbyes and thank-yous to Mohan, tipping him enough to make Ramesh grumble, and we stepped out of the complex.

I'd barely taken a step when three little kids came near me and started talking. Ramesh said, "They're just begging, Luke bhai. I shoo them?"

Shoo them?

"No, man. Wait," I said and pulled out my wallet.

Thankfully, I'd exchanged dollars for Indian rupees when I landed in India.

I pulled out three fifty-rupee notes and handed them to the kids.

"What did you do?" Ramesh asked in horror.

"Ramesh, I don't mind."

Before he could say anything, the little kids' excited shouts led to ten more kids running toward us.

"We have to go. You help one, and now all come."

For the life of me, I couldn't take a step in the opposite direction.

As I looked around, entire families had their tiny shops lined up outside the temple complex. Little kids carried their even tinier siblings in their arms as they begged in front of me.

Their faces were sad, defiant, and unflinching.

Hope shone in their eyes as they stood facing me, and my heart cracked.

The brutality and unfairness of life glared at me.

A lump rose in my throat at seeing a father trying to come near me, carrying his small child in his arms, hope and fear of rejection waging war behind his eyes.

I just couldn't leave without helping.

I opened my wallet, pulled out a few five-hundred-rupee notes, and turned to Ramesh. "Could you please get me the change for these?"

Ramesh seemed to want to argue with me, but I did not give him a chance. He huffed, took the money, and went to all the little shops to get me the change.

I started giving the money I had to the little kids.

Some kids had brought balloons or garlands of flowers or toys to sell to me. I took everything they had brought and gave them the money. Ramesh was soon back with more change, and I gave money and bought whatever they wanted to sell till every face around us—child and adult—was happy.

Once I'd given money to everyone, and the crowd around us thinned out, Ramesh and I carried all the gifts and toys to the car. On our way back, I asked Ramesh, "Why were all those kids begging outside the temple?"

Ramesh shrugged, his eyes never leaving the road as he weaved us through the traffic. "There are always people outside temple. People go to God and beg to God. People outside temple, the beggars, beg to people. The people from temple always give more money to do good deeds."

Despite his limited English, I understood the essence of his words. Most of the beggars outside the temple sold prayer items from their small carts, their torn clothes and thin bodies revealing their daily struggles with hunger. My heart ached as I contemplated the irony of a place of worship becoming a gathering point for people of vastly different social statuses.

It struck me that even within the sacred grounds of the temple, there were such stark disparities. The sight of these beggars outside the temple, the little kids carrying their younger brothers and sisters in their arms, was a heart-wrenching reminder of the inequalities and challenges faced by those less fortunate in society. The humbling experience left me with a renewed commitment to be more compassionate toward those who were less fortunate.

We reached home, and Ramesh helped me bring in everything I had accumulated.

Meera's mom looked up from where she sat in the living room. I shrugged my shoulders in an embarrassed smile and raised the bags of stuff in my hands. She gave me a small, puzzled smile in return, obviously not understanding what I'd done.

Ramesh entered right behind me and launched into an animated conversation with her, his gestures and expressions so exaggerated I knew he complained about my gullibility. I felt no regret; I did what my conscience demanded. Again, I shrugged my shoulders and, with a smile, climbed up to my room.

We arranged everything in the corner of the hallway outside my room. And soon, Ramesh took off on his motorbike.

My room was unbearably hot, but the power had come back, so I switched on the air conditioner and headed to the shower. Even though the water was perfectly cool, the sadness and helplessness lingered, refusing to wash away so easily. When I returned to my room, the air conditioner had kicked in, and the room was significantly cooler. I couldn't help but wonder about the people I'd met today: those little children with no shoes on, walking on the hot land, begging for money in this heat, while I sat thinking about them in an air-conditioned room.

My insides prickled in guilt and helplessness.

Why was the world divided so unevenly? Why were some born of fortune and some destitute? Were they happy in life despite the poverty? What brought them joy? Or was their life an eternal struggle of survival that I would never be able to comprehend?

Before I drove myself insane with all my thoughts, I picked up my phone and called Mom.

She picked up after a few rings. "Luke, sweetheart!"

"Hey, Mom. It's so good to hear your voice."

"Everything all right, honey? You sound upset."

Our family knew and understood pain, sadness, and unfairness of life. Since childhood, Mom and Dad took me to countless cities and countries where they participated in service projects. Today wasn't the first time I had witnessed poverty. Today, I reacted the way I had seen my father react countless times in the past.

I pulled on my hair in the hope that the physical sting would overpower the overwhelming hurt. "I sort of tried to help out a few poor people today. It's just sad, this suffering. Pain. Loss."

Mom's voice came out a little hoarse. "That's life, Luke. An endless circle of loss and gain, sadness and joy, life and death."

"You doing all right, Mom?"

"Yes, sweetie. I'm okay. Staying busy these days. I have the Mental Health of Teenagers charity event in two weeks."

"That's great, Mom. I'm sure it'll go great. And how's Dad?"

A soft sigh came across the phone. "He stays busy too."

For years, I've heard the same answer. But Mom continued, "But what's important, Luke, is that we're together. We're here for each other. We're stronger. We find joy in the smallest of things. And that's what's important."

"I understand."

"And I love you, honey. Always." *Not always.*

I pushed that thought away, and said, "I love you too, Mom."

She tsked. "If you weren't all the way in India right now, I would demand you come home and let me cook you dinner."

I chuckled. "I'll be there as soon as I'm back."

"I'll hold you to that, Lukey."

I groaned. "Mom, anything but that."

And we chuckled.

"Thanks, Mom. I feel a little better."

"Of course, honey. I'm just a phone call away."

"I know. Talk to you soon."

"Bye. Love you, Lukey."

I ended the call with a chuckle, thinking how far they've come.

At one point, my parents' relationship had been a mess. I was young back then, but I remember the shouting, the crying, the blaming, and the agonizing silence for days on end. It took a few years and a lot of therapy, but things improved between them.

They took their grief, their agony, and their hurt and turned their relationship around. They've become stronger.

But when your family had a giant hole, it never stayed the same. It never looked the same. And you just learned to live with it. Overcome it. Escape it.

6

Song: *Tujhse Naaraz Nahi Zindagi*
  - *Anup Ghoshal*

Meera

The moment I stepped into the house with Hari, I knew something was up. That feeling of impending doom had a way of crawling under my skin. Since I'd seen Luke's car in the front yard, I knew he was back from his site visit.

I had just put Hari's school bag on the sofa when Maa looked up from her knitting and said in Gujarati, "We have still not received the compensation money for the past five months."

As if paying the loan sharks wasn't enough, I had to fight to even collect our rightful compensation from the government as a part of the promised financial aid. We were supposed to receive three lakh rupees when my father died. We had to prove to the government that he had committed suicide and it wasn't a family squabble. After everything, the municipality told us we would receive a small monthly amount until we received three lakhs in full.

They never told us I'd have to keep begging for that money every month.

No, I couldn't behave like the loan sharks that demanded money from us every month. I had to *beg*. Not meet the eyes of the officers. Not raise my voice. Not do anything that would drive them to throw me out of their office. Just beg.

So when my mother reminded me about the pending money again, after I'd just come home, hungry and wilted from the burning heat outside, I snapped, "We are never going to get that money, Maa. Stop expecting the government to do anything."

Maa threw her knitting needles and yarn aside and shouted, "What else do I do? We deserve that money. Your father died trying to earn some money. Maybe he even died so we could get that money. Tell me what to do."

Hari sat on the sofa, playing with his water bottle. His tiny ears heard everything, understood everything, things I never wanted him to worry about. Maa believed he needed to learn what life was about early on and what he had to do as he grew up. That was another of our countless ongoing fights.

I ruffled Hari's hair and said, "Go freshen up, Hari. Wash your hands and face with soap and cold water. I'll get the food ready."

Hari nodded and ran off into the bathroom without meeting anyone's eyes.

I turned to Maa, fire in my heart, ice spreading in my veins, teeth clenched to stop words that could do more damage than good. "Why? Why always in his presence?"

Angry eyes turned away to look at the wall, her voice hoarse. "He needs to know. Understand."

No, he didn't. He needed to be a ten-year-old kid and have a normal, happy childhood. Frustrated tears clouded my vision. I blinked them away, jaw tight to keep from hurting my mother further, and said, "You know what? I'll call Surbhi didi. Ask her if she's heard anything."

Maa nodded. Her hands clutched her arms as if holding herself from breaking. I breathed out my anger, sat beside her, and put my head on her shoulder. I held her in my arms and said, "Don't worry, Maa. This time, our situation is not too bad. Luke has already paid five hundred dollars this month. That is thirty-seven thousand rupees. Plus, my salary of fifteen thousand rupees. We will have more than forty thousand rupees this month. Have we ever seen that much money?"

Maa shuddered and clutched my hand. She shook her head. "That's only for three months. What will we do after that?"

"Stay calm and relax for these three months. We'll figure out the rest. Things will be fine."

A little shuffle at my side made me turn. Hari stood there, his eyes filled with doubt, confusion, and hurt. Without hesitation, I extended my hand and drew him into our embrace. He huddled between Maa and me in a flash, his thin fingers gripping my dupatta.

Choking back tears, with a heavy lump in my throat, I made a promise to myself: I would protect my family, and Hari would have a normal childhood. They were the only two people in the world I had to care for, and that's precisely what I would do.

I kissed the top of Maa's and Hari's heads before saying, "Maa, I'll call Surbhi didi. Could you heat lunch and get the rotis ready? And Hari, make a list of all your homework."

Once they nodded, I rushed into the downstairs restroom, locked the door, and finally allowed the tears to fall. Why was I dealt this hand in life? Why did we have to rely on others for our sustenance? Why did I have to work so hard to keep just two people happy? My chest ached with helplessness.

But no more.

I wiped my tears, washed my face with soap and cold water, and looked at myself in the mirror. Over the next three months, I would find a way to rid us of all our problems—the debt, the compensation, the ruined farm, everything.

Walking outside the house to prevent little ears from hearing anything, I called Surbhi didi, the founder of our local community organization who advocated for widows and children of farmers who committed suicide. Five years ago, they reached out to us, helped us file for compensation, explained all the policies, and stood by us when we applied. They had helped over seventy-five families in our local district. Surbhi didi herself had lost her husband twelve years ago when their child was just a few months old. She fought for herself then and, frustrated at the government's injustice toward the widows of farmers, started her Life for Widows Organization.

Her story, strength, and resilience had kept me going all these years. So every time she needed me for anything, I was there.

She answered on the third ring. "Meera. How are you?"

Her warm voice brought a smile to my face. "Surbhi didi, I'm good. How are you?"

A small chuckle on her end as she said, "Same as always. Busy. Running around. I pray for us to be not needed anymore, but sadly, here we are."

So many more families just like us, some in circumstances more dire than our own. Guilt bubbled up in my heart. But, for Maa, I had to ask. "I'm sorry, Surbhi didi. If there is anything I can do, please don't hesitate."

"I know, Meera. I'll call you when things get out of control here. So, tell me, how can I help you?"

"Uhh... We haven't received the severance package for the past five months. Maa is getting antsy."

"How's the financial situation? Do you need money? Loan

coming up soon?" Her questions were on point without the slightest hesitation to help.

Just knowing she was available soothed me. "No, Didi. We are okay, financially. In fact, we have an American friend living as a paying guest for three months. So things should be fine for now. I just wanted to know if you've heard of others having the same problem, the reason behind the delay, or if we need to go to the municipal office."

Her tired exhale had already answered my questions before she said, "Yeah, I've had multiple complaints. Let's wait for two to three weeks, and if nobody starts receiving the money, we'll go to the municipal office."

"Okay, Didi. Call me if you need me."

"Thank you, Meera. Take care of yourself. Not just your maa and little brother."

"You too, Didi," I said, and we ended the call.

Although our conversation didn't yield much, at least we had a plan. I was content with that. Once inside the house, I asked Hari to call Luke downstairs for lunch. After he left, I quickly relayed our conversation to Maa as we set up the mats in the living room.

Luke's strong, gentle footsteps followed Hari's energetic ones. Hari hopped onto the mats and took a spot beside Luke. Luke wore a light orange shirt over blue pants, his shirt looking soft and well-worn. His hair was tousled, there was a crease between his eyes, and his usual smile was absent. Had he overheard our commotion downstairs? Could he sense the tension in the house?

As I served him some hot dal and rice, his gaze met mine. He gave me a faint smile, but it didn't reach his eyes. He ate quietly, seemingly lost in thought. Occasionally, he smiled at Hari's questions and antics.

Maa and Luke sat at opposite ends while Hari and I sat in

the middle. We had all the food containers sprawled between us for easy access.

I couldn't stop glancing at Luke, and he returned the looks with a hint of a smile that never fully materialized. The silence cast a heavy cloud over our heads, and even the amount we ate was less than usual.

After our late lunch, Hari coaxed Luke outside, but his steps lacked enthusiasm. Maa retreated to her bed, turned the table fan toward her, and went to sleep. By the time I finished cleaning up, Hari had come inside, and Luke had retreated to his room. For the rest of the day, I helped Hari with his homework, checked my children's school assignments, and spoke to Kriti, sharing the constant excitement of my life.

Dinner was another quiet affair.

After Hari fell asleep, I changed into pajamas, filled a pot with water, and climbed to the terrace. The cool night air and the open sky welcomed me, and the sweet smell of jasmine drifted from a nearby tree.

Luke's warm yellow light peeked from under his door, but I didn't linger. Instead, I filled the water pot, fixed my bed, switched cassettes on my player, and settled in for the night.

"Ude Jab Jab Zulfe Teri" played on my cassette player. After my day, I needed something upbeat to make me smile. As the music played in the background, my feet moved in rhythm with the tune.

I gazed at the sky, taking in the twinkling stars and the half-moon, and finally felt the day's tension slipping away from me.

Suddenly, a voice interrupted my reverie. "May I?" he asked.

Luke

I couldn't resist. The moment I heard the tinkling, upbeat song playing outside my room, my feet dragged me to open the window and peek out at the terrace. Meera lay on her back, with one leg crossed over the other, tapping her feet to the music as she watched the stars.

She looked at peace, and my desire to bask in that peaceful moment overpowered my need to leave her be. So I walked out to the terrace, but since she hadn't heard me approach, I had to ask, "May I?"

Meera jumped a little at the sound of my voice and turned to look at me. I automatically put my hands into the pockets of my sweatpants to stop them from fiddling. I must have passed her inspection because she nodded and said, "Sure."

The empty bed beside her already had a mattress and a pillow laid out.

"You'll have to get your own blanket," Meera said, her eyes closed as the gentle breeze blew through her hair.

I breathed a sigh of relief that her eyes were shut, because I couldn't stop staring at her. Her curls danced in the breeze, and a thin blanket outlined her slender figure. A small smile curved her lips as the upbeat tune played on her old-fashioned cassette player.

I retrieved a blanket from my room and silently lay down on the bed next to her. We were separated by about six feet of space as we listened to the music.

When the happy melody ended, a soulful song began, causing my heart to race. Meera's feet stopped tapping to the rhythm, and a sudden sadness hung heavily between us.

"What does the song mean?" I asked, yearning to understand the lyrics that weighed down my heart.

Meera reached for the player, rewound the tape, and lowered the volume. The intro music started again, and I turned to face her. She gazed at me with eyes brimming with restrained emotions and sadness before looking back up at the night sky. Then she began to translate the lyrics for me.

> "I am not angry with you, Life
> Simply baffled
> By your innocent questions."

She waited as the lyrics for the first stanza began in Hindi.

My heart pounded at the words, the punch of emotions rendering me speechless.

Once the music began again, Meera translated the lyrics to the next stanza.

> "Never thought that in order to live
> I would need to hold on to pain
> Never thought life would extract
> A price for every smile
> Now whenever I smile
> It feels like these lips are pursed in debt"

Every word was laced with pain, and her voice was hoarse as she translated the song's meaning out loud. Tears welled up in my eyes as the male voice sang the words. The song seemed to truly reflect Meera's feelings, and I regretted asking her to translate the lyrics.

I remained silent. Meera began to speak again as the music started, her voice trembling with emotion. I wanted to ask her to stop, but when I turned to look at her, tears streamed down her face. I felt a strong urge to comfort her, to hold her and share her pain, but I stayed still. She began speaking again, and I didn't look away this time.

> "Today my eyes have welled up with tears

Soon they will burst forth, I'm sure
Tomorrow, who knows, these sore eyes perhaps
Will long for the sight of more –
Where have I lost that lone drop of tears
Which I had tucked away so safely?"

And then the chorus began, and it was so hauntingly real that my own past kept rising to the surface. It reminded me of when my own family grieved.

Once the song faded out, I said, "Can I just say that was one of the most powerful songs I've ever heard? But please don't play it again for a few days."

Meera chuckled, wiping away her tears with the edge of the soft blanket covering her. "It always makes me cry."

I wiped a lone tear from my cheek with the sleeve of my T-shirt and turned to face Meera. She was watching me, her eyes red-rimmed.

"Well, it made me cry too," I admitted.

She gave me a small smile, and I knew my eyes were probably as red as hers.

The cool breeze felt good on my face. I didn't ask her to translate the next song. I was just glad that it sounded upbeat.

After a moment of silence, Meera said, "Maa told me about your shopping spree this morning."

I chuckled. "Well, I couldn't say no to those kids. They looked at me with such hope."

She smiled, but her eyes seemed to convey that I was hopeless. I hoped it was a good thing. "You do realize that you'll now have to buy things from every one of them every time you visit the stepwell, right? They remember the people who give to them so easily."

"Then you'll soon find the terrace and the hallway filled with toys and prayer items."

She chuckled, and I quickly turned to look at her, not

wanting to miss the smile on her face. When our eyes met, the cool, jasmine-scented air and soft tunes wrapped around us. For that moment, life seemed beautiful.

She turned her head back to look up at the stars while I kept looking at her. "Tell me what you're thinking," she said.

"Is everything all right? I sensed some tension in the house today. Anything I can help you with?"

"Everything's fine. You living here is beyond helpful."

With a deep breath, I said, "I'm sorry about your father."

I heard her sharp intake of breath and then silence. "Who told you?"

"Akira and her cousin Ria. Last year. I had found an article on the subject in a newspaper, and they had mentioned it."

"Of course. It's not like you don't see the absence."

I didn't know what to say to that. Meera had gone silent. Her secrets and private life had been laid bare, while she barely knew anything about me. Not many people knew about my past except my best friend Sam, but it only seemed fair to share it with Meera.

"My sister committed suicide when I was ten."

A gasp escaped her lips. After a few moments of silence, she asked, her voice thick with emotion, "Does it get easier?"

Sharp pain, long forgotten and deeply buried, rose afresh. It was a gentle yet painful reminder of its existence. "The loss or the guilt?" I asked.

Meera didn't answer, and I didn't repeat my question. I knew she had heard me, though. Her uneven breathing and silent sniffles were proof she was awake. I shouldn't have brought up her father when today had already been a tough day. But I needed her to know that I understood what was going on in her life, that I was there for her, and if she needed someone to talk to who might understand, I was here.

I *needed* to help Meera. I wanted to help her overcome her sadness, guilt, and any other troubles that held her back from living the life she desired, from smiling freely, from laughing loudly. Perhaps supporting her would help me heal, too.

One step at a time.

We didn't speak for the remainder of the night. Speculative silence and weariness of life dragged us into sleep while the slow melody playing softly from the cassette player tried to soothe the jagged edges of past pains.

7

Song: *Piya Tose Naina Laage Re*
  - *Lata Mangeshkar*

Meera

Loss or guilt?

What did I feel more?

Every day, I felt the loss, the emptiness, and the ache of our life without Pappa. I wonder if I would miss him, remember him, or even curse him every day if I wasn't drowning in the debt he left behind.

Along with the loss came the guilt. I keep thinking, if only I had earned on the side and continued studying, maybe he would still be here. Maybe if I had lived with my family, I would've noticed something was wrong. If only I had known about the dire situation earlier, I could've dropped out and taken up some work.

Would I hurt less if I didn't feel the guilt? Would I remember Pappa less once I paid off my debt?

Vicious cycle. That was where I was stuck.

Luke's simple question had circled in my head for the past two days.

The morning after our conversation, I had woken up to find Luke sleeping on the cot beside mine. A blanket all the way to his head, his face buried under the pillow. He slept as if nothing troubled him. As if his life was perfect.

But that was far from the truth, wasn't it?

I still couldn't fathom what he had shared about his sister. He must have been as young as Hari when he lost his elder sister. How did he cope with the loss? Did he realize the magnitude? Did he feel the pain as acutely today as he must have felt back then? How long did he keep waiting to see his sister again?

Suddenly, a loud slam beside me made me scramble to hold the edge of my desk. I looked up to find Kriti looking down at me, her face amused. "You seemed miles away. What's so captivating that you couldn't hear the recess bell, me calling your name thrice, and the fight between Seema Madam and the head of department?"

My eyes widened with each of her questions. "I missed all of that?"

Kriti gave me a teasing smile and nudged my shoulder. "So... what were you thinking about? Or should I ask, *who* were you thinking about?"

I rolled my eyes at her antics but couldn't stop the smile—or the embarrassment of getting caught daydreaming. Not that my thoughts were even remotely of the happy kind.

Kriti's eyes twinkled in delight as she clutched my hand and leaned in close to my face. "Why are you blushing? Is it the foreigner, Luke? Did you talk to him?"

I let go of her hand on mine and began tidying my desk. "Well, we live in the same house. Of course, we talk."

"So... what do you guys talk about?" She had a dreamy expression on her face.

I lightly patted her head. "What's with all the questions? Luke and I...Well, we're just sort of friends. Well, maybe even that's too much. He's just a decent guy. And he plays with Hari while I cook with Maa, and he eats with us. And when everything is quiet at night, we've had a conversation or two."

"Ahh... Meera and Luke. Luke and Meera. How romantic." Kriti sighed.

Again, I couldn't help but roll my eyes, which I hated—especially when Hari rolled his eyes at me—but this line of questioning left me no choice. "Didn't you just hear what I said? We're not even friends. And why are you so excited about this?"

Kriti chuckled and shook her head. "Well, at least one of us has something interesting going with a man. Some of us are just going to have an arranged marriage. Not that I mind. I've seen enough men in this village. My parents are my only hope to find a good enough guy to meet."

"How's the search for your dream man going?"

She shook her head, exasperation and mirth in her eyes. "Well, some guys run away when I tell them I'd continue teaching after getting married. Some run away when I tell them I won't let them touch me for at least the first six months of the marriage. And the few who have been sort of okay with the first two conditions run off when I tell them that I would hold power over money that I earn, and that if I want to buy gifts for my family or donate them or buy something pretty for myself, that's my call."

I laughed at her brutal honesty with the suitors. "That is the least you can ask for. Are your parents okay with your requirements?"

"They are. And since my salary significantly contributes to our family income, my parents don't really mind that I'm taking my time."

"You'll find someone. You're perfect."

Kriti scoffed loud enough to garner a few teachers' snooty looks. She coughed and turned her attention to me. "I am far from perfect. I'm thirty, which is six years too old for the regular demand. Also, a few kilograms heavier," she muttered the last part in a softer voice.

"Screw the guys who have such superficial demands."

"I'd rather not."

I chuckled, and so did she.

"Did something happen, though?" I asked. My firecracker of a friend doesn't often talk negative about herself. She's all about positivity.

She scrunched up her nose while removing her lunch box from her bag. "Ugh. A guy and his family came to see me last weekend. And the guy's mother blatantly said they were under the impression that I was slimmer."

"No, she didn't! Did the guy say something?'"

"Do they ever? Always hiding behind their mama's saree. But still, there was no need. The moment she said that, Pappa got up, clasped his hands in front of him in a *Namaste*, and told them we were done. It was a total badass moment."

Wow. "That's awesome. Good for you."

At that moment, Kriti opened her lunch box, and a look of pure disgust crossed her face. "Look at this. My father might be on my side, but my maa takes things personally. Look what she packed for my lunch."

She extended her lunch box to me, and I couldn't stop the chuckle. It was cucumber and tomatoes—and that was all.

I opened my bag and got my lunch box. My lunch was bataka-poha. It's flattened rice, cooked and stir-fried with onion and potato with a little bit of turmeric, red chili powder, and sugar.

"We'll share," I said and gave her my lunch. When she offered her lunch to me, I picked two slices of cucumber.

After eating it, I added, "And don't worry. You'll find the right man."

She nodded confidently. "I know. It's my mom who worries. I'm completely happy with my life for now. And you'll find the right man too."

I scoffed. "Marriage isn't for me."

Kriti stopped eating the poha. "What do you mean? Don't you want to get married?"

I shook my head and ate another slice of cucumber. "To marry a person, I need to believe in their strength. Emotionally. Mentally. Financially. I never want to end up like my mother. And even if I find such a guy, what well-to-do family would want to associate themselves with my family and me? I have absolutely nothing to offer them except debt, a young brother, and a mother who I will take care of till Hari becomes capable enough to take over. And that would take at least fifteen more years. So, no. Marriage isn't for me."

Kriti clutched my shoulder. "I still stand by my words. You'll find the right man who might not only accept your situation but embrace it, tolerate your negative, cranky ass, and even make you laugh. Imagine that."

I squeezed her hand on my shoulder and smiled. My always optimistic friend. "Sure. Imagine that."

Right then, the recess bell rang, indicating the end of the break.

I grabbed my bag and my books, and headed to teach my seventh graders.

Luke

A week passed after my conversation with Meera. Every night I fell asleep listening to the beautiful melodies she played, though I didn't return to sleep outside after that. The only time we met was in the early morning when we had tea together.

Meera sat silently reading her newspaper while I sat on my cot reading the latest news about the US on my phone. The internet speed was terrible, so whenever it started buffering, I would just disturb Meera and talk to her about pointless things.

For the most part, I initiated our conversations, but in the past two days, Meera had begun our conversations without a newspaper in sight. I had also started running early in the morning to combat the lethargy that came from spending most of the day in my room after going to the site for three hours.

Meera was still asleep when I left for my jog this morning. It was Saturday, and their school began an hour later than usual. Hari and his mother slept on the double bed in the living room downstairs, so I quietly left the house and began running on the empty dirt street outside.

Meera's house was located on the edge of their farm. As I ran toward the main road a few kilometers away, I passed by other farms with houses set in their lands, some along the street and others in the middle of their farms. All of these farms had crops growing, and I saw farmers and their wives working on them. Meera's was the only farm with nothing growing.

As I ran along the main road, I passed a street lined with shops and restaurants. Over the past few days, the delicious aromas emanating from some of these establishments had tempted me to go in. However, I always ran back at the thought of missing out on my morning chai and breakfast with Meera.

Outside a small restaurant that resembled a café, I paused to consider going in for a little treat. But what if Meera had already prepared chai for me? Would she be waiting for me or missing me? And what if I invited her to join me for breakfast to try something new?

After debating for far too long, I finally called Meera. The call rang four times before she answered. "Luke?"

Every time she said my name, my heart gave a happy little skip.

I quickly cleared my throat, suddenly nervous about asking her. "Hey, Meera, I was out for a run, and I've been running along this street for the past few days. It always smells so deliciously divine every time I pass through this café that I just had to stop. I was hoping we could have breakfast out here today?"

There was silence on the other end, and my hand started to sweat as I waited for her response. When she took too long, I prodded, "Meera, are you there?"

She cleared her throat. "Uh, yeah. I'm here. Are you sure?"

I felt like I almost had her. "Yes, Meera. I'm completely sure. Come on, let's try some new dishes together. It'll be fun. Please?"

There was a soft sigh from her end. "Okay. What's the name of the place? I'll be there in ten."

I told her the name of the café and said that I would get us a seat and wait for her inside. The place was already bustling with people, and I didn't want to lose a seat by waiting outside.

By the time she arrived, I had already ordered us a cup of chai. I suggested that she could order our food. As soon as she sat across from me, I gave her a grateful smile and said, "Meera."

She smiled back and replied, "Luke."

Hearing her say my name made my knees weak and my stomach flutter. I wished she would call me by my name more often, but it was a rare occurrence. I couldn't help but smile, and my cheeks felt hot. I shook my head and looked down at the handwritten menu, trying to contain my happiness.

A server placed two cups of chai on the table, interrupting my thoughts. Meera quickly ordered a few items off the menu, and the server left us alone.

We took a few sips of the chai, which tasted different from how Meera prepared it but was still delicious. I said, "I'm really glad you agreed to join me."

Meera blushed and replied softly, "Me too."

She cleared her throat, and I looked at her, knowing that was her signal for when she wanted to call me or when she needed my attention. Or sometimes she would send Hari to call me.

"What's up?" I asked, sipping the strong, minty chai with a hint of spice.

"So how is Akira doing?" Meera ran her finger over the rim of her cup and met my gaze.

Akira. My best friend's girlfriend.

"She's doing well. Happy. Sam and Akira are starting their second year in the grad program, and Akira has an intern position with Sam at our company in New York." Leaning forward, I spoke as if sharing a secret.

Meera leaned in with a smile, and I couldn't help but admire her warm brown eyes, long lashes, and soft brown skin. Her brownish-pink lips were so tempting that I had an inappropriate urge to bite them. My heart raced, and I held my breath. I focused solely on her, as everything else around me blurred. Arousal pulsed through my veins, and I struggled to keep myself composed and not reveal how she affected me.

With great effort, I managed to smile and recall what I would say. "Don't tell anyone, but Akira has practically moved in with Sam. Her family has no idea."

Mischief and excitement twinkled in Meera's eyes, but a hint of envy also seemed present. "How do you know?" she asked.

We were still leaning toward each other, closer than ever before, when our server arrived and placed three plates of food between us, effectively separating us. One of the plates had spongy yellow steamed cake-like items. Meera pointed at it and said, "This one's called dhokla. It's a steamed cake made with a fermented batter of gram flour."

She picked up a piece, dipped it in a green chutney, and took a bite. As I followed suit, she said, "This green chutney is coriander-mint chutney. Isn't it delicious?"

As soon as I put the savory cake with chutney in my mouth, a loud groan escaped me. "Oh my God, Meera. This is amazing."

I picked up another piece, gave it a hearty dip in the chutney, and ate it up.

Between bites, I continued our conversation. "Sam and I share a two-bedroom apartment in New York, and five out of seven days, I find Akira in our house."

A slight frown appeared between her eyebrows, but she quickly turned it into a smile. If I hadn't been observing her so closely, I would've missed it.

"I see. So you must spend a lot of time with her. I mean, with them?" she asked, taking a bite of her dhokla. Red dotted her cheeks, and she averted her eyes.

Before she could become more flustered and run away, as she seemed ready to do, I reassured her. "Sort of. Sam and Akira usually do their own thing. I'm usually in my class working. But sometimes they invite me to join when Akira has cooked some good Indian food."

Meera nodded and began serving the next two dishes: poha and khandvi. A few sips of chai completed the experience.

As I made appreciative sounds with each bite, Meera kept smiling. She then picked up the roll-like spongy pastry on the third plate and handed it to me. "Try this. It could be a hit or miss for you because of the texture."

Our fingers brushed as I accepted the savory yellow pastry from her, sending a jolt of electricity down my hand and swooping low in my stomach. I tried not to reveal the effect her touch had on me.

The pastry had the texture of thin slices of jelly wrapped in a roll. I kept my eyes on Meera as I took a bite. Once again, the food was divine, with the savory roll melting in my mouth.

I kept rambling about my life in NYC. She sat back, occasionally eating a few bites and drinking chai, a small smile on her lips.

And just to make her smile even more, I said, "Once, Akira cooked something called bhaji pav, and it turned out to be *so* spicy. I didn't tell her, but the next day, I had to take a sick day from all my lectures and spent the entire day making trips to the toilet."

And she laughed.

She *laughed*. At *me*.

And I knew I was in trouble.

Because that laughter was music to my ears.

I'd have to tell her more embarrassing stories of myself and thank God I was me. I had racked up plenty of them in my lifetime.

Just to keep her smiling, I joked, "Yes. Yes. Laugh at my pain."

And she chuckled some more. "It's just, you handle my cooking fine. And my food isn't bland."

"Exactly."

And she laughed some more.

Just to keep her laughing, I continued, "Don't get me wrong. Akira cooks great food. But apparently, she was not satisfied with the gravy color. She wanted it to be dark brown with oil floating on top, but in reality, it was light brown with no oil on top. So she kept adding red chili powder and her different masalas even though Sam and I warned her that it would get too hot."

Meera kept chuckling. This was my favorite morning already.

"Poor Akira," she said.

"Poor Akira? *Poor Akira?* No. Poor me, Meera."

She just shook her head at me, a big smile on her face, and picked up her cup of chai.

We spent the next half an hour talking, laughing, and eating the decadent breakfast, exchanging glances that spoke far more than words.

After returning home, Meera and Hari headed off to school. I had intentionally planned to visit the stepwell on weekdays to avoid crowds. After a week of visiting every day with Ramesh, I had most of the dimensions and decided to spend the day in my room drafting all the drawings in the AutoCAD file.

The happiness from the morning lingered with me throughout the day.

Although I had tea with Meera in the morning, I usually had a cup of coffee at around 11:00 a.m., either at the site or in my room. I had even purchased a single-cup drip coffee maker for my room.

Meera's laughter still echoed in my heart; her hoarse chuckle played in my ears, making my heartbeat faster.

I spent some time drafting on my laptop before taking a shower—or more accurately, a bucket and tumbler bath. I had grown accustomed to this method of bathing, which consisted of four quick steps: filling the bucket with water, pouring it over my body from head to toe using a tumbler, soaping up, and rinsing off with ten more tumblers of water. The tumbler released more water than a shower, and I relished the strong rush of water hitting my body.

Once I was ready to return to work, I poured myself a cup of coffee and sat at the desk near the window. I became engrossed in drafting, but the temperature began to rise, so I closed all the windows and doors and turned on the AC in my room. The room quickly cooled, but I heard loud, muffled voices from outside.

I turned off the AC to stop its loud whirring, and the

shouting became clearer. Meera's voice and her mother's kept interrupting each other. I got up from the chair and slowly opened the door to my bedroom.

The shouting grew louder, but since I didn't understand their language, I had no idea what it was about. I poked my head out to look out and saw a small figure huddled at the top step's railing. Hari clutched the railing with one hand, his shoulders shaking, and his soft sniffles pierced my heart amid the chaos of the shouting.

It reminded me of my own childhood, where, like Hari, I would sit on the steps listening to my parents fight, shout, and cry. My sister's death had broken something inside them and between them, and I was lost, swept up in the chaos that followed.

The utter loneliness.

The bone-aching terror that they, too, would be taken from me.

The helplessness.

Every emotion roared back at me as I watched Hari try not to cry, not to be another burden on his already broken family.

And I couldn't stop myself.

I quietly walked up to him and sat beside him. He held himself tight the moment he noticed me, clutching his little shorts tighter and turning his face toward the railing to hide the tears that ran down his face. My throat closed up at the grief and confusion of the little boy.

I saw my younger self in him—how I'd wished for someone to come and make the shouting go away.

How I'd wished for my parents to hold me and tell me everything would be okay.

They hadn't.

But *I* could.

I placed my hand on his tiny back and held his tiny hand that clutched his shorts.

I could barely hear his sniffles amid the shouting match downstairs.

When Meera shouted especially loud, Hari made a hiccupping cry, and I clutched his shoulder tighter.

And without meeting my eyes, he hid his face in my chest, letting out the tears that he tried so hard to hold.

8

Song: *Haal Kaisa Hai Janab Ka*
   - *Kishore Kumar and Asha Bhosle*

Meera

I ran out of the house and into our farm.

Angry tears, helpless tears, tears of frustration ran down my face.

Suddenly, a sharp pain shot through the sole of my foot, causing me to almost lose my balance. I realized that I had forgotten to put on my sandals, but I kept running nonetheless.

Despite the scorching heat of the late afternoon assaulting my eyes, I ran.

I ran, knowing deep down that there was no escape—no escape from the suffocating burden of debt, my mother's unrelenting expectations, or the endless sacrifices required to make ends meet in this life.

"*We've still not received the check. Why aren't you talking to Surbhi?*" *my mother shouted.*

"If we could just sell the farm, we might get enough money to pay some more debt," I tried to reason.

"Have you lost your mind? Just sell everything that your father has worked on? Sell the very thing that he gave his life for?"

"No. Sell the very thing that killed him."

"Meera!" she shouted. "Watch your mouth."

"Why don't you understand, Maa? We can sell it off. Get rid of the debt. Move to the city. Make a new life."

"And what? You'll stay with us forever? No intention of marrying?"

"Of course, and who would marry me and the debt? Who will agree to take care of you and Hari?"

"We don't need you. And maybe a good husband would take care of all of us. Have you thought of that? If you treat him well, maybe he will take care of your family," she said, every word a stab to my heart.

"And what if he can't? Burden him with more people to care for? What if he can't handle it? What if he ends up like Pappa?"

A slap hit me out of nowhere.

Tears streamed down Maa's face. *"Respect your father. He gave his everything to take care of his family. It is not his fault the world wasn't kind to us. He tried and tried and tried. He wasn't weak. Do you understand?"*

I simply nodded, her words tearing apart my defenses, my cheek on fire, my pride burned to ash.

After running for several minutes, I arrived at the banyan tree that held a thousand memories.

Memories of me tagging along with my mother, bringing lunch to my father, and the three of us sitting under the tree, sharing a meal almost every day. Memories of me sitting under the tree with my father, doing my schoolwork while he worked nearby, and showing him the pictures I drew of him farming.

Tears streamed down my cheeks, stinging on one side, as I sat under the tree. The shade provided some relief from the heat as I gazed at our now-barren farm, once a place where my father tended to his millet crops.

As the temperature started to cool, the burning heat became more tolerable, almost soothing.

Lost in the memories, I wondered when everything started to fade—when the hope and happiness of those times began to slip away.

As I sat there, I heard a rustle and looked up to see a figure approaching.

It was Kriti, wearing a brown salwar kameez that blended in with the surroundings. In one hand, she held a book wrapped in newspaper, while the other hand clutched a bottle of water. I turned my head away, uninterested in any conversation.

But since this wasn't our first time in this place for this reason, she took a seat next to me, placed the water bottle between us, and began to read.

For what felt like an eternity, Kriti read her book while I sat in silence. Eventually, I picked up the water bottle and took a drink, struggling to swallow with the lump in my throat.

Kriti interrupted my thoughts. "Guess what my mother cooked for lunch today? Dal tadka and jeera rice. But for me? Cucumber, carrots, and boiled dal. She's still hung up on the weight thing. I had to steal some food from my dad's plate."

A sound escaped my lips, starting as a laugh before turning into a sob. I held my face in my hands, trying to regain control, and Kriti wrapped her arms around me.

"It's okay, Meera. It's okay," she whispered.

"It's not," I cried. "Why do I have to live like this? Why do others have it so much better? Why is life so unfair?"

Kriti didn't say anything but held me close as I cried. As always, she was there for me. Her warmth gave me the strength to stand up and wipe away my tears.

Together, we made our way back to the house.

"Maa called you?" I asked.

"Yeah. She was crying. So I just knew."

"It's always the same. She refuses to sell the farm but expects the debt to go away."

"All her memories are attached to the farm. I can't imagine how hard it might be for her to let go."

"I know, despite the fact that she hasn't stepped on the farm in five years. But it's just... It might make our lives easier if she agreed to sell, you know?"

She held my hand as we walked. "I know," she said, squeezing my hand in support.

Finally, I noticed the pink-blue sky, the absence of sun, and the cool breeze soothing the slight burn on my cheek.

"It's almost dinnertime. I didn't realize I was gone so long," I said.

"Aunty called me after two hours had passed and you hadn't returned."

"You're having dinner here."

She lightly pushed my shoulders, her eyes turning mischievous. "Oh, I definitely am. I need to see Foreigner Luke."

I couldn't help but chuckle. "Stop calling him Foreigner Luke."

She giggled, and asked, "What should I call him? Jiju?" Jiju means brother-in-law.

"Oh God, please, no. Why would you say that?" I groaned. "Just behave yourself, or you're uninvited."

She pouted and sighed dramatically. "This is what I get for being the best friend in the world?"

I put my arm in hers and pulled her toward home. "Shut up, you drama queen. Let's go."

Well, my best friend would meet the beautiful man living in my room—the man who had charmed his way into my heart a bit, if I was willing to be honest. He would see my slightly swollen cheek and my red eyes and nose. He must have heard the shouting. What must he think about our family?

Embarrassment licked at my insides.

I had barely entered the room when I was enveloped in Maa's hug.

I clutched at her, and we both sighed in relief that things were fine.

"Dinner is ready. Call the boys from upstairs. I hope Hari isn't giving any trouble to Luke bhai."

"I didn't even think of that," I said, running toward the stairs. Kriti offered to help my mom set out the meal while I fetched the boys.

Hari wasn't on the terrace or in the hallway between the terrace and Luke's room. I could see the light under the bottom of Luke's door. Cool air touched my feet as I approached, and I knocked twice.

I heard heavy footsteps approaching the door. With a soft click, Luke opened the door. Our eyes met, and his face turned from warm to fierce. His eyes roamed across my face, and I looked away, feeling ashamed.

Luke inhaled sharply, and in a tone I'd never heard before, which was protective and furious at the same time, he said, "I heard shouting. What happened?"

I took a deep breath, turned my spine to steel, and met his eyes. "Things are fine now. Where's Hari?"

Luke's hand tightened on the door, two red spots appearing on his cheekbones as he pressed his lips together. As if he was restraining himself from asking more. From demanding answers. Good. I didn't owe him answers. He couldn't solve anything.

He opened the door to his room, and I found my little brother there, sleeping peacefully on Luke's bed, a blanket covering his small frame. Colored pencils were strewn around him. The chair at the desk was turned like Luke had gotten up from his desk.

"He was upset when you and your mother were fighting,

and I found him sitting on the stairs. So, I took him to my room, turned on the AC, and drew him a picture to color in. I hope that's okay," Luke explained.

How could it not be okay? I felt a pang of shame, and tears welled up in my eyes. Luke was breaking down the walls of my heart, and it was hard to keep his presence transactional when he did such kind things for my family. I clenched my jaw, trying to keep my composure, but a tear escaped.

"Thank you, Luke. Thank you," I managed to say.

Luke's hand reached out to touch my face, but I recoiled. I couldn't handle his touch. His hand dropped down into a fist, and he muttered, "It's okay," before turning to let me into the room.

Cool, heavenly air enveloped me as I stepped inside. I gazed at my sleeping brother and said, "It's not. I know it's not. I try not to have arguments when he's home, but sometimes things get out of hand."

Luke stood beside me, almost within reach, his arms folded across his chest. His eyes darted between Hari and me as he sighed and said, "Believe me. I understand."

I didn't have the capacity to discuss it further. Instead, I went over to Hari and gently woke him up. The moment he saw me, he climbed onto my lap and hugged me tightly.

I could feel Luke's eyes on us, and it sent shivers racing along my spine and goose bumps along my arms. I hugged Hari tighter and kissed his cheeks. "Everything's okay now, Hari. Maa has cooked a nice dinner."

"Is Maa still angry?" he asked in a small voice.

We spoke in Gujarati, so Luke had no idea what we were saying, but he stood at the edge of the bed, watching over us.

I reassured Hari that everything was fine and lifted him in my arms. He was too big for me, but he still wrapped his arms and legs around me.

"You want some help carrying the little guy downstairs?" Luke asked.

Hari just now realized Luke's presence and instantly smiled at him.

"You had a good nap, little Hari?" he asked.

Hari did not understand anything, so I translated it for him. He quickly nodded, turned to Luke, and pointed at the AC behind me.

"Ahh. You love the AC?" he asked.

Hari quickly nodded, looked at me, and asked in Gujarati, "Can we get one too?"

"Maybe later," I answered.

He nodded and rested his head on my shoulder as we walked down the steps. Luke walked a step ahead of me, ready to catch any of us in case I lost my balance. I couldn't help but smile at his thoughtfulness but quickly wiped it off when I heard Kriti's voice. I didn't want her to get any ideas.

The five of us had a pleasant dinner, during which Kriti behaved herself but continued to elbow me in a way that wouldn't catch Luke's attention.

Luke gave extra smiles to Hari and, if I wasn't mistaken, fewer to Maa. Not that Maa cared about it, but secretly, I liked it. It felt like someone was on my side.

After dinner, Luke went upstairs, and Hari rushed after him to "check" the air conditioner. Kriti left shortly after we finished cleaning up the kitchen. Maa was already asleep when I was ready to go upstairs, and I once again found Hari asleep by the time I got up there. I carried him from Luke's room to his spot beside Maa and kissed his forehead.

Quietly, I climbed upstairs. Luke's bedroom door was shut, with light shining from the bottom.

Under the moonlight, with the cool breeze blowing my hair, I made my bed, climbed under the blanket, and turned on the cassette player. I breathed out the day, but I couldn't help noticing the empty bed beside mine.

The silence, darkness, and the smell of night-blooming jasmine lulled me into a calm state, and with each soft song that played, I felt lighter.

Every night this week, Luke had stayed inside. Every night, I missed him, knowing I shouldn't.

But tonight, I didn't want to be alone. It felt like he needed to be in the empty bed beside me, talking to me in his soft baritone and soothing the raw emotions that threatened to overwhelm me. Yet I had no right to ask that of him.

As the next song played, I closed my eyes and focused on the cool breeze. I took a few calming breaths when I heard the door click open.

Relief and happiness rushed through my veins, but I still didn't open my eyes. Turning my head the other way so he couldn't see my face, I let the smile that had bubbled to the surface slip out.

Luke

As soon as I opened the door, Meera turned her face away from me. Perhaps she didn't want me there. Nevertheless, I needed to ensure she was okay.

I cleared my throat and asked, "Meera?"

She turned her head toward me, raising her eyebrows in question.

"May I?" I gestured to the empty bed.

She smiled and nodded slightly. A wave of relief washed over me, realizing she wanted me there.

Before she could change her mind, I retrieved my pillow and blanket from the room and settled into bed. The sweet scent of jasmine and the cool breeze were heavenly. While we both faced the overhead moon, my attention remained on Meera. She lay still, inhaling and exhaling.

"Can I say something?" I asked.

She tensed up as though anticipating the worst. Still, she nodded.

"I don't want to offend or hurt you. I merely wanted to share a bit about my past. Is that okay?"

She eased up a bit and nodded, avoiding my gaze.

I seldom revisited my past or spoke to anyone about it. But I couldn't help empathizing with Hari. "I was about Hari's age when my sister passed away. Old enough to remember her presence but young enough to forget most of the memories. I still recall her laughter, her tight hugs, and all of us having breakfast together before Dad dropped us off at school."

I gazed up at the sky, sensing Meera's eyes on me. It gave me the courage to continue and not be bogged down by the memories.

"But after she passed away, everything changed. My parents stopped smiling. Initially, they either fought a lot or didn't even talk to each other. Sometimes my mom hugged me a lot, and some days she couldn't even look at me. I felt like I had lost everyone. But I didn't want to, you know? So I always stayed where I could see my mom or dad. I loved the days when my mom would keep hugging me."

I had to look at Meera, just to see her expression and determine what she thought of me.

I didn't know what I expected, but her face held so much compassion and heartache that my throat closed up, and I looked away from her piercing gaze.

"Did it get better?" she asked, her voice hoarse.

"It did. It took years and years of therapy. My mom's sister is a psychiatrist. She suggested a grief counselor. My parents have gone to countless therapy and counseling sessions. Grief coun-

seling, couples therapy, child counseling, family counseling.
You name it. They still occasionally go for counseling sessions."

"And it helped?" she asked, hope and wonder in her tone.

"It helped. It took time, but eventually, we started cele-
brating my sister instead of only grieving her. My parents
started smiling and laughing without feeling guilty. And
instead of fighting, my parents became each other's rocks. They
started getting involved in tons of charities, helping people
with mental illness. My sister had been depressed, and no one
had realized it. I guess they got involved in helping people with
mental illness to assuage their guilt, but they've stuck to the
cause for the past seventeen years. It all taught me the impor-
tance of just being alive. To enjoy every moment, to just do
what I wanted, and not end up with any regrets. "

"Some of us don't have the luxury to follow our hearts," she
murmured, and my heart sank.

"I'm sorry," I replied.

"You don't need to apologize for your life. I'm glad you got
your parents back and found your own happiness. It gives me
hope. I don't want Hari's life to be sad. I want him to have a
normal, happy childhood. That's all I want. And I'm trying
really hard, you know."

"I know."

A soothing melody played in the background as we sat in
silence. It tugged at my heartstrings but did nothing to uplift
my spirits. Turning to Meera, I asked, "Do you have any uplift-
ing, happy songs in there?"

Her eyes twinkled as she turned onto her stomach, her
curls spilling over her shoulder. She reached for the cassette
player and deftly switched out the cassette, hitting play.

With an excited smile, Meera looked up at me as a playful
duet began to fill the air with the voices of a man and a woman.
As the lines playfully ended with "oh, oh, oh" and "ah, ah, ah,"
Meera began to sing along with them.

Then she surprised me by *yodeling* along with the male singer. And she did it again and again.

Caught up in the moment, I was half up, sitting on the cot, grinning from ear to ear. Meera cackled at my delighted expression. But when instrumental music started to play between the verses, I reached down and hit the pause button.

"Meera, you can yodel?" I exclaimed in amazement.

Frowning for a moment, but with a big smile still in place, she replied, "What is that?"

In my hoarse, out-of-tune voice, I tried to demonstrate by yodeling myself. "Oleiyo you oo... Oleiyo you oo... That is yodeling."

And she cackled, like I'd never seen her do before, then said, "Yes, it is so fun to do!"

Excitedly, I asked, "What are they singing? And please, please do it again."

She laughed and agreed. "Okay. The song's name is 'Haal Kaisa Hai Janab Ka.'" She translated it for me, explaining that it's a duet between a man and a woman.

> "How's the gentleman doing?
> What do you think?
> You were being stubborn and got caught.
> I just slipped and fell."

"Awesome," I exclaimed, sitting up on the cot, not wanting to miss a single moment of the playful and adorable Meera. She hit play, looked at me, and began to sing the peppy tune while swaying with the music. Her face lit up with the biggest smile as she yodeled once again, and I eagerly joined in.

Soon, a romantic trumpet started to play, and Meera playfully sang another verse, her expressions matching the banter between the man and woman.

I was lost, completely entranced by the joy on her face.

As the music continued, it was Meera's turn to translate, and she blushed. Intrigued, I kept looking at her expectantly, not wanting to spook her yet eager to learn more.

After clearing her throat, Meera said, her voice a little softer than before,

> "Crazy woman, O Crazy woman, did you ever
> consider how we met on the street?
> Crazy man, O crazy man, why does my heart
> pound with every word you say?"

Did she feel those words deeper than the others?

I expected her not to sing the verse, but she did.

With a small, shy smile on her face and her gaze avoiding me, she sang the words of the song, causing my heart to race. Before I could ask for more, Meera yodeled again, leaving me breathless.

Blushing even more, she translated the lyrics, which asked if she could enjoy my company every day. Despite the fact that it was part of the song, I nodded in agreement.

She shook her head and continued singing,

> "Listen please, listen please—if you could under-
> stand, please understand this yourself, what
> should I even tell you?"

This time, when she sang the verse, she looked directly at me, asking if she could enjoy my company every day. Helplessly, I nodded again.

No one had ever wooed me with a song before, and I could feel the heat rising in my face, burning up my chest, and a million butterflies taking flight in my stomach.

She quickly looked away, but I caught the wide smile on her face. Before I could ask her to play the song again, she jumped to the next song, intentionally avoiding my eyes. Nevertheless, I couldn't help but smile because I knew she liked my company.

Soon, another song with even more yodeling began, ending with a guy's crazy cackling laugh. And Meera repeated it.

With mischievous eyes, she said, "It's called *'Zindagi ek Safar.'* Life's a journey. Do I need to translate this?"

I met her gaze, smiling wide, and shook my head. "Just promise to play this three times, and if you could yodel the entire time, I'd really, really appreciate it."

She hit play.

> "Arre orleyi oouu...
> Orleyi orleyi oo
> Orleyi orleyi oohoo
> Ah ha ha ha..."

And she cackled, and I followed.

We replayed the yodel. Over and over again.

Made funny voices.

Laughed and howled and cackled in the darkness.

Yet when I finally closed my eyes, Meera's laughter shone brighter than ever before.

9

Song: Yeh Raatein Yeh Mausam

- *Kishore Kumar and Asha Bhosle*

Meera

I woke up alone. Yet after a very long time, I didn't *feel* alone.

For the first time in a while, I woke up with a smile on my face.

The air smelled fresher. The approaching dawn, and the chirping of the birds seemed to greet me with a good morning. As I made my bed, I saw the moon fading at the horizon.

Once I freshened up, I quietly prepared some snacks and a few cups of chai in the kitchen. Maa and Hari usually do not wake up before eight on a Sunday, so today seemed like a great day to take Luke to a nearby lake.

I prepared a picnic basket, packing the snacks in aluminum foil and pouring the chai into an insulated container.

Luke arrived in my life three weeks ago. Just three weeks. Still, it felt like more. If Luke hadn't been there for me last night, I would've wallowed in my grief, replaying the sorrow in the songs.

Why did Luke affect me so much? Why did I want to smile every time he smiled at me?

Maybe because he'd suffered a similar tragedy as mine, and still, he smiled, laughed, traveled, helped people, and just *lived*.

Seeing him made me realize I have put my life on a hold. I didn't *have* to think about my responsibilities and burdens constantly. It wouldn't be entirely awful if I smiled, laughed, and occasionally played happier songs. Maybe if I tried, I could reclaim some of my joy too.

I went to the terrace and waited for him to get back from his run. A low, thumping sound pulled me out of my thoughts. I looked at the stairs, and in a moment, Luke entered.

Sweat dripped down his neck, his sleeveless T-shirt soaked with sweat around his chest and stomach. His hair wet and plastered to his forehead. A wide smile came over his face the moment our eyes met.

He pointed a finger at me and said, "I'll be right there."

"Luke," I called out.

He immediately halted and turned toward me. The more he looked at me, the more it made me wonder if it was a good idea to go to a lake with him. Would he think it's a stupid idea? What if he said no?

"Meera? What is it?"

I pushed a few strands of my hair behind my ear, and said, "I wondered if you'd like to have breakfast at a nearby lake. Since the weather is pretty good right now, and it's a Sunday, I thought..."

"Yes. Definitely, yes." His immediate response caused relief to wash over my mind, and a tsunami of excitement flooded my body. I couldn't contain my smile, even if I'd wanted to.

He rushed into his room, and I tried my hardest not to look at his retreating back.

He was the first man I had ever developed this...this *attraction* for, and it was messing with my mind. When I was in school and college, I focused entirely on getting the highest marks and making my parents proud.

Yes, I wore my first jeans, pants, and T-shirts in college. But even in college, I never talked to any boys, just worked and studied. I had gotten a part-time job at a beauty parlor, waxing and threading ladies. I did not have any guy friends, and the girls I called friends were only there for the sake of having backup if I was unsure on assignments.

And in my last semester... Well, Pappa passed away, and I returned. Kriti was already working in the local government school then and convinced the directors to hire me. I finished my degree in the first year of my teaching job.

And now, looking at Luke and spending time with him, made me wonder if I missed out on having guy friends. On having a boyfriend.

No. I never needed one, then.

And now?

I definitely didn't *need* one.

But Luke.

I liked looking at Luke. Conversation with him was the highlight of my day. Singing with him last night was the highlight of the past five years. His easily given smiles, his playfulness, his care and thoughtfulness for Hari, his passion for his work, and his past so similar to mine all made me feel infinitely closer to him. Made me want to share all my joys and sorrows with him.

The moment he stepped out of his bedroom, my body lit up, and a smile came over my face. My heart pounded as he returned my smile, utterly stupid thing that it was.

We took my two-wheeler with Luke sitting behind me holding the picnic basket between us.

I had to stifle a laugh as he kept reminding me to drive slowly since he wasn't holding anything for support.

I couldn't stop my eyes from checking him out in the rearview mirror, his hair blowing in the wind, his jaw clenched tight. He kept stealing glances at me, and his gaze sent this giddy sort of excitement bubbling up in my heart.

Soon, we arrived at the lake and walked along the narrow dirt lane path lined by trees on both sides. We found a spot under the shade of a large tree near the bank of the lake.

"It's so quiet and peaceful out here," Luke said with a happy sigh as we laid down a carpet.

Taking a seat side by side, our arms almost brushed together. I kept my eyes on the lake, and said, "It is. Once in a while, when life gets too chaotic, I come here for a few hours just to get away for a while."

Luke pulled out all the contents from the picnic basket as he listened to me talk. He poured chai in one of the cups and handed to me. "It's understandable. You deserve some peace and escape, just to keep your sanity intact."

Luke poured some chai for himself, then leaned back on his arm and folded his leg so our knees touched. Surprisingly, he did not move it away.

Neither did I.

The feel of his leg against mine had goose bumps break out along my arms, and all I could do was clutch my cup tighter so it didn't slip from my shaky fingers.

Dragging my attention away from our knees, I looked up at his face. A glint of mischief shone in his eyes, and he said, "So... last night was fun."

Where I howled like a monkey and did what Luke called yodeling.

My cheeks heated in embarrassment, but last night *was* too much fun not to smile. So I looked at him and chuckled. "It was."

"We should do that more often."

"Of course. And then, we'll climb on our cots and break into a Bollywood dance, and the stars and moon will join us."

He snorted and the hot tea went into his nose, causing him to sputter and cough for a whole minute.

He sucked in a big, noisy breath, looked at me with his sharp eyes, and said, "My dear Meera, was that a joke?"

I tried, really tried, to stop the smile, and said, "Well, if you had to ask, it must not be a good one."

"Didn't you see me hack up my lungs? You could've killed me with that joke," he said, and winked at me.

Winked. At me.

And like a lovesick fool, I blushed, so I quickly hid my face by drinking tea.

"So what's the plan for today?" he asked.

I put my cup down on the blanket and plucked some grass from near my feet. "Well, nothing much. Spend time with Hari, get him to do his homework, correct my students' homework, and rest. You? Going anywhere?"

He shook his head. "Nah. It's too crowded at the stepwell on Sunday. I have realized weekdays are the best time to visit any landmarks."

"You're right. So just working from your room then?"

With a small smile, he said. "Well, maybe I'll join you and Hari for a while?"

I looked away at the lake, hiding the delight at his offer. "That would be good."

"Good."

And that was what we did. We spent an hour at the lake, talking about nothing and everything. When we got home, we played board games with Hari. Luke and Hari played cricket while Maa and I prepared lunch, which we all ate together. Luke was in his room, working, and Hari was doing homework with me when my phone rang.

Surbhi didi calling...

I quickly picked up the call, hoping for some news on the subsidy payment.

"Hello, Surbhi didi."

"Meera, so glad I caught you."

"Of course."

"So do you have some time to visit my house to talk about the subsidy payment issue? I've asked a few other people to come as well."

"Okay. I'll be there. What time?"

"How about five?" she asked.

Three hours from now.

"Okay. See you then, Didi."

"Bye, Meera."

She hung up before I could tell her goodbye.

I helped Hari with his homework for the next hour and a half, and then got up to start preparing for the meeting.

First task, prepare twenty cups of chai to bring to the meeting. I decided to have some before going, and Maa asked me to make one for her.

Since I was already preparing chai for myself, Maa, and twenty others, I decided I should also ask Luke if he would like some.

I put a lot of water on low heat and hurried upstairs.

Luke's bedroom door was closed, and as I stood outside it, cool air touched my feet. Even the tile flooring outside his room had become cold.

I knocked twice. "Luke?"

A rustle and thump on the other side, and then the door opened.

Luke, with a black pencil stuck behind his ear, his eyes red and tired, in a hoarse voice, said, "Hey, Meera. What's up?"

I couldn't help but notice how warm and inviting he looked in his gray T-shirt and loose black bottoms. My body almost swayed toward him, needing to be enveloped in his broad chest and thick arms. A throat cleared, and now I couldn't look up for entirely different reasons.

So I continued to stare at his chest, and asked, "Would you like some chai?"

His chest moved and puffed a little, then shook in laughter. "Meera, will you please look at me so I can talk to you?"

Bracing myself, I looked up to see a mischievous twinkle in his eyes and a small smile on his lips. "We don't usually have chai at this time. What's the special occasion?" he asked, his eyes betraying the playfulness he tried to conceal.

The reason brought me back to reality. "Well, I need to go to a woman's house for a meeting to discuss why we haven't received our subsidy money for the past five months and what to do about it. A few others will be coming too, so I'm taking chai for everyone. Maa and I will be having it before I leave, so I thought I'd ask if you'd like some."

Luke's eyes, which had just been red and tired, turned sharp and laser-focused on me. "Would it help if I joined you? And if you don't want me, would you like to go in the car? I can call Ramesh."

My cheeks felt like they were burning, and I couldn't discern whether it was due to embarrassment or anger. My stomach churned, and I struggled to speak, as if rocks were lodged in my throat. After several attempts at swallowing and gulping, I finally managed to force out the words, "I... I don't need your help."

A gentle smile crept over his face, his eyes softening. "I know. I'm offering. I want to help you. I want to support you, if you want it."

Support. Offer. Want. Very few people have spoken those words to me in my life. Those words made me look back at how infrequently I was offered support and how rarely someone asked me if I wanted something.

And how I *wanted.*

Luke patiently observed my inner turmoil, and I hoped he wouldn't notice the effect his statement had on me. His words were infused with genuine care and so much warmth that I couldn't find the words to express my gratitude. All I could do was nod my head and hope my gesture conveyed what I couldn't put into words.

I turned around to go back when he called out to me.

I turned, and he said, "I'll have the chai. Thank you."

The chai. Oh God, it was on the stove.

I nodded and ran downstairs, trying to escape the flood of emotions bursting in my heart.

Luke

It was pouring outside, so we had to drag the cots into the covered hallway before leaving the house. Fortunately, Meera agreed to take the car. Despite the wipers being turned to their maximum capacity, I could hardly see anything from the windshield due to the heavy rain. The constant potholes on the road only made Ramesh angrier.

Meera sat in the back seat with a large bag of bhajiya, as Ramesh and Meera called it. When I informed Ramesh on the phone about where we were going and that we were bringing chai for everyone, he had shown up with a big package of bhajiya, which he told me was the special fried food to be eaten with chai during the rain. Although I had yet to see or taste them, the spices infusing the car had me excited. I was glad he had gotten them for everyone on our behalf. After all, Ramesh and I were a team, right?

After a twenty-minute ride filled with potholes and expletives, we arrived at a gate. A few scooters and motorbikes were parked outside, and the smaller half of the gate was open.

We parked our car a little farther down the road, outside what looked like an abandoned property, and walked to Meera's friend's place. Ramesh kindly offered to carry the tea thermos, and Meera carried the bhajiya, while I walked beside them empty-handed, feeling like a foreigner out to have fun.

The house appeared to be in a dilapidated state. I saw several cracked roofing tiles, the plaster on the walls was peeling off, and a few walls had cracks. A low hum of conversation could be heard coming from the back of the house. Meera led us to the side of the house, down a narrow dirt passage that opened up into a yard big enough to hold around fifty people.

We noticed a crowd of about fifteen people already engaged in a tense conversation as we approached. Meera and Ramesh placed the food and chai on the covered porch that led into the house. Meera's friend excused herself from the conversation and hugged Meera.

After a brief chat, Meera called me to where they stood. As I approached, I introduced myself, "Hi, I'm Luke."

She gave me a small smile and shook my hand. "I'm Surbhi. Meera mentioned that you've been living in the village for a few weeks. I hope you're enjoying your time here."

I glanced over at Meera, who seemed to blush at the question. Was she thinking about the singing from last night? Our morning tea time? Meeting Surbhi's gaze, I replied, "Yes, very much. Thank you."

Before we could continue our conversation, loud voices interrupted us. Surbhi sprang into action, standing in front of the crowd with her spine straight and her voice strong. She fearlessly confronted a group of angry men and women while keeping her cool in the midst of it all.

Meera joined me, her focus on the meeting at hand.

At the far end of the yard, two women cried while three

others tried to console them. One of the crying women held a little child in her arms. The intense emotions emanating from the people around us felt like a sharp blow to the gut, and a heavy weight settled in my heart.

Meera tapped my shoulder. When I looked at her, she said, "Surbhi didi is the founder and the head of the Life for Widows Organization. She was the one who helped me navigate life after what happened. She helped me apply for all the documents for claiming a subsidy and provided a community for all of us to help each other out. When my father passed, a lot of these ladies brought food and clothes and such. Some just came to watch over Maa and Hari when I was busy running around municipality offices with Surbhi didi."

My heart broke for Meera and for all the people gathered here.

At my silence—because what could I even say?— she continued. "The only time I consider myself lucky is when I come to these meetings. I lost my father, but at least I have a job. Hari is studying. And we have food on the table most days. A lot of people here have lost their fathers, husbands, and sometimes both. They have no education. Their entire livelihood is dependent on their farms that they now tend alone. The price of fertilizer continues to increase, they don't get fair prices for the crops they sell, and they barely have food on the table. The loans that our fathers and husbands took still hold us in debt. These government subsidies should help us pay this loan, but when does the government ever do anything on time?"

Meera said she felt *lucky* among a lot of these people.

She could at least imagine their situation. I couldn't even comprehend it. The helplessness. The loss. The burden on these women to keep their families afloat. All amid an unreliable government.

Fuck.

The overwhelming sadness and fear in the air suffocated me, compelling me to do something. Even Meera seemed to be standing a little closer to me.

My heart pounded, and I grazed my hand against Meera's. That small touch grounded me and brought me back from the spiraling thoughts of helplessness.

She looked at me, and I said, "I want to help, Meera."

She frowned, and a sad smile appeared on her lips. Those were the worst smiles. "You can't."

"Can't a donation to the organization help some of them temporarily?"

"I didn't bring you here for your donation."

"I know. But I wouldn't have blamed you even if you did."

She nodded, her eyes downcast, her feet drawing circles in the mud. "Let's talk to Surbhi didi after everyone leaves. They're deciding to go to the municipality office the day after tomorrow. The office clerks don't take women seriously, so a few men have decided to go."

"Are you going?" I asked.

She shook her head. "I can't miss work."

"Of course."

Meera got back to listening, and I stood there beside her, hoping she found as much support from me as I found in her.

An hour later, we were on our way home—silent, exhausted, and drained of emotions.

Even Ramesh was silent, despite the same number of potholes on the return trip.

At least the rain had stopped.

"Luke," Meera said.

I turned back to where she sat.

She looked somber, and her lips trembled as she said, "Thank you."

The intensity of it squeezed my heart. My hand shook with

the need to squeeze her hand. Her hand that clutched the edge of her dress. But I couldn't.

I just nodded and looked ahead, clenching my hand in a fist.

I thought I always knew my privilege. I hadn't even realized just knowing that I could eat a healthy meal every day was a privilege.

Education was a privilege.

An income was a privilege.

The knowledge that I could stop thinking about these people's situations when the hurt got too overwhelming was a privilege, as was donating an exorbitant amount of money to sleep better at night.

THE MOMENT I heard the soft music playing around midnight, I jumped out of bed. My leg got stuck in the comforter, causing me to almost fall, but I quickly recovered and rushed out of the room. I found Meera sitting on her bed, looking at me.

"Can I join you?" I asked.

A tiny smirk formed on her lips. "Don't you like your cool, air-conditioned room?"

I like you more. My cheeks heated in embarrassment for intruding on her private time.

"I'm sorry. I didn't mean to impose," I said, turning around to go back to my room.

But then I heard her say, "Stay."

I couldn't hide the relief on my face as I quickly turned back around. "Are you sure?"

She rolled her eyes, a small smile on her lips, and said, "Yes, I was joking earlier. Clearly, I need to work in the humor department."

"No, I thought it was a joke. But you know how sometimes

people tell you what they really feel and try to pass it as a joke? I didn't want to disturb you if you needed space."

"I don't." Her eyes widened, and she sputtered, "I mean. I didn't. I like your company. Oh God. Do whatever you want."

And if that didn't completely melt my heart, the way she lay down on the bed facing the other way did it.

She didn't see the giant smile on my face as I carried my pillow and blanket to my cot and made my bed. She *did* catch me when I dragged the cot slightly closer to hers. When I raised my eyes in permission, she smiled and rolled her eyes. Her eye rolls with a smile seemed to be her own version of approval.

I dragged the cot closer to hers, leaving just a one-hand distance between us.

I lay down and asked, "Can we play a happy song today too?"

Meera fumbled with her cassette player on the floor between our cots and hit play.

A chirpy melody started to play. Meera tapped her foot along with the rhythm, a small smile on her lips. She laid on her stomach and pulled out an unwound cassette tape from a pouch, along with a pencil.

I looked up at the now clear sky. The smell of wet mud from the farms around us infused the air. The happy tunes and the sweet hint of jasmine managed to soothe my heart, and Meera's quiet presence beside me soon pulled me out of my melancholic thoughts.

She stuck the back of the pencil in the hub on the cassette and started turning it. With gentle maneuvers, she unwound the tangles in the magnetic tape. Every now and then, her sharp nose twitched, and her lips thinned in concentration. Just adorable.

Without looking at me, she said, "You're staring."

I turned my body to directly face her, and her lips twitched in response. "If you don't mind me asking, why do you still use a cassette player? It requires so much maintenance and caring. Especially those tapes."

She kept untangling the tape as she answered, "It's my father's. Every night, he used to play his favorite old songs on the player. When I was a kid, Maa, Pappa, and I used to sleep on this terrace in the summers, where he would play these happy songs. I didn't even realize when we stopped doing it. After I moved back, I found it in the corner of the hallway, just gathering dust. When Maa saw me cleaning it, she handed me some of these tapes."

"Does it hurt to keep reliving these memories every night?"

It seemed like she held on to her past with every part of her being. She hit forward when a sad song came on, her finger lingering on the stop button.

"It used to. For the first few months, I cried myself to sleep. I also only played sad songs. But then, I started playing happy songs. And I don't even know when it just became my thing. I got some new cassettes made to suit my moods. Yes, the memories always feel fresh when I play these songs, but now it's a good memory. I can smile about those days. I'm glad that we had a chance to be a happy family once."

Meera hit stop and then pressed the play button. Her hand lightly played with the cassette player, and I couldn't resist any longer.

I brought my hand down near the player and inched it toward hers, slowly enough for her to move it away if she wanted to.

Her hand stopped moving, and so did mine.

My heart pounded in my chest as I inched my hand forward again, our hands so close to each other. I didn't look up, not wanting to scare her away from the intensity of my need to hold her hand, to feel her hand in mine.

I moved my hand a little closer, but her fingers twitched,

and I stopped. My breath turned heavy, but I could still hear hers rushing out.

And then, she moved her fingers slowly toward mine and closed the short distance between our hands.

Sparks raced across my body at the contact as her hand glided in my bigger hand, the contrast in the color of our hands stark under the moonlight. Her fingers moved gently over mine, and warmth flooded my heart, igniting the spots where she touched. Her breath came out in loud rasps, but I could barely hear them from the way my heart beat out of my chest.

The feel of her fingers tangling with mine had my stomach doing somersaults. Her soft exhale made my heart race, and goose bumps raised along the length of my arm.

I didn't look up to meet her eyes, afraid of breaking the spell, afraid she would take her hand away if I looked at her.

So I let her explore, let her take what she wanted from our touch. Relief. Companionship. Warmth. Contact. Joy.

Because I got it all from her touch.

Our fingers played their own music, dancing to their own tune, while we lay there as spectators, holding our breaths, marveling at the beauty of it.

I moved my hand and intertwined our fingers, our hands closed around each other in finality, in comfort, in belonging, in peace.

And we slept a little more closely than before.

10

———

Song: Khoya Khoya Chaand, Khula Aasman
  - Mohammed Rafi

Meera

For the past three days, I woke up to my hand intertwined with Luke's. His hand was so much softer than mine, so much paler, so much bigger, and so full of warmth. We only held hands right before sleeping because every time we held hands, we stopped talking. I could not form words, let alone utter them, when he was touching me.

His touch soothed and exhilarated me, comforted me and created havoc in my mind. It brought a smile to my face and tears to my eyes, making me want to touch more of him and, at the same time, run far, far away from this overwhelming need to get closer to him.

For so many years, my only dream was to be debt-free, earn a living, and take care of Maa and Hari. Now, my mind has wandered into dangerous dreams that would break my heart and shatter my hold on reality. Dreams that consisted of Luke.

Just thinking about him made me smile, even in the most mundane moments.

In the middle of washing dirty utensils in the kitchen after our lunch.

In the middle of helping Hari with his homework.

In the middle of checking my students' assignments.

In the middle of having afternoon chai with Luke.

Yes, I started to offer him chai in the afternoon—just one more excuse to spend more time with him, and he readily accepted my offer.

On one such afternoon, we were discussing my favorite subjects to teach—history and civics—when my phone rang. I apologized to Luke with a smile and answered the call.

Manju Aunty calling...

"Manju aunty?" My heart pounded, because there could only be one reason for her call.

"Oh, Meera. Baldev came to collect money. He just left. I just wanted to let you know that he might be arriving at your place soon."

Only one word looped through my mind.

Protect. Protect. Protect.

"Thank you, Manju aunty. How was he?"

"Like every time, beti. I gave him all that I had. Still wasn't enough for him." Beti means child.

"It's okay. We'll talk to Surbhi didi. I think she would be able to help soon," I said, recalling the substantial donation that Luke had made to her. He'd told her the transfer would take some time.

"Let's pray she can," Manju aunty said.

As soon as we ended the call, my chest tightened, and my hands shook as I tried to hold on to the cup of chai in my hand.

Luke immediately came to my side, gently taking the cup from my grip. "Meera, darling, what happened? You're panicking. You need to take a few deep breaths. Let's sit down."

I pushed his arm away. "I don't have time."

My heart beat a mile a minute, but I had no time to dwell on the impending panic that crawled up my legs and arms, trying to pull me down.

Two severe lines formed between his eyebrows, his eyes sharp. "What happened?"

My voice shook as I answered, "Baldev, the man who gave us the loan, is coming to collect his monthly payment."

He quickly nodded, his hands on his waist, and asked, "Do you have enough? How much do you need? How can I help? Is he dangerous?"

His questions dropped on my shoulders like boulders, questions he had no right to ask.

I never have enough money. I need lakhs of money. It's not your responsibility to help me. Yes, he is dangerous.

"Yes, Luke. I have enough for now. And the best way for you to help me is for you to stay hidden in your room with Hari. And do not come out, no matter what."

His eyes burned with intensity and defiance, and I knew what he would say even before he uttered a single word. "Absolutely not. Does he misbehave? You didn't answer if he's dangerous."

My stomach churned with wanting him by my side. *No.* I glared back at him. "You are our guest. It is my responsibility to protect you. You are not coming out."

"Like hell I won't. If he does something to you... You know what? I'm not even going to entertain that thought. I'll just stay quiet and stand in the corner of the room."

He was talking nonsense, and I was running out of time. "And do what? Disappear into the wall? You think Baldev wouldn't notice a foreigner? Listen, Luke, I don't have time for your unhelpful protective feelings. You will stay in the room and keep Hari occupied."

His eyes narrowed, and his jaw clenched. "Meera! Look, I

know you've been handling this person on your own just fine. But I want to be there for you."

Why? Why did he want to be there for me so much? Why was he so hell-bent on making me rely on him? He would leave this place in a few weeks anyway, and then, I would be handling it all alone again.

With every word he spoke, my temper flared. "Exactly. Let me do this. You being in front of Baldev would just ruin everything."

"But—" he said, and my glare shut him up.

"But what? What do you think will happen when he sees you? You think he won't ask for more money?"

"If he asks for more money, we'll give it to him."

Of course. "Because you have all the money in the world. What do you think will happen when you aren't here? You think he won't ask for more interest on the loan we owe him? That he wouldn't make my life a living hell once you're gone? He would forever hold it over my head and *never* let me out of debt."

His face fell, and defeat was written all over his face. Helplessness poured out of his eyes. I could tell; I've been helpless for a long time now. And I hated it. "Luke, you have no idea how much it means to me that you want to help me. But Baldev can't know you're here. You can help me, though. Keep Hari with you. Distract him or play with him. Just don't let him make too much noise. Can you do that for me?"

He clutched his hair, his eyes in turmoil, yet he finally listened. And eventually nodded. "And you'll be fine," he stated, as if willing his words into reality.

Despite the situation, I smiled. I closed the distance between us and touched his hand. He tightly closed his hand around mine, like he needed it. Like he needed *me*. "I'll be fine," I said, and meant it.

Once he nodded, I squeezed his hand and ran downstairs.

I quickly stopped and turned to him. "Oh, and could you move the car at the back of the house so it's out of the sight from the front?"

Luke nodded and rushed downstairs.

After Hari settled, I dressed in my shabbiest salwar kameez —that covered every inch of my skin—and arranged the dupatta to cover my entire chest area. Maa was already prepared, wearing her own ugly saree. It was always better to appear in a worse situation than we actually were. Only then would Baldev show some pity.

We waited on our porch, knowing there was no need to invite him in. Luke had already moved the car and was with Hari in the room upstairs. Less than ten minutes passed before we heard a car approaching. Maa tensed up beside me, and I clutched her shoulder. "Everything will be okay, Maa," I reassured her.

She patted my hand gently but remained silent. Before she could speak, Baldev sauntered through our main gate, full of arrogance, as if he owned the house.

Looking at my mother, he said, "Maa*ji*, how are you?" My stomach clenched at the false respect in his tone. Ji is a term added behind a name of a person to show them respect.

I stood protectively in front of my mother as Baldev's lecherous eyes shifted toward me, sending a chill down my spine. Despite the discomfort, I maintained my composure and greeted him respectfully, "Baldev*ji*, Namaste."

"How's work, Meera*ji*? Making good money?" he asked. His *Ji* behind my name was just a mockery, said in a lecherous tone while his gaze lingered far too long on me. I tightened my dupatta around me and handed him the stack of money. "Here's our monthly payment."

He grabbed the money from my hand, slowly brushing his fingers against mine, making me shiver with revulsion. I quickly pulled my hand away and watched him count the money. As he looked back at me, he put his finger in his mouth, causing a sickening feeling in my stomach.

Although I knew he wouldn't do anything serious, it didn't stop him from testing my strength and trying to wear down my spirit with his lascivious gaze. Each glance felt like another assault on my dignity.

He looked at me, and said, "This is missing five hundred rupees."

It was not. I had counted and recounted. It was the full amount.

I met his gaze, and asked, "Can I count myself? I know it was in full."

Evil shone from his eyes, anger drenched in his words. "You think I'm lying?"

"No, but..."

"But what? You think I don't know how to count?" He came near me, clutched my arm hard enough to leave marks, and continued, "You think I need your little money?"

I tried to pry his hands off my arm, pain cracking my steady voice. "Leave me, please."

He jerked me around by the arm and growled. "Or what?"

Maa tried to pry him away from me. "Leave her, Baldev*ji*. We'll give you the money."

He glared at Maa, shook me in front of her, and said, "Teach some manners to your daughter, Maa*ji*. If I was a bad man, I wouldn't let her rudeness slide."

Maa joined her hands in front of her, yet he didn't remove his hands from my arm. Instead, he came near me, his stinking breath making my skin crawl. "Where is that brother of yours? I'll teach him to be a man. Show him where a woman stands in front of a real man."

I tried to loosen his hold on my arm. "He's at his friend's house. I'll give you the money. Please let go of my hand."

"What is going on here?" a voice boomed from somewhere behind Baldev.

The three of us turned around toward the gate, and there stood Aakar.

His eyes fixed on the spot where Baldev had grabbed my arm, and with a voice laced with fury, he rumbled, "Let go of her arm."

My arm was immediately released as Aakar strode over to us, his fists clenched tightly in anger. He stood between Baldev and me, a towering wall of strength that separated me from that vile individual.

Relief washed over me, my heart thudding with every beat.

"Who are you?" Baldev asked, who stood a few inches shorter than Aakar.

Aakar, in his fancy blue shirt and black pants, his muscles bulging as he crossed his arms over his chest, said in a calm voice, "Doesn't matter. What do you need?"

"I'm here to collect the loan amount. In full. Five hundred rupees are missing."

"No, they're not," I said from behind Aakar. He turned to meet my eyes and nodded.

"Can I count?" he asked Baldev. Aakar spoke in a calm voice, but every word was threaded with fury.

Baldev's cruel eyes met mine, and he glared at me with a vicious poison in his eyes, as if he couldn't wait to get me alone. I shuddered, and once again, Aakar moved to become a physical barrier between us.

"I'll be back next month," Baldev said, and I heard his retreating footsteps.

None of us moved till we heard his car taking off.

And I couldn't stand on my feet any longer.

I dropped to my knees and kept breathing. Maa clutched my head, words of relief and gratitude pouring from her mouth to Aakar.

And all I could think about was Hari's and Luke's safety. Relief that Aakar helped me keep my promise to Luke. I was fine. I was completely fine.

Aakar was about to sit down right beside me on the ground when I quickly got up. "Please, Aakar bhai, don't sit on the floor. Please come inside."

He nodded, and as soon as we were inside, he asked, "What was that? You didn't tell us that you owed money to someone like that?"

Our fathers used to be good friends when they were young. They helped us get our house renovated and expanded when Hari would be born. They even helped us out when Pappa passed. But I wasn't going to keep taking advantage of their kindness. "It is what it is, Aakar bhai. It's my responsibility. We're slowly paying off the debt."

"How can I help?" he asked.

"You helped today. Your offering is help enough."

He was about to say more, but I interrupted. "If I really need help, I'll ask, Aakar bhai. Please let me do this."

His shoulders slumped, and he nodded.

Before he could say anything further, I said, "I'll go call Luke."

I heard Maa ask him if he'd have chai or coffee as I dashed up the stairs.

The moment I reached Luke's door, it flew open as Luke stood at the entrance holding on to the doorknob, his eyes filled with worry. I looked inside his room and found Hari with colored pencils.

"Hari, go downstairs. Aakar bhai is here."

His eyes lit up with excitement, and he leaped off the bed, rushing past Luke and me in a frenzy. "Slow down," I called after him.

As soon as he was out of sight, Luke led me into his chilly

room, his grip firm around my hand. I could no longer stand on my own.

Collapsing onto the bed, I watched as Luke sat on the floor beside me, gazing up at me intently while caressing my hand with his thumb, attempting to comfort me.

"I'm okay," I murmured.

Though his eyes remained tense, his fear for me was a warm blanket around my lonely soul. I placed my other hand over our joined hands, stroking his soft, smooth skin. "I'm okay, "Luke."

He shook his head. "Don't lie to me, Meera. Please. Something was happening, I heard it. And then I heard Aakar's shout, and the only thing that kept me here was Hari. Tell me what happened."

"It was nothing. Baldev wouldn't release my arm."

"What?" Luke shouted, his hand automatically holding my arms gently. I flinched when it made contact with what would be a small bruise.

He quickly let my arm go and held my hands tightly. "You should've let me be there. He hurt you. God," he rambled, visibly upset.

I couldn't help but brush my fingers against his jaw, and I felt the tightness in his muscles ease slightly. His breathing became harsh, and he held my hand with a firmer grip.

"I'm fine, Luke. Aakar came, and Baldev ran away like the pathetic coward he is."

"And you're fine? Does it hurt? Of course, it hurts. I'm so sorry, Meera."

"You did what I asked you to. You protected Hari. You stayed inside. And I am so relieved that you both were safe. That he didn't see you. Things would have been far worse for me in the future had he seen you."

He nodded but didn't release my hand.

And I couldn't help but smile at his blatant display of care and affection for me. "I'm fine," I reassured him again—this time with a smile.

Finally, he smiled back at me. "I know. Just... let me look at you for a minute. Okay? And you're crazy."

The way he looked at me, as if his eyes could eradicate all my hurt, made me want to curl up in his arms and burrow my face in the crook of his neck and just breathe him in. "You don't have the time to look at me. Aakar is waiting for you downstairs. He might wonder what's taking us so long."

He nodded, his hand running circles on mine. "You're right."

I got up and, with a heavy heart, released his hand. "I'll tell him to meet you on the terrace."

And with one more look at him and his worried face, I gave him a smile and left his room.

Luke

The moment Aakar stepped onto the terrace, I reached up to him and pulled him into a hug. "Thank God you were here, man."

He slapped my back twice, and we stepped away from each other. "Yeah, I'm so glad I was there on time. Meera shouldn't have to do this on her own."

"Tell me about it."

We went and sat on the cots across from each other. The tense situation from before still hung in the air, and both of us sat there, lost in our thoughts. What would have happened if Aakar hadn't been there? I shuddered at that thought and reminded myself that Meera was fine. I just saw her five minutes ago.

I turned my gaze to Aakar. He was dressed in formal clothes

as if he had just come from a meeting. The glare from the sun behind me hit my eyes, and I turned the cot a different angle.

"What brings you here?" I asked.

He chuckled, not meeting my eyes. He ran his hand in his hair, and said, "Well, I came here to see a girl."

"Man, I didn't know you were seeing a girl."

This time, he met my eyes and shook his head. "Oh, Luke. I came here to see a girl who my parents suggested for an arranged marriage."

I knew arranged marriages happened in India. But he was the first person I'd met who was pursuing the option. What did you even say to that? Congratulations? I'm sorry? Are you okay? How was the girl?

"Oh... umm. Cool?" I said.

And he laughed. "You can ask me if you have any questions."

"Are you okay with the arranged marriage thing?"

"I mean, yes. I'm busy with work the whole day. I don't have time to find a woman myself. If my parents are showing me options, I don't mind meeting them. It's just another form of dating. I would meet the girl. We talk. Drink chai. And then, we decide if we want to meet again or not. Isn't that essentially dating?" he asked.

Spot-on.

"Except your parents have chosen the girl for you."

"Suggested."

"Did you like the girl you met today?"

A slight frown on his face gave me the answer. "She was nice. But not what I'm looking for in my partner."

"And then you can just say no to the girl?" I asked, curious about the process of rejection. I hated those parts of dating: the awkward conversation at the end of the date, when you knew there wasn't going to be a second date but didn't want to hurt the woman's feelings.

He smiled and shrugged. "Perks of an arranged marriage. Your parents reject them for you."

"I need to try this thing for myself. Doesn't sound so bad to me."

Gentle footsteps had us looking at the stairs. Meera carried a tray of chai and snacks. I instantly got up as soon as she neared us. She looked at me in shock, raising her eyebrows in question, reminding me of Aakar watching us. And all I could think was she *looked* fine. Normal. She had to be rattled. I was, and I wasn't even there.

She put the tray between us, turned to Aakar, and asked, "Do you need anything, Aakar bhai? Would you stay for dinner?"

He took the chai from the tray, and said, "Oh no. Please don't bother. I'm here with Maa, Pappa, Abhi, and Ria. They're all at our place."

"Are you sure?" she asked.

"Yes, absolutely. Don't worry at all. In fact, Abhi, Ria, and I are going to a friend's house party in the city. Why don't you join us?"

Meera was already shaking her head before Aakar could even finish asking the question. "No, no, Aakar bhai. I can't."

And then she looked at me and said, "You guys carry on."

I really was tempted to go. It would be good to catch up with them and let loose a little, but I really wanted Meera to join me. So I looked at her and gave her my best puppy dog eyes. "Come with us, Meera? After the day you've had, it would be good to be with friends."

Aakar, the smart guy that he was, piped in. "I insist, Meera. It's only a few of us. There will be good food, some light music, some drinks, and just talking."

She bit her lip as she looked back and forth between the two of us. "If you're sure?"

I quickly nodded while Aakar said, "Absolutely, Meera. Ria would be delighted too."

She met my eyes and, with a voice that was still hesitant, said, "Okay. I'll go."

I gave a wide smile to Aakar, trying to show excitement for both of us. "We'll go in my car so we can leave whenever we want."

That made her smile, and she gave me a nod of thanks. I gave her a quick wink before she turned and went downstairs, shaking her head.

"So you sure about that?" asked Aakar.

Huh? I turned to Aakar, who was looking at me with a serious expression on his face.

"Sorry, sure about what?"

A smirk came over his face as he said, "Trying out for arranged marriage for yourself. Seems like you already have someone in mind."

I picked the chai and took a sip. I nodded at him. "I do."

"I hope you know what you're doing, Luke. She's been through enough."

"All I want is to make her smile. Make her laugh."

He gulped down his chai. "I believe you. Just be careful. I'll see you guys around eight? I'll send you the address."

"We'll be there. Thanks for inviting us, man. I appreciate it."

He got up from the cot, and I followed. "Of course. And I'm glad you're here. I didn't know the situation was so bad," he said.

A sharp pang of anger and hurt sliced through me at the reminder. I clenched my jaw to stop the scream that kept wanting to come out. I nodded at Aakar. "See you soon, man."

He nodded, and with a quick hug, he left.

I stayed on the terrace, looking at the darkening horizon.

∼

RAMESH and I waited by the car when Meera stepped out of the house, stunning me. She wore jeans that molded to her legs and a tight, full-sleeve top that delicately hugged her curves. I had never seen her in such clothes; they left little to my very excited imagination and my even more excited parts down south.

As she approached the car, I could see her eyes were lined with kohl, and she wore light brown lipstick that spun vivid scenarios of what those lips could do, and how badly I wanted to taste them on my tongue. My mouth went dry, and my hand shook as I opened the back door of the car.

Stopping her with a soft touch at her elbow, I had to clear my throat to speak. "You look breathtaking, Meera."

Her cheeks darkened at my compliment, and her lips curved into a small smirk, telling me that she knew exactly what she did to me. "Thank you."

We got into the car, and by the time I distracted myself from how hot Meera looked, we'd arrived at the address Aakar had provided.

I asked Ramesh to get some dinner for himself and gave him extra money for taking us around at night. As soon as Meera got out of the car, I walked beside her, trying hard not to put my hand on the back of her waist.

"You're staring," she said, looking at me with a shy smile.

"Damn right, I am."

And she laughed, causing my heart to stutter.

We climbed the three steps to the house, and sounds of music and chatter could be heard from outside. Meera pressed the doorbell, and Abhi's wide smile greeted us in the next second.

Abhi's eyes widened the moment he spotted Meera, and he blurted out, "Wow, Meera didi, you look great!"

Meera smiled at Abhi, and a pang of jealousy shot through me.

My hand clenched into a fist at the appreciative look in Abhi's eyes, but I had to remind myself that he was barely an adult and had no interest in Meera. Abhi led us inside the house, where we were greeted by enthusiastic hellos. Ria ran up and pulled Meera into a hug after giving a friendly shove to my arm. Then she dragged Meera to the dining table lined with all sorts of food and drinks.

Aakar was right behind Ria. He quickly handed me a drink and hauled me with him to introduce me to his friends. I took a sip of the scotch and instantly remembered something. I turned to Aakar. "Isn't alcohol illegal here in your state?"

Aakar chuckled and put a finger on his lips. "Shh..."

All of us chuckled, and my eyes gravitated toward Meera. She stood with a slice of pizza, talking to Ria, occasionally giving her a polite smile as she nodded her head along with whatever Ria chatted about.

My feet automatically dragged me to her, my mind unable to resist the pull she had on me. The moment I neared her, Ria instantly took notice. Whatever she saw on my face triggered a sly smile on hers, and with a sneaky wink at me, she turned to Meera and said, "I'll be back in a minute. You guys carry on."

Meera barely noticed since her full attention was on me. I noticed *that* because I could not, for the life of me, look away from her.

As I stood closer to her, I noticed she didn't have anything to drink, just her pizza slice. "You want a drink?" I asked, offering the scotch in my hand.

She looked at the drink and took the glass from my hand, deliberately brushing her fingers against mine.

Heat rushed through my body, and my cock stirred in arousal as Meera held my eyes and took a sip of the stiff drink.

She cleared her throat and coughed the moment she took the sip, causing me to laugh.

She chuckled and beat at her chest with a fist. "Wow, it's been a while since I had a drink."

"Oh, I should've asked if you drank alcohol." Regret swarmed my gut as I looked at the drink in her hand.

Meera smiled and shook her head. "You offered. I accepted. And yes, I drink. Well, I used to occasionally drink when I was in college. But I haven't had one in a very long time."

She took another sip from the glass, and my eyes followed from her lips to her throat as she swallowed the drink. My throat went dry, and without looking away from her eyes, I took the glass from her hand and took a sip from the same spot of the glass where she just had her lips.

Her eyes darkened as heat pooled low in my gut, and my cock stirred in my pants. I took another sip of the scotch, and the burn of the scotch paled compared to the heat burning up my body as Meera looked at my lips.

Ria soon returned and pulled Meera to meet some of her friends.

I refilled my glass, and when my eyes met Meera's across the room, I raised my glass at her, not in cheers, but a reminder that she knew where to get her drink if she needed one.

And whatever she saw in my eyes and my gesture, she understood, because she gave me a small smile and rolled her eyes. In the next forty-five minutes, as she talked with Ria and her friends, she excused herself twelve times from the group to come and have a few sips from my glass that I kept filled.

Every time she returned to me, her smile got wider, her body loosened up, and the thirteenth time—yes, I was counting —she clutched my hand that held the glass in hers and took a sip while my finger brushed her chin.

My heart pounded in my chest at the touch, and my blood heated in my veins as she gave me a wide smile and swooned closer to me, almost snuggling into my chest.

She was drunk.

I bent my head lower to hers, my lips almost brushing her ear, causing her to shiver, as I said, "Want to head back home?"

She met my eyes and pouted at me, and I just about melted at her feet. "Will you stay with me on the terrace?"

And I couldn't stop myself. I brushed her hair behind her ear, the feel of her skin causing electricity to rush down my fingers. "There's nowhere else I'd rather be."

She nodded, and I went to get her some water. I was glad we had Ramesh to drive us home because neither of us was sober.

I only had a few sips to feel the spot that touched Meera's lips. Today was for Meera. I needed to feel her let go, and I was more than happy to see her unwind. And unwind she did.

The moment I handed her the glass of water, she gulped down the entire thing.

We soon said our goodbyes, and I kept my hand at the small of her back in support as we walked to the car. Meera leaned closer to me, and her body brushed against mine, causing sparks everywhere we touched.

As I held her closer to me, I asked, "How drunk are you?"

She made a small pinch with her finger and brought it closer to my face. "This much," she said with a wide, unrestrained smile.

I shook my head, totally smitten by how adorable she was when drunk. I so badly wanted to press a kiss on her forehead that was mere inches from my lips.

Ramesh saw us approaching and quickly got the car ready for us. I put Meera in the back seat, and soon, we were headed home.

Once home, I helped Meera out of the car.

Her mind seemed clearer as she held my hand to get out of the car.

"Thank you," she mumbled, her eyes still tracking slower than usual.

Ramesh headed home, and the two of us crept upstairs as not to wake Hari or her mother.

"I need to change," she mumbled, and I let go of her.

"Me too. I'll wait on the terrace for you."

She nodded and went back downstairs to change.

Once I'd freshened up and changed into my sleepwear, I leaned against the parapet of the terrace to wait for her. A seemingly endless ribbon of darkness lay before me, with a tiny scattering of lights from other homes. I liked that. I liked how it gave us privacy as if we were the only ones in the world.

Quiet footsteps behind me had me turning around. Moonlight glinted off her warm brown skin, and a small smile stretched across her face, relief evident in the way her shoulders dropped.

I watched her walk toward me...well, toward her cot. She wore a short-sleeved T-shirt and salwar for pajamas.

She was about to start making her bed when I hurried over to her. "Meera, please, let me make your bed for you."

Surprised, she sputtered. "Oh...Oh no, no...You really don't need to do that."

"I want to," I said and stepped forward. I slowly took her hand in mine and got her to sit on my bed.

"But..."

"Just sit and relax. And talk to me. Do you feel better? Today has been a long day."

She chuckled. After the day she had, she *chuckled*. "You're making things very fine. Thank you."

"Anything you want or need, I'm here." I kept my voice strong, reliable, and trustworthy, I hoped.

"I'm seeing that," she whispered, her eyes slightly red. But in the silence of the night, I heard it. And it made me glad.

Once I'd made her bed, I flung my arms out theatrically and said, "Your bed under the stars and the moon is prepared, my lady."

She giggled and covered her laughter with her hand.

And it spurred me on.

I bent down at her knees and clutched her hand gently in both of mine. I stood with her and walked the three steps to her bed. Her laughs and giggles made me hope that, for a while, she continued to feel good.

"I hope the sleeping arrangements meet your expectations, madam," I said in a fake British accent, crouching down on my knees once more.

Her burst of laughter brightened the dark night. "My ancestors would have loved to see the day the British treated them like this, on their knees," she said, and chuckled.

I laughed in agreement. "Well, I'm at your service. What do you need?"

Her small smile stayed on her lips, and she grazed her thumb on my hands. She seemed lost in thought, and I would give anything to get a peek into that beautiful mind. At my raised eyebrows, she gave a little chuckle and said, "Let's lie down. It's getting late."

I stood and, with a question in my eyes, pulled my bed closer to hers. Close enough to hold her hand. Close enough to look into her eyes. Close enough to play with her fingers as the soulful, sweet melody from her cassette player surrounded us.

Close enough to want more.

Close enough to want to know if she, too, felt these rising emotions brewing between us. If she, too, was losing the fight against this bone-deep need for our lips to meet.

I watched as her eyes drifted shut, still clutching my hand, even as my own eyes shuttered with the image of my hand in hers and a soft smile on her face.

11

Song: Pyaar Hua, Ikraar Hua

  - Lata Mangeshkar, Manna DeyShankar Jaikishan

Meera

I woke up to a pounding headache and my hand encased in what felt like a burning stove. I closed my eyes and buried my head under the blanket, thinking back to what caused this excruciating pounding in my head. My mind flashed through the images of last night.

I'd worn jeans and a top after so long that I'd felt good about myself. And oh God, I'd shared drinks with Luke. Lots and lots of drinks. Just to keep finding the taste of him on the glass. Just to feel that much closer to him.

What was happening to me? Did I look desperate to him? Crazy? Smitten?

Could he tell that I would do just about anything he asked of me? That I was so weak for him every time he showed me a little bit of kindness and care?

My head pulsed in pain as my mind spiraled into an endless

loop of thoughts and desires that had no reason to be there in the first place.

Steeling myself for more pain, I got up from my bed. I moved downstairs and spent a while in the bathroom, slowly getting ready for the day.

As I prepared the chai in the kitchen, my mind kept circling back to how I'd kept drinking with Luke, the way he'd treated me so gently after we'd come back home, and the way I kept going to sleep with his hand in mine.

What was I going to do when he left? Because he absolutely would.

I poured our chai into the cups and took them to the terrace, where Luke was sitting on the bed, swiping through his phone.

The moment he noticed me, though, he put the phone away, and wore a wide smile that I was tempted to trace with my fingers. How could someone's smile make my heart flutter so much?

He'd moved our cots so close to each other that our knees touched when we sat across one another. Yet I didn't have the heart to move away.

And because the embarrassment from last night still lingered at the back of my mind, I cleared my throat and looked at my cup while I asked, "Was I a total fool last night?"

Luke's finger gently brushed my chin, his touch causing my heart to skyrocket in my chest. I couldn't stifle the gasp as he raised my chin to meet his eyes. What I found in them had blood rushing to my cheeks. "You were perfectly adorable— and gorgeous—last night. And I was glad you got to let loose a little."

My heart pounded at the words he used to describe me. Nobody in my life had ever uttered those words to me, and my mind was having a very hard time trying to catch up with the way my heart beat out of my chest.

My hand shivered as I closed them around his fingers that touched my face, and for the first time, I kept his hand in mine simply because I wanted to. Heat rushed my cheeks as I wondered what he thought of me.

"Something's happening here, Meera. Do you feel it, too?"

I felt his words penetrate deeply into my heart as a mixture of hope and fear spilled out of my chest—the hope false, and the fear all too real. Because he was *leaving*. Not today, not tomorrow, but entirely too soon.

"What difference does it make?" I asked, knowing in my heart that we had no hope to be together.

Luke's hand tightened around mine.

When I looked up at him from where I sat, he said, "That's not what I asked."

Just by asking a question like that, Luke had made himself vulnerable to me, leaving himself open to rejection and answers that could break his heart. It took courage to ask something like that.

Would I have ever gathered enough courage to ask him something like that? Knowing that he held the power to refuse the existence of these storms of feelings between us? Knowing that with one *no*, he could shatter the profoundness of my hand in his? Never.

I had no right to deflect this question. No right to lie because I was terrified of how it would change everything.

Despite standing on the edge of a cliff after that question, Luke still made the effort to soothe *me*.

I clutched his hand tighter, needing to borrow his strength. "Yes," I whispered, "I feel it too."

A heavy exhale rushed out of Luke, and his hand tightened around me even more. "You do?"

I couldn't meet his eyes, not after that acceptance. Heat rushed through my body, and I nodded.

"Look at me, Meera."

I'd never felt this shyness, this rush of a thousand butter-flies fluttering in my stomach, before. Taking a deep breath, I turned my head. And a huge smile, full of hope, relief, joy, and something extraordinarily profound, greeted me.

"I...I don't have words," I said, barely able to meet his eyes.

His eyes were shining with so much joy, and sheer happi-ness radiated off him. "I don't need any more words, darling."

Darling. Fire danced in my stomach, hot and burning. The early morning light and the chirping birds around us did nothing to calm my racing heart. And my lips, they'd never smiled wider.

He kept looking at me, engulfing me in the warmth of his gaze. And I kept smiling, trying to control my pounding heart.

After two whole minutes of his eyes on me, I leaned over and put my hand over his eyes. "Stop it."

His smile stretched wider, and his laugh vibrated through my hand, causing me to shiver. He clutched my arm and removed my hand from his eyes. "Never," he said.

He didn't release my hand, but instead brought it to his lips and pressed a kiss to my wrist.

And I nearly fell off the bed. This was the first time a man's lips had touched my skin. The first time a man touched me like a hero touched a heroine in the movies.

And just like the shy heroine in the movies, I shivered. Just like in the movies, the orchestra started playing in the back-ground, the sun shone a little brighter, and the breeze blew my hair as if I stood in front of those wind-blowing machines. All that, just by a whisper of a kiss on my wrist.

We slowly drank our chai. His eyes never left mine, and his smile never wavered. His smile made my heart sing.

The rest of my day went by in a daze, my thoughts stuck on the feel of his lips on my skin.

Even when I tried to teach my boisterous class, my mind kept circling back to the way Luke's eyes shone with delight when I admitted my feelings for him. I could recall every crinkle around his eyes when his lips stretched into his wide smile.

And his lips. His soft, full lips sent a storm of shivers through my entire body and goose bumps across my arms.

It was only during lunch break when Kriti shook my shoulders that I pulled myself out of my dream state. "Sorry, what?"

She dramatically rolled her eyes. "Where are you today? Are you all right? And why are you smiling?"

I quickly wiped away my smile, but then Luke's face popped into my head, and I lost the battle.

"That's it," Kriti blurted. "Tell me what's up with you. Right now."

But I really wanted this first brush of Luke's lips on my skin all for myself, so I shook my head. "Not today. But just know that nothing can ruin my day today."

Kriti chuckled and shook her head. "I love this new smiley Meera. You better hold on to her."

I laughed and did exactly what Kriti asked me to do for the rest of the day—held on to the happiness coursing through my body.

When I returned home and saw Luke, the happiness exploded into giddiness I could not contain.

So when night came along, I dragged my cot closer to his, not leaving any space between them at all. When he came outside and looked at the sleeping arrangement, his eyes twinkled in a way that was absolutely intoxicating.

I had my hand in his before he even had a blanket over his body.

I went to sleep with his lips peppering a thousand small kisses on my wrist, brightening my night under the starlight.

Today turned out to be the best day of my life.

I slept, promising myself that no matter what came tomorrow, I would forever cherish this day. I would forever cherish Luke, even if he became just a memory.

Luke

Sweat poured down my back as I climbed up the stairs to the second floor. I had left for a jog pretty early in the morning.

Meera was still asleep; her hand that had held mine was now curled below her cheek, and her soft blanket draped softly across her curves. She looked so fucking adorable that I almost kissed her cheek before leaving.

The moment I climbed up, my feet stopped moving. There she stood, leaning against the parapet, looking out at the fields, a cup of chai in her hand, the early rays of the sun turning her hair golden brown. Her T-shirt and pajamas showed off her slender curves.

Just as I stepped farther into the hallway, she turned toward me.

A shy smile came over her face, and it softened the hard edges she always carried with her. "Good morning," she said.

And I just couldn't go into my room to change my sweaty clothes without going to her first.

I stepped out on the terrace, picked up my cup, and stood close enough to her to let our arms touch. "Good morning, darling."

She turned her head away but not quickly enough. I caught her huge smile, the way she blushed, and how she held her cup tighter, how her arm shivered against mine.

Heat sizzled across my skin where it touched hers.

But then, she stepped a foot away, still looking out into the fields.

I kept my gaze on hers and followed, keeping our arms close enough to touch again.

She shook her head and smiled.

Her eyes met mine, and with her lips stretched into a huge smile, she shook her head once again. "You are crazy."

Crazy for you.

"Sleep okay?" I asked, the question far too casual for the way my heart pounded and my hand trembled.

And maybe she felt it too because she fumbled with a cup a moment before she nodded. "Yes. You?"

"Nope. How could I? You were snoring so loudly..."

She roared in laughter, head thrown back, curly hair bouncing. Her eyes shone with golden light as she turned her head. "Of course I snored. My days are stressful, and my nights are even *more* stressful."

My jaw hung open for a second, then I narrowed my eyes.

"Stressful? Stressful? Our conversations and listening to music together is *more* stressful?" I asked, clutching my heart.

She chuckled, met my eyes, and said, "Yes. So stressful I can barely keep up. My heart beats like a wild boar stomping on the fields, my stomach churns as if I have indigestion, I sweat like crazy even in the cool air, and I feel feverish every time you step near me. It's all *very* stressful."

My body turned to stone, desire curling in my stomach, then traveling south. I struggled to get things under control. My arms ached to hold her, my mouth desperate to meet hers. "You're right. I myself feel very stressed right now," I said, my voice a heavy rasp.

"Uncomfortable, isn't it?"

I nodded. "Very."

She smiled knowingly and sipped her chai. And I couldn't look away. I wanted this. Always. But time was ticking, and my departure loomed over my head like an anvil. How would I leave her? I was in India for only six more weeks. I was leaving for my other site visits in *two* weeks. Just the thought of flying back to New York sat like a rock in my heart. I wanted more, more time with Meera, more time to explore this connection. I was desperately trying not to fall, but I'd already jumped off the cliff last night.

I took a few sips, pondering whether to propose my idea to her. Bracing myself, I asked, "Come with me to visit my other sites. I have the entire itinerary planned. We will be gone for a month. We'll visit a few cities in Gujarat and Rajasthan and tour all sorts of historic places. Palaces, forts, stepwells, and markets. Come with me. Please."

She smiled, yet pain reflected in her eyes. Her voice shook when she said, "I can't."

I clutched her hand, and we gasped at the contact. It never got old. The heady, all-consuming need to be closer to her, to experience more with her, to *be* more for her. "I need to have more time with you, Meera. I can't just have this much. Don't you want that too?"

Her nostrils flared, and she clenched her jaw. "And what will we do with more time? It will only make me want this— want you—more. It will only destroy me more when you leave. It will *ruin* me."

My heart clenched, and I had no words. Only one. "Meera."

She turned around, her back tight with tension. "I can't leave everything here. I have responsibilities, people relying on me, not to mention my work."

"You deserve to take a break from all your burdens. Even if it's just for a month, I want to show you as much of the world as possible. I want to have more time with you, Meera."

"We can't get everything we want, Luke. I learned that pretty early in my life."

Disappointment flared in my gut. The chai turned sour in my mouth. I just couldn't fathom that I had only two weeks of time with Meera. I couldn't give up. "Will you please think about it? Whatever responsibilities you need to handle, I'll help you out. We'll make it work. Please don't just say *no*. Consider it. Think it through. Are two weeks all you want for us?"

"How are we an *us* if two weeks is all we have?" she asked, her tone defeated.

"Then let's figure out if we *are* an *us*. And if we are, we will make it work. I'll think of something."

She chuckled, but it didn't sound happy. She looked at me, her eyes shining with tears instead of joy. "You know what I like the most about you? Your hope, your optimism. You just go for whatever you want."

We only had this one life—this one chance. And I was privileged enough to go for whatever I wanted. So why shouldn't I? "Please say you'll think about it."

I gave her puppy dog eyes since they seemed to be effective on her. She shook her head, gulped down her chai, and said, "I'll think about it. And you are crazy."

"I am. I'm completely crazy."

For you.

12

Song: Jab Koi Baat Bigad Jaaye
- Kumar Saanu, Sadhana Sargam

Meera

"He said what?" asked Kriti, loud enough to attract attention and glare from a few teachers nearby.

"Shh! Yes, he invited me to go off traveling with him for a month."

"And you said no?" she asked, her eyes wide and mouth stuck open.

"Of course I said no. I don't have the time or the liberty to go. I can't take a month off work."

Her lips thinned. "Yes, you can. You haven't taken a day off in five years."

"I can't leave Hari and Maa alone."

Her eyes narrowed. "Two people are not alone."

"Baldev could come back and harass Maa and Hari."

This time, she paused. Her lips pursed in thought, and she

said, "Hari can stay at our place for a month. You can send your maa to her sister's place."

"All so I can have fun and roam around with a guy? Have you completely lost it?"

She clutched her hair as if I was the crazy one. "Meera... have *you* completely lost it? You have the offer to roam around the country for a month, all expenses paid, with a very, very, *very* handsome man who really likes you, and you're refusing? When will you ever get this opportunity again?"

Never. I would never get this opportunity again, which was why I needed to say no. "Kriti, he's going to leave. This trip would make everything so much harder. It will show me everything I'm missing in life and make me bitter."

Sympathy shone in her eyes. She clutched my shoulder and said, "Meera, you already know what you're missing out on. He is giving you something that will last forever. The memories will stay with you, and if you're going to hurt either way, let it hurt for loss of what you briefly had instead of something you've never known. Besides, you deserve a break. A moment of joy, laughs, travel, something naughty with a guy." And she winked.

My ears burned, and my cheeks heated. I looked around and whispered, "It's not like that between us. We just hold hands. And listen to music."

"Aww..."

I was about to say something to shut her up when my phone rang.

Surbhi didi calling...

"Hello, Surbhi didi."

A sniffle on the other end caused my stomach to clench. "Is everything okay, Didi?" I asked, concerned.

Her voice was strong yet wavering as she spoke, "Meera, I need you. And I will need you to be strong after you hear what I have to say."

My instincts began to prepare me for something as she continued, "There have been two farmer suicides this morning in Amargaam village. Their families need us. Could you be there at my place in an hour? I need to go to the bank to withdraw some cash."

I tried to speak, but no sound came out at first. After clearing my throat, I whispered shakily, "I'll be there, Didi."

Surbhi didi sniffled once more and gently said, "It's okay, Meera. I need you strong after an hour. I called you after I cried my heart out. It's okay."

"Mm-hmm." I agreed, and with a restrained sob, I said, "I'll see you later."

I ran outside.

I was at college, walking toward the canteen when my phone rang, my mother's name appeared on the phone. I'd asked my friend to go ahead, and I'd catch up with her later.

"Meera! Meera. Pappa! Your pappa, Meera."

My mother's wailing paralyzed me.

"Come home, Meera. Come home."

I ran. My phone clutched in my hand, glued to my ear, I just ran.

Someone was talking to me, calling out my name. I couldn't hear them, couldn't understand them. Couldn't see anything ahead of me. Everything looked like a blur. Horns were honking. The auto-rickshaw driver kept looking at me.

The crowd at the train station had led me to my train. Time seemed like an eternity as I sat in that train car taking me home.

Home.

Home, where my family lived. My mom, my little brother. And my pappa.

Memories chased me as I ran toward my home. Our farm.

Only one word echoed in my mind.

Only one man I wanted to see right now.

Pappa.

Pappa.

Pappa.

My feet carried me aimlessly, my eyes burning, my stomach crushed by an insurmountable weight, and my heart pounded like a hammer. My knees buckled, and I couldn't breathe. I tried to inhale, but my throat wouldn't allow me to take in air. I couldn't hear anything, and all I could see was the sun. Suddenly, arms came around me.

"Meera... Meera, it's me, Kriti."

Kriti. I turned to her, but she looked all blurry. Tears flooded my eyes and streaked down my cheeks, the crushing weight of my memories beating down my chest. Before I could utter a single word, Kriti pulled me into her arms.

"Shh...Meera, it's okay. I'm here."

"I need to go to Surbhi didi's place," I said, hiccuping my words.

The thought of facing the families who just lost their family members shook my hands, and my stomach tightened into knots. The wails of my mother and the tear-streaked face of Hari were forever imprinted in the back of my mind.

But today, the sounds of Maa's crying came roaring back, and my heart staggered with an ache so deep, I couldn't hold myself upright.

My tears soaked Kriti's sleeve as she ran her hand through my hair.

"What do you need, Meera? I'm here. Everything's going to be okay."

Her words did nothing. My heart raced, and I needed someone to take away this agonizing pain.

"I need....Luke. Call Luke."

I turned around to search for my phone, but all I got in my hands was hot, coarse sand and pebbles.

"I have your phone, Meera. Stay with me. I'm dialing."

I stared at the hazy fingers that clutched the phone. I couldn't see, and everything around me was a blur. I wiped my eyes, but they wouldn't stop leaking.

"It's ringing," she said.

I snatched the phone from her hand. I needed Luke. He would understand. He would know how to stop this pain.

I put the phone on my ear and clutched it tighter, but it rang and rang.

I screamed at the dial tone. "Luke!"

Luke

"Luke bhai, your phone is ringing," Ramesh said from where he sat on the steps of the stepwell, watching over my things.

I jotted down the measurement of the column's capital in my sketchbook and asked, "Can you tell me who's calling?"

"Umm... it says Meera."

My heart skipped a beat. Meera never called. *Never.* I ran toward the phone, climbing the steps two at a time and jumping to reach it.

"Meera?" I asked, my breath a little rushed.

All I heard was a gut-wrenching sob and a shaky cry that said, "Luke..."

"Meera, what's wrong? Where are you?" I asked, hastily shoving my things into my bag.

Ramesh was on high alert.

"We're leaving. Now," I told him.

My stomach dropped, and my hands shook. "Meera?"

Her sobs tore through the phone and punched my heart. "Meera, please, baby."

I heard some movement, and a new voice came on. "Luke, Kriti here."

I remembered meeting her friend. She had come when Meera had a fight with her mother.

"Kriti, what's wrong? Where are you? I'm coming."

"I'll send you our location on Whatsapp. Just hurry. She just keeps saying your name."

I received a message notification and quickly forwarded it to Ramesh. We ran out of the temple complex.

"Thank you, Kriti. I'm on my way. Can you give the phone to Meera? I'll stay with her on the phone."

"Luke?" Her voice wobbled, and her sobs faltered my steps as I ran toward the car.

"Meera, I'm coming, okay? I'll be right there," I assured her. And she continued to cry.

Once in the car, I urged Ramesh to drive as fast as he could. He became serious and responded, "Yes, Luke bhai," before tearing through the roads.

Throughout the ride, I continued to talk to her. Her gut-wrenching sobs and keening cries tore my heart apart. She couldn't speak; all I heard was my name, repeated over and over again. I never wanted to hear my name uttered with such pain from her mouth ever again. I kept repeating her name, telling her I was almost there and would stay on the phone with her. And she just cried and cried.

After what felt like the longest car ride of my life, I was there. I saw her hunched form near a tree, away from her school building, and Kriti holding her. Our car stopped right near her, but she didn't even notice.

I ran out of the car and dropped to my knees near Meera. Her face was tucked between her knees, her one hand still holding the phone at her ear.

"Luke?" she said into the phone, her voice trembling.

My hand shook as I touched her arm. "I'm here," I whispered.

Her head flew up, and our eyes met.

Her eyes and nose were swollen red, and her mouth trembled in grief.

"Luke," she said in a shaky voice. Her eyes watered more, and she fell in my arms.

Her hands clutched my shirt, and tears soaked the thin material where her cheek rested. Her body shook, and I held her tight against me. For the first time, I held her, and I hated that it was under these circumstances. "What happened?"

My eyes met Kriti's, who kept her hand on Meera's back. She shook her head and said, "She got a call. And she just ran out of the staff room crying. She said she needs to go to Surbhi didi's place."

I clutched her tighter in my arms, and her body fit against mine. I ran my hand through her hair, trying to soothe her. After five minutes of sitting on the ground in the midday heat, she said against my chest, "Two farmers committed suicide this morning."

"Luke, your sister has gone to heaven."

"What? Why?"

"She's an angel now, honey."

"I want her, Daddy. Where's Lucy?"

"She's our Lucy Angel now. She'll always watch over you."

"No! I want to see her."

My eyes filled with tears, and I couldn't hold them back. "Oh, sweetheart." This must have triggered all her worst memories. Memories that were better left forgotten. Memories that always brought pain.

She cried in my arms, and I let my tears disappear in her hair. "What do you need?" I asked, my voice strained.

She turned to look at me, her cheeks streaked with tears. She clutched my shirt in her fist and, with a trembling voice, asked, "Tell me how to stop this pain. Please, Luke?"

My chest cracked open, and I pulled her into my arms, hiding my face in her hair. Because that was all I could do. I rubbed her back gently, and answered, "I wish I knew how, baby. I wish I knew how."

After a few minutes of holding each other, she mumbled in my chest, "Surbhi didi needs me with her. I have to go to her place, and then we'll go help the families."

"I understand. Can I come with you?" I asked. I didn't want her to face this alone. Memories like this, seeing someone else go through the same shit as you, can rip open old wounds.

She sniffled, her face nestled under my neck, and asked, "You don't mind? I know it's painful."

This girl, always trying to protect others. "You need me, and I need to be with you. We'll go together. We'll visit the families."

"Thank you," she whispered.

She stopped crying after that, except for a few hiccups and sniffles, her hands still clenching my shirt. "When do we need to go?" I asked.

"We need to be at her place by one o'clock."

We still had some time. Soon, my leg cramped up after keeping them bent, and sweat gathered at my every crevice. "You want to sit in the car?"

She nodded, and we stood.

Her arms left me, and I felt empty. My arms ached to hold her again. Kriti told us she'd take care of Hari and Meera's mom while we were gone. Meera hugged her, and Kriti returned to the school while we got in the car.

I tucked Meera in my arms. I could feel Ramesh's eyes on us, inspecting us, trying to dissect our relationship. I knew by now what people thought about a couple showing affection to each other in public. It made them uncomfortable. But I didn't care. I needed Meera, needed to hold her in my arms, needed to make her feel less alone, and if at all possible, needed to chase away the painful memories.

"Ramesh, we're going to Surbhi's house. Remember where we took the chai during the heavy rain?"

He nodded and started driving. The air conditioner soon cooled down the car. Meera got up from my arms, sat straighter, and wiped her cheeks with her hands. I kept my arm on her shoulder. "Thank you," she said.

I held her hand with my other hand and squeezed. "Of course."

Soon, we arrived at Surbhi's place, and everything was a whirlwind from there. They hugged, cried, and spoke in Gujarati. They gathered all the documents they needed to help the families, and other families had packed food to send through Surbhi. When I offered some funds for the family, Surbhi declined and informed me that she was using the funds I had donated earlier. We loaded everything into the car, and I took the seat next to Ramesh while Meera and Surbhi sat in the back. They talked and murmured occasionally, none of which I understood. Even Ramesh looked sad.

We reached the first farmer's house in an hour, and the scene that greeted us made my knees weak. I hardened my heart and imagined it turning into a stone. I had no right to cry here when families sobbed and children stared helplessly at each other. The grief of the family, the cries of the farmer's wife and mother, were painful shards in my chest, and their poverty was a sharp reminder of why the farmer did what he did.

Meera and Surbhi took charge of the situation. The first thing Surbhi did was hand over a few bundles of rupees to the family. As insensitive as it seemed in the face of the loss, they still thanked them profusely. The money would reduce their worries about how they would manage to pay the loan sharks. Meera sat beside a man, probably the father of the farmer, and filled out some papers. She directed a few other men and Ramesh as to where to put the things we had brought along.

We sat with them for two hours in silence as Surbhi and Meera exchanged phone numbers with the family and offered their support. Then we left and continued to the next farmer's home.

"How are they going to earn money?" I asked, having only seen two young children with the wife and parents.

"The farmer's wife and probably his father will take up the farming. It's not uncommon for women to be involved in farming. Everyone often forgets that—the government, the families of the farmers, the community."

"Wow. That's... just wow." I had no words. These women, who had just lost their partners, would have to take on their partner's work as well as their own just to keep the bare minimum they had.

When we arrived at the next farmer's home, we repeated the process. Looking at Meera, no one would know she had cried heart-wrenching sobs in my arms just a few hours ago. She remained strong and provided unwavering support to all the people who had suffered such a tremendous loss. As for her, she stood tall, her demeanor softening toward the grieving family, her eyes conveying empathy for the pain they experienced.

And at that moment, I knew.

I knew *falling* had turned to *fallen*. There would be no parachute to save me now.

This incredibly strong woman ignored her own pain as she helped others bear theirs. Who cried in my arms and now let others cry in hers.

We left when it was turning dark. We dropped off Surbhi, and then Ramesh took us back to Meera's place. No one spoke. No words were needed. We'd all suffered similar losses at some point in our lives. We were all dealing with the deeply buried but now open wounds.

Once home, Meera hugged Hari and her mom before thanking Kriti for staying at her place. I looked at Meera and indicated that I was headed upstairs.

I got a change of clothes and went for a shower. Well, the bucket bath. I would have done anything for a shower right now. But I plucked up the tumbler, dipped it in the bucket, filled it with cold water, and poured it on my head.

The burst of cold water on my body jolted me awake and out of the spiraling memories. I turned the tap on and kept filling the bucket up with water. The activity of using a tumbler and the bucket kept my mind focused on the task, and the cold water started to soothe the pain.

Once done, I got into my softest sweats and T-shirt and left the bathroom.

I found Meera standing at the parapet, her hair tied up in a top knot, staring off at the dark fields around us. No music played today, and for once, I was glad. Her songs always made me more emotional, and I was already hanging by a thread.

I stood behind her, and her body went still.

"Can I hold you?" I asked softly.

She nodded once, and I closed the distance and wrapped my arms around her waist. Her back leaned against my chest, and I bent my head to breathe in her freshly showered skin.

"Can I hold you while we sleep?" I asked, not wanting to let her go.

This time, she answered with words. "Please."

And so I did.

I climbed into the small bed with her, covered us with her blanket, and wrapped myself around her. In the silence of the night, with her silky neck touching my arm and her scent surrounding me, my heart raced and calmed at the same time. The sadness of the day mixed with the joy of holding Meera in my arms.

My body yearned for more, yet my heart was content.

And as I closed my eyes, feeling the brush of her lips on my arm, I fell for her a little deeper.

13

Song: Gulaabi Aankhen Jo Teri Dekhi
- Mohammed Rafi

Meera

The entire week passed by in a blur. I barely knew
what I was teaching in my classes. Every evening, I
went with Surbhi didi to help prepare the documents for the two families. Since the widows of the farmers
lived with their husbands' families, the land ownership automatically went to the brother and father of the farmer. The
women were left with nothing of their own except their
children.

Surbhi didi was trying to help them. She knew how cruel
some in-laws could be when they didn't have to care for their
widowed daughter-in-law. Often, they ended up being abused,
made to work for everyone to earn their keep, and considered
an unlucky burden. It wasn't uncommon to hear stories where
the families threw the widow and the children out of the house
to avoid giving the inheritance to the farmers' children. That

was why Surbhi didi's first priority was always the widows left behind.

"I'm going to set up a bank account for these women. I'll only tell the women about it and give them strict instructions not to tell their in-laws. It will be their safety net to fall on," she had told me one evening.

"That's a great idea. I still remember when my father's family broke all their ties with us. They wanted our farm, but they, too, had no money to pay off the loan. At that time, we could have used the family's support. Instead, the three of us were left alone. Thank God for my friend Kriti, who got me a job in the school. And thank God for my father's friend in the city, who helped us keep our house and the farm by hiring their city lawyers. Our lives would have been destroyed without them."

I was well aware of my luck, in spite of the hardships we experienced. Not everyone was able to keep their farms and homes. Many farmers left behind children too young to work.

"We will take care of our fellow sisters left behind, Meera. I'll make sure of it," Surbhi didi promised.

I believed her. She was a determined woman and had the biggest heart that I'd ever known.

"Your friend Luke's donation has been very helpful, Meera."

"It has?" I asked.

"His donation was big enough to pay off loans for three families. But I need to use that money properly. We have many widows who have no jobs and no income. We take care of our women first. We need to put a monthly amount for their day-to-day life aside. A little for their loans. And set up jobs for them. I think setting up online donation facilities for foreigners would be a good idea. Their little amount can be big for us."

We had discussed more strategies as we worked on preparing document packages for the two families. Every evening, Luke took me to Surbhi didi's place. He, too, got involved in planning and offered more donations. Surbhi didi accepted some amount but asked him to let her have some time to better plan the finances.

Every night, we returned, had a quiet dinner with Hari and Maa, and went to sleep.

Every night, he held me in his arms. His warmth, his strength, his soft, murmured conversations became my anchor.

It wasn't the first time I had helped the family of a deceased farmer. Surbhi didi had first asked for my help two years after my father passed. And it had destroyed me. Yet it had also repaired me. For the first two years, I had wallowed in self-pity. But when I'd met the deceased farmer's family, discovering their situation was so much worse than mine, I'd felt blessed. For the first time, I felt the need to help others instead of expecting the world to help me. However, the memories that came roaring back—the loss, the difficulties, and the echoes of my mother's cries—had brought back all the grief, and the loneliness had crippled me.

This time around, though, I had Luke. For the first time in five years, I had someone to share my grief with. Someone who understood the pain.

In the past seven days, Luke had become my shore, my safety net. When I started to drown in the emotions, he pulled me back. He never asked me not to cry for the loss, mine and others. He cried with me. More than once, I'd felt his shaky breath, his tears sliding down my neck.

The past week had been one of the most difficult times in the past few years. Yet Luke made it a little easier. A little more bearable. Every night, his touch, his hold on my waist, and his body engulfing mine, were a balm to my bruised soul.

But soon, I would lose it all. He would leave for his site visit in a week and would be gone for a month. He would only return for another week to get things in order, and then leave this village—leave *me*—forever.

As I curled up into him and held him tighter at night, he didn't complain. And if I cried at the thought of losing him from my life instead of for the families who lost their loved ones, he didn't have to know.

Every night I slept in his arms, I memorized the feel of his strong arms around me, his soft breath along my neck, his chest rising and falling at my back, and his legs tangled with mine. His distinct scent of summer and ocean breeze infused every pore in my body.

I cried at the thought of losing him.

I hated him a little for making me rely on him.

I hated him even more for showing me I *could* rely on him.

I hated him the most because I knew I couldn't have him.

Luke

"Psst...psst..." The sound came from the crack of my bedroom door.

I had already turned to face the door when I heard it open with a loud creaking sound.

A small head poked into my room. "Luke bhai?"

I chuckled. Hari had stayed home today with the pretense of a stomachache. The moment Meera had left for school, leaving him behind, he'd jumped up from his bed and started playing.

"Yes, Hari?" I asked.

He stood by the door, a book and his pencil box in his hands. He looked anywhere but my face, as he asked, "I study here? In AC?"

Oh man, here I was, sitting in my cool room every day, not thinking about how people in this house cope with the heat.

Not to keep Hari waiting, I indicated with my hand for him to enter, and said," Come on in, buddy. "

He quickly stepped inside the room and climbed on the bed, his face full of relief and excitement. Once Hari settled down with his work, I returned to my desk and continued copying my hand-drawn details into my AutoCAD file.

A few minutes passed where we worked silently when I heard Hari get down from the bed. He roamed around, inspecting the things lying around. I kept the pretense of working, but all my attention was on him. Soon, his steps wandered toward the air conditioner fit in the window. And then, he stood there.

For one minute, two minutes. I slowly turned my head around to see why he stopped moving and quickly turned back around to hide my laughter.

Hari just stood in front of the AC, his shirt held up to his neck, basking in the cool air from the vents. I had to get this kid an AC in the living room downstairs, if only to see the joy on his face.

Now about the joy on his sister's face...I hadn't seen that in a week. For a week, she hadn't played any music at night. She'd slept huddled into me as if showing her back to the world around us, and I'd clutched her to me, wanting to shield her from the sadness.

I wanted to do something special for her. Something that would make her smile. Make her laugh. Something that would ease her burdens. Even if it was just for a day or a few hours.

Maybe I should cook for her. I was actually getting hungry. Yes, I should cook for her. Usually, her mom cooked lunch every day, and Meera cleaned up. Why not surprise her with some lunch? I was getting pumped just thinking about it.

Ideas started firing in my head, and I quickly called Ramesh to get started.

"Luke bhai? How can I help?" asked Ramesh, his English getting better and better each day.

"Ramesh, I need to go to a supermarket. I want to cook something for Meera and her family. Do you know someplace we can go?"

"Hmm... we have to go to the city. Big market there."

I checked the time. Meera would return from school in about four hours, enough time for me to go to the market and prepare lunch. "Can you pick me up in a few minutes? We need to go shopping."

"Yes, sir. I will leave now."

"Thanks, man. See you soon."

Hari looked at me as I talked in English, awe in his little eyes.

I smiled at him, and said, "I go. You stay here." I also acted out the bit to show him what I meant. He nodded and returned to his spot in front of the air conditioner, which left me chuckling and ruffling his hair.

Once I was ready, I went downstairs to inform Meera's mom I was cooking lunch today.

That was a challenge. We'd never really talked since she did not speak English, and my Gujarati was limited to words necessary for good manners like "Saru chhe" for it's good, "Aabhar" for thank you, and "Barabar" for alright, all thanks to Ramesh.

I opened my Google Translate app.

I made the necessary changes in the language input and output and cleared my throat as I neared her mom.

She looked up, a frown marring her forehead, her knitting paused. I gave her a small smile to show how harmless I was.

I raised a finger at her, indicating to give me a minute.

I raised the phone between us, and said into the phone, "Hello."

I pressed play for the Gujarati translation, and the Google lady spoke out the greeting.

Her mom's eyes brightened a little as she stared at the phone in surprise.

She greeted me back and stared at the phone.

Again, I said on the phone, "I want to cook today."

And when she heard the translation, her eyes widened, and she started shaking her head. Maybe she thought I didn't like her food? Or did she not want me to because I was a guest in the house? But I'd been living here for a month.

I tried again. I said into the phone, "I really want to cook for Meera. Can I?"

She stared at the phone as it translated. And when she looked up at me, her eyes shone. She nodded and smiled at me.

"Aabhar," I thanked her out loud, getting a small delighted chuckled out of her.

When I got outside the house, I started the car and switched on the AC to start cooling it. It was hot as hell.

Soon, Ramesh arrived on his motorcycle, parked it under a tree in the front yard, and ran up to the driver's seat. Then we were off. It took us two hours to go to the supermarket in the nearby city, shop for all the ingredients I would need today and groceries that they could store up for a while, and return back home.

Hari ran up to us the moment we parked the car, and the little man helped us carry all the bags into the kitchen. I picked the bag with the ingredients I needed and pulled them out. I had no clue where all the pots and pans were. I guess Google Translate had a lot of work cut out for it today.

I went out into the living room, where Meera's mom sat, and opened the app. A huge smile came over her face, clearly still delighted by the technology. I sat on my knees in front of her and brought the phone between us. Hari followed me and stood staring at us, curious about what was happening.

But the minute we started conversing via the app, Hari squealed.

By the time I asked her to help me find the cooking utensils, he was bouncing off his feet, wanting to try the same with me. Meera's mom got up from her bed, and we all entered the kitchen. She showed me where everything was by opening the shelves and pointing. Once she was gone, Hari stayed in the kitchen with me.

I picked him up and placed him on the countertop, away from the stove. I opened the app and showed him how to translate. And that was how we talked while I cooked.

He said something on the phone, and then pushed play. "You play with me?" said the speaker.

I knew I had to be precise with the translator app. "Yes. After lunch."

I put the pasta on a boil on one side of the stove. I washed the tomatoes, bell peppers, and onions and started chopping.

When he pressed play, he giggled. So I asked, "What happened? Why are you laughing?"

And he laughed louder when it translated. "This sounds like dirty," the speaker translated his answer for me.

And I nearly dropped my knife. *Dirty?* What the hell was it translating for me? What if he told Meera I was talking *dirty* to him? Oh God. She would kill me.

I bent down to where he held the phone and spoke *clearly* into it. "No, buddy, I am not talking dirty."

Perspiration dotted my forehead as he pressed play on the phone. And the moment it translated, Hari howled with laughter.

Oh man, why was he laughing? "Is it the accent?" I asked.

He frowned at the translation and raised four fingers in question. Now, what in the hell did that mean? Either I had to sit and learn Gujarati or teach him English.

"Four?" I asked.

We looked at each other, neither of us understanding what the other was trying to say.

And then I heard it. The sweet laughter that always seemed to scramble all my senses and got my heart pumping.

I turned around to look at the kitchen door. I wished I could walk over to her, greet her with a kiss, and ask her about her day. Wouldn't that be something?

Instead, I asked, "How long have you been standing here?"

She wore white salwar kameez with small colorful prints on the borders of the kameez. She held the edge of her dupatta as she walked over to where Hari sat, and said, "Since you've been talking dirty with Hari."

A desperate groan escaped my mouth. "Meera, you know I wasn't."

She chuckled. "I know. Hari kept laughing because Google's translation is very formal. Like no one actually talks like that. Hari actually said that the speaker is talking like a crazy person. And it translated to dirty."

"Oh... that makes more sense. I thought you would kill me if Hari told you that I was talking dirty to him."

She laughed and looked at me, her chocolate-brown eyes shining with warmth and twinkling with delight. It had been a week since I'd seen that laughter on her face. A week since her eyes shone in excitement, in hope, and in that beautiful something that we only shared in the darkness of the night.

And how I had missed it.

14

Song: Aap Ki Nazaron Ne Samjha
  - Lata Mangeshkar

Meera

Luke stood in my tiny kitchen, cooking something while he talked to Hari and made him laugh. The moment I stepped inside the house, something felt different. Lighter. Happier. Maa had smiled at me, and I could hear giggles and murmurs from the kitchen. At the question in my eyes, Maa had told me to go take a look.

And here I stood near Hari while Luke chopped tomatoes. "Need some help?" I asked.

He gave me a huge smile that warmed me from the inside and said, "Absolutely not. I'm cooking for you."

For me. He was cooking *for me*. When was the last time someone had done something for me? Something bubbled inside me, rising, swirling, the emotions incomprehensible. What was this that I was feeling? This...this knowledge that someone thought about me.

"I... I don't understand," I mumbled, trying to figure out my own feelings.

"Meera, darling, I am in awe of what you've been doing and helping others for a week. It's your turn to feel special."

Special. That was what this was.

I was feeling *special.*

"Oh, Luke.... I've not felt that for a long time."

He gave me his big, joyful smile, focused back on his chopping, and said, "Well, that's a shame. I'll have to work harder at making you feel special every day."

My heart jumped in excitement and hope as bright, vivid dreams spun in the deepest corners of my mind. "Please don't. My heart won't be able to take it."

He glanced up at that. "We'll see," he said, and winked at me.

My cheeks heated at that tiny gesture. I flushed and failed to meet his eyes. I focused on Hari and played the translation game with him. Luke joined in with his translations, and Hari laughed and laughed and laughed at the silly accent. Luke cooked food for my family, and I stood beside him and simply felt special.

I can't have him. I can't fall for him. I repeated that sentence as a mantra and begged to my heart to understand logic, but that foolish organ was hell-bent on giving itself to this wonderful person, beating faster every time he smiled and thumping harder every time I felt his touch.

The three of us stood in the kitchen, watching the pasta cook. Soon, the bright red tomato sauce in the pan bubbled, and Luke added the boiled pasta to the sauce. He stirred it while Hari watched him, curiosity in his eyes.

I bent near him, and asked in Gujarati, "Why are you looking at him like that?"

He turned to me and brought his face close to my ear. He put a hand over his mouth to whisper, not realizing the fact that

Luke wouldn't understand him even if he spoke out loud. Luke smiled at us, realizing the same thing, and I returned his smile, as Hari said, "He is cooking. Can boys cook?"

"Of course they can cook. Do you want to learn?"

He nodded, so I turned to Luke, and asked, "Luke, Hari would like to help you. Is there something he can do?"

Hari looked at him expectantly, and Luke's eyes brightened. "Of course, little man. Let's get you a little closer to the pan."

He dragged Hari closer to the pasta pan. He gave the wooden spatula to Hari, held his hand over his, and started stirring. Luke encouraged him, constantly praising him by saying things like *That's it, Very good, You got it.* Hari couldn't wipe the smile off his face. Once they finished stirring and mixing, Luke served the pasta on five plates.

Soon, Hari, Maa, Ramesh bhai, Luke, and I sat in a circle in the living room eating pasta. I'd had pasta before and liked it enough. But I highly doubted that Maa and Ramesh bhai would be enthused. However, as I looked around, everyone ate it and made appreciative noises for Luke that made him smile.

He looked at me, eyebrows raised in question. I smiled at him and ate a big spoonful of it to show him how I loved it. He turned to look at Hari, and I followed his gaze, and what we saw had us both bursting into laughter. Hari had abandoned his fork and was pulling aside all the capsicum and onion pieces. He ate each piece of pasta with his hand, smearing the sauce all over his face.

"Hari, why aren't you using the fork?" I asked in Gujarati.

He frowned, glaring menacingly at the fork, and said, "The pasta keeps falling off. I can eat faster with my hands. See?" And he took a fistful of the pasta and shoved it in his mouth.

Luke chuckled. "I take it he loves it, then? No one has ever eaten my food with such passion before."

I chuckled and continued eating.

Once the dinner was done, I got up to clean up everything.

Luke stopped me, and said, "This is your day, Meera. I'm cleaning up."

"Absolutely not. You cooked; I'll clean." I could see he was about to argue, so I continued, "No, no, don't argue. You are not cleaning if you ever want to cook for me again."

He huffed. "You're so stubborn."

"I'll meet you upstairs later tonight," I said, and heat sparked in his eyes. Goose bumps covered my arms, and I looked at him, matching the intensity of his gaze. I showed him my need for him and my desperation to have his arms wrapped around me.

His fists clenched around his plate, and sparks ignited where I grazed his fingers to take the plate from him. With a rough exhale, his voice hoarse, he said in a whisper, "Hurry up."

I nodded and ran off into the kitchen.

By the time I cleaned everything up, Ramesh bhai had left, and Maa and Hari had returned to their knitting and doing homework respectively. The temptation to go upstairs to Luke was unbearable. But I stayed put in the living room as I finished my work and helped Hari with his studies.

The four of us had dinner together in the evening, and every glance from Luke had my stomach doing somersaults. Maa and Hari were already in bed, ready to sleep, by the time I cleaned the kitchen and changed into my pajamas.

Anticipation curled low in my belly. My body craved the feel of his strong arms wrapped around mine, and the memory of it sent shivers to the parts of my body that had never been awake before.

Just the thought of being in Luke's arms had me rushing up the stairs while the intensity of my feelings for him tried to drag me back.

Just a week of this.

He was leaving in a week.

My heart hurt at the thought, yet it compelled me to return to his arms, take everything he was willing to give me, and be a little greedy. I wanted to clutch him against me and never let him go. I so badly wanted to ask him to stay.

But I wouldn't.

He deserved more than a shitty life in a tiny Indian village. Luke was made for bigger things in life, finer things. And I'd let him go.

But I would take these moments of happiness and savor them. Cherish them. And then let my heart hurt when I lost them.

Luke

A flutter of approaching footsteps caught my attention, and I looked toward the staircase. As soon as Meera stepped out onto the terrace, our eyes locked. She rushed over to me in the next heartbeat and jumped into my arms. I wrapped my arms around her, lifted her off her feet, and held her tightly against me.

Her curves fit perfectly against my body, and her grip around my neck was tight enough for me to lose myself in her. We stood there, suspended in time, for seconds, minutes...as long as our hearts beat together.

Darkness enveloped us, the sweet fragrance of jasmine filled the air, and the creatures of the night sang their melody.

All I felt was an unyielding desire; it was feverish, bone-deep, and unending. I had the world in my arms, yet I still craved more.

I wanted to give more to Meera. More pleasure. More laughter. More passion.

"Can I play some music?" Meera's breathy murmur sent

shivers down my spine as I nuzzled her neck. She clutched my shirt in her fist, her voice turning sharp as she asked, "Luke?"

"Yes, please. I've missed it," I replied, instantly regretting my response as she let go of me. I wanted more of her touch. I needed her to be wrapped around me, desperate for me like I was for her.

A noise of despair might have escaped me because Meera's arms tightened around me again, and her laughter touched my neck. "We'll hug on the bed."

Gently, I released her and put her back on the floor.

She retrieved the cassette player stowed under the bed, and I plugged it into the outlet. "Do you have a preference?" she asked.

"Whatever you want, darling."

She glanced down at the cassettes, a small smile forming on her lips.

I had pushed our beds together so I could hold her for as long as possible, and then roll over to sleep properly in my own bed. But for now, she placed the cassette player on the floor near the head of the bed, and I climbed onto her bed, positioning myself right behind her.

I extended my arm, and she used it as her personal pillow.

She pressed play, and we looked at each other, our faces nearly touching. Her breasts brushed against my chest, quickening my heartbeat, and our legs tangled under the comforter. Her nearness drove me crazy. If she moved her hips even an inch closer to mine, she'd discover how much I desired her, how much I wanted to consume her every breath.

A slow tune started to play, and Meera shivered. Her fingers twisted in my T-shirt, and her gaze didn't move above my neck.

I knew the song meant something to her. It had to be for her to avert her eyes. I let it play, and its soothing quality was almost wistful. Once the song was done, I asked, "Would you translate it for me?"

Her breath caught, and she finally met my gaze, a mix of fear and hope in her eyes. They screamed at me not to ask her, yet she nodded. She stretched over the edge of the bed, pressed rewind, stop, and play.

She got back in my arms, just the way we were, just the way I loved.

And again, the same soft tune from earlier began.

She kept her eyes on mine when she translated what the lady sang.

"Your gaze deems me worthy of your love,
Stop, oh beats of my heart, for I have found my
destination."

As soon as the music began between the verses, I whispered, "You know it's the other way around, right?"

She clutched my T-shirt and came closer. Our bodies fit together, and I felt like we swayed with the music.

The moment she turned down her gaze, I gently lifted her face to meet mine. She smiled at me in mock exasperation, but her eyes were the softest I'd ever seen. And then she sang,

"Yes, this decision of yours is acceptable to me,
my every glance is thanking God as you
brought me into your life with a smile."

And I just couldn't help but lean forward and kiss her forehead. This song, these lyrics, her eyes that spoke even louder than these beautiful words. I clutched her tighter, my hand tangled in her hair, my eyes lost in the emotions pouring from her. My other hand held her waist, anchoring myself to her.

She rubbed her hand on my chest, placed it on my heart, and continued.

"I am your destination. And you are my
destination.
Why should I fear the storm? You are my shore.
Someone go tell the storms that I've found my
shore."

I rubbed my cheek against hers and placed soft kisses underneath her ear. Her body shook, and the whoosh of her breath on my neck sent shivers down my spine. My hand moved lower to her hip, traveled up to her shoulder, her back, and down her hips. I wanted to consume her. I wanted to *be* consumed by her. The agony of the distance, the truth behind her words, and my ever-increasing need to care for her and protect her from the darkness in her life slowly rearranged my heart.

She pulled me back from my thoughts with a kiss on my jaw, and the desire swirled between us, erotic, passionate, and so fucking painful. I met her eyes, and they declared her feelings for me with courage and acceptance.

She continued the song.

"Your shadows have cast upon my heart,
In every direction, hundreds of musical instru-
ments are playing in celebration;
Today, I've gained the joys of both the worlds.
Your gaze has deemed me worthy of your love."

And the notes of the song drifted away.

The silence was deafening. She had stolen the words from my heart and sung them back to me. What more could I possibly ask from the world?

"Can we play it again?" I asked, my voice a soft whisper, almost touching her lips.

She nodded, and I stretched my hand over the bed, pressed rewind, stop, and then play.

I pulled her closer than ever before, the moon shining down on her face, making her appear like an angel of the night. I closed the distance between us, and whispered near her lips, "I feel the same, Meera. Every word you said, believe me, I live those words. You *are* my destination. And you too have cast your shadows upon my heart."

"Truly?" she asked. Her words fell upon my lips, and I nearly leaned forward to catch them.

I brushed my thumb on her cheek, turned her face up so our eyes met, and nodded.

And then she smiled. And I just had to taste her smile and feel it on my own.

"Can I kiss you, Meera?"

Her heated eyes met mine, and her voice shook as she asked, "On the lips? Like in the movies?"

A breathy chuckle escaped me, and I nodded as I gently ran my thumb over her lower lip, mesmerized by its softness.

"I've never kissed before."

My heart pounded, and a primitive sort of want bubbled inside me at the thought of being the first guy to kiss her. The *only* guy to kiss her. "Would you like to?" I asked, my voice shaking at being so close to her lips.

"Yes. Will you go slow?"

I stared at her lips as she bit them and nodded. "I will."

She nodded back and said the words I'd been dying to hear. "Kiss me, Luke."

And I slowly closed the short distance between us.

I grazed my lips against hers, and sparks danced behind my eyes.

I closed my arms around her and pulled her into me, lightly pressing our lips together.

A moan escaped her, or maybe it was me, and she pressed tighter against me.

She clutched my hair and deepened the kiss, making me groan in her mouth.

She quickly pulled away from the kiss and looked at me.

"Well?" she asked.

"That was the best kiss of my life. Did you like it?"

A shy smile came over her face, and she nodded. "I loved it. Can we do more?"

My heart melted at her innocent question. "Oh, baby, yes, please. We can spend the whole night kissing. Maybe even tomorrow morning."

She giggled and pulled my face to her.

She kissed me, and I forgot my own name.

I kissed her, and I forgot the whole world.

Under the starlight, hidden beneath the blanket, we kissed, and kissed, and kissed.

15

Song: *Aise Na Mujhe Tum Dekho*
  - *Kishore Kumar*

Meera

My eyes opened the following morning, yet I still dreamed of last night. Was it all a hallucination? Did I kiss Luke? On the lips? I tried to raise my hand to touch my lips but couldn't. A heavy arm was draped around my waist, and now that I was fully awake, I could feel every inch of Luke sleeping behind me.

Did he forget to go back to his bed last night? Of course, he did. And here he was, holding me while he slept peacefully. My entire body buzzed with pleasure as I felt his hard body wrapped around mine, and all I wanted to do was burrow deep into his arms and never leave.

Slowly, I pushed myself back deeper into his embrace, and his arm tightened around me, causing my heart to beat out of my chest in delight. He nuzzled at my neck, and a breath of a kiss touched my skin.

"Good morning," he whispered.

A thousand butterflies took flight in my stomach. My body was so paralyzed by his nearness and the way his words touched my skin that I could barely utter a word. I cleared my throat, and said, "Good morning."

"Sleep well?" he asked, his mouth so close to my ear that it sent shivers down my spine.

I automatically pushed back my hip and bumped into a very hard *something*. I quickly pulled forward with a loud squawk. Red-hot embarrassment rushed my cheeks, and I covered my face with my hands.

Luke shook with laughter and kissed my hair.

"Shut up," I grumbled and rushed to get out of the small bed we'd shared throughout the night.

"Please don't go," said Luke, his hair disheveled, his warm brown eyes bright with amusement, his cheek creased with a pillow line. He looked like everything good in the world.

"I need to get up. I'll come back with chai."

"Can you give me a kiss before you go?" His eyes swirled with heat, turning darker.

I couldn't help but be disgusted by the thought of our non-brushed mouths meeting. I might not have been able to hide it well because he laughed and shooed me away. "Fine, I see how it is. Off you go, freshen up. I'll meet you all minty fresh when you come back with chai. I'm gonna take a power nap."

"You slept the entire night. Why do you need a nap?"

"Shut up."

I chuckled and left the terrace. I should have kissed him on the cheek.

As soon as I was back on the terrace with our cups of chai, I found Luke standing at the parapet, looking out at the fields.

I put our chai trays on the table, walked up to Luke, stood on my toes, held his face, and kissed him on the cheek, just like I wanted to. He held the hand cupping his cheek, brought it closer to his mouth, and brushed his lips along my wrist, making my heart beat faster.

Our eyes met, and he pulled me even closer and kissed my lips.

Desire curled low in my stomach, and my body involuntarily moved against his, trying to get closer. He groaned in my mouth, his tongue grazing my lips. I let him in, and we both hummed as our tongues touched, our mouths moved, and our bodies rubbed against each other. Pleasure hummed in my veins, and I was floating.

"Meera," Luke said, his voice ragged.

I looked at him, and his eyes were a dark brown, need and love and adoration shining through. With a gentle smile, he tucked some of my wild curls behind my ear, and said, "Come with me, Meera. Please."

That brought me back to the ground.

I let go of him, picked up my chai, and sat on the bed. "Luke." I sighed, tired of saying no when all I wanted to do was jump up, pack my bags, and go on the month-long trip with him.

He came and sat on his knees in front of me, his hand holding my leg. "Meera, I don't want this to end in four days. I just can't. I need more time with you."

The harsh reality of our inevitable end sent a sharp pain through my heart. Four days or thirty-four days. It was eventually going to end. The only question was which one would be less painful.

I touched his forehead, tucked a stray lock of his hair back, and said, "Letting you go would be even more painful after a month."

He took hold of my hand and clutched it in both of his. "Who said it has to end? We might decide to make it work long distance. Don't you want to try? Wouldn't you regret losing an entire month we could've spent together?"

"At least it would be less painful if it doesn't work out."

"Regret hurts far worse than heartbreak."

"I'm scared," I whispered.

"Of what?" Luke's tone was gentle. Always gentle.

"Of leaving Maa and Hari behind. What if I fail in taking care of my family?" *Just like my father.* I hated myself for that thought.

Maybe he heard my thoughts, maybe he didn't. But his eyes softened, and he placed a soothing kiss at my wrist. "You haven't failed in five years. One month away won't make you a failure. You deserve this break, sweetheart."

I nodded, repeating his words in my mind. "I'll think about it," I said.

His smile widened, and hope shone through his eyes. It made my chest hurt. How could I disappoint him? How could I make him sad? For so many years, I'd only felt responsible for Maa's and Hari's happiness. And now, Luke slowly crawled his way into my heart, breaking my resolve bit after bit. "Please don't get your hopes up," I implored.

He chuckled and leaned closer as if telling me a secret. "If thinking about making me sad makes you come with me, I'm going to look at you with the most hopeful and saddest eyes I can manage."

"I hate you."

He laughed. "No, you don't."

I shook my head in mock exasperation and gulped down my tea.

Soon, I was off to work with Hari, and I kept thinking about Luke's offer the entire time. It terrified me to think of what would happen to Hari and Maa while I'm gone. What if they need something and I'm not there? What if Hari gets sick?

A loud thud pulled me out of my thoughts. Kriti dropped in her chair beside me, a severe frown on her face. She flipped through notebook after notebook, slashing tick marks on the pages, her movements rough and jerky.

"Kriti," I called her name.

She jumped on her seat. "Oh, Meera. Sorry, what?"

"Are you okay?"

She groaned, slamming her pen between a notebook, and turned to me. "No, Meera. My mother has made my life hell. Every time we talk, it's all 'Kriti, you need to lose more weight. Kriti, you need to learn how to cook undhiyu. Kriti, you need to be more polite with the prospective suitors.' Ugh! I'm so done with her."

"That sucks. Isn't Uncle saying anything to your mom?"

She made an exaggerated eye roll and said, "When it comes to these meetings with men, Pappa seems to always lose in verbal combat with Mummy. Look at what she sent me for lunch."

She opened her lunch box, and it was filled to the brim with carrots, cucumber, radish, and tomatoes.

"How colorful," I said, trying to make it sound appealing.

"Ugh... Don't start. I have another man coming to meet me on the weekend. I just hope I find the right man soon so I can be done with this stupid raw food diet."

It was just last week that I received that awful call. Just last week, I was reminded of my past again and thrown into those memories. But the moment I looked around me, life seemed to just...move on. Then why was I stuck in the past? Why couldn't I move on?

Or could I?

I turned to Kriti, who was still grumbling under her breath. "Uh, listen, Kriti," I began. "Can I ask you something?"

"What's up?"

I fumbled with the notebook in front of me. "Uh... I'm considering going on the trip with Luke. Do you think that's okay?"

She put her arm around my shoulders, and gave a low, excited screech. "Meera, of course it's okay. You have to go on the trip. Take this break. And how are things with Luke?"

I averted my eyes, and she gave an even louder screech and shook me like a rag doll. "What are you not saying? Meera, what's going on? Are you together? I'm gonna kill you if you don't start talking."

I laughed, apologized to the other teachers glaring at Kriti, and dragged her into the courtyard outside the staff room. We sat on the steps, and I told her everything that happened in the past week. She kept interrupting with really raunchy questions that I left unanswered. By the end, we decided —she ordered— that I was going on the trip.

She dragged me to the principal and we sat together to discuss the logistics of my absence. I thought I would have to beg him to let me leave on such short notice, but he just said he was glad I finally decided to take a break. He talked to a few teachers, including Kriti, to assign my classes, and I was all set to leave for an entire month.

As soon as I was home, I sat on the bed across Maa. When she looked up at me from her knitting, I said, "Maa, I was thinking... Uh... Luke invited me to go on a one-month trip with him. Jaipur, Udaipur, Patan. He said he would love to have some company, and I'll get a nice trip out of it."

She kept staring at me, her eyes unblinking. So, with a deep breath, my heart pounding, my face red, I asked, "So, uh... can I go?"

The longer she looked at me, the faster I spoke. "You and Hari don't have to stay here alone. Maybe you could go to Masi's place? Or I could ask Kriti to come here for a few days. I won't go if you need to stay here. I can't risk Baldev showing up."

"Meera, beta," she said. She clutched my cheek gently. "For the first time in the past five years, I've seen you smile. I've seen hope and warmth in your eyes. And if that boy makes you laugh and sing—"

At my shocked expression, she laughed then continued, "Yes, sometimes I can hear you sing on the terrace. As I was saying, if Luke has brought back joy in your life, you *have* to go. Hari and I will go to Sudha's place."

"Really?" A sob stuck in my throat.

She chuckled. "Yes."

"What will people say if they find out that I've gone with a foreigner alone? For a month?"

Her jaw hardened. "I don't care. Nor should you. It wouldn't matter to those who truly care about you, and if what you do—who you go with, what brings you joy—makes them frown and talk behind your back, those people shouldn't matter to you."

I hugged my mother. "Thank you. Thank you. Thank you."

She laughed and patted my back. "Go, have fun. All these years, you took care of me and Hari. It's time you took care of yourself."

I kissed her cheek and ran upstairs to inform Luke.

Luke

Ramesh dropped us at the railway station in the nearby city, his face sullen and his movements brisk. He slammed the trunk of the car after silently dropping our luggage at his feet.

"Ramesh, man, you know that if I could, I would've asked you to come with me for the tour. We don't have enough time to take a car journey."

"Why's he not talking to me?" I asked Meera, who stood beside me, silently chuckling.

She came a little closer to me, and said, "Maybe he got

attached to you. Maybe he's jealous you'll find another favorite driver? Could be anything."

I went to Ramesh and placed my hand on his shoulder. "Ramesh, you are the best driver I've ever had. And here is the tip for your excellent service. I am coming back in a month, and if you don't mind, I would love it if you would be there for me for my last week."

His eyes finally brightened, and he gave me a firm handshake, a salute, and off he went with the company car, leaving Meera and me in the middle of a swarm of people rushing past us.

Five men in red clothes stormed around us, asking something and snatching my bag from me. I was about to push him away when Meera said, "Hold on, Luke. They are porters. They're asking if you want them to carry our luggage up to our platform and help us get settled in the train."

"Oh, wow, so we don't need to carry all this? Let's hire them."

She rolled her eyes at me, and said. "We can carry our luggage."

"But this way, we can help them earn money. And we can walk hands-free."

"Fine. But we just need one person. So you'll have to choose."

"But we have four huge bags. One person can't carry it."

One of the porters said something to Meera, and she made a sign asking them to hold on a second.

"Luke, one person can carry it."

"But they don't have to. We can hire two. What do they charge?"

She turned toward the five porters around us; each one looked powerful enough to crush me in their arms.

After talking to them for a whole minute, Meera turned to me, and said, "Forty rupees per bag."

I instantly handed my bags to one of the porters and asked another to pick up Meera's bag. That was not even a dollar per bag.

The porters got excited and in a millisecond, swung the bags and put it on top of their heads. Two bags on each of their heads and they were off walking—more like running—through the crowd of people. Meera and I ran after them, Meera keeping her handbag, and me toting a bottle of Glucon-D, the best energy drink on this hot day.

We barely kept up with the porters. The entire way I worried that they would surely take off with our stuff, but nothing of the sort happened. We reached our platform, and they put the bags on the floor. We were about fifteen minutes early.

Our platform was about fifty feet wide, with small tea and snack shops at regular intervals. Hundreds of people covered just our platform: men carrying suitcases, women dragging their children, students standing in groups around the tea stalls, porters rushing past people with families running after them. We'd made a small space of our own, our bags in front of us, and the porters standing in front of them, protecting them. A few people stared at us but kept moving along.

It was humid, and I was already sweating. A train arrived on the opposite platform, and people hung off the doors. One wrong move from behind, and a fellow might get pushed out of the train. I quickly turned away and looked at Meera. She was far less frightening to look at.

She wore a yellow kameez with tight pink pants. Her long, pink dupatta hung over her shoulder. She'd pulled her hair in a low ponytail, but some of her curls were already poking out. She looked around, touching her purse now and again.

"Everything all right?" I asked.

She smiled and nodded. "Yeah, it's been a while since I've

traveled. And I've never traveled in an AC train. I'm a little nervous."

I gently grazed my finger with hers. "You shouldn't be. It's my first time traveling on an Indian train. If you get nervous, who's going to guide me?"

She touched her arm to mine in thanks and gave me a big smile.

Soon, an announcement played overhead that I didn't understand. At all.

I turned to Meera with a raised brow, and she shrugged.

"How do you not understand it?" I asked.

"It sounded like the person on the speaker was speaking with his mouth closed."

She turned to one of the porters and inquired about the announcement. He said something, and Meera nodded. She turned to me and said that the train would be arriving in three minutes.

The moment the train arrived, it felt like the population on the platform immediately tripled. People swarmed around us, and I pulled Meera closer to me. The porters had already swung our bags in their hands. They asked me for our compartment and seat number, and then we too rushed off into the crowd. I kept a tight hold on Meera, dragging her with me.

In a minute, the porters entered the train compartment, and we followed. As soon as the door to our compartment opened, a rush of cold air blasted on my face.

We entered a narrow passage with sleeping berths on both sides. The berths were arranged in two tiers, four across the width of the coach and two longways along the corridor. There were curtains at each berth for privacy. We stopped where our porters arranged our bags under the bottom tier of the berth along the corridor.

As we reached our berth, Meera bent slightly to avoid hitting her head on the top tier and settled cross-legged on the bottom tier. I followed suit after paying our porters. Once they left, I mimicked her actions and positioned myself across from her. The train had yet to depart, and the corridor was filled with people searching for their seats or berths and children who were screaming at the top of their lungs.

I pulled the curtain on my side and closed off our section from the bustling corridor and other berths. Meera did the same, and it became just the two of us, sitting across from each other, with the bottom tier resembling a twin-size bed and the windows on our side providing a view of the platform outside.

Now that we were enclosed in our little noisy cocoon, Meera seemed to relax. She smiled at me, reached out to touch my leg, and gave it a squeeze. "I'm really excited. I've never been to Jaipur before."

Leaning closer to her, I held her hand and intertwined my fingers with hers. "I've never been on a trip with a girlfriend."

She blushed, her cheeks turning a delicate shade of pink. She averted her eyes, focusing on anything but me in the confines of our tiny space, and asked, "Is that what I am? Your girlfriend?"

I brought her hand closer to my lips and kissed her wrist, feeling her delicate pulse. "I would love for you to be. Would you like me to be your boyfriend?"

She looked at me, and I could see the hesitation and fear but also the want shining in her eyes. I implored further, "Let me be your boyfriend, Meera. Please, darling."

Her cheeks instantly turned red and her lips stretched into the biggest smile I'd seen on her face. "I can't believe I'm saying this. I have no idea how it would work and for how long, but yes. Let's be girlfriend-boyfriend."

She giggled and shook her head as I kissed her palm. "My dear girlfriend, let's not think about how we can't be together, and let's focus on *being* together. Deal?"

She bit her lip and nodded, her smile still wide with happiness. "Deal."

Before she could say anything further, the train lurched forward. It was scheduled to depart at eight but had been delayed by fifteen minutes. Not bad, given the chaos I'd seen outside. We had approximately fourteen hours until we reached Jaipur—a blissful stretch of uninterrupted time with Meera, *my girlfriend*.

Just then, a boisterous voice echoed from the train corridor, incessantly repeating something. Curiosity piqued, I decided to take a peek. I parted the curtain slightly and stole a glance. A man with two large stainless steel cylinders occupied the adjacent berth, serving tea and coffee to passengers.

Turning back to Meera, I asked, "Would you like some tea?"

"Sure," she replied, opening her side of the curtain.

The moment the man got free from his customers, he walked to us. Meera said something to him, and they started discussing the rates. She paid him, after glaring at me when I insisted I'd pay. Chastened, I quietly took the cup from her while she settled everything.

Once again, we closed the curtains, enveloping ourselves in our little cocoon.

I took a sip of the chai and immediately wanted to spit it out. It tasted bad.

Meera chuckled at the expression on my face. "What? You thought all chai tastes the same?"

"No, but what is in there?" I put the cup on the window's ledge, refusing to take a second sip of that concoction.

"It's cardamom and too much water. That's train chai for you. Some people love it; some hate it. There's no middle."

"Yeah, I'm the hater."

She chuckled and extended her hand toward me. I understood her intention yet placed my hand in hers.

Rolling her eyes playfully, she flashed a wide smile and shook my hand. "I was asking for the chai."

Our fingers intertwined, and I smiled back. "I know."

Just then, another man's voice boomed through the corridor, advertising and selling something.

I was about to open the curtain when Meera said, "You don't have to open the curtain every time someone arrives. This goes on the whole day."

"What's he selling, though? It smells good."

"He's selling omelet. But I don't think you should eat that. Train food isn't really of the highest quality, and you don't want to upset your stomach this early in the journey."

I was about to protest, claiming that I was hungry and eggs couldn't possibly upset my stomach, when she released my hand, retrieved her heavy purse from her lap, and pulled out a stainless steel container.

"Whoa. When did you pack this? And what is this?"

She opened the container and held it out for me. It was filled with round, thin flatbreads. I took the container from her and picked one up.

"It's called thepla," Meera explained. "Wait, I have some dried pickle."

She rummaged through her bag, searching for the pickle.

"You cooked this for me?" I asked, my chest swelling with affection.

She looked up from her bag, a soft, teasing smile on her face. "I didn't want you to get sick. I've heard that outside food isn't suitable for foreigners. Can't have my boyfriend fall sick on our trip now, can I?"

As she handed me the small container of dried pickle, I clutched her hand and kissed it gratefully.

To my surprise, the tea tasted better when paired with the flatbread. We enjoyed our meal, sometimes in comfortable silence and other times in fits of laughter.

Our berth was a tight space, only three feet by seven feet. Once we had tidied up after our tea, Meera retrieved a deck of cards from her bag. She taught me a game in which we each created our own hands. I attempted to teach her poker, but neither did I explain it well, nor did she play well. Eventually, we landed on rummy. One game we both knew.

For lunch, Meera unveiled yet another container with something called dhokla. It was a soft, savory cake. She pulled out the pickle from this morning and raw green chili, which I declined because I did not want to spend my time on the train in the latrine, which Meera had warned me was fairly primitive.

The combination of the delicious food, the cool air-conditioning, and the gentle rocking motion of the train made me feel pleasantly drowsy.

"Do you want me to climb on the upper seat so you can sleep for a while?" she asked.

"What? No. Stay here. I just need to stretch my legs, and I'll be good."

She didn't look so sure, but she scooted a little, making space for me to stretch my legs out. I did the same so she could stretch her legs by my side, and just like always, we fit.

I put on my neck pillow, clutched her leg near me, and closed my eyes.

Soon, Meera shook me awake.

"Huh? What? Oh, hi."

She chuckled, and said, "You've been asleep for four hours."

And? We still had some time.

At my bewildered expression, she chuckled and gave me a small pout. "Talk to me. I'm so bored."

I was unreasonably pleased at her words. It wasn't often she asked me to talk to her or spend time with her. So when she said it, I felt compelled to comply. I quickly got up.

"I'll freshen up and be right back. And then, we'll talk." I bent closer to her and whispered, "I so want to kiss you right now."

She blushed, and without meeting my eyes, whispered in my ear, "The curtains are closed."

For a second, just for a second, I was shocked still.

In the next second, my lips were on hers. I held her neck and kissed her deeper. Her tongue grazed my lips, and I almost moaned. She whispered, "Shh..."

The kiss ended too soon, and I was *so hard*. On a public train. God. This woman would be the end of me.

"Weren't you going to freshen up?" she asked, all wide-eyed innocence.

"In a minute," I said, and looked down pointedly to indicate what her kiss did to me.

Her cheeks turned red, a large smile came over her lips, and shaking her head, she looked out the window.

The world passed by us—the acres of farm, the trees, villages and cities—and we stayed in our little berth, soaking up our time together.

16

Song: *Roop Tera Mastana*
- *Kishore Kumar*

Meera

"It was awful. Just disgusting," said Luke, as we sat in the taxi taking us to the hotel.

He had been on a roll ever since he used the train restroom.

And every time he complained, I couldn't stop laughing.

"I told you to expect the worst," I said, wiping the tear from the corner of my eye.

"I did! It was just..." He shuddered beside me.

"You need to forget about it. Or else you'll keep stewing in horror."

He shook his head as if expelling the images in his mind. "I need a shower," he grumbled.

Since it was late evening, we couldn't see much outside except for heavy traffic. Cars and two-wheeler vehicles were inches from our taxi, the horns beeping constantly, and big concrete buildings with fancy restaurants and shops surrounded us.

The taxi soon turned onto a narrow road that opened to a towering building with a grand entrance. It stopped right in front of the hotel, a massive, overhanging glass canopy lit in thousands of shining, golden lights. The moment we got out, two men in a maroon uniform rushed to us and greeted us profusely. They opened the trunk of the car and got the suitcases out.

Soon, a few men in Rajasthani attire of kurta and dhoti started playing the traditional music while a woman with a prayer dish approached us. She first put a red dot on Luke's forehead and then on mine.

Wow, the service here made me feel like a queen. I tried to smile at everyone, I truly did, but I was pretty sure they made more money than me, and seeing them greeting me like a celebrity messed with my head.

As if that wasn't enough, two more women came where we stood, each carrying a marigold flower garland. They put it around our neck and started to sing folklore I'd only heard in Hindi TV serials. I couldn't take my eyes off the scene. Luke, too, was mesmerized, his eyes wide with delight, reveling in the culture and the traditions.

So this was how the privileged were welcomed in the outside world: showered with music and flowers, a grand celebration of their arrivals, with attendants rushing to cater to their every need.

I couldn't help but feel a pang of embarrassment for how little attention I had paid to Luke when he first came to live with us. No songs and no garlands awaited him. Just simple, homemade meals and the chatter of a ten-year-old.

As we approached the entrance of the hotel, Luke applauded the staff with great enthusiasm and left them a big, fat tip. He placed his warm hand on my lower back, guiding me inside the lavish foyer. And what a sight it was!

Opulence surrounded us, with thousands of oil lamps illuminating the space. Vibrant rangoli patterns created using colored powder adorned the floor.

"Are you seeing this?" I whispered, not wanting to disturb the rich silence around us. Only a few people lingered in the foyer, some reading books, some listening to a live tabla player in one part of the foyer.

"Do you like it?" Luke asked. He sounded nervous. I looked at him, and doubt filled his eyes.

"Like it? It's like I'm a queen returning to my palace after years of exile."

And he laughed. "Feels like that, doesn't it? It's just that you haven't smiled since we've arrived."

"Oh. I'm just...taking it all in. I've seen rich people—heard about people's wealth, read it in the news, and watched it in Bollywood movies. I've never lived it."

We'd stopped near the reception desk. Luke's hand moved from my lower back to my neck. I hadn't even realized when I'd turned my gaze away from him, but the solid touch of his hand had me turning to look at him. Something shone in his eyes, but the golden light from the candles and the shadows they cast on his face made it hard to read his emotions.

Before I could ask him what he was thinking, he pressed a kiss on my forehead, squeezed the back of my neck, and led us to the reception desk.

We were soon in a hallway, headed toward the elevator, which was draped in ruby-red fabric with golden threads woven into it. Even the elevator buttons were golden in color.

Our room was on the twelfth floor, and we walked down a wide hallway that overlooked the city on one side and was covered in beautiful paintings of kings and queens on the other.

Two men in maroon uniforms walked ahead of us, carrying our luggage. They opened the door, gave the keys of the room to Luke, and entered our room in front of us. I stepped in last, and my feet came to a halt.

This wasn't just a place to sleep. This was a small apartment. There was a small living area, two chairs, and a sofa in a C-shape facing a big flat screen television. There was a tiny platform with a coffee machine and a teapot and a variety of teas in a basket. Beyond the living area, a wood and glass partition separated the sleeping area. A giant white bed sat along the wall, facing the windows and the balcony.

"All okay?" asked Luke, his voice pulling me out of the trance the room had put me in.

I shook my head. "Luke, this is too much. Wow. Is the room very expensive?"

He led me with a gentle push to the sofa. We sat next to each other, my hand in his, grounding me. He touched my chin with his finger and lifted my face to meet my eyes. A small, teasing smile appeared on his face. He bent closer to me, and said, "If you must know, I have gathered a lot of points in hotel credit. Our stay here is almost free."

"Are all the hotels going to be like this?" I asked, still looking around the room. One of the walls was painted red, and the others were warm white and gold.

"Actually, no. I had planned to explore different types of stay. Here, I chose the nice hotel because it was the most affordable with my points. In Udaipur, we have an Airbnb, and in Patan, we have a pretty standard hotel room. This way, we get all types of experiences."

"Wow. That's....you've thought of everything."

He chuckled, his fingers playing with mine. "Yes. I love to travel, plan trips, visit all the beautiful architectural and historical monuments of a city. And with travel, I want to experience everything, you know."

His passion brought a huge smile to his face that made me forget about my feelings of not belonging in such opulent places. I belonged where Luke went for now, and maybe if I, too, focused on travel and experiencing new things, I might enjoy this trip more freely.

Luke got up and opened his bag. "Does it feel like we're still moving? It's like my mind and body are still on the train."

I chuckled. "Yeah, we'll feel normal by tomorrow morning. Wait until you try to sleep. You'll feel like you're still sleeping on the train."

He pulled out a set of clothes and placed them on a chair. And I realized what he was about to do.

Shower. He was going to take a shower.

I looked at the bathroom door, which was just a few feet away from the living area.

He would be naked in there.

Was it hot in the room? I wiped the sweat on my forehead with my dupatta.

"Do you want to go first?"

Huh? He looked at me expectantly, a sly smile on his face. His eyes had that wicked delight shining in them as he leaned against the wall.

"Uh...no. I'll go after you."

His smile was all but gone, and his eyes were pools of hunger, just like they got when we kissed.

He walked closer to me, and closer, and dropped to his knee where I sat. Our eyes met, and I wanted to clutch his shirt and pull him closer. My fists tightened in my dupatta. His thumb grazed my cheek, and he cupped my face gently. Slowly, he kissed me. Once. Twice. Deeper.

I was about to kiss him harder when he quickly got up, a bulge evident at the front of his pants. "I'm going to shower. We will continue this in just a bit."

And he was gone.

In the next minute, the shower turned on, and I heard a loud groan.

I almost melted into the floor as my entire body erupted into goose bumps, and blood thrummed through my veins.

Before I could hear more noises threatening my heart, I opened my bag to get ready for the shower.

～

Luke

My lips still tingled with Meera's kiss as hot water rained down on me. I was in heaven. I didn't know what gave me more pleasure: a hot shower after over a month of bucket bathing, or Meera being here with me.

Definitely Meera.

After a rigorous shower, washing away the worst parts of my train journey, I got dressed in the bathroom. Normally, I would've stepped out in a towel, but if I did that, Meera would probably run out of the room. Or maybe not.

Maybe she would look at me with heated eyes. Maybe she would come over and kiss me. Maybe she would remove my towel and take me in her hands.

I shook my head and got dressed before I had to take my problem in my own hand. After a minute of calming down, I stepped out.

I found Meera just where I left her, except she had some clothes tucked in her lap.

I rubbed my hair with the towel and said, "Bathroom's free."

She couldn't even look at me, and dark red dotted her cheeks.

To lessen her discomfort, I went to the bedroom area, pretending to be busy while doing absolutely nothing.

Why were we getting weird? Why was there a sudden awkwardness in our silence?

I got under the warm blanket, the soft mattress dipping under my weight, and I groaned in the sheer relief of sleeping on a cloud-like bed. The bed reminded me of my bed in New York.

Soon, I heard the shower in the bathroom turn on, and vivid images of a very naked Meera sliced through my mind. Her naked, just on the other side of the wall, water sliding down her neck, her breasts, her hips. *Fuck.*

My mouth dried up, and my cock stood at attention at the mere thought of her. She had never even kissed anyone before me, so I needed to go slow. But my body was too far ahead, hungry for her touch, dying for just a taste of her.

I heard a click of the bathroom door and quickly turned on my side to hide the tent under the blanket. She entered the bedroom space, her hair wet, the curls pulled into waves that framed her beautiful face. She wore her well-worn T-shirt and loose cotton pajama pants.

She hung the wet towel on the back of the chair and looked around our room.

She stood back, not getting into bed.

"You're being weird," I said, wanting my Meera back.

She snorted. A smile came over her lips, and she shook her head. "I am, aren't I? Everything is just so pretty and perfect. I'm scared I'll ruin it. And seeing you fit right in to all of it so well makes me even more nervous."

Oh, Meera. This woman. "Come here," I said, extending my hand toward her.

She hesitated but then moved toward the bed.

"Not like that," I said, stopping her, an idea taking root in my head. "Run and jump on the bed."

She laughed. "Noooo, never. I'll dent it."

And now I laughed. "You won't dent it. You'll feel like you're on a cloud. C'mon. Run and jump."

She took a few steps back, shaking her head. Her lips were stretched wide in a smile, and I saw the temptation swimming in her eyes. "No. No. Not doing it."

I sat up on the bed, the thick white comforter bunched on my lap. I couldn't stop my smile as she bounced on her feet. She just needed a little nudge. She needed to own this bed. "Run and jump, Meera. C'mon, baby. You can do it."

"Luke," she warned, "I'm gonna do it."

"Yes, you're gonna do it. C'mon, baby."

Her eyes sparkled, her lips stretched into a wide, ecstatic smile. She assumed a runner's stance, and I couldn't help but join in her excitement. "Come on, Meera!"

Like a bull about to run toward the red cloth, she moved, her leg pawing at the carpeted floor. And then she took off toward the bed. Toward me.

I braced myself, gripping the comforter tightly with my hands, prepared to catch her.

She soared through the air, a joyful squeal escaping her lips as she landed on the bed with a whoosh, droplets from her wet hair splashing onto my arms.

Quickly rolling onto her back, a mixture of delight and excitement gleaming in her eyes, she let out a contented moan and extended her hands to caress the bed. "It feels so good, so soft."

I couldn't stop looking at her. Her wet black hair spread over the white sheets, her skin velvety smooth after her shower, her eyes alight with excitement and pleasure, and her smile radiating pure joy.

She was breathtaking. I bent closer, my whole body taut with desire. Her breath quickened, her chest rising and falling with each inhale. My heart went wild. I was dying to touch her, to kiss her.

Gripping the comforter near her head, I leaned in closer, giving her the chance to pull back and stop me.

Instead, she clutched my T-shirt with both hands and pulled me to her, rising up halfway to kiss me.

I groaned, and my hand moved to her waist, her hips, squeezing, touching, pressing her more tightly against me.

She guided me until my entire body enveloped hers, her delicate fingers entwined in my hair while her other hand rested firmly against my back.

Our lips met again and again, her tongue explored mine, and my skin flared with need. Our bodies melded together, not an inch of space separating us, her curves fitting seamlessly against mine.

"Luke," she moaned, her neck arched, and every time her body undulated against mine, I had the irresistible urge to just press down on her and get fucking lost in her.

"God, Meera." I kissed her neck, wanting to consume her, and she moaned louder. Her grip on my hair tightened, and she arched her neck further, surrendering herself to the moment, to me.

And I took every inch she gave me. I sucked below her ear, and her hips arched up and grazed against my cock, sending shivers down my spine.

"Meera," I groaned in her neck.

"Oh Luke. You. This bed. Oh your... your—" she said, but every word was a moan against my lips.

I slowly moved lower down her body. My body shook with restraint as I bent down and kissed her covered breast. She whimpered.

"Do you want more?" I asked, my voice barely a whisper, electric pleasure racing through my veins. I wanted to devour her, consume her, get lost in her curves, her scent, her moans.

She nodded, over and over. "Yes, yes, please."

Roughly pulling my hair, she dragged me back to the wet

patch at her breast, and I groaned, sucking the now-pebbled nipple through her T-shirt. I clutched her waist and squeezed her hip, trying not to grind into her.

But she rose up and pressed into me, making me groan. "Meera, baby, we need to stop."

Her eyes were clouded with lust, a dark red flush to her cheeks, and her lips were swollen from our kiss.

She looked at me in confusion. "Stop? You don't want it?"

I went up to meet her eyes, my cock brushing between her thighs. My eyes rolled back, but I held myself still. I dragged my fingers against her cheek, kissed her, and said, "I want it more than anything, sweetheart. But if you keep moving your hips like that, I'm gonna come."

I didn't think she could get any redder, but she did. Flustered, she asked, "Really?"

"Yeah. I'm too close."

"Can you show me?"

I froze. My mind stopped working, but my cock stood at attention.

"Show you?"

She turned her eyes to my neck, her fingers playing with my hair. "I've never seen someone do it for real."

"For real? What do you mean?"

She blushed, her lips lifting in a smile. My cock hardened ever more against her thigh, and she gasped.

"Meera?" I gritted my teeth as ugly jealousy slithered down my gut, twisting my insides at the mere thought of Meera seeing someone else pleasure themselves.

She nodded, a shy smirk pulling at her lips. "One day, Kriti was alone at her house, and she invited me over. She loves reading these romance books where they have sex. And she decided to watch sex videos. So the moment I reached her place, she pulled me to her bedroom, closed the curtains, and gave me one earphone. She had already loaded the video. It wouldn't stop in between. And then, well, we, you know, watched it."

Just imagining Meera watching porn made my body clench harder. Her eyes widened when she felt my cock rubbing against her hips. "This excites you?"

A breathy chuckle escaped me, my body in pain from trying to restrain myself from mindlessly rutting over her. "No shit. I thought you talking would calm me down. But imagining you watching porn..."

I groaned and kissed her on the neck. "You're killing me," I said.

"So?" she asked.

"So what?" I had no idea what she was talking about.

"Will you show me?"

Those four little words lit my body up. Pleasure. Anticipation. Need. My blood hummed in my ears. I nodded in her neck, and asked, "Are you sure?"

"Yes," she said as her fingers roamed over my back, driving me wild with need and ready to explode.

"Okay, can I make you come too?"

Her fingers stilled. "You know how?"

Her question was so shockingly innocent, I couldn't stop the laugh from escaping my lips. "Well, I sure hope so. Have you made yourself come?"

She hesitated, but her cheeks darkened, and slowly, she nodded. Just imagining her in the throes of pleasure—her back arching, her fingers caressing herself, her toes pointed in ecstasy, the sounds she would've made—had me aching with a riot of pain and pleasure.

"Can I make you come? Fuck, say yes, baby," I begged.

Her voice shook slightly as she asked, "Would I have to remove all my clothes?"

"Not if you don't want to. But I would like to put my hand in your underwear. And then, after I make you come, I'll put the same hand in mine and make myself come. How does that sound?"

She shivered, and her hips arched. "Yes, yes. Please. I want that."

"Are you sure?" I asked, almost struggling to believe my dreams were coming true. I was desperate to see her writhe in pleasure, hear her little moans, touch her softness, taste her wetness.

She glared. "Why do you keep asking? I wouldn't ask if I didn't want it."

"Okay, okay!" I chuckled and kissed her.

She kissed me back, her hips bucking under me.

I shifted a little so my body was half sprawled on her, not wanting to move even an inch away from her. She tried to follow me, but I held her still with my hand on her stomach. I kissed her, sucked her tongue, and moved my hand over her stomach. She tried to arch up, but I didn't let her.

"Luke," she growled.

I kissed her with a laugh, placed my lips on her neck, and dipped my hand under her waistband. She sucked in a breath and tilted her hips up so I moved my hand over her underwear. Soaked. I squeezed her gently, and her moan echoed in the room. I moved my fingers in circles over her clit, and she whimpered.

She chanted my name. In pleasure. In need. And it had never sounded more beautiful.

"I'm going to touch you, Meera."

"Yes, yes. Something's happening. I'm feeling—" She stopped and moaned.

I dipped my hand inside her underwear. Hot and soft and soaking wet, she drenched my fingers, and I could just imagine sliding inside her.

My balls ached, and my cock leaked, wanting to feel her around me.

I swirled my fingers around her clit, and her hips rocked with my movements.

She clutched both of her hands around mine, trying to stop me, or guide me, or just feel me.

"Meera, open your legs wider, baby," I said, and she instantly obeyed.

"Good girl."

She whimpered at those words, and even more of her arousal dripped down my fingers. I spread the wetness seeping from her to her clit and rolled my finger.

She moaned louder and tightened her hold on me. She clutched my hand in a vise-like grip and rocked her hips on my fingers. "This. This. This," she chanted.

She writhed on my hand, and my cock ached. I couldn't help but begin to stroke myself as well, relieving the pressure.

"Don't," she said. "I want to watch later. Please."

"Oh God." I groaned at the sheer agony of letting go of my cock and held her throat. I ravaged her mouth and swallowed her moans and whimpers and the little breaths she let out every time I moved my finger against her clit.

I sucked her neck, and then her thighs clamped around my hand, her body shuddering. Her eyes rolled back as she came on my fingers, rocking against them in mindless pleasure as she tried to push them inside her.

She looked divine, a goddess taking pleasure from my hand just the way she liked.

And I was so close to exploding in my pants. "Meera, Meera, I need to... Fuck," I moaned.

"Yes," she said, her eyes wide open and dazed with pleasure.

I climbed on top of her, my knees enclosing her hips. I quickly pushed down my sweats and pulled out my cock. She rose on her elbows, and her eyes widened, which only made me harder. "Is this what you wanted to see, baby?"

I stroked my cock, and a loud noise echoed in the room. I didn't know if it was her or me.

Her cheeks flushed a dark red and she let out a low moan. "Yes, you're so beautiful," she whispered, her eyes glued to my cock.

Meera's words, her eyes watching my hand stroking my cock drove me to the brink of madness and pleasure. I pushed my hips forward into my fist, my fingers still wet from touching Meera. "I can feel your cum sliding on my cock."

She whimpered, bringing her fingers closer to my cock, making it jump in anticipation of her touch.

I switched my hand and sucked on the fingers coated with Meera's arousal, and my brain short-circuited. "Fuck," I groaned, my voice raw and hoarse.

Her taste coated my tongue and all I wanted to do was dive between her thighs and have her writhing on my face.

Mind-numbing pleasure raced down my spine and my balls ached and tightened at the impending release racing through my veins.

"Meera...So close, God, Meera."

My jerks turned faster and harder.

The moment she pulled her T-shirt up until it only covered her breasts and grazed her fingers against my cock, I completely lost it.

I bent forward and ropes of cum erupted on her stomach. Watching my cum drip on her skin had me shooting even more.

Our moans and groans echoed in the room, and I fell on my back beside her, my mind floating in the earth-shattering, life altering haze of making Meera come and watching her shatter on my fingers for the very first time.

After a few moments of blissful, post-orgasmic silence, she said, "Uh...Luke?"

I turned to her, and she had her T-shirt clutched in her

hand, undulating her stomach, balancing the cum so it wouldn't fall on the bed. I roared in laughter.

"Stop laughing! I'm gonna ruin this magnificent bed," she screeched in worry. "Luke, do something. Tissue. Cloth. Wipe it."

I looked around, and the tissue box was on the other side of the bed. I climbed over her, making her squawk in fear of losing the balance, and got a few tissues. Quickly, I wiped it off her stomach, and said, "There. Your precious bed is safe."

She smiled and rolled in the bed. "Thank you."

"You're welcome."

She turned to me with a smile and said, "I was thanking the bed."

I couldn't stop the big-ass smile on my face. "Why?"

"It made me feel so good." Her eyes shone with the lightness and mirth I so rarely saw.

I pulled her in my arms and gently bit her neck, making her shriek. "It was the bed, huh?"

She nodded. "Yes. Best bed in the world."

I pulled the comforter over us and held her waist under her T-shirt, wanting to keep feeling her soft, warm skin against mine.

I kissed her neck, and we slept like that.

We had an entire month of this, and I already felt like it wasn't enough.

17

Song: Humne Tumko Dekha
  - Shailendra Singh

Meera

Our first destination was two hours away from the city of Jaipur. We were headed to Chand Baori, one of the largest stepwells in the world.

"It is the largest and the deepest stepwell of India. Meera, it is thirteen floors deep. And holy shit, it was constructed in the eighth and ninth century. That's more than a thousand years ago!"

Luke had been like that for the past hour. His voice rising in pitch the more he read from his travel guide book. His book had pages that opened into larger pages. He had spread it over both our laps, tracing his finger over the lines he read.

The hotel had their own taxi service, and that was how we met our driver of the week in Jaipur, Jagdish. At Luke's excited muttering, he looked at me from his mirror, and asked me in Hindi, "Sister, where has sir come from?"

Luke turned to me, his eyebrows raised in question. I smiled and shook my head at him. I looked at the back of Jagdish's head, and said, "America."

"America? And you, sister? Where are you from?"

"A small village in Gujarat."

"I can speak some Gujarati. Kem chho? Saru chhe?" he asked. *How are you? All good?* His eyes shone in delight, a soft teasing smile on his face.

I chuckled.

Luke was silent as he watched our exchange. A small smile tugged at his lips as he looked at me. "What?" I asked.

He chuckled, shook his head, and gently grazed the back of his fingers along my cheek. My heart fluttered within my chest, and a rush of warmth surged to my cheeks as I glanced at the driver's seat.

"Luke, what are you doing? Someone will see."

At that, he smiled. "Do you know anyone here?"

I shook my head.

"Does anyone know you?"

"No."

"Then does it matter to you what anyone says or sees or thinks?"

Crazy, sweet man.

I shook my head and grazed my fingers on the back of his hand. Heat bloomed in his eyes, turning darker. He turned his hand, allowing our fingers to intertwine, creating a sense of comfort and warmth. Luke had a way of grounding me, of pulling me away from the dark and melancholic corners of my mind and filling my heart with light, joy, and a riot of fluttering sensations in my stomach.

I was so lost in his touch, in the scenery and the villages passing, I was taken by surprise when Jagdish stopped and announced that we'd reached our destination.

I looked outside the window and couldn't see anything

monumental. It was just houses and shops and tiny buildings like my own village. Jagdish asked us to get out of the car so he could go park it somewhere cool.

It was a beautiful, cloudy morning. It wasn't so cloudy that I'd worry about rain, but the sun hid in the clouds and wasn't hitting my head.

I got out first, clutching my purse on my shoulder. I wore my green kameez, with pink salwar and dupatta. Little mirrors were embedded in my dupatta, and pink flowers were embroidered in my kameez. It was one of my favorite salwar kameez, and I just had to wear it on the first day of our trip. It felt like a celebration—happiness, a ray of sunshine.

Luke got out of the car right behind me. He wore a white shirt with dark brown pants that folded at the bottom, sunglasses hung in the V of his shirt, his camera slung on his neck, and he carried a bunch of things in his brown backpack. In all, he looked like a proper foreigner tourist. And like the most handsome man I'd ever seen in my life.

And when he smiled at me, just like he did now, my heart all but dropped down at his feet. He clutched my hand and led me down a dirt road separating two small buildings.

A few people stared, but I ignored them. I was here with Luke, with a goal of having the best time of my life, and I intended to soak up every second I got with this wonderful man.

As we walked a little farther down the path, we reached a stone structure that looked like a long one-story temple. We entered the complex through a metal gate. On our right side, a small stone structure with a metal plaque was engraved with the history of the stepwell. We stood there and read it.

Luke played with my fingers the entire time. He might not be aware of what he was doing, but my heart raced a mile a minute, and if anyone asked me a question about the history of this stepwell, I wouldn't be able to answer a single fact.

He snapped a picture of that stone and began dragging me in the one-story building that served as the entrance to the stepwell. At first glance, it hardly looked like it was an entrance to the deepest stepwell in India. But I guess that was the nature of stepwells. They were like a surprise to the human eye.

The moment we stepped through that one-story structure, we entered into an open hallway beyond which was a massive courtyard. On the other side of the courtyard was a palace, and right in the center of the courtyard was the gigantic stepwell.

Luke gasped as we stepped closer. I clutched his hand tighter, almost dizzy at the sheer number of steps going down, down, down. Each set of six steps meticulously aligned, leading downward into the depths. Thousands of them formed a symphony of architectural symmetry, culminating in a small, square body of water at the bottom. There was a metal railing halfway down the steps, restricting access beyond that point.

"The guide book says that since this is in the middle of the desert, when it would rain, the water body would fill up as high as that metal railing, and in the ancient times, it would've been even higher. People from the village would come here to collect water for their house. And all this water in the middle of the desert would keep the palace cool. It might even be the coolest place in the village."

He talked, but his eyes were glazed over as if looking at a centuries-old scene. His eyes burned with passion for the architecture, for the history of the place, for the thought behind this structure that held little meaning for me today but something he seemed to find precious.

He walked forward, leading me closer to the steps, holding my hand. The steps were hot despite the cloudy weather. Luke released my hand and clutched his camera. Soon, he was lost.

I sat on one of the steps, watching *him* instead of the architecture. He was captivating, his every little movement, the way he captured the images, bent at the waist, trying to get the right angle. The way he checked the pictures in the camera, a lock of his hair falling over his forehead. The way he put on his sunglasses and wiped his hand on the back of his pants every time he touched the dirty walls.

The way he was trying to hold his sketchbook, the travel guidebook, his camera, and still trying to sketch.

I couldn't help but laugh at him. I got up from where I sat and walked to where he fumbled. "Let me hold something."

"Oh. Uh." He chuckled, his face all red, and said, "Thank you. If you could hold my bag and maybe the guidebook?"

I took the guidebook and put it inside his bag. "Do you need your camera right now?"

"Uh. No. I just wanted to sketch a little."

"Do you feel comfortable giving me your camera to hold?"

He hesitated for a second and asked, "Would you mind putting the camera strap around your neck? I'm sorry; I'm just really touchy about my camera."

He didn't meet my eyes, and then his ears turned red. I gave him a gentle smile, nodded, and said, "Of course. You put it around my neck."

Relief washed over his face, and he quickly made me sit on one of the steps.

I put his bag on my lap, and he put his camera around my neck.

And with just his sketchbook and pencil in hand, he sat and lost himself to sketching.

I watched him while he sketched, his hand moving like a flash on the pages, his hair falling over his sunglasses, his eyes taking in every detail.

Soon, he got up and started walking a little farther. Not wanting to be left behind, I followed him, carrying his bag on my shoulder, camera around my neck, and handling my dupatta so that it didn't get in my way. I was panting in the few steps it took me to reach him.

"I wonder if that's how my ancestors felt like serving yours."

He gasped. Then choked. And turned entirely red.

And I couldn't help but roar with laughter. "I'm just joking. Relax. I'm happy to help."

He shook his head, still sputtering, and said, "You're. You're so. Your humor sometimes..."

"You treat me like a queen, Luke. Do your sketching, and let me admire you."

A shy smile came over his face. "Admire, huh?"

I nodded, deliberately looking at him from top to bottom, letting him see how much I admired him.

He turned his head away, all red this time for entirely different reasons.

"You're awful," he groaned.

I preened. "Thank you."

We spent the next three hours there. Luke clicked pictures, did his sketching. I soon moved under one of those open hallways around the courtyard for shade. Every now and then, some kid would approach him to ask questions and try to get in the pictures. Luke humored them, and arranged them on the steps properly to click their images. A couple of times, teenaged girls and boys neared him and clicked selfies with him.

He turned to me in question, and I just shrugged. He was a novelty here. His skin, his clothes, his entire demeanor exuded otherworldliness. People knew he had come from a faraway land they'd only dreamed of visiting. A land where everyone was fair and rich like him, where they didn't worry about money and were always happy. It was all just a fantasy for most people here. It didn't matter that the foreigners' lives in their country might not be as perfect as we imagined. Yet we imagined. We dreamed. We prayed. We studied. And people who could afford it went to make a life of their own in this faraway land that they never left to return home to India. Surely, it would be a better world. Why else would you not come back?

I was pulled out of my thoughts when Luke sat beside me. Sweat dripped down his forehead, and he looked exhausted and dehydrated. I opened my purse and handed him an orange candy. "Here, just put this in your mouth, and I'll get you a Glucon-D."

He looked at me, a weird smile coming over his face, but he did as I told him. I opened my water bottle and put a pack of orange-flavored glucose powder. I closed it and shook it well. All the while, Luke held my dupatta in his hand and played with its edge.

It was just a cloth, I knew it. But I felt his touch on my skin. My body went into overdrive the more he played with my dupatta.

I looked at him. He looked at me. Heat and desire coiled in my stomach as goose bumps broke out at the back of my neck. It felt like he was pulling me closer to him just by my dupatta, and I badly wanted to be near him.

I remembered where we were, and quickly brought the bottle of Glucon-D between us. "You need to keep yourself hydrated if you're going to stay out in the sun like this," I said.

"Yes, ma'am," he said. He opened the bottle and drank half the bottle in one long gulp. "Wow. I *was* dehydrated. Thanks, love."

Love. He called me *love.*

I couldn't have stopped the stupid smile on my face even if I'd wanted to. He gently nudged my shoulder with his in acknowledgment, his lips curled in a cheeky smile.

"I got everything I needed. You ready to go back to Jaipur and explore more?" he asked.

"Yes. Let's go."

Luke

She looked radiant in her pink-and-green salwar kameez, her eyes lit up in excitement and wonder. Ever since we'd started our trip, she smiled more, she joked around more, her every step had a bounce. She truly looked happy.

It was almost evening when we returned to the main city, so we decided to explore the market. She walked beside me, her hand in mine. We passed through shop after shop, exploring the traditional souvenirs. Handcrafted decorative lamps, pillowcases, bedsheets, each more colorful than the one before lined the shops. Purses and bags of leather and fabrics hung from top to bottom, traditional footwear with pointed toes hung at the entrance of the shops, locals and tourists trying different pairs.

Soon, we passed a jewelry shop. The storefront held thousands of colorful bangles, and Meera stopped walking. I silently stood beside her as she looked at the collection, her gaze taking it all in.

"Do you want any?" I asked.

Without looking at me, she shook her head with a scoff. "I'm not going to start shopping on the first day of the trip. I'm just looking. We can shop later on."

She was not *just* looking; her eyes couldn't stop moving over the hundreds of colorful bangles twinkling under the yellow lights of the shop. I clutched her hand in mine and dragged her into the shop before she could argue or glare at me with those pretty eyes that made my heart pound.

"What are you doing?" she whispered, subtly trying to remove her hand from mine.

I greeted the shopkeeper with a smile, and from under my breath and keeping a wide smile on my face, muttered, "We're getting you some pretty bangles. How about you ask him in Hindi to show you some?"

She glared daggers from her eyes, and fuck, it made me want to kiss her right then and there.

I smiled at her, not letting go of her hand. "If you don't stop glaring at me, I'm going to kiss you right in front of this nice shopkeeper."

Instantly, her eyes narrowed and slowly turned softer. "Luke, I don't need to buy these right now."

I pressed a kiss on the back of her hand. "I know. Just let me get you some. I want to see you wearing them. C'mon, baby."

And then I turned on the puppy dog look.

She scoffed. "That won't work every time," she said with a sniff, then turned to the shopkeeper and started talking to him, pointing at different bangles.

The shopkeeper brought out a few bangles and held my girl's hand to put them on her.

Acid burned my stomach as she so easily gave her delicate wrist to him as he clutched her hand in his and started to rotate and twist the bangles around her knuckles, pushing the bangles to her wrist.

A soft smile came over her face as she moved her hand this way and that, admiring the bangles.

Meera pointed at another set after that, and this mother-fucker again clutched *my* girl's hand, and that was it.

I pulled her hand away from his. "Let me handle this," I said and extended my hand, asking him to hand me the bangles.

The shopkeeper frowned at me while Meera bit her lip, trying not to smile. As I glared at the shopkeeper, Meera cleared her throat, and asked, "Do you even know how to help me wear the bangles? They're really tight."

I glared at her. "How hard can it be?"

She chuckled as I took the bangles from the shopkeeper and turned to my girl.

I raised my hand and looked at her while she giggled and placed her hand in mine.

Just like the shopkeeper had done, I held Meera's arm, but gentler than him, and started pushing the bangles over her knuckles. And boy, these bangles were so tight around her knuckles, they refused to pass over.

I muttered, "They're not your size. You need bigger bangles."

Instantly, the shopkeeper piped in. "No, no, sir. This is the right fit. Let me show you."

Meera snorted as I glared at him. "Umm. I'll handle it, thanks."

The shopkeeper shrugged, and I got back to pushing these over her knuckles. I was afraid if I applied too much force, they would hurt her.

"Just push it in."

My mind instantly went to thoughts of pushing something else inside her, and now my jeans were very, *very* uncomfortable.

I looked at her and realized how close we stood to each other as I held her hand with both of mine. I could see the dark gold specks and the reflection of the yellow lights in her dark brown eyes. I could feel her heavy breathing and notice her cheeks turning redder by the second.

I slowly applied more pressure to push them over her folded hands. "Did I tell you how beautiful you look today?"

She shook her head, never moving her gaze away from mine. "You didn't."

I pushed a little, and a few bangles slipped past her knuckles, making her gasp. "I'm sorry. You look breathtaking, baby."

She shivered, and I tightened my hand around hers, pushing a few more bangles over her knuckles. "Does it hurt?"

She made a small noise at the back of her throat in denial. I nodded and pushed a few more bangles over her knuckles, making her gasp out loud.

I could just imagine her making these breathy gasps when I finally pushed inside her. I was dying to hear her moans on my tongue and feel her gasps on my neck as I pushed and gave and devoured her.

My body was on fire as I slowly pushed every bangle over her knuckles and onto her wrist, causing them to jingle together.

"All done," I said, still not leaving her hand from mine, my voice husky as I managed to utter the two words from my clenched jaw as I tried to control the riot of heady need choking my body.

Meera's eyes were glazed over as she looked at the bangles adorning her arm. A small smile came over her face as she let go of my hand and touched them, her fingers caressing each of them lovingly, making my hands clench into fists to try to stop them from grabbing her and pulling her into me.

She looked at me with knowing eyes, desire swirling like a tornado between us, as she turned to the shopkeeper, and said, "We'll take these."

The shopkeeper asked if we'd like to remove them and pack them, but Meera shook her head and looked at me.

I nodded at her and quickly pulled out the wallet and paid for them, thanking the shopkeeper.

As we walked out of the shop, I grazed my fingers against Meera's arm and the bangles, feeling the cool metal against my skin, and glanced at the shy smile on Meera's face.

"Thank you," she murmured, grazing her fingers along mine.

I linked our hands, and brought our intertwined hands to my lips and kissed her wrist and the colorful bangles. "I'd give you a thousand more bangles if I'm the one putting them on you."

She turned to look back at the street with a shy smile, and we continued to walk farther along the markets. Two-story buildings with shops on the street level and houses on the floor above lined the market. Every shop and house in the area was painted in the same brick-red color, giving the market a beautifully red undertone, and maybe that was why Jaipur was known as the Pink City of India.

We walked more, admiring the nightlife of the crowded city. A hundred different smells assaulted me—spices and oil, sweet perfumes from shops we passed, sweat from the people around us—and made me want to stop and just take it all in. But we couldn't stop even if we wanted to. Thousands of people moved around us, carrying us forward.

Meera's warm touch made a simple walk feel like the time of my life. We stopped at a place that sold a famous Jaipur food item called pyaaz kachori. It was sort of a fried flatbread stuffed with onions and spices, to be eaten with spicy and sweet chutney.

I was about to bite into it when worried lines appeared between Meera's eyebrows, and she asked, "Are you sure your stomach can handle it?"

I chuckled, despite the way my heart warmed at her worry for me. "Meera, Meera, Meera. I really have a high tolerance for Indian food."

I'd lived with Akira and Sam for a few months now, and those two ate a lot of Indian food, both trying to cook all sorts of Indian dishes, some epic fails and some out of this world.

Meera smiled at my answer, shrugged her shoulder, and took a huge bite out of her kachori. I followed her and bit into mine, and flavors of onion and spices and chili and sweet tamarind sauce burst in my mouth. I groaned out loud, and Meera laughed.

We stuffed our faces with the kachoris, standing outside the small shop with a few others. Soon, we dragged our feet to the car, where our driver waited, our stomachs heavy with the greasy food. The moment we were back in the hotel room, Meera rushed to change into her sleepwear and dropped on the bed like she fucking owned it.

By the time I came to the bed after changing, she was already asleep, spread-eagled, her hair in disarray, and her mouth slightly open.

Adorable and *mine*.

The moment I slid inside the comforter beside her, her hand made her way to my chest, and soon her body followed. Before my eyes had shut, she was cradled in my arms, where she belonged, as if she'd been doing this forever.

THE NEXT DAY was more or less the same. We went to Amer Fort, a massive palace of red sandstone and marble sitting atop a small hill with a lake on its side. We took an elephant to get on top, despite Meera's numerous protests. She was terrified to climb the ladder up to the elephant's back and screamed my name with every step she climbed.

"I hope you scream my name just like that in the bedroom," I'd said once she sat beside me, her hands tightly clutching the railing of the carriage.

"I doubt it. You're not as big as the elephant," she'd replied, a smirk on her lips.

And that had shut me up for ten whole minutes as I sat there trying to figure out whether I wanted to kiss her or show her how big I was.

We entered the palace through several huge ornamented gates. The entire complex had a number of small and big court-yards, a huge charbagh-style garden with a highly ornamental lotus-shaped fountain in its center, ornate rooms of the king and his queens, and intricately carved colonnades and walkways overlooking the entire city of Jaipur. We walked, following a guide who regaled us with stories of the kings and queens that had lived there, Meera rolling her eyes at some of the more improbable ones.

We laughed, we roamed where kings walked, we talked nonsense, and she deliberately made me uncomfortable with her brutal humor of colonial India. I captured her smiles, her laughs, her wonder, her glares, and her sly smirks in my camera. I even captured her shying away at my blatant appraisal of her beauty when I pointed my camera lens right at her.

We visited the small stepwell right near the fort. The walls of the stepwell and the steps running along those walls were all in yellow-colored stone, with brown and black soiling streaking at the side of the steps. We sat there for a while under the approaching sunset. I clicked tons of pictures, and Meera sat on a step holding my bag and sketchbook.

I didn't expect our trip to be as comfortable as it was turning out to be. Meera had no demands, she didn't tire easily, and her purse was a well of endless snacks. She didn't get bored of my constant explanations of architectural features; in fact, she seemed to really enjoy them.

"It makes me know you better," she had said when I'd asked her if I was boring her with my architecture talks.

On the fourth day of our trip, we had to rush back to our hotel room early in the evening. My stomach had started to revolt.

"I told you not to eat so much street food," Meera called to me from the living room area while I sat on the toilet, clutching my stomach.

"I told you I could handle it. Something we ate must have been bad."

"I seem to be perfectly fine," she shouted again, her voice holding a hint of superiority.

"Good for you," I grumbled under my breath as I tried not to die.

"What was that?" she shouted.

I cringed. "Nothing, Meera. Now go away and let me shit in peace."

A loud snort from outside and then finally blessed silence.

When I finally emerged, Meera was right there on the sofa, ready to catch me if I dropped. She'd changed into her T-shirt and pajamas. She came near me, clutched my arm, and led me to the bed.

I felt well enough to walk, but she was just so sweet, a ball of anger and worry, that I couldn't utter a word in protest. I went along with her, enjoying her hands on my arm. She held up the comforter as I lay down and pulled off my shirt and pants. She didn't even ogle me in my boxers, just glared at me as she filled a glass with water from a store-bought water bottle.

"You know, you're not supposed to be mean to sick people," I whined, my voice cracking from my dry throat.

She put the glucose powder in the water and thrust the glass toward me, and said, "Drink this."

As I sipped the glucose water, she sat beside me, her hand on my bare shoulder. "I just... I don't like seeing you sick. It hurts me."

My heart thumped louder at her words. Her voice shook with so much emotion, so much worry, and all that for *me*.

"It's just indigestion, Meera. I'll be fine."

She glared at me. Again. "If you hadn't insisted on eating street food every day, this wouldn't have happened."

"But then you wouldn't be giving me so much attention."

She shook her head, her eyes filled with something so strong, emotions so potent, that my stomach tightened. "Luke, you are like the sun. You are all I can see."

And how I *loved* her.

My stomach lurched. In fear. In terror of letting her go. In grief for the day when I wouldn't have her by my side.

I jumped out of bed and ran into the bathroom, emptying my stomach into the toilet.

Yet none of the fear, none of the grief left me.

Just an overwhelming awareness of love for Meera lingered and bloomed in the pit of my stomach, taking root and clutching my heart in a vise.

Meera was right outside the door when I opened it and again clutched my arm as she led me to the bed. She ordered coffee and buttermilk and juice from the reception desk to keep me hydrated and ran her fingers through my hair, gently lulling me to sleep.

The last thing that I saw was her face lined with worry.

The next time I opened my eyes, it was in the middle of the night, and her face was tucked into my back, her arms tightly wrapped around my waist.

Yep, my heart gave that swift push of its overwhelming feelings for her, a stark reminder of love.

I drank some of the fluids she'd left beside me, tucked myself around her, nuzzled my face into her curls, and went back to sleep.

The entire time, my mind kept shouting *I love her.* This wonderful person fit perfectly in my arms and cared for everyone around her, ignoring her own happiness. All I wanted was to give her everything her heart desired, and if there was one more thing that I could ask for from whoever and whatever higher force was up there, then it was this—I really, *really* wanted to keep her.

18

Song: Bheegi Bheegi Raaton Mein
  - Lata Mangeshkar, Kishore Kumar

Meera

It was in the late afternoon the next day when Luke came out of the shower and looked more like himself. He had slept all day, only waking up to have a lot of orange juice, electrolytes, buttermilk, and coffee.

So while he rested, I called Maa and then Kriti. Maa sounded happy, and her sister's voice laughing in the background was reassuring. I guess she also needed to get out of our house for a bit. Hari seemed to be in a great mood too. He regaled me with all the mischief he's been up to with the grandkids of my aunt. I had worried that he would miss me too much and beg me to be back soon, forcing me to cut my trip short, but I guess I overestimated their need for me. It tugged at my heart a little but also provided a sense of relief. Now, I wouldn't feel guilty for being on this trip.

The moment Luke stepped out of the bathroom, wearing

only his boxers and his eyes shining with mischief, I knew I was in trouble. I didn't put too much mind into his almost nakedness when he was sick, but now, he looked fresh, energetic, and small water droplets glided down his chest. He walked to where I sat on the cozy wooden armchair lined with maroon fabric. He stood over me, his waist and boxers right at my eye level.

And I could not stop staring at the little drop right where his black boxers began.

A finger came under my chin, and I pushed it off.

A chuckle somewhere, and the body moved lower, and I was face-to-face with a very happy Luke.

And I realized then that I was supposed to look at his face, not his boxers.

"Oh God. I was staring," I groaned, and covered my face with both of my hands.

Luke roared with laughter. "You looked really into it. I almost didn't wanna disturb you."

"Shut up," I said from behind my hands, refusing to look at him.

But he seemed to be feeling all too well because he pushed my knees apart and walked on his knees to sit between my legs. His large, warm hands held my thighs, the strong grip heating up my body. I wanted more, needed him to close the distance between us and put his lips on mine. It had been so long since we kissed. Well, only two days. But it felt so long.

And the way he had given me an orgasm, that high, sublime feeling that held me in its grip until my mind and my body were pulsing with relief and ecstasy.

I wanted that again. So much so that I wanted to push Luke down on the floor and climb on top of him, demanding he repeat what we did two nights ago.

I didn't say it out loud.

But maybe Luke understood it. Maybe he felt the same need racing through him because he bent down and nuzzled my neck. He placed hot, wet kisses on my skin, and shoulder, and below my ear, making me whimper and arch my neck up further for more.

"Does sex feel as good as what we did last time?"

He mock-sobbed into my neck, his grip on my thighs tightening. "Meera, you're killing me. Yes, it feels as good. Maybe even better. Well, I don't know about women. It can be a little painful the first time."

"Just a little painful?" I asked.

"Could be more. But if we do it, I'll try to make it as good as possible for you."

"So once we do it the first time, it would not be painful the other times?" I wanted to know what I was in for. I wanted to have sex with Luke. I wanted to feel that close to him. I wanted to feel him inside me, consuming me. But I was scared of the pain.

Luke looked at me. His eyes were heated, his warm brown eyes almost black. He pulled me forward on the chair with his hands on my hips, and I could feel his arousal between my legs. "It will always be painful if a man enters inside you without preparation. Before making you wet. Before stretching you a little. Before you're desperate to want it inside you."

"And you'll do all that?"

His eyes heated further as he moved his hand dangerously close to the apex of my thigh and ground against me, causing an involuntary shiver to race across my body. "Yes," I whimpered, a rush of need flooding between my legs.

"You'll make me desperate to want you inside me?" I clarified, despite knowing that I already was desperate to feel him inside me, my heart pounded so hard I was afraid Luke could hear it.

He bent closer to me, his lips grazed mine, his mouth brushed my cheeks, and he whispered in my ear. "Yes. You would be so desperate that you'd beg me to push inside your pretty little hole. Fuck, I can't wait to see you laid out completely naked in front of me, *just for me*. What're you doing to me, baby?"

I clutched his shoulder, his *bare* shoulder, and pulled him closer. My knees held him tighter between me. "I'm not doing anything. You're the one with all the words. You looked so innocent and harmless when you were lying sick in bed. Look at you now, whispering naughty words."

"You started it," he mumbled, his lips brushing mine, his tongue grazing my lips, demanding entrance.

"I missed you." My eyes widened at my own words. I didn't mean to say that. Even though we were together the entire day, I had missed him. I'd missed talking to him, listening to him talk, his kisses, his eyes always twinkling in mischief and delight. Looking at him sick in bed, unmoving for hours, I'd hated it.

He cupped my face, his brown eyes pools of delight, and kissed me. My embarrassment all but forgotten, I clutched his hands and kissed him back. His tongue grazed my lips, seeking entry, and I readily opened for him. Wanting him. Wanting everything he was willing to give me.

His hands roamed over my body and under my clothes. Touching. Squeezing. My body followed his hands, undulating under his touch, craving more. We didn't stop kissing. I didn't even realize I was leaning so far back on the armchair, and Luke was over me, no space between our bodies, as his tongue brushed against mine, his mouth devouring mine like he could consume me whole.

"Bed," I said against his lips, kissing him, pulling him in deeper, needing that press of his hardness between my legs.

He picked me up, all the while kissing me, and dropped us on the bed.

I needed to feel more of him, needed to feel his skin on mine.

I stopped the kiss and pushed him off, making him sit on his knees. "I want to feel your skin. Can I remove my clothes?"

His eyes darkened, and he groaned as he clutched my thighs, his thumb brushing me down there, making my toes curl with pressure. "Oh, Meera. Can I help you?"

I nodded, lost in the building pleasure of his touch. My body heated as I started to remove my T-shirt and felt Luke's hand untying the knot of my salwar. The cool air of the air conditioner and cold blanket on my naked skin had me shivering. I was just in my bra and underwear, and Luke sat on his knees, his hands on my naked thighs, looking at me, his eyes ablaze with passion. I could see the evidence of his arousal in his boxers. His hair was disheveled, his breathing was fast, his eyes dark pools of heat and want.

"Meera," he whispered.

"Come closer," I said, embarrassed to see so much emotion in his eyes as he looked at me. "Please."

He glided his hands from my thighs to my waist as he moved over me, mapping every dip and curve of my body, leaving behind electric sparks of pleasure and hunger for more. He stopped at my breast, and my body arched for more. "Luke," I cried out, my hands clawing at the sheets under me, needing *something*.

Slowly, his breath came hot on the exposed skin, and I wanted more. I couldn't get in enough air as I looked at the burning desire in Luke's eyes.

"Can I kiss you here?" he asked, his eyes darkened and riveted at my covered breast.

"Yes, please. Kiss me. Touch me. Just *do something*."

With a loud groan, he kissed me there. The warm wetness of his mouth had sharp tingles travel down my body, right between my legs, making me ache with need.

He rubbed his face between my breasts, and his hands

tightened at my waist. He groaned, and I shivered. I wanted more. Needed more.

I pushed down my bra cup and exposed myself, needing his mouth on my skin. With a sharp curse, he took me in his mouth, and I almost came off the bed, entirely blinded with pleasure by the feel of his tongue. He sucked, kissed, bit, and squeezed me as he tugged down my bra straps and unhooked it. His hips kept moving between my legs, turning me wetter and wetter, to the point that I felt an aching emptiness at my entrance, and all I needed was to get closer to Luke.

My hips started to move with his. "Luke." I moaned his name.

He touched my underwear, and I automatically lifted my hips, wanting more, needing to feel him moving inside me.

He groaned in my neck and slowly removed them. He moved his boxer-clad hips right where I needed them the most, and the friction of his hardness against my sopping-wet entrance had my body curl in bone-deep pleasure, so close to the feeling of euphoria.

I clutched his shoulder and moved my hips with his, needing more friction. "Luke. Luke. This is. Oh my God. So good. Luke. More."

"Meera. Just—can I remove my boxers?"

"Yes. Yes. Fast. I'm so close. Please, Luke."

He pushed his boxers down without lifting away from me, and I pushed them off with my feet. Call it instinct, but I needed them off without letting him get away.

The moment his thick, hot cock slipped between my legs, pleasure rushed down my spine, my toes curled, and shivers raced along my body. Everything was so wet and slippery, and I couldn't stop myself from rocking against him, *needing* him to just slip inside me.

Luke groaned out loud, his pleasure fueling mine.

I felt empty, my core clenching every time he moved his

hips. I needed more. Him. Inside. He was right. I was desperate for more.

"More, Luke. Inside. God." I didn't even know if I was making any sense, but my hands clutched his back and shoulder, clenching in the raw, aching hunger to feel him moving just like this inside me.

"Yes. Need condom. Fuck."

He tried to get off me, but I followed. He chuckled and said, "You need to let go, baby. I need to get a condom. And lube."

"Where is it?" I asked, kissing his neck, shoulder, chest, leaving behind marks on his pretty skin. Kissing him wherever I could. *Because* I could.

He held me tight, groaned, and said, "In my bag. Let go and I'll get it."

"In your bag?" I hissed, the thought of letting him go too much to handle. "Why didn't you get it out before we began?"

With great difficulty, I let him go, and he jumped to his feet, his hardness swinging in the air, making me chuckle. It looked ridiculous.

"Hurry, will you?" I asked, as I lay back on the warm sheets, the aching need still ever present.

In the next minute, he was on me, a bottle in his hand, a condom wrapped around him.

He squeezed transparent liquid on his finger from a bottle and put it on the side table. He sat between my legs, looking at me down there. My legs wanted to close, but he held my thighs open, his hooded eyes dark with desire. He rubbed that liquid in his hands and glided his fingers to my opening. Pushing his one finger inside me, he made me clench tight around it.

I gasped. He groaned. His hips moved in the air as if he imagined himself inside me. I clenched around his fingers. I couldn't help it.

"You're so tight. So wet. God, Meera."

I was already soaking, and now, I was so slippery down

there. His hands basically floated across my skin, sending bolts of sparkling pleasure down my spine every time his finger brushed that little spot at the crest of my pussy. "Oh my God, what is this?" I asked.

His voice was like gravel when he answered, "It's lube. It makes you even wetter and will make you more comfortable when I push inside this tight pussy. You ready for me, baby?"

I nodded, more than ready. "They didn't use this lube in the sex videos."

He grunted. "Of course they didn't."

"Trust me?" he asked, pushing two fingers inside me.

"Yes, always," I moaned out loud because I did. I trusted him with everything I had. He had proven himself over and over again. And I would do this, be this vulnerable, only with him.

I whimpered, feeling so full already. How would he even fit?

Right then, he moved his fingers deeper and hit a spot inside me that had my back arching with mind-numbing pleasure, making me scream his name.

I was dying to feel him move inside me just like his fingers; the fullness from before was so much more manageable now.

It felt like I would burst. My hips moved with his hands, wanting him deeper. More. I held his hands and moved faster against his fingers, clenching around them with raw-aching need for something deeper.

"More, Luke. Please, please, please, I need you," I sobbed and begged.

He gently removed his fingers, climbed on top of me, enveloping me entirely in the cocoon of his warmth, held my neck, and kissed me, pushing his tongue inside my mouth, fucking my mouth, showing me what was to come. "I'm right here, baby. Fuck, I'm dying here."

Before I could beg him for more, he held my hips and brought the head of his thick length at my entrance.

He took the bottle of transparent liquid and poured it on him and me.

I tightened at the anticipation, frightened of the pain.

"Relax, baby."

I breathed out, and he said, "Good girl."

I whimpered at the praise. I wanted more of those sweet words. I needed him to need me, want me, as much as I needed him.

He held one of my hands near my head and placed a hot, open-mouthed kiss on my wrist as he slowly pushed inside me.

I gasped. In pain. In pleasure. At the thought that he was *inside* me. And I moved my hips. Wanting more. This wasn't too painful. I felt the stretch and a slight pinch, his long length dragging pleasure out of my body. I felt so incredibly full that I could only hold on to Luke and focus on the feel of his skin brushing against mine.

His breathing was fast, and sweat beaded on his forehead. His body shivered above me as he tried to stay in control.

"Slowly, Meera. Don't move. Please," he gritted the words out.

And I stilled, obeying his every word, clinging to his back with one hand as I squeezed the life out of his other hand.

Slowly, he pushed into me more. We groaned and shivered, both of us hanging on by a thread.

I clutched his shoulder, pressing my mouth at his neck and sucking at the corded muscles at his shoulder, consuming everything he had to offer. His warmth. His strength. His passion.

I wanted to claim him and never let anyone else have him like I had him right now.

He pushed all the way inside me with a loud groan, and my mind all but shattered.

∾

Luke

She was so tight. So wet. I held absolutely still, letting her adjust. I counted backward from a thousand, trying to get back in control. If she moved even a little, this would be over real fast. "Don't move, Meera. Not even a little. Just for a minute, okay?"

She nodded in my neck, yet a shiver rocked through her body, which I felt inside her and all around my cock.

I moaned, and my body vibrated with the need to move. "Ready for more?" I asked, holding her hips steady, not allowing her to move, building her pleasure.

"Yes, please," she whimpered, her eyes glazed over and her skin flushed with sweat and pleasure.

I moved and pushed inside her. She gasped and bit my shoulder, her nails digging into my back. I clutched her hair and pushed into her deeper. "Yes, baby. Fuck, bite me harder."

She whimpered and clenched around me, and bit me harder. Pain and pleasure raced down my body, and I moved faster. Meera's name was a chant on my lips. I kissed her neck and sucked the skin between my lips, unending need for this woman coursing through me and riding me hard. I fucked her like I was her first and her last. Because I *was*. "Mine. You're *mine*, Meera. Aren't you? This body. This tight little pussy, these lips, these warm brown eyes, all of you. All mine, aren't you, darling?"

I clutched her hips tighter and thrust deep and hard, needing to feel Meera all around me. She moaned loudly, dragging her nails down my back, nodding and moaning, "Yes. Yes. Yours. All yours."

I went wild with her confession. I pulled her thigh higher around my waist, and went in deeper, needing to burrow deep inside her.

She felt like heaven and home. I never wanted this to end. I never wanted to leave this. Leave her. And at the best moment of my life, my mind whispered *You are going to leave her. Soon.* And my body rebelled.

I thrust inside her deeper. My heart chanted *no*, refusing to believe Meera and I had an expiration date.

We belonged together.

We didn't make sense, but we *did*. To me, we were perfect. The way we fit was perfect. She was a rock for her family, but I wanted to be *her rock*.

The way she moved, her legs around my hips, pushing me deeper with the heel of her foot on my hips, chanting my name. We *belonged. I* belonged to *her*. I pushed harder, needing to crawl inside her, claim her, mark her, *keep* her.

Her hands tightened on my back, her hips pushing forward, and I was as deep as I could go. And then, she tightened around me. She squeezed the fuck out of me and stilled, her neck thrown back, her eyes closed, her mouth open in blinding pleasure, and I pitched over the edge into oblivion. My mind emptied, electricity raced down my body, and pleasure like no other sizzled on my skin. I erupted once, twice, three times, pressing all my weight into the cradle of her hips.

I dropped down on her, and she held me, our breaths loud, our skin damp with sweat. The smell of sex was heavy in the air.

I tried to move out of her, but she held me closer. "Just two more minutes."

I nodded and laid my head on her chest while she played with my hair, while I stayed inside her.

Her body was dotted with sweat and covered in goose bumps. I slowly rubbed my hand along her arm, gently placing kisses on her chest.

"How do you feel, baby? Did I push you too hard? Too sore?"

I almost climbed off her to check, but she tightened her

legs around me and kept me between her legs as she played with my hair. "I'm a little sore. You didn't push me too hard. You were perfect. Just absolutely perfect. I feel like... a changed person, in the sense that I never knew my body could experience pleasure like this and still survive and desperately want more."

"You're not the only one who feels like their life turned on its axis. I'm just glad I'm not the only one," I admitted, running my hand through her curls. I couldn't stop looking at my girl.

She kissed me, and I lightly nipped her bottom lip.

My cock slipped out, and I had to quickly hold the condom not to let anything spill. I gave her a few soft kisses and went to the bathroom to throw the condom away.

After cleaning up quickly, I rushed back into the bedroom with a washcloth. Meera still lay there with a soft smile on her lips. I climbed on the bed right between her legs.

She instantly tried to close them, but I held her knees open. "Let me take care of you, baby."

Her cheeks turned red, but she got up on her elbows to look down at what I was doing.

There wasn't any blood on the sheets, but when I gently wiped between her legs, a bit of the blood came on it.

She shrieked. "Oh no, you don't need to be seeing that."

I quickly kissed her knee close to my face to calm her down. "It's all done, baby. Relax for me. It's okay. Just a little blood."

"Oh God," she moaned and dropped back on the bed, covering her face.

I chuckled and went back to the washroom.

An idea struck me.

I turned on the tap in the bathtub, added some bubbles and bath salts, and rushed out to the bed where Meera lay naked. Gorgeous. When I kept staring at her, a small smile came over her face, and she raised her eyebrows.

"Wanna take a bath?" I asked. I should've asked her before I started filling up the bathtub. If she said no, it would all go to waste. I wasn't going to take a bath alone.

"What?" she said in a rough voice.

Not what I was hoping for, so I continued. "Um... Bath in the tub. There are bubbles. Bath salts. It will help soothe your body after your first time."

"Oh. That's a good idea."

"I already started the bath."

A grateful smile came over her face, and she went under the covers. After a lot of movements where it felt like a white ghost was moving on the bed, she came out, fully clothed.

"Wow. That took skills."

"Shut up," she mumbled, and smiled.

I gave her my hand to climb down the bed. Not because she needed it but because I wanted to touch her. "You know my hands and mouth were just on your naked body, right? You could've walked to the tub without going through the whole ghost routine thing."

She gasped as if scandalized and then looked down at my naked body. She blushed but managed to sputter out, "Me, naked? All the way to the bathroom? No way."

"You are gorgeous. Sexy. Completely blow my mind."

We went to the restroom while she shook her head in exasperation and gave me her little amused smile. She came to a stop when she saw the big bathtub with bubbles rising over the ledge of the tub.

"Get in, Meera," I whispered in her ear.

She all but nodded, her eyes riveted to the tub. After a few seconds, she turned to me and frowned, as if expecting something from me.

"What is it?" I asked.

"Well?" she asked back.

"Well what?"

She huffed, and said, "Aren't you leaving so I can bathe?"

And okay. Wow. Um. Why did I think she would just *know* that the bath was for the two of us? God, this was embarrassing.

"Why are you blushing? Are you imagining me naked?" she asked.

Oh God.

"Uh. No. This is embarrassing. But I thought we would take a bath *together.*"

Understanding dawned on her. Now, she turned red, and asked softly, "Like in the movies?"

I nodded. And a shy smile graced her lips. "That sounds romantic."

"It will be."

She nodded, her eyes resolute, and said, "Okay. Turn around."

"What? Why?"

"I need to get in the tub first, and then you can follow me."

"But we're going to be naked in the tub together. And we were just naked together a few minutes ago." How did she suddenly get so shy around me?

She blushed a deep maroon, and said, "That is different. We were in that state of passion. Now, it is different."

She was adorable, trying to get the words out. I kissed her head and turned, facing the opposite wall of the tub. A few rustles and a splash later, she said, "I'm ready."

I turned back, and she looked glorious. She'd pulled her hair up in a knot, a few curls still framing her face, a few lingering on her bare back. White bubbles covered her up to the neck, her brown skin a vivid contrast to the white foam. Her eyes dropped to my cock, which stood at attention and showed the evidence of its appreciation. I smiled and climbed in behind her in the tub.

I turned off the tap, and there was silence. I plucked the loofah from the side and roamed it over her back. After a few circles, she relaxed and gently shifted her weight on my chest.

Her hips met my cock, and she quickly jerked forward. And I don't know what happened, but her hips slid, and she slipped under the water.

She pulled herself out at once, sputtering and clutching my knees around her. And I won't lie. I laughed. She turned to me with a glare, and still, I couldn't stop picturing the whole thing over and over again. Her hair was all wet, and she had white bubbles all over her cheek, forehead, nose, and neck. Fucking adorable, like a wet kitten.

She splashed some water on my face, trying to retaliate. But I pulled her back to my chest and firmly held her waist. "Now, let me hold you properly. We don't want you sliding back under."

And as soon as I said it, I laughed again.

"It's not that funny," she grumbled, but I could sense the humor in her tone.

"It is. If I had slipped in like that, you would've laughed too. Admit it."

"Maybe."

I placed kisses on her shoulder, neck, and back, knowing that talking time was over. I moved the loofah over her body, the hot water sluicing down. And she forgot all about her reservations and her shyness. She leaned her back on my chest, her eyes closed in pleasure, and her moan echoed in the bathroom. I kept rubbing and swirling the loofah, and she pushed out her boobs, asking for more. For so long, I'd dreamed about this. Meera in my arms. Meera kissing me. Meera moaning my name. The reality was so much better.

We made out like that. Touching. Kissing. Savoring each other's bodies. We sat in the tub, our hands entwined, our fingers flirting and playing with each other, a sharp reminder of our time on her terrace during our midnight conversations.

We lay still in the tub, looking at our fingers. At the contrast in the color of our skin. Her rich, warm brown and mine a pale white. "What are you thinking?" I murmured.

"How different we are. How I don't *feel* different when we are together. What an impossibility we are in reality. Yet here we are."

"We belong together," I whispered, too scared to voice that out loud, my heart a pounding drum, waiting to hear what she thought of my words.

She let out a sigh, almost wistful. "Belong? I feel that too. But for how long, Luke?"

Her words were gentle. They stated her thoughts, her hope —or lack thereof. The thought of saying goodbye to her still hurt, of never having the midnight conversations under the stars and the moon, of not listening to the old songs with her. It was agony.

I pulled her closer to my chest, her face near my neck.

"I wish I had an answer."

I couldn't possibly give up my degree and stay here forever. I couldn't leave Sam with our construction company. And do what in Meera's tiny village? Nothing made sense. Except the two of us together.

"I know. That's why I decided to have sex with you."

"Meaning?" I asked, genuinely confused as to how the topic of sex came about.

She squeezed my fingers and kissed my knuckles. That gentle touch of her lips gave me a million fucking butterflies in my stomach.

"If I would trust anyone enough to be that vulnerable with, it would be you. According to our customs, people should only have sex after marriage. Especially women."

"We too have such a custom in Christianity. To be celibate before marriage. Not many of us practice it."

She nodded. "In India, I've seen the groom's family ask the bride and her family if the girl is a virgin when they go to see the bride for an arranged marriage. And on the first night of the marriage, many families still put a white bedsheet to check if the woman bleeds as a proof of her virginity."

Fuck. My stomach turned sour at the next question. "Would they ask you too? In case you get an arranged marriage?"

I hated asking this question. Hated imagining a scenario where Meera would marry someone else, her being asked about her virginity, her having sex with her husband. I hated myself for giving voice to such thoughts.

"I'm not the best deal in the marriage market. No father. Barren farm. No dowry. Also, since my father committed suicide, the people of the village would consider me a bad omen if I were to marry in the family. And I wouldn't want to marry into families like that. I wouldn't want to marry a family who would restrict me from taking care of Maa and Hari."

"And how does having sex with me come into this reasoning?"

"Well, the possibility of me getting married is slim to none anyway. Why should I care what the customs say? I don't know what good deeds I'm getting blessed for, but I'm just so happy and grateful that you came into my life. You showed me what joy feels like. You gave me the chance to experience this care-free feeling. You gave me my first kiss. My first trip. My first sex. And I'll happily take everything you're willing to give me, Luke. Every moment, every day, for as long as I can have it. I'll take these moments with you. And they'll always stay with me, whether you stay or not."

My heart rejoiced at her declaration, but it broke too. *I* broke. How would I ever live without her in my life? How would I stay happy with just the memories? Knowing how powerful a kiss could be with her, would I ever want to kiss someone else again? Or was I completely ruined?

19

Song: *Kabhi Kabhi Mere Dil Mein*
   - Lata Mangeshkar, Mukesh

Meera

I shouldn't get used to this. To him. We left Jaipur last week and reached Jodhpur, the Blue City of Rajasthan. We walked down the narrow streets of the old, walled city, hand in hand, exchanging glances, laughing, talking. Most of the houses along the streets were painted blue. Old women sat on the small porches gossiping, observing, and chopping vegetables. Small shops lined the streets, selling everything from groceries to ornaments to snacks and tea. Stray dogs roamed everywhere. And Luke seemed to get unreasonably happy and sad at seeing them. I didn't understand. They were just common street dogs.

We had already spent two days visiting the stepwells of Jodhpur. At one of the stepwells, a small café overlooked the entire structure. Luke had gone crazy happy. "You can easily sit here and have coffee and rest in shade. We'll keep the tab open.

I can click all my pictures and do some sketches down there, and you won't need to follow me around."

"You just don't want me to keep joking about being your servant."

"Yes, that is the primary reason you'll sit in the café and order anything you want while I toil down there. And then you can tell me how I treat you like a queen."

I had rolled my eyes, but we did exactly that. I could see the entire stepwell from the café up above, while Luke clicked pictures of every corner of the stepwell. We had spent about five hours in the café. Even the staff working there had become comfortable with me.

They told me about how foreigners from all over the world kept clicking pictures of the place. Soon, they moved me from the hard chair and table to one of the traditional beds on the balcony, lined with soft cushions and small tables in front of them.

When Luke came back to the café after clicking pictures, that was where he found me. Lounging on the bed, sipping tea, and looking down at the people hanging out at the stepwell. A huge smile came over his face, and he dropped on his knees, took my hand in his, placed a kiss on my fingers, and asked, "May I join you, my queen?"

And I couldn't help but laugh. "You may."

"What an honor," he exclaimed, and sat beside me.

He had a large sandwich, and I ordered a masala dosa, which was essentially potato-stuffed South Indian savory rice crepes. Since Luke had ordered a non-veg sandwich, I did not taste it. But I did break off a small bite from my dosa and gave it to him for a taste. He loved it so much he ordered a whole new one for himself.

Every day seemed to be the best day of the trip.

There was too much happiness. Too much light. Too much laughter. What was I going to do once he left? I'd told him I would always cherish these moments. And I would. But I would always long for them too. Long for *him*. I knew I wouldn't feel happier than this in my life. Because it just wasn't possible. My heart was full, and like a glutton I was, I kept eating it all up.

We stopped our walk when the narrow street opened up into a large public square; a statue of someone was in the center surrounded by the shops that sold all sorts of souvenirs. We knew it was all for tourists because so many foreigners were around us. A few greeted Luke, and they exchanged hellos as they passed. We often found such sections in the city where we would come across a lot of tourists, and Luke would get this same smile on his face.

"What's that smile for?"

He turned to look at me. We kept walking, maneuvering the crowd around us. He shrugged, and said, "I guess it feels nice to see people who look like me. It's not often I'm in the minority at home."

I couldn't help but chuckle. He was crazy.

We walked slowly along the shops. Countless colorful, traditional Jodhpuri footwear hung on top of each other, covering the entire front of the shop. The leather sandals with pointed toes, each in a unique bright color with mirrors sewed in them, were captivating. I wanted them all. The best thing about them was that any Jodhpuri sandal would go well with almost anything. Even one pair would suffice, and I would be able to wear them with any of my salwar kameez.

"Can we go in?" I asked Luke.

He dragged me out of the crowd to right in front of the shop. I looked at all the different options. Some had really pointy toes, and some had simple round edges at the toe.

"They have a men's collection too, Luke."

"Oh yeah. Look at that," he said, pointing at a rich brown leather sandal with intricate patterns at the top and open from the back. He'd just have to step in them, and he'll be ready to go. He pointed at another which had a strap at the back. They would look good on him.

We were discussing options when a man came out from the shop with a big smile on his face. He spoke in both Hindi and English. I guess since the shop was in a tourist area, the shopkeepers would learn English to attract more tourist customers. He called another man outside, and after testing some shoes for our size, he brought in our selected shoes in the right size.

While I tried some—well, many, because I was only getting one, so I wanted the right one—Luke talked to the shopkeeper.

It was when I was thinking about getting a pair for Maa and Kriti that I heard Luke ask the customer, "Sir, do you have these Jodhpuris in a size that would fit a young boy? Say ten-year-old."

My nose tingled with the incoming tears, and for the life of me, I couldn't stop them from slipping down my cheeks. I tried so hard to keep the walls around my heart strong, but they shattered. He *cared*. Not just for me but for Hari too. I quickly wiped my tears, my hand shaking, and I turned around to look at him.

He was looking at five small Jodhpuri shoes, asking questions, in intense conversation with the shopkeeper. And I was done for. At this moment, if he asked me for anything, I'd move heaven and earth to give it to him. He deserved my adoration. He already had my respect. And love, he didn't even have to ask for it. My love was his. Today. Tomorrow. Everyday. No matter what.

And I hated him for it. Just a little.

Because I could never have him, and I would never want someone else.

⁓

Luke

Time flew by.

Hours. Days. Weeks.

We moved across cities. Jodhpur to Udaipur to Patan. Step-wells, temples, palaces, forts, markets, lakes. I saw it all, captured as many pictures as possible in my camera. Created as many memories with Meera, lived every moment of the trip with her, and dreamed a million more.

Time still flew. I tried to stop it. Extend it. Slow it down. And I failed.

We woke up early, just to spend more time together. We stayed up late, talking into midnight just like we did on the terrace, stealing kisses when talking was too much, and making love when kissing wasn't enough. Sometimes we went slow and deep, in each other's arms, never letting go. Sometimes, it was frantic, rough but not enough, as if we were racing against time and losing. Whatever it may be, we always ended up holding each other.

Tomorrow, we left for home. The trip was nearly over, and I was so deeply in love with Meera, I was terrified. Terrified to say goodbye. My stomach turned sour every time I thought about living my life without her in it. I wanted to cancel my ticket back to New York. I wanted to take Meera away with me.

I wanted to tell her I loved her. The way my heart skipped a beat every time I made her laugh. The way she cared for me— or glared at me when I lost control over the street food—and constantly reminded me of the days I was sick. I wanted to tell her I would miss her. But the fact that for me to miss her, I'd have to leave her, made me want to take her in my arms, tuck us under a blanket, and turn off the world.

I had no idea what I should do. Whether to confess my feel-ings or not. Whether to ask her to come with me. Or wait for me. And would she?

We silently packed our bags in our Airbnb room. There was nothing to talk about. Nothing to discuss. No confessions that would change the outcome. She didn't look at me as much as I wanted her to. She didn't smile at me as much as I needed her to. She just packed. Folded her clothes. Folded the stupid towels that didn't need folding. Cleaned the bathroom. Ironed her clothes for tomorrow.

Once I finished my packing, I got in the bed and just waited. Waited for her to sort through her feelings. Waited for her to get back in my arms, so I could have one more night of *us*. Of her. So I could remember how she felt. Her wild curls over my chest, her dark brown eyes when they looked at me with heat and desire. Her laugh on my lips.

I watched her as she moved around the tiny room for hours. Until she finally looked at me. Fear. Heartbreak. Loss...all of it reflected in her eyes. Her eyes were red, but she didn't shed a tear. And when I stretched my arm in calling, she dove into them.

She felt right. She felt perfect. Like I never wanted her to leave me, never wanted her to let her out of my sight. I placed soft kisses along her neck, and in a whisper, I voiced my deepest—my only—desire. "I want to take you away with me."

She stilled. Her back straightened. "I wish it was that simple."

I braced myself before I *finally* touched what seemed like the forbidden topic. "It could be. I can pay off all your debt."

She immediately tried to move away from me, but I held her waist and turned her to face me, my arms clutched her tight against my chest. She glared daggers at me.

"You know I can't accept it. I won't."

"Please, Meera. Just take the money. It would make things so much easier."

If eyes could throw daggers, it would've gone straight through my mouth that uttered those words. She clutched my shirt in her hand and pulled me closer. *"Easier?* You think it's *easy* to just spread my hands and accept money from the guy I... You think it's *easy* to know day in and day out that just one yes from me, and all my problems would be solved? You think it's fucking *easy* to let every sacrifice I've made in my life just go in vain?"

How could she be so stubborn? I glared back at her because she needed to understand. "Haven't you sacrificed enough? Haven't all your misery and debt been enough? What the hell are you waiting for? What could possibly be more important to you than paying off your debt and seeing what life has to give you? What we could be?"

She pushed at my chest, trying to get away. I clutched her tighter to me, and glared at her to stay put. She glared back at me harder. "My self-respect. My principles. You think I can't do it on my own?"

I held her neck, compelling her to look me in the eye. "I only wish to give you the money because I care so goddamn much about you. I wholeheartedly believe that you can do it on your own. But for how long, Meera? And at what cost? At *whose* cost? Isn't that important?"

"Not more important than never being able to look at myself in the mirror."

There was no convincing her otherwise. I didn't know what to say.

Meera must've misunderstood my silence as me giving up because she continued, "I've never had much of anything of my own. I grew up knowing I had to make something of myself. The only thing I could rely on to improve our situation was myself. I've grown up knowing I have to study hard, get good grades, get admission in a good university, and get a degree. Everything I've done is to improve our situation.

"After my father passed, that responsibility just grew. I took a good job, and I've spent the past five years of my life trying to pay off the loan. Every dent I made, every sum of money that I put aside, sacrificing a hundred little things, was to pay off the loan. My life's focus, my efforts, all the hard work, my *everything* has gone into this. And with one little offer, my goal, all my efforts, sacrifices, would just vanish."

A soft whisper of her name came out of me. "Your struggles, your sacrifices, your hard work, all of it has made you who you are today. Me giving you the money does not invalidate your journey. It might just mean that you've reached the destination. It might mean that it's time for a new journey. Hopefully one filled with passion, ambition, love, and happiness."

Her eyes shone with tears. She didn't let them fall. Just took a deep breath and gave me a weak smile. "When you have no money, Luke, you stick to your strengths. You live by your principles. And all I've had for myself is my self-respect. My self-worth. How can I give that up when I know I *will* get us out of debt? Please don't ask me to give it up. It will take some time, but I believe in myself."

This woman would destroy me. I pressed my forehead to hers, my chest tight with hopelessness and heartache. "How can I ask you to give up something that makes you *you*?"

"Thank you," she whispered, rubbing her nose against mine. "I'll never ask you to wait for me, you know that, right? This time with you would still be one of the best memories for me."

I kissed her. Softly. "There's no one for me but you. I'll wait for you. However long it takes. No matter the distance between us. You have to trust me."

"I can't ask you to do that."

I kissed her again. Harder. "You're not. I'm telling you."

And I kissed her more, shutting her up before she tried to argue with me otherwise.

I dragged my lips down her neck, sucking at the junction of her neck and shoulder. I marked her, trying to show her how she'd marked me. My heart was already hers. *I* was already hers.

She moaned my name. I chanted hers.

Our love was frantic. I needed to be inside her. The sharp sting of her nails on my back demanded I never leave her. Demanded more from me than I could ever give her. We moaned our desperation as we moved. It was a dance of want and loss. Of heartbreak and desire. A reminder of what we were soon going to lose. A rebellion of taking more from each other. Giving everything we had to each other.

Maybe, just maybe, if we loved hard enough, the world would be kinder and grant us a miracle.

I prayed for that. I loved her as hard as I could. As softly as I could. She held me in her arms, unwilling to let go. And I stayed there. Happily. For now.

20

Song: Aaiye Meherbaan
 - Asha Bhosle

Meera

Hari's excited squeals welcomed me home. Maa and Hari had returned the day before yesterday. The moment I stepped out of the car— Luke had called his favorite driver and friend, Ramesh, to pick us up from the railway station— Hari ran toward me and clung to my waist. He was too big to pick up in my arms, so I hugged him for a long time.

"Did you have fun at Masi's place?" I asked in Gujarati as I patted down his ruffled hair. Masi means *aunt who is Mother's sister*. Wow, it felt so good to be speaking in Gujarati again. In Rajasthan, I had to keep talking in Hindi, and with Luke, in English.

He nodded at my question and asked, "Did you bring me anything?"

"I brought you so many things. Let's go inside, and I'll show you."

He nodded and turned to Luke, who was done getting our luggage out from the dickey, or as Luke liked to call it, the *trunk* of the car. He had a good laugh when he'd heard me call it a dickey. He'd explained to me what the first half of the word meant, tears streaming down his face. Now, every time I said the word, it felt like I was saying something dirty. But whatever. I wasn't going to start calling a dickey a trunk. Also, every time I said dickey, Luke laughed. It was the easiest laugh I got out of him.

Slowly, as if testing the waters, Hari neared Luke. The unfamiliarity between the two had sort of returned. That happened when you stayed away from a kid for too long. Yet like nothing was any different, Luke got on his knees and hugged Hari. To everyone's surprise, Hari hugged him back. To my utter shock, and Hari's, Luke lifted Hari in his arms as he got up. Hari laughed. It had been years since anyone had lifted him in their arms. He looked at me in delight, his arms holding on to Luke's shoulders.

I looked at Luke. His eyes turned to me, his lips stretched into a delighted smile, like he was genuinely happy to see my brother. He held my brother like it was natural for him. And he looked at me as if he had no clue what that did to me. As if it was normal for me to see a man holding Hari in his arms, to see a man support me, a man who wasn't bogged down by life and had the strength to share my burdens. And I would lose it all.

The moment I stepped inside the house, the reality started to creep up on me. Maa had her arms around me as soon as I stepped inside the living room. We looked at each other, in relief, in happiness, assuring ourselves that we were all right. The three of us were back in our tiny house, just like always, as if nothing had changed.

But it had.

Maa looked less tense. She wore a smile on her face even though worry lined her eyes. Hari clung to Luke, but he was still smiling. And I was in love with a man leaving soon, but I smiled. Because I had lived the best month of my life.

"How was your trip, beta?" asked Maa, her hands clutching mine as she dragged me to her bed.

"It was amazing, Maa. I saw so many palaces, forts, temples, and markets. Rajasthan is really pretty. I'll take you and Hari someday. You will love it."

"Really? I'd like that. Hari will too."

"How was your stay with Masi?" I asked.

Her eyes shone with excitement, and her grip turned tighter. "It was very relaxing. We talked and talked for days. Her children are all grown up. Almost your age. Her husband treats them well. He even agreed to send their younger daughter Pinky to college. Their older daughter, Reshma, is pregnant. Isn't that amazing?"

Both my cousins, Pinky and Reshma, were younger than me. Reshma was just a year younger, and she was pregnant. "That's great, Maa."

"God knows when you'll marry," she said with a dramatic sigh.

I couldn't help but scoff at that. "I'm not leaving you and Hari to take care of another family."

"We'll see. Let's not get into that," she said, a small frown on her face.

Before she could say anything else, Hari began dancing in front of me. "Where are the gifts, didi?"

Luke stood at the door, two bags in his hands. He smiled at Maa and greeted her with a *Namaste*. Maa laughed as Hari started to drag me.

I turned to Luke, and asked, "Could you pass me that maroon bag?"

He stepped forward to the middle of the living room and

laid down the bag. He murmured in English, "Should I stay here or go to my room?"

I could feel Maa's eyes on the back of my head. I very deliberately tried to ignore it and said to Luke, "Stay. You got so many gifts for Hari. You have to be there when he sees all his gifts."

He smiled, and if I wasn't mistaken, relief shone in his eyes. He wanted to be there. But not if I didn't want him there. This man. He took a seat on the floor, right beside me, as I opened the bag. Hari came over and sat between the two of us.

I rummaged through the bag and pulled out the first plastic bag and handed it to Hari. He quickly opened it and pulled out the Jodhpuri shoes. Not one pair. Three pairs. And his squeal might've been heard on the neighboring farm. He stood and started trying them on.

"Look, didi. Look! They fit. I'll wear them all the time," he cried out in Gujarati.

"You know who you should thank for it?"

A wide smile came over his face as he asked, "You?"

I couldn't help but laugh. I shook my head and pointed at Luke. "Thank Luke bhai. He insisted you needed three pairs. I was only going to buy one pair."

"Really?" he asked.

When I nodded, Hari looked at Luke, paused for a second, and then he ran into Luke's arms. Luke's shocked eyes turned to me, and I tried my best not to bawl right there. Luke put his arms around Hari, and I heard Hari mumble a carefully pronounced *thank you* to Luke.

"There's more, Hari," Luke said, and Hari flew out of his arms and looked at me in anticipation.

I pulled myself together and started pulling out more gifts. A *kurta*, toys, sweets, fancy pencils, a flute, a leather bag. I handed out the Jodhpuri shoes that I got for Maa to her, and she tried them right away. I also gave her three bandhani sarees, a very popular type of sarees from Jaipur. And she marveled at those. It had been years since she'd bought any new clothes for herself. When I told her two of those were from Luke, she thanked him profusely, while Luke turned red with all the gratitude coming his way.

Luke had even gotten three boxes of sweets for Ramesh, toys for his kids, and a saree for his wife. He was so happy he was in our kitchen preparing chai for us. It was already late afternoon, so it was the perfect time for it. Once we had the chai, Ramesh left, Maa insisted she'd cook dinner, and Hari was off playing with his toys. Luke went upstairs to get settled back in his room, and it felt very weird not to follow him.

Something felt off. Missing. Like I was supposed to be there in his room as he disrobed and went for a shower. And I was supposed to be there when he returned from the shower, and I took my turn. Instead, I took a shower in the bathroom downstairs and came out to sit with Maa even though thoughts of Luke preoccupied my mind.

Now, I sat on the bed beside Maa as she kept talking about her stay at Masi's place.

"Meera, are you even listening?" Maa's sharp words pulled me out of my thoughts.

"Huh? Uh. Yeah. Sorry."

"What is going on between you and Luke?"

Her question completely took me by surprise. I knew she noticed us, but I never thought she would outright ask me. "What?"

"I have eyes, Meera. And you two couldn't stop looking at each other."

There wasn't any point in hiding. "I don't know, Maa. I like him. Just look at him. And for some insane reason, he likes me too. We're taking it one day at a time. It's like we both know it's coming to an end, so what's the point in talking about it?"

"Oh, Meera. I wish you would have found some decent man

from our village. That boy is going to break your heart."

"I know, Maa. I know."

She clutched my shoulder in support. "It'll be okay. We'll be okay."

I had nothing to say to that. I could only nod.

Before I could say anything else, Maa pulled something out from under her pillow. "I found this on our door when I returned."

She handed me an envelope. It was torn. Maa must have already read it. "What is this?" I asked while I pulled out the letter.

Maa didn't even need to answer. Written in clear, bold letters, it said, "The next time no one is here when I come to collect the money, you won't like it. This is the last warning."

Fear slithered down my spine, my mind remembering the slimy hands that had clutched my arm.

Baldev. The letter wasn't dated, so we had no idea if he had made a visit recently or not. Whether he would make a visit soon, or did we still have time to prepare. I had Luke's two months of rent, so I had enough money to last me a few months if I gave it to him in small batches.

"Don't worry, Maa. The next time he comes, we'll give him two months of loan together. That should cool him down."

"When will this end, Meera?"

"It will. It has to, right?"

Maa had tears in her eyes. When she spoke next, her voice shook, as if the words were difficult to utter. "I know your father was trying to protect us, feed us, and keep us alive when he took that money from Baldev. But sometimes, I hate him for it. I hate him for leaving us with all this debt. Sometimes, I've wished I could follow him," she said, taking my breath away.

But before I could protest, she tightened her hand on mine, and continued, "I'm not that strong, Meera. I could never do that. I could never leave you or Hari. And every day, I wish your father hadn't taken that step. I think of the countless things that we could have done differently."

I laid my head on her shoulder. "Maa, what's done is done. I, too, keep thinking that if only he had waited and held on for a year, I would've gotten a job and supported you. I don't know. It just makes me more upset when I get into those thoughts."

These *what-ifs* and *if onlys* are the crux of never-ending misery. You try to stop the pain, you try to forget, and these two-word troubles rear their head into the weakest part of your mind and cripple you. And that's why I had decided to never use those words when it came to Luke.

Luke. He must be resting after the long train journey. And here I felt like I'd just woken up from a beautiful dream and was thrown back into the reality of my life.

Luke

I had already joined our beds, arranged them on the open terrace like usual, and plugged in the cassette player when Meera came upstairs. We had a simple dinner of khichdi, potato sabji, and buttermilk. Hari had talked nonstop; Meera had entertained him while she barely met my gaze.

Things seemed to be different from what we had become used to. I didn't have to think about kissing her or holding her hand. She didn't have other people to talk to or to be responsible for. It had been just us.

And now, we were back again, hiding our relationship from her mother and Hari. On some level, I felt like Meera's mom already suspected that there were feelings involved between Meera and me. But I guess none of us knew how we could possibly work, so she seemed not to be asking questions.

Meera placed the jug of water on the small table near the

bed. Gray clouds scattered across the dark, midnight sky, the half-crescent moon and stars occasionally giving us a peek. The moment I lay down on the cot, Meera was in my arms. She had changed into her fully covered nightwear of a T-shirt and pajama pants. She had slowly started wearing my boxers in the month that we traveled. I loved the feeling of our legs sliding together under the blanket. Even now, she tangled her legs with mine, and I missed the feel of her skin.

"I missed the view," she said in my neck.

My hands went in her hair, and I played with her soft curls. "I miss our trip even more."

She lightly bit my neck and met my eyes. "Me too. Especially the night parts."

I groaned and dragged her even closer so she was half on top of me. "You know what? We can sleep in the bedroom now that we're together. No one comes upstairs."

Her eyes widened. "You are so right. Why didn't I think of that? From tomorrow, we're sleeping in the room. Let's make do tonight. We can listen to songs."

"I've definitely missed those."

She gave me a quick peck on the mouth and crawled over the side of the adjacent cot where I'd placed the cassette player. She rummaged in her pouch filled with cassettes, and then I heard the click of the play button. It started.

The magic. The melody. The music. And Meera in my arms. I *had* missed this.

A slow, seductive tune began with playful notes joining in. A woman crooned and sang something.

"The song is 'Aaiye Meherbaan'. It's a very seductive song to this day." Meera's voice was a little hoarse, as if she too was trying to be seductive.

"What does it mean?" I whispered, not wanting to break the magic spinning around us.

And Meera described the song as the lady sang. She seductively whispered words of how lovely I was, telling me to happily take the test of love, and what a good-looking guy I was, a handsome guest. She ran her fingers over my chest all the while she sang about how wherever I looked at her, she felt like she was struck by lightning— and I all but kissed her right there— and how the lightning didn't care where it struck and who it burned.

That was when all thoughts left my body, and I clutched her seducing fingers that were way below my waist now, brought them to my mouth, and bit her.

For the next seven songs, I kissed her. She touched me. I clutched her waist under her T-shirt. She held my face as she met my tongue. She rubbed herself on me, and I helped her do it harder. We moaned in each other's necks, trying to keep it low. I reminded her that the last month was real. That nothing had changed. I mumbled it in her ear. *I'm here. We're good. Don't you forget, Meera.* And she clung to me tighter. Letting me hold her. Letting me love her.

After a while, our frenzied grabbing turned into calm, soothing caresses. Our kisses turned softer. My mind turned sharper. My heart, more wistful. It ached with the need to have this forever. It rebelled against all reason.

"I leave next week." The words were out of my mouth before I could stop them. Whether it was to remind Meera or myself, I didn't know.

I heard a gasp from my side. I realized that I was looking up at the moon. It was out. Her hold on my T-shirt tightened, and I remembered that I needed to face her. What would I see in her eyes? Disappointment? Sadness? Relief? I was terrified to find relief in her eyes. I'd rather take all the sadness. At least then, I'd know she felt the same as me.

"I knew that. It feels final when you say it."

I turned to face her. Our knees brushed, and I pulled her closer till our foreheads touched. "I don't want to leave you."

I was sure she could hear my heart pounding. Her hand rested on my chest, and my heart beat faster. She pressed deeper and said, "I can't ask you to stay."

"Can I ask you to go? With me?"

Her breath came out shaky, she looked up to meet my eyes, and for a moment, endless emotions reflected in them. Heartbreak. Loneliness. Deep, bottomless want. It passed away in a blink, hidden from me. But I saw. She wanted me too. Just as much. Just as fiercely.

Her eyes pooled with tears. "You can't. Not only will I not get any visa, I just can't leave my family. Don't ask me to come with you. You'll only get heartbreak. So will I."

My eyes stung, and I hid my face in her neck. "Without you, my heart is going to break regardless."

She held my head, and her warmth, the press of her lips, just her, soothed me and hurt me all the same. "If only things were different. In another lifetime, maybe things would've been easier. For me. For us."

I didn't want to think of another lifetime or the countless *if onlys*. I held her face in my hands and looked at her. I waited until she looked at me. "This, Meera. This is the life we have. Things are not different. I want you. In this lifetime. This. Not another. And *this* is what I want. You. Me. Together. You are it, Meera. And I can't believe I have to leave you."

A tear slid down her cheek. I wiped it with my thumb. I kissed the corner of her eye and breathed her in. She sniffled and clutched my wrist. "Your words. You. It's going to destroy me."

"I won't let it."

A sad smile came over her face. I hated this smile. It was a smile of surrender and acceptance. "What if you do? You've spent every day with me for the past two and a half months. You'll go back to your big city. To your friends. To your family. Your world. And in a few weeks or months, I will just be a distant memory to you. And yes, that will destroy me. It will probably destroy you too. But you'll find someone. Someone who belongs to your world. Someone with less problems. And I'll be happy for you."

With every word she spoke, I shook my head. I refused to accept the picture that she painted. My vision turned red—a painful, angry red. She didn't get it. How could she not get it? How could she even think she was that disposable to me? I clutched her hair, her beautiful hair, tight in my fist, and tilted her face so she looked me in the eye.

I was angry. Angry at the way those awful words flew so easily out of her mouth. As if what we felt was unimportant, insignificant, when it was the most life-changing, unforgettable, irrevocable feeling in the world.

"You don't get to say shit like that. You hear me?" I said, and she whimpered my name. I continued, "No. I won't destroy you. And I won't let you destroy us. And no matter where I go, or how long I go for, I will come back. We are meant to be together. I'll fucking make it happen. And don't you forget that."

Tears flowed down her cheeks, and she held my shirt tighter. Fire burned in her eyes, and she spat, "I hate you."

And I heard her words because I felt the same. "I hate you too. So fucking much."

And we crashed into each other. She kissed me and bit my lip. Hard.

I grabbed her waist and pulled her under me. We pushed and pulled. We moved and plunged deeper. The moon hid behind the clouds and reappeared, plunging us in darkness and in light. We didn't stop. Every moment, every minute, every day that we had left, was precious.

She showed me how she hated me. I showed her how I hated her more. And the entire night, we hated each other until I fell asleep in her arms.

21

Song: *Lag Jaa Gale*
 - *Lata Mangeshkar*

Meera

The recess bell rang, and before I had even stepped out of the classroom, the kids had already taken out their lunch boxes and started eating. I greeted the kids on my way to the staff room. I had missed this. The kids— some were genuinely happy to have me back in the class after a month's leave— and their questions, that feeling of satisfaction when my kids answered something right, the constant noise of children, and Kriti.

Speaking of, the moment I sat at my desk in the staff room, Kriti was on me. "How was the trip? How was Luke?"

Luke. Last night. His declarations. He *would* destroy me. Or I him.

"Meera," Kriti called again.

I met her eyes, full of joy and that ever-present excitement for romance, and said, "It was the best thing to happen to me. And probably the worst."

Worried lines appeared between her eyebrows, and she clutched my hand. "Oh no. What happened?"

Last night came back to me. The entire trip flashed before my eyes. Days full of adventure and laughter. Nights of endless passion. Just Luke and me. His smiles that lit up his warm eyes, the way he constantly held my hand, his take-charge attitude in planning the entire trip without me having to worry about a thing. The trip was an illusion of what life would be like with Luke. But it was just that. An illusion. Not real.

A lump lodged in my throat just thinking about what I was about to lose. "I fell in love."

My voice was a whisper, but Kriti heard it. "Does Luke feel the same way?"

I hate you too. So fucking much. His words hadn't stopped echoing in my mind.

I nodded. "I think so. We haven't said anything to each other but sort of circled around it."

Her eyes bulged. "Can't you guys work something out? If you both feel the same way, there has to be a solution. Has he said anything?"

I turned my eyes to my desk; children's books I needed to check were arranged in piles of pending work. "Well, he says he'll make it work between us. He has no plan. Just a lot of belief."

A small, hopeful smile returned to Kriti's face. "That's good, right? Long distance relationships are hard, but they do work."

How did she not understand? How did Luke not understand? I turned to Kriti, and said, "What happens when he goes back to America? How long do you think he will remember me? How long till he finds someone who has less problems than me? Someone who is near and there for him?"

She squeezed my arm and said, "Those things don't matter when you're in love."

"For how long, Kriti? You think I can just leave Hari and Maa? Or he can leave his life, his family in America, and what? Settle down in this village? I'm stuck here, Kriti. I can't make his life worse. He is so talented. He has dreams. He has his father's firm to run with his friend. I can't ask him or even allow him to give up his life to live in this tiny village. If not now, he'd eventually resent me when he realizes how limited life is here. I'd rather he love me and lose me than resent me."

"Meera, don't lose hope. When it's meant to be, things have a way of sorting themselves out. There's no happily ever after without hope."

"Hope only hurts, Kriti."

"Love also hurts."

"You won't hear me denying that," I mumbled.

A pause, and she whispered, "So... does sex hurt?"

I choked on air and coughed for a minute straight, all while Kriti patted my back and informed other teachers to carry on with their work.

She handed me my water bottle, cool as a cucumber, and waited till I felt better. "Why? Why do you think I did that?"

She shrugged her shoulders. "One month of just the two of you. Sharing a hotel room. It was bound to happen. It always does. In movies. Books. Was it like those videos we saw?" Thankfully, she whispered the last line.

Even if I hadn't coughed for a minute straight, I would've turned as red as I had now. "It was not that crazy. But yeah, it was good. Didn't hurt a lot. Like a pinch and a burn," I said, and without thinking too much, I continued whispering, "And I guess, the more we did it, the better it felt."

Her eyes shone in delight. She pushed my shoulder with hers and waggled her eyebrows. "How many times did it take to get better?"

"Shut up. This is it for the topic of discussion."

She pouted, and said, "But I had so many more questions. About size. Positions. Duration. Protection. How will I know what to expect from my future husband? And what if my future husband is a virgin? I'll be doomed, Meera."

Before I had to get into that, the bell rang loudly, indicating the end of recess. I quickly got up, grabbed my purse and books, and said, "We'll discuss it when you actually find someone to marry. Now bye."

I rushed out of the staff room without waiting for a response. On my way to the classroom, I realized what Kriti had done. Even for a few brief minutes, she helped me forget the impending heartbreak of my life. Because the moment I finished with my class, that dull ache in my heart returned. The painful stab was a ticking time bomb.

I wish I could believe Luke when he said he would make us happen, but he was a dreamer. He went after things he wanted, and he got them. I didn't have the privilege to go after anything, let alone get it.

SINCE MAA HAD ALREADY FIGURED out that something was going on between me and Luke, I found every excuse to go upstairs and talk to him. I prepared tons of dry snacks to send him off with, in the hopes that he'd remember me at least till the snacks lasted. And now that she knew about us, I couldn't even claim that it was a mosquito bite when she saw the hickey on my neck. She just shook her head at my poor attempt at hiding it under my dupatta.

"Whatever is going on between you and him, you have to be careful," she'd said.

I had just nodded and proceeded to cook a box full of dry puris, sev, and chakri. The more food he'll have, the longer it will last. And the longer he'll remember me. It hurt to think that he might eventually forget about me. But for the entire week, I cooked in the afternoon and clung to him at night in his bedroom.

Saturday came in a blink. Luke left tomorrow.

I parked my Activa in our front yard and rushed into the house. Hari trailed behind me, complaining about carrying his heavy school bag by himself. I ran back, grabbed it from him, and ran inside. Maa looked up from her bed at me, understood what had me frantic, and grumbled something under her breath.

Quickly, I changed into my comfortable salwar kameez and reheated lunch for everyone. My roti-making speed was unparalleled as I shouted at Hari to freshen up and get Luke. Today was our last lunch together. My hands shook as I rolled the rotis. My heart beat so fast, the world blurred around me. Or maybe it was the tears that dropped on the roti. I threw away that roti, wiped the tears on my shoulder, and rolled another one.

Soon, we sat in the living room, quietly eating the mediocre lunch like every day, pretending as if this wasn't the last day. I couldn't meet his eyes even when I felt them, prodding and poking, warm and loving.

I looked at Hari. He still didn't know. I had to inform him that Luke was leaving. He needed to say goodbye. Be prepared for his absence in the house. My heart already ached at the thought of what was coming.

Luke and Hari went upstairs to his room. To spend as much time as I could with Luke, I'd resorted to getting Hari to do his homework in Luke's room, where we spent the evening together. Luke working on his computer, Hari doing his homework, and me checking my students' homework. It felt cozy. A dream. A dream soon to be shattered.

I cleaned up the living room, and Maa followed me into the

kitchen. "Leave all the dirty dishes. I'll clean everything up. You go up. Take all the containers upstairs and help him pack those."

I *always* did the dishes and cleaned up the kitchen after lunch. My hands shook at the thought of spending my last afternoon with Luke. My body felt too tight—as if I'd break from one little touch. I clutched the countertop, steeling myself to face Luke. A soft hand squeezed my shoulder. "Everything will be okay, *beta*. You've handled far worse pains."

I squeezed her hand. My lips twisted into a sob. I bit my lip, trying not to let it out. "Why do people keep leaving me?"

A tear tracked down my cheek.

Maa had no answer. She kept rubbing my back while I collected myself. I didn't wait for her answer as I washed my face, wiped it with the edge of my dupatta, and grabbed the containers of snacks. I climbed the stairs and heard the murmurs coming from Luke's bedroom.

I took a deep breath, pasted a smile on my face, and stepped in the bedroom.

I joined Hari, who already sat on the bed to do his homework. Luke moved from the cupboard to an open suitcase laid out on the desk, packing things haphazardly. His awful packing almost made me get up and pack for him, but it went completely against what I actually wanted to do, which was return everything he was packing and keep him with me. I stubbornly stayed put.

Hari had a little frown on his face as he watched Luke. Luke met my eyes over Hari's head, narrowed his eyes, and jerked his face toward Hari, telling me to inform him. I glared at him, telling him to break Hari's heart himself. His eyes screamed helplessness at me. I let out a breath. Hari wouldn't know so much English. I patted the bed at him, asking him to sit with us. His shoulders dropped, he exhaled, as if steeling himself for the pain, and sat at the edge of the bed.

Hari, clearly picking up the vibe, looked back and forth between us. He frowned and turned to me. "Is Luke bhai going somewhere?" he asked in Gujarati.

I gave him a small smile, and rubbed his ear. "So, uh. Luke bhai is going home."

He looked at Luke, who sat absolutely still, who smiled at Hari in reassurance. Hari turned back to me, and said, "But he lives here."

"Only for a little while. He has to go back to America. That's his home."

My voice wobbled as I said that, my heart rebelling at every word out of my mouth.

"When will he come back?" he asked.

And I couldn't help but look at Luke. "He's asking when you will come back." My voice broke at the last few words.

Luke clutched my foot by his hip. His eyes glistened. He turned his gaze away from me and looked at Hari. His warm brown eyes burned with resolve. "Little Hari. I will come back in May. Do you have summer vacation in May?"

He nodded quickly. In the two months that Luke stayed with us, Hari had started picking up English better. He could understand what Luke said even though he still struggled to speak in English. He could string up a few words together, but he couldn't have an entire conversation. Hari got up on the bed, stepped over his homework, and sat right across Luke. He looked at Luke, eyes full of hope, and asked, "You promise?"

And I could feel the pain in Luke's heart. The agony of leaving us behind. His voice was gruff and shaky when he answered, "I promise."

Hari smiled, relieved to hear the answer, and returned to his spot and got back to his homework. I expected tears and tantrums, but nothing like that came from Hari. Luke looked at me, his voice unwavering, and repeated, "I promise."

I wished I could believe him as easily as Hari did.

Luke

Hari and Meera returned to their respective work on my bed as I continued packing. My packing style was proof of how much I despised leaving Meera. Every clothing item I packed was a sharp sting of a needle. The salt on the wound was how easily Hari accepted my leaving. I loved the little man. And fuck, I was gonna miss him. His adorable scowls—just like his sister—his constant murmurs while he worked, his delight at spending time in an air-conditioned room. I would miss it all. And it hurt a little that Hari was so chill about me leaving. I knew I was an asshole for wanting the little kid to feel a little hurt, but fuck, I at least hoped for a hug.

I turned to the seven steel and plastic containers that Meera had stacked on the desk. Warmth bloomed in my stomach at the thought of carrying a part of her with me. I would make them last as long as possible. And then I'll ask her to send me more.

Yes, I would make our long distance work. Just till May. Until I graduate.

Then we'll have time to figure everything out. I wasn't going to let her push me away. She thought I would forget all about her. She was crazy. She was all I saw, all I thought about, and nobody— not even her— had the right to trivialize my feelings.

I heard a murmur behind me.

"Luke? Everything all right?" Meera asked from the bed.

I turned to find the brother and sister looking at me with an identical expression of confusion, head tilted sideways, two little frown lines between their eyes. I almost chuckled at the cuteness.

"Yeah. Everything's fine. Why?"

Meera frowned, and said, "You looked really angry as you were stuffing the clothes in your bag."

I looked down at my hand and found them tightly clutching one of my T-shirts. I instantly rolled it into a ball and dropped it in the bag.

Hari said something to Meera, and she murmured something back.

Meera cleared her throat. When I looked back at her, her eyes were slightly teary but affectionate. "Hari was wondering if you would want to play cricket with him since it's your last day."

Little Hari *cared*. And my heart thumped and pounded and rebelled and just melted. My chest expanded with emotions, and I turned away and pretended to pack as I let the tears fall. One heartbeat. Two heartbeats. Three heartbeats. I breathed out the pain, the longing, the overwhelming affection for this little boy who'd been through so much.

I wiped away my cheeks with the front of my T-shirt and turned to face him with a wide smile. "Of course, I'll play. Let's go now."

A bright smile came over Hari's face as he climbed on the bed and jumped toward me. I quickly caught him and carried him downstairs like a football while he clutched my T-shirt and shrieked with laughter. Meera's laughter followed us as she ran behind us.

And we played. One hour turned into two. Two turned to three and a half. No matter what Meera said to Hari, he refused to let us stop playing and get back in the house. Dusk turned to dark, and I stopped seeing the ball he threw at me. I missed every shot, and still, he ran to get the ball, begging me not to go back inside the house. I obediently stood there as his tiny voice and stubborn little gestures broke my heart.

It was after eight when Meera shouted at both of us. With him shouting and screaming, I picked him up in my arms and told him we'd eat together and he could spend some time in my room. That seemed to calm him down. He hadn't even been in my room for ten minutes when he fell asleep. I gently patted his back, imprinting this moment in my mind. I softly pressed a kiss on his forehead and lay down beside him.

That was when I noticed Meera. She stood at the door, a jug of water in her hand, her hair pulled into a bun on top, small curls clinging to her neck. Her eyes were red-rimmed, tired, and sad. She stepped in, placed the jug on my desk, sat on the other side of Hari, and kissed his forehead.

"I'll take him downstairs," she said.

She was about to wake him up, but I stopped her. I got up and carried the little guy downstairs. He didn't even move when I placed him beside his mom.

Tonight was my last night in this room. In this house. With Meera.

Three months of my life.

They were the longest three months of my life, yet they flew by. Three months that shook up my normal, monotonous life and plunged me into a whirlwind of emotions. Happiness. Tragedy. Affection. Hurt. Laughter. Love. And *purpose*. Purpose to make my relationship work.

When I returned to the room, I closed and locked the door behind me. Meera had plugged in her cassette player beside the bed. She stretched her hand toward me, and when I clutched it, she pulled me toward her. I climbed on top of her, burying my face in her neck.

We stayed together, arms around each other, my hands traveling over her curves as I nuzzled against her neck, her chest. I memorized her smell, her silky soft skin, and the rhythm of her heartbeat. Our silent touches stretched for minutes. Neither of us had any words. I was not going to lose this.

"This is not a goodbye, Meera."

She stiffened. "I can't expect you to put your life on hold for me."

"I'm not. I'm going back. Finishing up my studies. Getting my degree. That does not mean we can't be together along the way."

"What if you find someone in your own city?" she asked. She didn't meet my eyes. Instead, she played with my T-shirt.

"Give me some credit, Meera. Just because I'm away from you doesn't mean I'll stop wanting you. You will have to trust me."

I held her waist, turned my head so I could lock my gaze on hers, and moved my hips between her legs so not an inch separated our bodies. She gasped but held me. I met her eyes and said, "I don't want anyone else. Not now. Not later. Will you want someone else once I'm gone?"

She shook her head, tears slipping down her cheeks.

I wiped them with my thumb, my voice hoarse when I spoke, "Then why would you think I'd move on?"

"I'm scared," she whispered.

I kissed her forehead, and she held me there. "Me too," I murmured.

She rubbed her cheek against my neck. She breathed in deep, and said, "Yes."

"Yes what?"

"Yes, let's make it work."

Hope blossomed in my chest, a relief so sharp, I couldn't hold myself up anymore, and dropped on Meera. She let out an *oomph* and chuckled.

I rolled off her and pulled her in my arms again. "You'll see. We'll talk every day. Message each other. Write emails. Send each other letters. Whatever it takes. We'll do it. And in nine months, I'll come back, and we'll figure everything out."

"Can you promise me something?"

"Anything."

She looked at me, her eyes unflinching, and said, "Promise me that you won't stay with me out of any guilt or obligation."

Anger and love fought within me. What would I have to do to convince her that I wasn't leaving her? I pulled her closer to me, and said, "I promise you. But that's never going to happen."

"It could. And I won't blame you," she said.

I said, "It won't. Because I love you."

A tear slid down her cheek. Again.

I wiped it with my thumb. Again.

She shook her head over and over again. "I wish you didn't," she choked out.

I huffed. "Don't lie."

She nodded, now crying, and said, "It would be so much easier not to love you. It wouldn't hurt so much when you leave."

My heart pounded at her words. I wanted to hear it. Wanted to hear the words. "So you do? Love me?"

She snorted, and a wet chuckle escaped her lips. "Yes, I love you, Luke. So much."

One moment, I was looking at her mouth, her lips telling me she loved me.

In the next, I had captured her lips in mine.

I tasted her love for me, so sweet, so full of want and need. I poured all my love into her, pulling her closer, clutching her tighter. She moaned in my mouth, and I brushed my hips against her. I groaned when she rubbed herself against me. I removed her T-shirt, and she pushed down my sweatpants and boxers. By the time I'd grabbed the condom from the nightstand and rolled it on, she had removed all her clothes.

She lay there naked, her long, curly hair spread across the pillow, her slight curves mine to explore, her warm, brown skin soft and blushing. My pale hands on her thigh were a stark reminder of the different worlds we came from, and how little that mattered.

I moved between her legs and brushed my thick length against her clit. She gasped and rose on her elbows. She grabbed the back of my neck and pulled me into a biting, blistering kiss.

I growled into her mouth and kissed her deeper. I sucked her neck, and she marked my chest, her lips and teeth leaving behind her presence.

I pushed inside her, and I was home.

Her arms clutched me tight as if never wanting me to leave. I pushed deeper into her, memorizing her touch, the way she clamped down on me, and the way her neck arched against my lips as I pounded into her. She pleaded for more, and I gave her my all. My wants. My need. My love. My desperate need to make her believe in us.

She kissed me. She loved me. She cried for me. She whispered promises of faith and hope in my ear. She moved under me, with me, in harmony with my heart.

I burrowed deeper into her, my body throbbing with my impending release but refusing to give in to it, never wanting to stop. I grabbed her hips and hiked her leg higher, climbing deeper into her, sucking furiously at the top of her breasts.

She clutched my hair and pulled me tighter, her keening whimpers making me want to burrow deeper into her.

The moment I thrust harder into her, she tightened and clamped down on me, her body arching off, her neck thrown back as she whispered my name over and over again. I clutched her thigh tighter, pushed it into her chest, and moved into her faster, chasing after her. Burning hot pleasure rushed down my spine, my balls tightened, and my release burst out of me as I saw stars and my vision blanked out. I clutched Meera in my arms, still staying inside her for as long as my body allowed.

We lay there. Still. Panting. Breathing in each other's scent. Memorizing the lines of our bodies. The feel of our skin together.

My gaze caught on the cassette player on the nightstand on her side of the bed.

I played with a strand of her hair, and asked, "Play me a song?"

I met her eyes and jerked my face toward the cassette player. When she turned and saw what I was referring to, she snuggled closer in my arms. "It won't be happy," she said.

"Play me your feelings," I said.

She rolled her naked body toward the cassette player, my cock slipping out from her. We both groaned at the loss, and slowly, she ruffled through her cassettes in her pouch, and pulled out a cassette. She put it in the player and after a few fast-forwards, she turned to me with a sad smile and asked, "You sure?"

When I nodded, she pressed play.

She got back in my arms, and I pulled the blanket over us. "The song is 'Lag Jaa Gale' which means *hold me in your arms*," she said.

A woman began singing, her voice hypnotic, the melody sharp.

Meera held me closer, and translated,

> "Hold me in your arms for who knows if we'll get
> this beautiful night again,
> Maybe in this life, we may or may not meet
> again."

The slow tunes between the verses were hauntingly beautiful, like a prelude to an everlasting separation. Like a final goodbye.

She continued.

> "Destiny has granted us this time,
> See me up close, to your heart's content,

> Who knows if destiny will grant you another
> chance."

I didn't look away from her. The song, the words, the melody tugged at my heartstrings. They cut me, hurt me, and brought tears to my eyes.

She tucked herself closer, her sniffles loud near my ear. Still, she continued,

> "Come closer to me, as I won't come to you again
> and again, hold me closer and let's cry a
> thousand tears, who knows if destiny will
> allow us these tears of love again, in this
> lifetime."

And we did just that.

She didn't translate any further songs.

She'd already poured her heart out. She cried her fears. I cried because she cried.

All night, I looked at her. I caressed her. I memorized every little detail about her. Her curly hair, the mole on her neck, the feel of her satiny skin against mine, the way her body held mine.

We didn't sleep, not wanting to miss out on a single moment.

She held my face and kissed my eyes, my nose, my forehead, my cheek.

She told me *I love you* over and over and over again, imprinting the echoes of those words on my skin and branding them on my heart.

We kissed and kissed, even when our lips bruised, even when we ran out of breath, even when we got aroused again, and even when I slipped inside her, and we shuddered with pleasure against each other.

I held her, a piece of my heart, my life, my future, in my arms, and watched the early light of dawn falling on her bare shoulders.

And I kissed her once more, memorizing how she looked in the early morning light, in my bed, in my arms, one last time.

22

Song: Abhi Naa Jao Chhod Kar
   - Asha Bhosle, Mohammed Rafi

Meera

We were having chai on the terrace when we saw a car approaching. Before I could prepare myself, Aakar and Abhi stepped out of the car. Luke stiffened beside me, his hand tightening on my lower back.

"This is not the end," he said, his lips near my ear.

I nodded, clutching his wrist. "I know."

Under different circumstances, I would've enjoyed their presence and jokes.

Today, they carried away all the things Luke had brought into my life, one piece at a time.

When the last box was carried out, Luke stayed in the now-empty bedroom. I watched them carry everything out. I watched Hari silently helping them. I couldn't move an inch. For the life of me, I couldn't help them carry out a single thing when all I wanted was to keep him locked up with me.

Once Abhi and Aakar went downstairs to pack everything in the car, I stepped into the bedroom and locked it behind me. Luke sat on the bed, staring at the ground. His eyes met mine with a wild sort of grief and need swirling in them. I stepped forward, between his legs, and held him. He clutched my hips, and brought me closer, closer, closer until I sat on his lap.

Our mouths met, our hands moving wildly, our breaths ragged, our chest heaving. His eyes were red when he pulled off my top, and tears slipped down my cheeks as I pushed open his jeans and pulled him out.

He was frantic as he rolled on a condom, and I pulled my panties aside. He grabbed my waist and pushed inside me. He latched onto my neck, his voice shaking as he muttered into my skin, "Fuck, Meera. I'm going to miss you so much," and he pressed his lips to mine. Once. Twice. He chanted over my lips *I love you, I love you* as his hips pounded into mine in a frenzy.

I clutched his shirt, moving my hips, tightening around his cock, holding him in.

I held his face, memorized the way he looked at me, and said, "I love you too. So much."

He pushed me down harder, his mouth swallowing my whimpers. He clutched my throat and thrust into me harder. "Promise me," he said with an especially hard thrust, "Promise me you'll always reply to my messages. You won't forget me. You won't push me away."

"I won't. I promise," I said, each word coming out as a sharp cry against his frantic thrusts. I didn't ask him to promise me back. I could never. But I would always write him back. I would always remember him. And for the life of me, I didn't have the strength to push him away.

He grabbed my waist with one hand and clutched my hair in a possessive grip, forcing me to meet his eyes. "You're mine, Meera. Today. Tomorrow. With an ocean separating us. I don't give a fuck," he uttered every sentence with a hard thrust.

I whimpered as he moved inside me, blinding pleasure racing through my body. "Yours. All yours," I said through clenched teeth, trying my hardest to not make any sound.

He pulled me down harder on his cock, grinding into me. "And don't you ever fucking give up on us. You understand, baby?"

I cried out at the pleasure coursing through my body as pain of losing him caused riot in my heart. Yet, I grabbed the back of his neck, and gritted out, "Yes. Yes. Yes."

His lips stretched in a feral grin, his eyes burning with satisfaction. "Good. Now come on my cock."

He rubbed my clit, his hand shaking with need and desperation. I bore down on him and came with a keening cry, biting his neck, squeezing around him, my body shaking with pleasure and pain racing through my heart.

He grabbed my hair, turned my face and pressed his lips to mine, his tongue invading my mouth for the last time as he groaned his pleasure in frantic jerks inside me.

I hugged him to my chest as he clutched me to him like his life depended on it.

I placed a kiss on his throat, licking and soothing the dark red patch that he wouldn't be able to hide for a while.

A loud honk outside had us flinching. He kissed me once more. I poured all my love into that kiss. One last time. For now.

He got up, and we righted ourselves.

He looked around the empty room.

Looked at me.

A tear slid down his cheek that he quickly wiped away.

He didn't look away as he opened the door.

I climbed down the stairs right behind him.

I watched him say goodbye to Maa using the translation app on his phone.

I couldn't stop the tears when Hari cried in his arms, clutching his neck, unwilling to let go.

I watched Luke tear up when he had to ask me to get Hari because he couldn't put him down.

He kept repeating *I'll be back soon, Hari, I promise I'll be back.*

I pulled off Hari's arms from around Luke. And with one last look at me, one moment where I heard my heart gallop and rebel and shatter, he turned around and left.

I followed him outside the house.

I stood back as he got in the passenger side of the car.

I watched the car as it left until I couldn't see it anymore.

23

Luke

I watched her from the side-view mirror of the car as we drove away.

For some inexplicable reason, my eyes stuck on the small text written at the bottom of the mirror. *Objects in the mirror are closer than they appear.*

A wet chuckle escaped my mouth. *Not close enough.*

I watched Hari tightly clutching Meera's hand as they watched us leaving.

I watched them until they were a speck of dust in the mirror. I watched them because I knew they were closer than they appeared.

I watched them until Aakar took a turn on the road, and they disappeared.

Only then did I allow the next tear to fall.

24

Song: *Wada Karo Nahi Chhodoge Tum Mera Saath*
  - Lata Mangeshkar, Kishore Kumar

Meera

Seven days down, 254 to go

Late nights were the most difficult. Listening to songs like I used to before Luke came along was barely tolerable. He flew home to New York two days ago. In the past seven days, we'd tried to keep messaging each other as much as we could. But the past two days had been the most difficult. His nights were my school time, his morning classes were when I had free.

This would be a challenge.

I slept on my bed, what used to be Luke's bed, and breathed in the smell of the pillow. The distinct, musky scent of Luke still lingered in the fabric, bringing me comfort tinged with an ache that refused to stop. It was ten o'clock in the night, and I'd just sent him a Whatsapp message.

Me: Hi...

He had sent me his class schedule last night and I had placed two clocks on my side table. One showed me Indian time, and another showed me Luke's time. A few minutes passed as I stared at the phone. I thought he would be free during his lunchtime.

I stared at the phone as the minutes ticked by. One minute. Two minutes. Five minutes.

Nothing.

It'd only been seven days, and we had to spend more than seven months apart.

I scrolled through the contacts in my phone and came across the one I hadn't used in a while, which I should have.

Surbhi didi would be awake right now. She usually worked on the Life for Widows Organization at night. I pressed the call button and prayed she would pick up. After four rings, the call connected.

"Meera?" she said. No hello, no how are you.

"Surbhi didi, how are you?"

"I am good. The usual. You tell me. How are you doing? How is your friend, Luke?"

I breathed out the pain that punched me in the chest at hearing his name, my hand automatically moving over the bedsheet— the one he had slept on— and I said, "I'm good. Luke is back in America. I...uh... I was wondering if you had any work I could help you with."

"Oh, Meera. Sure. How about you come to my place tomorrow evening? I can show you the forms and files I need packaged for a few families, a few letters and emails I need to write for banks and municipalities," she said.

I nodded even though she couldn't see it, and answered, "Sounds good. I...um...need to stay a little more busy."

"I understand. You know I'm here for you, right? Our entire community is."

"I do. Should I bring anything?"

After a pause, she said, "Umm... do you have some books? Fiction? Or Hari's old books? We have a few families where I think women would benefit from learning how to read and write. If not the women, the books could help their kids too."

"Sure. I haven't thrown away his books in the past few years. I'll get those."

"Great. Thank you, Meera. See you tomorrow."

"Bye, Surbhi didi."

And I hung up to find a notification.

Luke: Hey baby!! :-*

A stupid grin came over my face. Every thought flew out of my head at seeing those two words. With every beat of my heart, my mind screamed *Luke, Luke, Luke!*

Me: What are you doing?

Luke: (photo attached)

I opened it to find him holding a forkful of salad raised to his open mouth, his eyes twinkling with joy. A lot of people were in his background, so maybe he was in a restaurant? He looked so handsome; his T-shirt clung to his body, highlighting his toned arms. I zoomed in and out of the photo, trying to look at every inch of him.

Me: :-*

I clicked a selfie of me sleeping on his bed, tried not to have an awkward smile, and sent it to Luke before I chickened out.

> Luke: :-* :-* :-* :-* :-* :-* :-* *heart eyes* *heart eyes* *heart eyes*

And I giggled. He could make me blush even from across the ocean.

I played a love song on my cassette player and recorded a snippet and sent him the small recording along with the YouTube link of the song.

> Luke: I'll listen to it as soon as I'm done with my classes. Thanks, baby. :-*

> Me: I'm sleeping. You carry on. Good night, Luke.

> Luke: I miss you.

My heart melted at those three little words. Three words, yet so true. So powerful.

> Me: I miss you too

> Luke: I love you, Meera. Just as much as I did yesterday. A week ago. If not more. Sweet dreams, baby.

And that was what I did. I slept, clutching my phone in hand, looking at Luke's face, wishing he was here, loving him even harder.

THE NEXT DAY, Hari and I talked to Luke on a video call after returning home from school. It was late at night for Luke, but he had stayed up waiting for us. It felt good to see his face, and Hari's excitement had brought a smile to our faces.

After the call, Kriti soon arrived with a big box full of books and clothes. I had mentioned to her that I was going to Surbhi didi's place in the evening, and she'd enthusiastically offered to bring some stuff for me.

At around four in the afternoon, I left for Surbhi didi's place on my Activa with Kriti sitting behind me and the box full of books and clothes placed on the footrest in the front. Since we didn't know when we would return, she decided to accompany me. We reached our destination in about half an hour and found the main gate open.

Two women sat in the front yard talking, and a kid I hadn't seen before played with Surbhi didi's son, Jay. I parked my Activa, and Kriti grabbed the box.

"Do you know them?" asked Kriti, as we walked toward the main door of the house.

The ladies stopped talking and stared at us, their gazes worried. I smiled at them to put them at ease. A slight tension left their stiff shoulders, and I rang the bell. In a few seconds, the door opened, and a slightly frazzled Surbhi didi stood in front of us.

I hugged her, and asked, "How are you? Everything all right?"

She squeezed me tighter, and murmured, "I'll tell you inside."

I looked at Kriti and shrugged my shoulders. Surbhi didi led us to her living room, which was slightly bigger than mine. A three-seat sofa and two chairs were arranged with a center table. A small TV unit right across the sofa had shelves of medals and trophies, photographs, and a small idol of Lord Shiva.

Kriti placed the box on the chair adjacent to her, and we sat on the sofa. Surbhi didi got us some water from the kitchen and sat on the chair adjacent to me.

Once we had some water, she said, "You might have noticed the people outside. They're from the neighboring village, Shitalanagar. Their husbands committed suicide last year. They had been staying with their in-laws for the past year, but their farms didn't reap many crops. So not much profit. Not enough to sustain every member of the family. Three weeks ago, their in-laws threw them out of the house with two hundred rupees. No clothes, no books, none of their personal stuff. They used their money to take an auto rickshaw here. That's where we're at."

My heart hurt for those women. For the family who had lost their sons and had no money to sustain the people left behind. For Surbhi didi, who worked tirelessly to help people like them, like me. That was why she requested the books and the clothes.

I clutched Surbhi didi's hands, and asked, "What's the plan?"

She smiled softly, relief shining in her eyes. "Well, they don't have any identification proof. We need to file the paperwork for them to get their Aadhar card. Without that, they don't get any government benefits and can't open a bank account. We need to start on that. I need to find some jobs for them. Anything will do. Cooking, cleaning. And we need to get their kid admission to school in our village."

I can take up most of this work. I turned to Kriti, and asked, "Do you think we can ask school administration if they need someone to clean the school compound or have any similar positions open?"

She nodded. "Yes, we should definitely ask. We can also talk about the little kid who needs admission. The term has just begun, so maybe we can convince the school to admit him."

Hope filled Surbhi didi's eyes. "Thank you so much, Meera. You too, Kriti. This really takes a lot of burden off my shoulders."

I rubbed her arm in comfort and asked in a low voice so the women outside couldn't hear, "Have they been living with you for three weeks? Do you need any funds for groceries and everything? Do we need to get beds or pillows?"

She smiled in gratitude and shook her head. "Thanks to your lovely American friend Luke, we have what we need."

Warmth and love infused my heart. Even here, even after going back, pieces of his heart are still here. His generous, caring, wonderful heart. How could I ever stop loving him?

"I'm glad," I whispered, as Kriti bumped her shoulder with mine.

Kriti turned to look at Surbhi didi, and said, "Is there any other way we can help? To be honest, I'm a little surprised it's the first time women have shown up at your place for help."

A wet chuckle escaped Surbhi didi, and she turned her gaze away from us. "It's not the first time. I just could never afford to help them before. I used to give them some money and ask other organizations to help them out."

My heart dropped at those words. I squeezed her knee, in support, in comfort. She shook her head and wiped the tear that had slid down her cheek. "I'm just glad that I can finally help a little. It's just that this house is small. And every time someone comes to my place for a meet or questions, they see them here, and they think I can provide for others too. I can probably keep one or two more women in my house but what happens after that? The more the people who know about them, the more women who will show up."

"Maybe we all can do something," I said, even though I had no clue what that would be.

"What if we rent a house for the women and children?" Kriti asked.

Surbhi didi shook her head. "That would be too expensive. It is more affordable for me to help them out when they're staying here. If we rent a new house, we would need to pay all sorts of bills and provide money to run the house. I have a significant amount saved up, but I can't do all of that without thinking of the future."

Maybe I should talk to Luke and see if he has any ideas. What if he was really busy with work? Should I disturb him with village problems? What if me sharing compelled him to send more money? As nice as that would be, he didn't owe the village people anything.

What if he felt burdened by my problems? What if he just wanted to focus on our relationship?

What if he felt forced to help the village?

No. I couldn't do that to him. We barely had time to talk. I couldn't add more things to worry about for him. I had to wait and see how our relationship progressed.

For the next two hours, the three of us talked. Gayatri, one of the women who had started staying with Surbhi didi, prepared chai for all of us. Kriti and I talked to the ladies about their skills, what they were willing to work on, and what they needed. Considering they had grown up on a farm and married a farmer, all they knew was farming. But farming itself gave a broad array of work experience, and Kriti assured them that she would find something for them.

Soon, we were on our way back home, and later that night, I went to bed, texted Luke, and waited. I was already asleep, looking at his pictures from our trip, before I got any reply from him.

~

Luke

243 days to go

I woke up to three missed calls and ten new messages from Meera. Fuck. I quickly called her back, but nothing. She must be busy. I kept the phone with me as I freshened up and went to the kitchen to get the coffee started.

I sat at the breakfast bar, scrolling through the messages I'd exchanged with Meera as I waited for the coffee to brew. Sunday was my least busy day of the week. I didn't need to go to the studio or any classes. I knew that the last year of my course would be busy and tough, but I had no idea it would kick my ass. For the first week itself, the faculty had been upon us with one assignment after another. Models, papers, designs, reports, group discussion. There seemed to be no end.

I already had a few notifications and emails from our group discussion last evening, but I wasn't checking them for at least a few hours. I filled a full cup of my black coffee and added a pack of sugar. I had just taken a sip when Sam and Akira walked out of their room. Even though October had just begun, she was already in a sweater, and it had barely started to cool down. On the other hand, Sam was in his usual sweats and T-shirt, cleaning his glasses.

"We smell coffee," Akira mumbled.

She grabbed two mugs, poured plain black in one, and added a dollop of half and half and three packets of sugar to another. The two of them sat across each other at the dining table and looked at me pointedly.

"What?" I grumbled.

Sam frowned, and asked, "Have something to share?"

"Nope."

I hadn't shared anything about Meera and myself with them. I just couldn't. It was too painful, and they looked too happy—too *together*—when Meera and I weren't.

"How's Meera?"

My finger hovered over her picture on my phone. I looked up at Akira, who'd asked the question—because of course she would.

"She's good," I said.

Akira pursed her lips, and said, "Oh come on, Luke. Tell us what's wrong. It's been two weeks, and you don't talk. You don't laugh. You just work and work. This is the first time we've seen you drinking coffee in the kitchen."

And how I regretted it.

Sam placed his hand on Akira's shoulder, calming her down. He looked at me, and said, "When Akira and I had problems, you were there for us. Let us be there for you, man."

They, too, had been separated for a while. For a month. And they had to fight Akira's parents, unlike Meera and I. We had no one to fight to be together except circumstances.

I let out a sigh, got up from the breakfast stool, refilled my cup of coffee, and took a seat at the table. They both simply kept staring at me as I rubbed my head, trying to gather words.

How do you explain to someone how you fell in love?

"I'm in love with Meera," I said. Plain and simple. Truth.

Akira shrieked and hugged me. "Tell me everything. Does she love you too? How did you fall in love? When did it happen? Who said the words first? Oh my God. Sam, didn't Luke tell you that he would never fall in love with an Indian woman?"

I glared at him. "You told her I said that?"

Sam's eyes twinkled, and he said, "Shut up. I tell her everything. You're free to tell Meera whatever you want."

"Yeah, well, I already did," I muttered.

Akira laughed, squeezed my hand, and said, "You have to tell us everything."

And so I did. For the next hour, I recalled the little moments when I fell for Meera. The connection we shared. The grief that brought us together. The midnight conversations that transported us to a world of our own. Her unbending loyalty to her family, her warmth for her brother, her laughs for me. I talked about the times when I got a glimpse into her world, got to *be* there for her, and the joy I got when she finally started to rely on me a little. Trust me a little more. And damn the world if I would let that go.

I told them how we decided to be in a long distance relationship, how I was going back to the village next May to figure everything out.

By the time I was done, we'd emptied the full pot of coffee, Akira was huddled closer to Sam, and Sam had a big smile on his face.

"I'm so happy for you. How are you handling the long distance?"

"It's fucking brutal. It's like we can't seem to meet at one time. It's missed calls after missed calls. And my course schedule doesn't help either."

"That's rough. I remember when Akira had gone back to India for a month. It's like we had schedule appointments to talk in peace for fifteen fucking minutes."

I glared at him. One month.

Akira poked him in his chest with her elbow and gave him a glare too.

Sam flinched in apology. "I didn't mean that our situation is the same, you guys. I just meant I understood the communication problem. And just one month was frustrating, you have what, eight more months? Fuck."

"Tell me about it."

Akira squeezed my hand, and asked, "What's the plan moving ahead?"

I shrugged. I didn't have any answer. "I have no clue. I wish I could tell you that everything would be a breeze for the next few months, and then I'll bring Meera to America, and that would be it."

"But that wouldn't happen," Akira said.

"I wish. *She* could come if I marry her, but she would never leave her mother and brother behind. I wouldn't want her to. And how do I move to her village? What would I do with my life? People don't need an architect in a village. I just don't know what to do."

"Have you guys talked about it?" Sam asked. He was a guy who needed plans, organization, and a rule book to follow.

"To be honest, our first step is to get through the long distance part. Once I graduate, I'll go back to Laxminagar, and we'll go from there. Maybe we'll move to Canada. It's a good country. They'll allow everyone to move, right?"

"Do you even want to move to Canada?" Sam asked, again with the tough questions.

"I don't know, man. I don't even know if Meera would want to go to Canada. Leave her village, her country behind. I told you, we haven't talked about this. We're just trying our best to find each other on a video call once or twice a week."

Akira looked at Sam, her eyes narrow slits as she said, "They'll figure it out. You need to stop asking these questions."

"I'm just trying to help," he mumbled and looked at me apologetically.

I was about to respond when my phone rang. Loudly. I had kept it on full volume. I didn't want to miss Meera's call, at least not on a weekend.

I picked up the video call, quickly got up from the chair and ran to my bedroom, all the while shouting to Sam and Akira, "See you later."

I locked the door behind me and jumped on my bed.

And there she was. Dark brown eyes shining at me, her brown skin so smooth. I wanted to kiss it. Rub my cheek against hers. Her hair, her beautiful curls, were spread across the pillow— the same pillow I'd used when I lived in her room— and all I wanted was to clutch them in my fist and devour her. Just looking at her turned me on.

"Meera, Meera. How I miss you, darling."

A smile lit up her eyes. The video pixelated a little, but I remembered. I felt her smile inside me. "I miss you too, Luke. So much."

"How's Hari and your mother?"

"Everyone's good. Hari was asking about you. I'll try to call a little earlier someday so you can talk."

"That'd be nice. How are you doing? Anything new?"

She paused, her eyes tightening, but she said, "It's the same at work. But I started helping out Surbhi didi a little more than before. Remember Surbhi didi?"

She turned on her side, and some of her hair came over her shoulder. I mirrored her position on my bed so it felt like we were facing each other and not seven thousand miles apart. I focused back on the conversation.

"Yes, I remember Surbhi. Of course, I do. And that's great, baby. What are you helping out with? Can I help with something?"

Her eyes softened, and she looked at me like she wanted to kiss me. She slowly shook her head, and muttered, "I'm just helping with paperwork and stuff. Kriti and I donated a few old books and clothes." She looked down, and said softly, "I needed to stay busy, you know."

A sharp pang hit my chest. "I know."

"I wish I could hold your hand," she said.

"I wish I could do so much more than that."

She gasped. Her blush deepened. "I'd like that."

God, she killed me. I was so turned on.

"You're aroused, aren't you?" she asked. Her soothing voice was a fuel to the fire. Her eyes brimmed with heat and passion, her breath heavy and loud in my ears. She held her hair, trying to keep them off her face, and it just turned me hotter.

I nodded. My voice stuck in my throat.

"Your cheeks go all red. And your light brown eyes turn so much darker. And you bite your lip like that."

I couldn't stop the groan. "Meera, you're killing me. You

need to stop this line of conversation or I'll have to take matters into my own hand."

Her breath turned faster. "Do it. Take *matters* into your own hand. But don't show me. I've heard it's not safe, and the government always monitors everything."

I pulled down my sweatpants and did just that. Pleasure rocketed in my veins. "Oh God. I love you."

"I love you too. I really like seeing you like this," she said, her eyes stuck on my face, her lips slightly parted. Her eyes were dark with lust.

"Like what? And do you want to join in too?"

She shifted around, and she was on her back again. "I'm touching myself," she whispered. It took me all the strength in the world not to spill right then. I needed us together like this. Needed more time with her like this.

"You were saying, Meera? What do you like about seeing me like this?"

Her words turned me on. Her mind, her own arousal for me, her feelings for me, all of it burned me hotter and made me crazy. Desperate.

"This. The way you look at me. So passionate. Your eyes burn me. Like you want to tear off my clothes and push inside me."

"I do. Fuck, I do. So much. So. Much." My hand moved, and my hips thrust in my fist with every word that I uttered.

"Yes. I love that *I* make you feel like that."

"You do, baby. This. God, I don't need anything else. Just this. Just you. Fuck." My hips moved off the bed, my hands tight around my arousal, my blood hot under my skin. I was so close.

"Luke. Luke, I'm close. I'm so wet."

I could see her shoulder moving, and I was dying to touch her. Feel her wetness on my fingers. My tongue. My cock. And I came. And came. And came some more, with her name on my lips.

Her hand moved faster, her neck arched, her eyes rolled back, and she bit her lip as she shuddered. Once. Twice. A soft exhale passed her lips as she opened her eyes and looked at me.

I grinned wide at her. And she shook her head in disbelief. "I can't believe I did that on the phone," she said.

"High five," I said, and raised my wet hand to the camera.

She snorted but gave me a virtual high five with her glistening hand.

"Did I say I love you?"

She yawned, but nodded. It was almost midnight on her side of the world.

"Wanna play some music for us?" I asked.

Her smile stole my breath away. I wiped myself with the tissue from the nightstand and settled in.

"You'll stay with me till I sleep?" she asked.

"There's nowhere else I'd rather be."

And she played her songs. The sweet melodies and her sleepy eyes brought me back to her terrace. I could almost smell the night jasmine and feel the cool night air.

She looked at me, an ocean of love in her eyes.

I watched her till she fell asleep and far longer after that.

25

Song: Pyaar Hamein Kis Mod Pe Le Aaya
  - Kishore Kumar, R.D. Burman, Gulshan Kumarehta, Sapan Chakraborty

Meera

2 <u>28 days to go</u>
Just like last time, just like *every* time, Maa and I stood on our porch. Baldev's car entered the open gate of our front yard. Maa neared me and clutched my hand. I wore my ugliest, full-sleeve kurta. Baldev parked his car, got out, and walked toward us.

Shoulders rolled back, his shirt stretched over his pot belly, he walked like he owned the ground he walked on. In a way, he did. But it still grated my insides.

"Where's your bodyguard?" he asked, an evil smirk on his face.

Before I could say something, Maa answered, "Baldev bhai, you know how it is. People come and go. We have no body-guard. Nobody to rely on. My poor daughter works at school and saves every penny to pay you."

The helpless act always cooled him down. As if the weakness of others soothed something inside him. The sick sense of satisfaction that he was better than us. Better than someone. I said nothing. I just stood beside Maa with my head down. This is the one aspect of our life that Maa handled better than me. She knew how to show our weakness, just enough for Baldev to take pity on us, but not too much that he would prey on us.

Maa handed him the bundle of money. "Here, Baldev bhai. That is everything."

He started counting them. Once he was done counting the first bundle, he said, "You all weren't here for last month's rent. I had to go to Surbhi's house to collect it."

Maa stammered, "Please forgive us for the inconvenience. We were at my sister's place."

He hummed. I could feel his eyes boring down on me, yet I did not look up.

Once he finished counting, he took a step toward me. I refused to step back but held myself still. "I'll be back next month," he said, and chuckled.

He stepped back, and after looking over me once more, got into his car and left.

We stood there till his car disappeared.

Only then did we release our breath.

Maa stepped inside the house and went into the kitchen to prepare lunch. I rushed upstairs to my room to get out of the hideous clothing and everything that it represented. Helplessness. Disgust. Debt. I closed and locked the door of my room and changed into my T-shirt and pajama pants.

My eyes snagged on the two sketches and a photograph on the wall Luke had left behind. The photograph was of Hari from the day we visited the stepwell for the first time. I sat on the chair he'd occupied for months and looked at the wall. At the desk. My fingers moved over the wooden surface, imagining

Luke working on his laptop right here. I picked up the stray pencil on the desk and opened the top drawer to put it in.

And I froze.

A plain white envelope rested there.

I picked it up, and just by the thickness of it, the weight of it, I knew what it was.

I didn't even have to open it, yet I did, to find hundreds of 500 rupees notes.

My heart beat like a thunderstorm, my vision blurred and sharpened. So much money. It wasn't often that I'd get to hold these green-colored notes. I fanned the notes. The smell of money, the green paper dipped in privilege, wafted around me. Did Luke forget his stack of money?

I looked at the envelope again. A letter was tucked inside it. I shook the thing, and the letter dropped out. I opened it, and with my heart hammering out of my chest, I read the words written in English, the writing full of sharp lines.

Meera,

If I haven't told you already today, I love you.

I'm writing this to you because you would never accept it otherwise. Now, don't be mad at me. But I had to leave the money for you. Not for your sake, but for my peace of mind.

You don't ever have to use it. You can keep it. Give it away. Use it.

It's yours to do with as you please.

But you just need to know that it's there.

I'll wait for you for as long as it takes. I'll come to you once I finish my degree, regardless.

I can deal with you indebted.

I can deal with you working hard for your freedom.

I can deal with you paying off everything little by little.

What I can't deal with is you thinking that you're helpless and bound.

What I can't deal with are your tears and sacrifices.

What I can't deal with is your heartbreak over denying Hari's wishes.

If this is the only gift you'll ever take from me, if this is the only thing you'll allow me to do for you, please let me do this. It kills me that I'm not there with you. Let me stand behind your back. Let me lend you support and strength. Because you are mine.

I love you, Meera.

Yours,
Luke

Tears streamed down my face, a few drops blotting the paper, spreading the ink at some words. I wiped my tears and quickly dialed his number. Not a video call this time. I couldn't look at him, couldn't face him. He was right. He would be taking away my life's biggest burden. Just like that.

I didn't know why it made me cry, or my heart rebelled against accepting the money. Because it was too easy for him? The same thing would take me years to accomplish. Was I taking an easy way out of my life? What about others who didn't have their own Luke? Did the money make me feel cheap? I didn't know. I just couldn't make sense of anything. Yet I couldn't lose the tight grip on the bundle.

The dial tone rang in my ears. My head spun, my hands were clammy, and the phone clicked on the other side.

A hoarse voice, as if woken from sleep, murmured, "Meera, what's wrong? Everything all right?"

I looked at my clock set to New York time. Three in the morning. *Shit.*

"I don't know," I said, my voice shook with restraint, too many emotions trying to burst out.

"What happened?" His voice was soft, reminding me of our nights on the open terrace, him gently holding my fingers, coaxing hard truths out of me like only he could.

"The money. In the drawer."

"Oh."

"Yeah."

"You finally found them. I've been waiting for this call for a while."

"Why, Luke? God, I don't know if I can take it. But dangling this in front of me, making me reject it. Luke, that's cruel. Why did you give it to me?"

"Meera, fuck. I don't *want* you to give it back. That's the whole point of leaving the money behind."

"Luke. I'm so tempted. But I don't know. I feel sort of cheap. Like I'm using you for money. Like you're buying my love. My loyalty. But then again, you actually don't need to buy *my* love. You could just not bother. Gosh, it's like I have too many thoughts running through my head, but my brain refuses to make sense."

"Meera, sweetheart. If I thought you were in it for money, I wouldn't have to hide it in a desk drawer and wait for you to find it. And just think about it. If our situations were reversed, wouldn't you do the same thing?"

I couldn't help but snort. But if I think about it, I would have. "If I was in your place, I would've given you the money in your hands. Not left it behind like this."

A loud scoff came out of him. "And I would've accepted it. Like a gentleman. You wouldn't have. You're still thinking over it. And I did give you the money way earlier. Even before I asked you to let me give you the money. You just found out tonight. That money has been in there since the day I donated to your friend's organization."

My stomach swooped for a second as if I was falling. My fingers tightened on the phone. "Since then?" I whispered.

"Of course. Don't you know it by now, Meera? My utmost loyalty lies with you. Before anyone else, I want to take care of *you*. Try to share *your* burdens, and if at all possible, get rid of those burdens. Because I know. I know you'd do the same for me."

Tears streamed down my face. My lips turned down in that horribly, ugly face that I always got when I couldn't stop crying. "If it was a game of who is a better lover, you'd easily win."

"Ahh, you'll catch up."

A growl escaped my lips. "You were supposed to say no, and that I'm equally good."

He laughed, and said, "Well, you woke me up from my beautiful dreams of us doing some really amazing things, and then made me talk on the phone for an hour, and completely ruined my sleep, so now I'll be tired the entire day tomorrow. Clearly, you're losing the game of a better lover."

This wave, or more like a tsunami, of love rushed over me. I wanted to hug him, kiss him, hold him in my arms, and never let him go far from me. But I couldn't. I could just clutch my phone tighter, as I said, "I love you. I love you so much."

"I love you too, darling. And please consider using the

money. Nothing would make me happier. But I'll respect whatever decision you make."

I nodded along every word he spoke. "I will consider it. Thank you. The two words seem too insignificant, but thank you, Luke."

"You're very welcome."

A sigh of relief seemed to escape him as he yawned loudly in the phone. Just imagining him yawning, with his mouth wide open and his eyes closed, brought a smile to my face. After a second yawn, he murmured, "Now play me some soothing sound and help me sleep, will you?"

It was late afternoon for me, but I sat at his desk and played him a song. A soothing melody that crooned about undying love, the lonely nights, and a hope of meeting again soon.

Luke

209 days to go

The door to my childhood home opened the moment I pulled the rental car into the driveway. I lived in the city and just used the subway system, so I had no need for a car except for when I visited my parents. I usually got myself a rental car.

Mom rushed down the stairs as soon as I got out of the car and was in my arms, clutching my shoulders. "Oh Luke, it's been so long."

I pressed a kiss on Mom's forehead, and said, "I missed you too."

I kept my arms around her shoulders as we walked inside the house. "How's Dad?" I asked.

"Busy as always. He's in his office right now."

The woodsy aroma in the living room from the fireplace, the leather couches, and the colorful blanket and pillows thrown on one side of the couch brought back so many memories. The large photograph of my sister laughing hung over the fireplace was a sharp reminder of who we loved and lost.

We moved to the dining and kitchen space. One wall of our dining room was filled with black and white pictures of our entire family tree, starting from my great-great-grandfather. The old photographs, their faces, their clothes, and a glimpse of a time so far in the past made me feel like I was a part of something. A part of history, present, and a future. I took a seat at our round dining table and placed my bag on another chair. Mom brought me a coffee and a piece of banana bread from the kitchen. It's like no time had passed, like nothing had changed in my life from before I met Meera.

"Oh, Mom, you're the best," I moaned as I stuffed my mouth with a huge bite.

She sat across from me and sipped her coffee, which was more milk than coffee. "It came out of the oven just an hour ago."

"I missed this," I said, after a gulp of coffee.

She put her mug on the coaster. "Now tell me all about your trip. How was it? Did you get everything that you need for your thesis?"

I got so much more.

Meera's smiling face, our early morning tea time, her eyes glazed over in passion, and her laughter that made my heart beat faster—it all flashed through my mind.

"You're smiling, Luke. What is it? What're you hiding?"

I chuckled. "I'm not hiding anything, Mom. Just remembering."

"Remembering what?" Mom leaned forward and looked at me without blinking, as if her creepy stare down would just make me spout all my secrets.

"Umm... Meera," I said and closed my eyes. God, her creepy stare down always worked.

"Oh, Luke. Who is she? Is she your girlfriend?"

Right then, Dad walked in. He placed a soft kiss on Mom's head and took a seat beside her. "Luke, been a while."

I nodded. "How are you, Dad? How's work?"

He waved off. "All good. I'm good. I was just talking to Daniel the other day—"

Before Dad could continue, Mom placed her hand over his and interrupted, "James, hush now. Luke was just telling me about his new girlfriend."

Dad's eyebrows rose to his hairline as he looked between me and Mom. "Since when do you have a girlfriend?"

I had always shared my relationships with my parents. But for some reason, I was nervous. My instinct was to protect Meera, and she was the most important person in my life. I needed my parents to like her. "Umm... Since I went to India."

Mom gasped and clutched my hand. "You met her in India?"

I nodded, remembering the day I first arrived at her place. "Yeah. I actually stayed at her place for two months. It's her, her little brother, and her mother. Her father—well, he committed suicide five years ago."

Silence. Mom released my hand and sat back in her chair. "Oh, dear. I'm so sorry, Luke."

I couldn't meet their eyes, afraid to see the memories that would inevitably flash behind their eyes and the sadness it would bring. I looked down at my hands. "Yeah. It was for financial reasons. He was a farmer who couldn't pay back his loan. Ever since then, Meera has been paying off the loan and supporting her family. And when I was there, every night, we would talk, and listen to songs, and just *be*, you know?"

I looked up and saw the sadness. The understanding of that loss in their eyes. "She must be a very strong woman," Dad said, his hand on Mom's shoulder.

I nodded. "She is. A bit jaded, though. Naturally. And I melt every time she laughs. She's fiercely protective of her family and friends. When we heard about two more farmers committing suicide, she immediately went to help the families out any way she could. Even though it destroyed her emotionally, she was there. And I was just, completely, a goner."

"You love her," Mom said, tears shining in her eyes.

"I do," I said.

"How, uh, how does it work between you two? Is she coming here? Are you in a long-distance relationship?" Mom asked.

I nodded. "Right now, we are. And well, once I graduate in May, I'm going back to India. We'll figure things out then."

"What about our business, Luke? You're part of Wilson & White Construction. You're studying and getting your architecture degree so you can carry forward our company with Sam. Have you thought about your role here?"

Wasn't that the crux of my problem? If I hadn't had any responsibility toward my family, I'd be out there in India right now, living with the love of my life. "I am thinking about it, Dad. That's why I'm here. But I need to have a plan. I just, you know, I just can't live without Meera. She's it for me."

Mom clutched my hand, and asked, "But honey, can't she come to the US?"

I held my mom's hand. Her fingers had more wrinkles than I'd last noticed. "Unfortunately, no. Even if *she* can, her family can't. And she just can't leave them alone."

"But you can leave us alone should you choose to go away?" Mom asked, her eyes hurt as if I'd betrayed her.

"That's not what I'm trying to do, Mom. But it would be simpler."

She turned her face away from me even though her grip on my hand was firm. A tear rolled down from her eyes. "I've already lost one child; I can't lose another too."

My heart pounded like a drumbeat, and flashes of my childhood looped in my mind. A hundred different moments when I needed my parents, and they weren't there. So many times when I wanted to celebrate my success—the time I won the art competition in school, or when I had parent-teacher meetings, sports days—but it was too difficult for them to laugh and smile with me. When they made me feel guilty for being happy.

"Ma, you're not going to lose me. It's not like we see each other every day. I can visit whenever you want. A US passport doesn't stop me from moving between India and the States. Also, I need you to give Meera a chance. You'll love her. And who knows, you might even find another daughter to love."

"Oh, Luke."

Tears ran down her cheeks now, and Dad sat even closer to Mom, holding her. I clutched her hand with both of mine. "It's okay, Mom. But I really love Meera. And even if not as your daughter, I think you would really love her."

I looked at Dad and continued. "And I know we have the company, and I plan to join you. I just need to go back in May to figure everything out with Meera. I'm not going to make any major decisions while we're apart. It's difficult to catch each other to talk as it is."

Dad nodded, a small smile on his face. "I'm happy for you, son. Not many are able to find someone they'd move across the world for. And I would love to meet Meera. Such a beautiful name, isn't it, Olivia?"

Mom nodded and held her palm up to my cheek. I pressed a soft kiss to her hand and said, "Thanks, you guys." Before Mom could get even more emotional, I looked at her and asked, "What's for dinner?"

A chuckle escaped her, and she shook her head. She got up from the chair, and on her way to the kitchen, said, "It's roasted chicken, roasted veggies, mashed potatoes, and brown rice."

Dad and I sighed in anticipation, and Mom laughed all the way to the kitchen.

26

Song: Mera Saaya Saath Hoga
  - Lata Mangeshkar

Meera

1 66 days to go
   I missed Luke. Managing the long-distance relationship was getting easier and harder at the same time.
Easier because I had a person in my life, an anchor, who I went
to and talked about everything and anything. Harder because
he wasn't here. He wasn't near. I could see him laugh, hear him
laugh, but couldn't touch his lips when he did. His eyes still
warmed my blood when he looked at me, but his hands, his
body, his touch never enveloped me in their safe cocoon.

He said he'd booked his tickets to India for May 18. I had
already marked my calendar, and the fact that the school had
summer vacation at that time was a boon in itself. He had also
informed me that Akira was coming to India, and to my place,
next week. With a gift from him. A Christmas present, he'd
said. So, naturally, I, too, had prepared a package for Akira to

take back with her. Luke was already preparing and planning for our next trip, and this time, he was involving me in the discussion. We spent many of our video and voice calls looking at pictures and discussing locations.

Every day, every minute when I wasn't teaching in class, my mind constantly chanted Luke's name. I had begun to relate to my namesake more than ever before: A woman madly in love with an unattainable god, forever waiting for him, lost in thoughts of him, always praying and chanting his name.

With the thoughts of Luke and Meera, my namesake, in mind, and the constant chatter of Hari in my ears from behind me on the two-wheeler vehicle, I parked in our front yard. Before I could ask him to carry his own bag in the house, Hari jumped down from the back seat and rushed inside the house, leaving me shouting at him.

"Next time you don't carry your own bag, I'm going to leave it out in the sun," I shouted as I entered the living room and dropped his bag on the double bed where Maa sat. More like where Maa would be sitting usually, but wasn't there.

She was always here. For the last five years, every day, she has been on this bed when we returned from school. Where was she? I checked my phone, and nothing. No missed calls, no message.

Hari came running back from the bathroom, all changed out of the school uniform. He instantly picked up the cars and trucks Aakar had brought for him and started to play.

"Hari, did Maa tell you if she was planning to go somewhere?"

He thought for a second and shook his head. Small lines formed between his eyebrows, his lips scrunched up in worry. I brushed my hand in his hair and said, "Don't worry. I'll call Kishan Kaka, and ask if he saw her."

I called our neighbor, who lived a little farther down the road from us, far enough to feel isolated but close enough that Maa would have to pass their house to get on the main street. But when I talked to him, he told me he hadn't seen her.

I thanked him and dropped the call. I'd have to go look for her myself. I turned to Hari, who silently played with the toy truck, and said, "Hari, I'll give you some snacks, and go to find Maa. I'm asking Kriti to come here, but in the meantime, you will quietly play in the upstairs room. I'll even turn on the AC for you. You won't be opening the door, no matter who knocks. I'm taking the key with me. Kriti already has the key. Can I leave you alone for a while?"

He looked at me, his eyes focused on me, and he nodded. "I promise. I'll stay in the AC room."

I kissed his head and quickly prepared a plate of his favorite snacks. We went upstairs, where I closed all the windows and turned on the AC. I placed the snacks on the desk, and he sat on the chair. With one last look, I assured he was fine and went downstairs to let Kriti know about the situation. She agreed to leave right then and said she would be at my place in fifteen minutes.

With a thank you, I was out of the house. I got on my two-wheeler vehicle but had no idea where to go. Where could Maa go? She'd not left the house except to go to her sister's place in the past five years. I had no idea where she would go.

I still started the vehicle and went in search of her. I circled all the roads around our house, as if I'd find her just strolling down some road. Hoping, praying, begging that I'd find her quickly. That I'd find her *safely*. That I'd just *find* her.

Minutes passed with me on the vehicle, under the hot sun, the cool, December wind chilling me to my bones. Or maybe it was the fear. But, I kept driving. Circling around all the roads I could remember. My heart pounded, and sweat gathered over my lips even though it was just so cold. I couldn't—I just couldn't lose her. Not her too. What had happened? Why wasn't she home? Where could she go? Where would she have gone five years ago?

Five years ago.

And something clicked.

I had to check it. Just to be sure. I drove back home and, without stopping, drove the vehicle on the dirt road of our farm, following the path that Maa and I had always taken. Tears streamed down my cheeks as memories assaulted me. Happy. Sad. Bone crushing. Some full of despair. Some, full of hope.

When Maa and I walked to the tree to have lunch with Papa.

Where I'd first learned how to use a rake, and explained which rake was used for what.

Where we planted seeds together.

Where I'd first announced that I'd gotten admission to the state university.

Where Papa had killed himself.

My hands shook as I neared the tree. The tree of our memories.

And I saw the small form of my mother huddled under it.

My heart squeezed so tight I had to clutch it.

I quietly parked the vehicle and made my way toward her. Slowly. Steeling myself for more pain. Preparing myself to be the support Maa needed. The crunching of the leaves and the rocks beneath my feet had Maa looking up.

Red, tear-streaked eyes met mine for a second, but quickly looked away, off toward our farm— our wild, barren farm— in silence. I rushed toward her and took a seat beside her under our tree. Gently, I placed my hand on her shoulder, and placed a soft kiss right beside my hand.

She clutched my hand and started to cry again.

A lump lodged in my throat, my lips turned down, and

words refused to come out of my mouth. I swallowed the lump, and asked, "What's wrong, Maa?"

"I miss your father," she said, wiping the tears with the edge of her saree.

Pain sliced my heart. My father's face, the memories that we shared right here. And I realized I missed him too. "He used to always give the first bite of lunch to you," I said, the memory coming out of nowhere.

Maa nodded as she breathed out, controlling the tears.

"Sometimes, well, most of the time, I wonder. What if our life was easier?"

Her question was the same I'd asked myself all these years. Even when my father was alive, I'd wondered the same thing. What if our life was easier? Easier than who? Easier than what? Our life before Papa passed was so much easier than today. Life when Luke was here seemed so much easier than today. Our life itself looked easier than so many women and children who are left with absolutely nothing and have to rely on donations and goodwill of others.

But this was Maa's pain, her questions, her musings, her journey. Who was I to dictate her feelings about life?

"It could be worse, Maa. At least I have a job. Luke has given us the money to pay off all the debt. We can finally live without that Baldev breathing down our necks. Life *will* be easier, Maa."

She listened to me. Hung onto my every word. Nodding along every little good thing coming our way. And then she asked, "I've been really bad to you, haven't I?"

Her words stunned me. "What? Uh, why would you think that?"

She looked back toward the open land, her hand still clutching mine on her shoulder. "All these years after your father passed, you begged and begged to sell the farm. Get rid of the loan. And I just—just never agreed with you. I was lost, Meera. Blindly holding on to the thing that was dearest to your father, the place that was your father's life, and well, also his death."

I clutched her shoulder. Five years, and this is the first time she has shared her feelings without us fighting.

She turned to me and held my face, and continued. "You understand me, right? Without this farm, all the memories, no matter how happy or sad, they would all be gone. And I wasn't ready to let go of your father yet. Because without him, what even is my existence?"

I clutched her shoulder. "Your life doesn't end with him, Maa."

A sad smile came over her face. "I know, beta. But I was brought up with one goal drilled into my mind: to be a wife. And then I married your father. A farmer. So I became a *farmer's* wife. I found a purpose. And then, he was gone. Our farm was gone. And I became nothing."

Tears pooled in my eyes. My mother, this gentle, loving yet tough person. Life had not been kind to her. I hugged her as we cried. I clutched her, trying to hold her up as she'd held me up all my life.

"You're not nothing, Maa. You're *everything*. You are the reason I'm a teacher. You've fought for me, always. You've stood by Papa, in his life and even after his death. And it's okay to be lost, Maa. You'll find something new. A new purpose to life. I promise. Just hold on, okay? I'm always here."

She held me tighter with every word. She cried harder. I cried harder.

"I'm ready, Meera," she said, as she pulled out of the hug and wiped her tears.

"Ready for what?"

"To let your father go. He'll always be in my heart, in my memories, but I don't need to hold on to this farm anymore."

I shook my head. "We don't need to sell it anymore, Maa. Luke has given us the money, remember?"

She smiled and held my cheek. "I know. But if you want to sell it someday—today, tomorrow, a year or ten years from now —I'll be ready. And you know, you can use that money for something else, too, if you choose to sell the farm."

"We'll see. We don't have to make any decisions right away. Now let's go. Hari and Kriti will be worried. I had to call Kriti to watch over Hari while I was out searching for you."

Lines of worry appeared on Maa's forehead as she quickly got up. "Oh no. I completely lost track of time. One moment I was knitting, and then I just had to come here."

We walked to where I'd parked the vehicle. "Don't worry. Everything is okay."

Before we got on the vehicle, we turned around to look at our farm. Barren, with wild grass and weeds spread everywhere. Yet the afternoon light washed it in gold, the hot rays burning off all the stress, while the cold breeze provided a respite after the tears. Millions of memories played before my eyes, disappearing one after the other, permanently etching themselves in my bruised and battered soul. Forever mine to keep.

We made our way back to house, Maa sitting behind me on the scooter, holding my shoulders for balance. Hari ran out of the house to greet us and flew in Maa's arms. Kriti stood at the door and gave me her solid smile in support as she called out, "C'mon in. You guys took so long, I already prepared lunch for us."

Maa laughed, a little embarrassed, and I hugged her tight.

That night, my body ached to feel Luke's arms around me. That night, I wanted to be lost in his heat, his smell, his strength, his humor, and his touch. And all I could have was his T-shirt, his smell in it all but a distant memory, as I drifted off to sleep, hoping to meet him in my dreams.

∾

Luke

138 days to go

> Sam: Akira's back home

I read the text over and over again as I ran from the studio to our place. The harsh snow and cold wind against me made it difficult to hold the umbrella still. But nothing mattered. Akira was back from India—after meeting Meera and giving her my present. I had sent her some classic American cookies and candies, mostly for Hari, and a white gold charm bracelet. Some of the charms that I'd sent with it were two twin beds, a cassette player, a teacup, and last, a heart— as cheesy as it was, she had my heart, and I wanted to show that to her, and wanted her to keep it.

I burst inside the living room and found Akira and Sam cuddling on the couch. Three huge bags lay on the floor, and three steaming cups of hot chocolate were ready on the coffee table.

A teasing smile came over both of their faces. Honestly, they were starting to look similar in the year we'd been living together. They laughed together, they frowned at the same things, and they looked at me with the same raised eyebrows right now.

"I made three cups. Knew you'd come running," Sam said and looked at Akira. "He's been more excited than me for you to come home."

Akira laughed and got up from his arms to hug me. I squeezed her in welcome, and said, "Welcome back. How was it?"

"It was so good. Met all the relatives that I had to, went to all the restaurants that I was missing. I'm sure I gained four to five kilos, but I dare anyone to make me stand on a weighing scale."

I laughed because she looked the same as before but better rested and happy. Now, it had been five minutes since I was home, and I had controlled myself from asking about Meera to my limit while Akira talked about her visit.

Sam looked at me with laughter in his eyes, and said, "Akira, sweetheart, put the poor man out of his misery, would ya?"

Akira's eyes widened in apology, and she rushed to open a suitcase. "Oh, I'm so sorry, Luke. I totally lost myself for a second there. Now where did I put it?"

"Where did you put what? Tell me about Meera. Did she like my present? What did she say? Did she look okay? How were Hari and aunty? What are you trying to find?"

Akira mumbled, "Just hold on a second, Luke. Now where is it?"

I looked at Sam in frustration, complaints about his girlfriend in my eyes, while he kept looking at Akira's unorganized mess of a suitcase with all the fondness in the world. Normally, he would be getting uneasy with all that mess. When I raised my eyebrows at him, he just shrugged, and said, "I haven't seen her in a month. I missed all of it."

I raised my hand in defeat and sat on the couch as Akira shouted, "Ahah! Here, Luke. Meera sent this for you."

My heart jumped, and I was off the couch and kneeling beside Akira. My hands shook as I accepted the plastic bag from Akira's hands. I was glad she didn't mention it, but her eyes turned softer.

She said, "She's well, Luke. She had tears in her eyes when she saw the present. And Hari literally ate five chocolates the moment he opened his present. I spent about half a day at her place, and we talked about a million things. But mostly about you."

And I didn't even realize when I had taken a seat on the ground, my legs folded, my arms clutching Meera's present. My mind was entirely conflicted between wanting to hear what Meera and Akira talked about versus running to my room to open the present.

Yet I sat still, rooted to the spot, while Akira told me all about her visit, how Meera told her she missed me, how Hari told her all about the time Luke bhai came to visit them and now he was his best friend, how I was awful at cricket and that he would teach me how to play it properly when I was back with them.

Every conversation with Akira made me want to book the next flight and go to Meera. Every story made me miss her more. My heart yearned for Meera. Just the fact that Akira had *met* Meera, spent time in that little house, hugged her and laughed with her made me insanely jealous. Yet I know she went there for me, and I could never thank her enough for that.

I hugged her and kissed her forehead in gratitude, "Thank you, Akira. You've no idea how grateful I am that you saw her."

"Anytime, Luke. I'm so glad you both found each other. After talking to her, I realize you're meant for each other."

After quickly gulping down the hot chocolate, I rushed into my room to open Meera's present. I quickly checked the time in India. It was three in the morning. Shit. I just didn't have the heart to wake Meera up.

I emptied the plastic bag on my bed. A few letters dropped, plus a small cassette player with the slot for earphones, five cassettes, and a thick bunch of papers with handwritten translations for each song. Each cassette was numbered, and I instantly put the first one in the cassette player and plugged in my headphones.

Before pressing play, I opened the letter labeled with the numeral one.

Luke,

Words cannot express how much I miss you. We talk, we chat, and we video. But I know you would agree, it is not the same. I miss your touch. I curse myself for not falling for you sooner. I would have had more time with your arms around me.

I miss holding your hand while we listen to songs under the stars. The nights are lonely without you. Each song hits me harder. Yet the music doesn't feel the same without you. Life has gone back to the time before you were here, but what used to be my normal life has now become a lonely existence. Too much is happening. I have hope. You've given me the opportunity and the means to hope. Hope for a better life. Hope for a happier and burden-free life. Hope for a life with you.

I miss you. But you're not forgotten. For every important and unimportant moment of my life, I remember you. I feel you. And someday soon, I'll touch you.

Till then,

I hope the music, the words, the letters, and the phone calls keep you company.

I love you, always.

Merry Christmas,

Meera

A few tears escaped my eyes. I read and reread the letter.

Over and over again. I smelled the paper and traced Meera's handwriting with my fingers. Memorizing the words. Feeling them deep inside me. I folded the letter and placed it under my pillow. Because God knew I would reread it every moment I got. I didn't know I needed those words from Meera until I read them.

Each day was getting more difficult.

The fears, however irrational, kept creeping up more often than not. Would she still want me? Does she even need me? Does she love me as much as when I was with her? Does she too feel like she'd die if she couldn't kiss me? Was she as desperate as I was?

Her letter was the validation I needed. And she'd sent me five cassettes, with twelve songs in each. Sixty songs to tell me how she felt. I couldn't have asked for a better Christmas present.

I found the stack of papers that had lyrics for all the songs, turned to the first page to the song "Mera Saaya Saath Hoga", took a deep breath, pictured Meera, and pressed play.

> Wherever you go, my shadow will follow you
> Wherever you go, my shadow will follow you
> My shadow will follow you
> My shadow will follow you
> If you shed your tears remembering me
> Then my tears will come out to stop them right
>   there
> In whichever direction you go, my shadow will
>   follow you
> If you'll be sad, then I'll be sad as well
>
> I'll be close to you whether you see me or not
> Wherever you live, my shadow will follow you
> Wherever you go, my shadow will follow you

Don't be sad if we ever get separated
Don't bring tears in your eyes remembering
    my love
Whenever you turn around to see, my shadow
    will follow you
Wherever you go, my shadow will follow you
My sorrow has always been involved with your
    sorrow
My love has always been there for you in
    every life
Wherever you go, my shadow will follow you.

27

Song: Intehah Ho Gayi Intezaar Ki
  - Asha Bhosle, Kishore Kumar

1 25 days to go

Meera: You're absolutely CRAZY!!

Luke: What?

Meera: I got your letter and a package

Luke: Oh.

Meera: Yes. Oh.

Luke: Did you like it?

Meera: It's a dildo!

Luke: I know. I sent it. Did you like it?

Meera: Maa and Hari almost opened it!

Luke: Did you like it, though?

Meera: I'll have to try it to know if I liked it.

Luke: DO NOT TRY WITHOUT ME.

Meera: Hmm. Maybe I should break it in before I call you.

Luke: NOOOO. PLEASE DON'T.

Meera: I wonder what would make me reconsider?

Luke: I'M SORRY I DIDN'T WARN YOU ABOUT THE PACKAGE.

Meera: That's better. See you tonight. Your noon. Will you be able to get free?

Luke: Everything else can go to hell today.

Meera: You know, I might not like it.

Luke: Oh, you will. I did my research.

Meera: See you later :-*

Luke: See YOU later ;-)

~

97 DAYS TO go

Meera, My Love,
Reading your handwritten letter touched my heart. Not just touched, it punched my heart. I

could not stop tracing the ink on the paper, could not stop breathing in your words. The paper that you'd touched and poured your heart on. And I just had to write you back a letter. I know I thanked you over the phone and the video, but those are just a memory now. The letter, though... I hope it gives you something to hold on to until you have me.

I had never imagined myself in a relationship where I wouldn't be able to touch my love. To be oceans apart. I never imagined that I'd find you, the person I'd want to spend my life with, in a tiny village in India. And I thank the universe, the God, whoever is up there, for bringing us together. For putting me on the path that would eventually cross with yours, that would give me you.

I miss you. Every minute. Every day. But I wouldn't change this for anything else in the world. Even if it takes us a few more months, a few more years, to finally be together. Because I know. I know we'll survive all of it and come out together.

Waiting to hold you again with my every breath.

Love,

Luke

PS: Have you heard the song "Talking to the Moon" by Bruno Mars?

72 DAYS TO GO

> Meera: Check this out… (Photo attached: Hari dressed in traditional clothes and wearing the sandals that Luke had gifted)

Luke: He looks precious. What's the occasion?

> Meera: Just a Republic Day celebration at the school. He's participating in singing the national anthem with the other kids

Luke: Please send me a video of him singing.

> Meera: Will do :-*

Luke: :-* What're you wearing?

> Meera: Sends photo (In a saree)

Luke: Sends photo (Tented pants) See what you do to me? :-*

> Meera: Dead

> Meera: Be free in ten hours.

Luke: You're on (eggplant emoji)

> Meera: (eye-roll emoji)

> Meera: (water drops emoji)

31 DAYS TO GO

Luke: Only thirty-one days to go before I kiss you.

Meera: I don't think I remember how to kiss.

Luke: I'll remind you. Thoroughly.

Meera: I'm counting on that. How is the thesis coming along?

Luke: Really good. Thanks for getting me those photos btw. :-*

Meera: Anytime. Brought back memories... :-*

Luke: Me too. Maybe I should move up my trip. Screw the graduation ceremony. I can take a flight on the last day of my semester.

Meera: Don't you dare. This might be your last graduation ceremony. How many more degrees are you planning to get?

Luke: But I miss you.

Meera: Only thirty-one days to go

Luke: Don't say "Only"

Meera: Sorry. "Still" thirty-one days to go.

Luke: A little better.

Meera: :-*

Luke: :-*

～

19 DAYS TO go

Luke: I really don't want to go.

Meera: You should. They're your friends.

Luke: It's not fair of them to ask me to spend three fucking days in a campsite right before graduation. They knew I planned to spend all the days talking to you. It's been so long since we video called.

> Meera: I know. But they're your friends. They know you're leaving for India and won't be back for a while.

Luke: But we had a celebration date, baby. You, me, your dildo, my fleshlight. ;-)

> Meera: We can have that once you're back. And if not, we won't need our replacements when we'll be together.

Luke: I won't be able to call you or text you for three days.

> Meera: I've spent 242 days without touching you. I'll survive not talking for three days with you.

Luke: Brutal, baby. You're supposed to be angry and upset and forbid me to leave.

> Meera: Lol. I'll be angry and upset if you miss out on spending time with your friends for me.

Luke: You really want me to go?

> Meera: Yes.

Luke: Fine. And you'll miss me.

> Meera: Very much.

Luke: Okay. TTYL. Back to thesis.

> Meera: Off to sleep. Good night :-*

Luke: :-*

~

3 DAYS TO GO

Luke,

You did it.

You finished your thesis. And I am so proud of you.

I've seen how tirelessly you've worked. How much heart you've poured into presenting your best work. And you did it.

I can't wait to jump into your arms and kiss you crazy.

And Luke,

WE did it.

We survived this never-ending drought.

Soon, I'll see you.

I'll touch you.

I'll feel your heartbeat against mine.

Your laughter against my lips.

Your hands in my hair.

Your body alongside mine.

Yes, every time I start to write something to you, my mind wanders off, and my body gets a little demanding ;)

This is hopefully my last letter to you before we meet. I know we will be meeting soon, but I just had to send you this letter. As a token of this journey. Of our fight to be together again.

I never thought we'd make it. I had resigned myself to loving the memories you gave me. Never did I imagine that I'd still be making those memories with you.

This letter. It is the proof that we did it.

Thank you for making us work.

Thank you for making me believe in our love.

Thank you for loving me.

We survived the separation. We will soon meet. And I will never ever let you be without me for such a long span of time.

Soon. Very soon, we will meet.

Waiting for you,

Your Meera

28

Song: Yeh Kahaan Aa Gaye Hum
  - Lata Mangeshkar, Amitabh Bachchan

Meera

My heart pounded as I walked among the crowd of people, some Indians, but mostly foreigners. Announcements blared overhead, people talked and laughed, and hugged each other. And all I could do was look around and try not to feel alone and lost.

"Meera!" A shout broke me out of my melancholy and my rising panic.

Akira ran toward me. Her long, black hair was in a gorgeous ponytail, a thin jacket over her blue blouse and black jeans. And here I was in my old, faded jeans and a thick, old-fashioned sweater, certainly not flattering my body. I wasn't even going to think about the status of my hair.

A thirty-two-hour flight with three stops doesn't leave a person in a sane state.

Akira enveloped me in a warm, fragrant hug, almost

bringing me to tears. I didn't know why I felt like crying. But I wished Luke was here to welcome me. I would've bawled my eyes out in his arms and not have felt so weak.

But he wasn't. He didn't even know I was here. He was out camping somewhere with Sam—the plan specifically made to surprise Luke on his graduation.

"Oh my God, Meera. I can't believe you're actually here," Akira said in Gujarati, taking over the trolley with my suitcases.

"I'm so glad you found me in this crowd. I was sure I was lost."

She laughed and gave me a side hug. "Luke is going to lose it tomorrow."

My stomach fluttered, and my heart pounded. "I would've never thought of this idea. It's all thanks to you."

"It's a pleasure, Meera. I'm just happy you were willing to go through all the months of paperwork and the visa interview. That process almost had me canceling my plans for the US altogether."

I couldn't help but laugh. It was only the hope of seeing Luke and surprising him that had me going through that process. When Akira came to my place in December, she proposed this idea. Initially, I had refused. I had no money for the tickets. But well, once Ma and I talked, she convinced me to use the money Luke had left me. So here I was. In America.

"I know we talked about it, but you don't mind staying with my old roommates, right? They're all Indian and of our age, so it shouldn't be awkward."

For the past six years, I'd not met more than three new people in my life. And all of a sudden, I was thrown into a world of strangers. Why was I doing this again? *Luke. Luke. Luke.* I kept chanting his name in my mind as I answered, "It's okay."

Akira clutched my hand tighter. "Everything is fine, Meera.

Trust me. I'll drop you at my old place, and in the early morning, I'll be there to pick you up."

I could only nod because Akira was leading me to two people, one who distinctly looked like an older version of Luke. *Oh no.* My steps must have faltered because Akira looked at me and instantly turned guilty at my horrified expression.

"Uh. Sam mentioned our plan to Luke's parents, just to prepare them for tomorrow. And they insisted on picking you up. Actually, they insisted you stay with them, but I convinced them you'd be more comfortable with my roommates. But I couldn't stop them from coming here. They'll just drop us at my old place."

Akira rambled on, and all I could think about was my mussed hair, my tired eyes, and the frumpy clothes I'd been wearing for the last thirty-six hours. "Akira, look at me. How can I meet his parents like this? They're totally going to reject me."

She laughed. "They're not going to reject you. The entire way to the airport, they've been telling me how excited they are to meet you."

"And now all their excitement is going to be in vain."

Before Akira could reply, Luke's mom rushed forward and hugged me. *Hugged* me. My eyes met Akira's, and she looked at me with an I-told-you-so expression. Nervousness and embarrassment had my body stiffening, and I willed myself to relax. I awkwardly patted her back, and the moment she released me, I instinctively bent down to touch her feet out of respect.

"Oh goodness," Luke's mom blurted, and I quickly got up, my cheeks turning red. I was losing it. I had no idea how to behave with a boyfriend's parents, in the absence of the said boyfriend, much less American parents.

Akira quickly came to my rescue and explained, "Olivia, touching feet means asking for a blessing."

Olivia. Akira called her by her name. No Aunty, no Mrs.

Olivia. Just plain Olivia. She might be twice our age. Luke had never called my mother by her name. Before I could think much over it, Olivia aunty clutched her necklace, her eyes full of surprise, and dare I say, warmth, and said to me, "Bless you, dear."

I extended my hand in a formal introduction—if only to show her that I wasn't an uneducated, village girl but a teacher and someone who could stand by Luke— and said, "I'm Meera."

Luke's mom smiled and shook my hand. "Please call me Olivia."

She turned around, and Luke's dad approached with a broad, welcoming smile that looked a lot like Luke's. "It's such a pleasure to meet you, Meera. Call me James. Luke has talked about nothing else for the last year."

"Hello, James." *Uncle,* I added in my mind. My mind wouldn't let me just call them by their names.

After the introductions, Akira took over my trolley, and Luke's mom came on my other side and led me out of the airport. "Meera, I'm just so happy you agreed to come. I have been dying to meet you. But this is even better. Luke is going to be so happy."

"How could I not come? It's Luke," I answered. Because there was no other reason. Just him. And if seeing me here would make him even half as happy as it would make me, I needed nothing else.

"Once you're settled in with Luke in a day or two, you both must visit our place," she said, her tone totally serious as if she hadn't just shocked my mind.

I turned to Akira and raised my eyebrows in question. A question that didn't need to be uttered out loud. *She knows I would stay with him? How is she okay with it?* Akira winked at me, and just like with the lack of using the labels *uncle* and *aunty* for elders, I decided to go with the flow and keep quiet.

The moment I stepped outside the airport, a cool gust of wind sent shivers down my body. How could the month of May be so cold? Thank God Akira told me to wear a sweater. Olivia aunty must have seen me tug my sweater tighter because she started walking faster and asked James uncle to get the car ready. Soon, we were seated in the car, Akira and I in the back seat of a big SUV, James uncle driving, and Olivia aunty turned around in her seat to face us. Or more like watch me.

I smiled at her, but I had no idea what to say. Oh God.

Akira, once again, came to my rescue as she reiterated the plan for tomorrow morning. Outside the car was nothing but passing vehicles and darkness. No buildings, no people walking along the roads, no two-wheeler vehicles. Only cars. Thousands of cars driving in the opposite direction than back home, which caused somersaults in my stomach at every turn.

I closed my eyes to stop myself from minor freak-outs and focused on Akira and Olivia aunty talking. "Poor thing must've been tired," someone said.

And I really must be tired because I wanted to deny it and sit up and talk to Luke's mother and impress her with my amazing English. But no words came out of my mouth and my eyes didn't open.

A sudden jerk to my shoulder had me gasping awake. "What? What happened?"

"Meera, relax, honey. I just had to show you the view," Akira said and pointed outside the window.

And now, another gasp escaped me. This one full of wonder and awe. We were driving toward a bridge, and beyond that, the skyline of Manhattan emerged from the horizon. Slowly. As if welcoming me in this city. The city that never slept. A city I'd seen a thousand times in the movies. A city every person in the world recognized and aspired to visit. And I was entering it. Towers as tall as mountains emerged, every window in them lit up in yellow and white lights, a light for every person living in this city. This formidable city stood like a beast that could inhale you and spit you out.

My heart beat with a wild excitement that I'd not yet felt in the entire trip. *This. This* was Luke's city. Where he lived his life. Where he studied. Worked. Had friends. And he wanted to leave all of this and come back to India? How would he survive? Why would he even want to leave this place? And how long would he last without it? My chest felt heavy, and I suddenly felt like crying. I bit down on my near trembling lip and scolded my mind not to think such thoughts.

As we entered the city, the towers reached the sky. Glass buildings, lights everywhere, so many trees, people walking along wide, wide footpaths, cars and buses ran along the roads. The city was a beast. Alive. Roaring in its energy, its endurance. Thrumming with the hustle and bustle. "I feel like nobody, yet so powerful. Just by stepping into the city," I murmured.

"Huh. It kinda does feel like that," Akira said.

My gaze was stuck to the city that passed by. Some full of beauty and elegance and power. Some full of small houses and quiet streets, all brown in color, for some reason. It had to be said that the color coordination of all the buildings in the city was astounding.

An hour flew by in a minute.

Then Akira was climbing out of the car. Luke's parents helped us get my bags out of the car and hugged me. Both of them. "See you tomorrow, Meera," James uncle said.

"I can't wait to see Luke's reaction," Olivia aunty squealed, reminding me of my teenage students, and I couldn't help but join in her excitement.

Once they took off, Akira and I carried my bags to the third floor. As sweat dripped down my body, and my heart pounded with carrying a 25-kg bag for three floors, I cursed the country for boasting about its economy but not having a single elevator in their building.

"Do buildings here not have elevators?" I gasped.

Akira, like me, breathed out with a pained chuckle. "I know, right? Most of these four- and five-story buildings are really old, so they don't have such facilities."

"And they can't renovate it?"

She gasped. "It's a historic building. It has value."

A value that had no good comfort features was beyond my understanding. I kept my mouth shut as we entered her house. We kept everything in the living room, and she introduced me to her roommates. One of her roommates, Shruti, was from the town where I did my college, and I thanked God for little blessings. I would at least have something to talk about to someone.

Before I could ask them where I could sleep, Akira said, "You're sleeping in my room. It's clean, and you will have your privacy. I'll sleep at Sam's place."

A relieved smile came over my face, and I thanked Akira.

She waved her hand in welcome and said, "Sam and Luke should be back home soon. I should leave. They don't live too far from here, actually. Just a fifteen-minute walk."

I would be sleeping a mere fifteen-minute walk from Luke. My heart ached with that sweet agony of longing and separation. Of the knowledge that he was close, he was *here*, and I had to wait. Wait. Wait. One more night. A few more hours.

I nodded at Akira and bid her goodbye.

Once she was gone, I got my essentials from my travel bag, took a long, hot shower after thirty-six hours of flight, and had a warm bowl of soup and toast that Shruti prepared. I soon went to sleep, a burning anticipation pounding through my body, nerves firing through my brain, and prayers to every god for everything to work out fine tomorrow.

And a heart full of hope for a kiss.

A kiss I'd been waiting on for the past two hundred and sixty-one days.

Luke

The entire university campus was covered in Columbia Blue. I stood near the assigned spot for the architecture students with Sam. I'd dressed my best, in a sharp, light gray suit over a white shirt. The Columbia Blue-colored graduation gown reached a little below my knees. I clutched my cap under my arm because no way would I wear it right now.

"I hope Mom and Dad arrive soon. I was hoping to meet them before I need to get seated."

He frowned at the clouds above but turned to look at me when I spoke. "Yeah, man. They should be here soon. Don't worry. Just enjoy this day. You're finally fucking done with assignments for life."

Just hearing those words had relief rushing through my veins. I slapped him lightly on the stomach, and said, "Yeah. Can't believe it. No lectures, no deadlines. No more thesis. No more presentations."

"Fuck you. I still have a year to go."

"Should've started the cohort with me."

"Nah. Wouldn't have met Akira then."

"Thank God for that. Because without that, I wouldn't have met Meera."

A mischievous glint shone in Sam's eyes as he said, "I still remember a time when you told me you'd never date an Indian girl."

My response was lost in a grumble when I heard my name from somewhere around. Sam pointed behind me, and I turned to find Mom and Dad striding toward me. I rushed closer and pulled Mom into a hug.

"I'm so glad you guys made it on time," I said and exchanged a hug with Dad.

"Barely. We knew the parking would be trouble, so we thought we'd take the subway. But what do you know? We got held up on the subway for twenty-five minutes."

If I didn't stop Dad, he would go on and on about the awful subway system and a need for better management. I quickly turned to Sam and asked, "Where's Akira?"

For some reason, he looked startled. "Oh. Uh, she went to her place. She needed some accessories and heels for her dress. She said she'd meet me here."

"Where is she? I was hoping to see her too before joining my classmates."

He ran his hand through his neatly combed hair, completely messing it up, and said, "Let's click a few pictures with your mom and dad, and if she still isn't here, you can see her after the ceremony."

For the next ten minutes, I got some pictures with my parents. Mom clicked some with Sam, some with just me, and some with my classmates hanging around near us. But it was time, and Akira wasn't here.

"It's time, Sam. I'll catch up with Akira later."

I hugged Sam, then my parents, and said, "See you later. Please stay with Sam. We'll catch up right here after the ceremony. And keep your phones on. It's going to get super crazy and crowded."

If I didn't give a long list of instructions to Mom and Dad, they'd just do their own thing and I'd be left running across the entire campus. There were five other graduation ceremonies of different grad programs happening at the same time. I looked at Sam and tipped my head toward my parents. He gave me a thumbs-up in assurance, and I joined my classmates to head to the building where we were supposed to gather.

The entire way to the building was filled with students in blue huddled close to their families. Everyone was joyful, bursts of pride emanating from them. People had their partners in their arms, looking at them with such adoration, and a surge of loneliness pierced my heart. Meera would be proud of me too. I thought about calling her, but it would be her midnight. I'd received her letter, as well as her text this morning, wishing me luck.

Two more days.

And I'd be in her arms.

Two. More. Days.

With a renewed determination, I walked faster.

When it was time for our cohort, our entire batch of classmates poured out of our assigned building in line, wearing our caps and big smiles, and walked toward the outdoor seating space. I couldn't see where my parents and Sam sat, but there were loud cheers and claps from the entire friends and family section. The air of accomplishment and excitement to go out in the world was palpable.

Once everyone was seated, the speeches started. And of course, we cheered and hollered. This was the last time we'd hear a lecture from some of our favorite professors. And when the dean said we'd always be welcome in the community, I felt that. This connection that I'd formed with all my classmates and this university. This network that I'd be able to rely on for future opportunities. It was a ray of hope that things would work out, even if I was in India. And maybe the idea that Sam and I talked about during our little camping trip could actually work.

With the conclusion of the last speech, it was time for students to get a certificate from the dean. We slowly started moving along in the line toward the stage as I looked around to find my parents or Sam, just so I could wave at them. But God knows where they'd taken a seat. I just couldn't find them.

I could only hope they could see me.

Once my name was called, I climbed the three steps to the stage. As I shook my hand with the dean and got the certificate,

I turned around to wave and hopefully get a glimpse of my parents, Sam, and Akira.

Thankfully, Akira had climbed on top of the chair to wave, and she was holding someone's hand and waving like a madwoman. I started to laugh when my eyes dropped to the person whose hand she held.

And I tripped and fell flat on the stage. My mind was still stuck on one face. For the life of me, I couldn't move myself, too afraid that if I looked again, she'd disappear. Someone clutched my arm and pulled me up, and my eyes returned to where she stood.

There she was. Her lips parted in shock, eyes wide in horror, hands clutched in her wild curls, and I laughed. I jumped down from the stage, and I ran. All I could see was her, across a sea of faces that were all but a blur.

Her eyes followed me, her lips trembled. And my legs pumped faster. People parted for me, or maybe I pushed them out of the way as I got closer. And she finally moved away from where she stood and ran toward me.

In a blink of an eye, she'd jumped into my arms. Her arms clutched my neck, my face hidden in her curls. How I missed her. My heart soared and pumped and went wild within my chest.

I breathed her in, and I finally felt like I was home.

I squeezed her tighter to me. She was real. Real. Meera was in my arms. We pulled away from the hug, and my hands clutched her face.

"You're here," I whispered as I felt the softness of her cheeks, the wild curls of her hair, and the tears that brushed my thumb. I wiped them gently and pulled her closer. She laughed and wiped at my cheeks, and I realized I was crying. And I was laughing. And she was laughing.

"Surprise!" she said, and her voice, after so long, washed

over me, soothing me and filling the raw, aching emptiness within me.

And before I knew it, my lips were on hers. It wasn't slow. It wasn't gentle. It wasn't like a first kiss. This kiss was a storm of all the missed kisses. It was all consuming and raw with need. It was a warm ray of sunshine after two hundred and fifty-nine days of a frigid, cold winter.

I kissed her like I reminded her of my love, my touch. She clutched my hair and deepened the kiss, reminding herself, and me, that she owned me. Because she absolutely did.

Loud cheers and hoots broke our spell. I pulled off the kiss and found a hundred faces looking at me, laughing and cheering us. And before anyone could say anything, I clutched Meera's hand, pulled off my graduation cap, and threw it in the air with a loud whoop.

And then I ran.

Our hands entwined, I ran out of the ceremony, pushing away anyone who got in my way. I kept glancing at Meera, who kept up with me, her smile so bright I couldn't look away.

"Where are we going?" she shouted, looking around with her gorgeous smile.

"I don't know," I shouted back, and she laughed.

And for the life of me, I couldn't help but stop and kiss her again. Feel her laugh on my lips. And I was lost again.

Meera laughed and pulled away. "Luke, we're in everyone's way."

"Then stop laughing. I can't help myself."

She laughed again. And I kissed her again. And when she moaned, I had to drag myself away from her and run faster.

"We're going home," I said, and that was all we said the entire way.

I cursed the stairs for the entire two floors of my building that we climbed.

But the moment we stepped inside the house, all bets were off.

I hauled her in my arms and rushed to my room. I dropped us on the bed and took a deep breath, just staring at her.

Her eyes shone with excitement, nerves, and the adoration I could never get enough of. Her fingers traced my forehead, my cheek, my lips, my neck, my hair. She bit her lip before she whispered, "I missed you."

I held her waist with one arm while my other got busy exploring her. Her beautiful hair, her smooth, brown skin, her adorable, pointy nose, her long earrings, her slender neck. I looked at what she wore. A saree. A gorgeous maroon saree with a thin golden border. My finger moved along the border. Slowly. Trying to make my brain work.

Meera was here. In America.

"How? God, when did...? I mean, just...how?"

She chuckled. "Akira. Remember when she came to my place in December? She asked me if I could."

"If I'd known you could, I would've invited you. I promise."

She placed her finger on my lips and said, "I know. I had told her no, actually. But, well, things changed. And I used some of the money you left me for the tickets."

I dropped my forehead on hers, guilt slicing through me. If she used the money for this, she wouldn't have enough to pay off the loan. And it's so difficult to make her accept money as it is. "You shouldn't have. What about the loan, Meera?"

She moved her fingers along my jaw, and my body shuddered in pleasure. How I missed her body along mine. Her soft curves, the way we fit. Adding her soft silk saree to the mix, I wanted to devour her.

Seeing my turmoil, she said, "Hush now. I know what I'm doing. Things are going to work out. Now, enough talking, Luke. Kiss me."

I didn't have to be told twice. I clutched her waist,

dropped my weight on her, and kissed her. With every swipe of her lips on mine, I turned harder. My hips rocked against her saree-covered hips while she kept trying to put her legs around me.

"Shit," she muttered, "shouldn't have worn the saree."

"Let's get it off, shall we?" I asked, holding the part that draped over her shoulder, but for the life of me, I couldn't pull it off. "Why is it all so wrapped around you?"

She giggled and kissed me. "Let me up."

I got off her and climbed down the bed. I noticed I was still wearing my graduation gown and my suit. I quickly removed the thing, took off my suit, and pulled out the belt from my pants. I sat at the edge of the bed as Meera turned around, and said, "Can you remove the safety pin from the underside of my blouse at the shoulder?"

I pulled her on my lap and kissed and sucked her exposed back. I suckled at her neck and the way her body moved against mine. The way her back looked in her little blouse, I couldn't help but suck harder and leave a little bruise.

"You're so fucking hot, baby."

She rested her head on my shoulder, her hand clutching my thigh, and she moaned. "Luke, hurry."

Right. The safety pin. I quickly found the pin tucked under her blouse and removed it. The entire part across her shoulder dropped, and all I could see was her blouse, tightly molding her breasts. My body hardened even more underneath her, where she sat on my lap. Her hips moved over me, and she moaned my name.

"I need to touch you, Meera. Fuck. Can I?"

"Please," she whispered.

My hands covered her breasts, and I squeezed. A loud groan burst out of me, and I sucked her neck to stop more noises. Meera pulled at my hair and brought me even closer. She ground her hips on my lap, her moans pumping up my arousal. I quickly turned her around and pulled at the saree around her waist. Again, it got stuck at the front pleats.

"Fuck, why won't it come off?"

Dazed, Meera opened her eyes and patted around the front. "Pins. Just a sec."

Quickly, she removed the front thing, pulled out the safety pins, and I quickly pulled her saree. Meera turned a full circle as I got her out of the bloody thing, and another skirt-like thing appeared from underneath the saree.

"Meera," I groaned. "You came here to kill me, didn't you?"

She laughed and kissed me. With a quick tug on the lace at her waist, the skirt pooled at her feet, and she climbed over my lap, now only in her blouse and underwear. Clutching her, I rolled on my back and kissed her. She ground herself on me and placed open-mouthed kisses on my neck. "You looked incredibly hot in your suit. This shirt and pants are driving me crazy," she whispered, rubbing herself against my tented pants.

I groaned, and she captured the sound with her mouth.

With a quick work of hands, she opened the buttons of my shirt, and I lifted myself to take it off. Holding her to me, I laid her on her back and traced the edge of her blouse. Slowly, I unhooked the buttons that revealed her bare breasts to me. No bra.

At my raised eyebrows, she said, "It's a padded blouse."

"Good."

And the next thing I knew, I'd pulled off her underwear and we were both naked and kissing.

My hands were everywhere, clutching, squeezing, grabbing. Her body moved beneath mine, pulling me closer and closer until no space was left between us. Her hands branding me, her nails digging into my back, her lips burning me where they touched, and I lost myself to her warmth, her smell, her hair.

My cock moved between her thighs. So hard. So painful. The only relief was her wetness and heat gliding against me, soaking my cock. More. More. More. I needed to be inside her. Needed to belong to her. Without moving away from her, I stretched my body toward the nightstand.

Meera, however, did not stop. While I looked for a condom, she kissed and sucked my neck, grazing her teeth against my shoulder. Pleasure rocketed through my veins and my hips kept rolling in her heat. If she didn't stop, I would come right between her legs.

Where the fuck were my condoms? My hands couldn't find the damn things.

At that point, Meera ground hard against me and moaned. And fuck, *fuck.* "Meera," I groaned.

"I can't, Luke. I'm too close."

And fuck it. I clutched her thigh and ground harder against her.

My cock slipped against her wet folds, and I felt the tingle of the impending orgasm at the base of my spine.

My hips jerked faster, and she moaned, "Right there, Luke. Please. Please. Just like that."

I couldn't look away from her. Her head tilted back, hair spread across my pillow, hands clutching my bedsheet, hips jerking with mine. "Meera. Baby, I love you. So. Fucking. Much."

With every word, my hips jerked faster, harder, needing to be buried inside her, but unable to do so. Desperation clung to me as pleasure and need rocked my body farther and farther against her, as my balls drew up and I gritted my teeth, needing to feel Meera come on my cock. "Come for me, Meera. Oh, fuck, baby. So. Fucking. Close."

With the next slide of my hips against her clit, she screamed out her orgasm. Her legs tightened around me, and her spine rose off the bed in pleasure, and I lost it. With quick, jerky movements, my orgasm rushed through me, sliding between her pussy in a hot, pulsating mess.

"Meera, Meera, Meera." Her name was a prayer on my lips.

She shivered and pulled me up over her. I quickly cleaned us up as best as I could using the tissues from my nightstand because I refused to move away from Meera even for a second.

I pulled my blanket over us and remained on top of her, warming her up, and placed kisses along her shoulder. "I still can't believe you're here."

"Me too. I so wanted to tell you. But then, I also wanted to surprise you."

Something finally registered. "Did I actually face-plant on the stage?"

She cringed at that, but a mischievous spark lit up her eyes as she said, "Yeah. Sorry about that."

I moved beside her and brought her in my arms. "You don't look sorry at all."

She giggled and cuddled closer, her face tucked in my neck. "I'm not. It made me realize how much I missed you."

My hands moved across her naked back, memorizing the feel of her skin. "Tell me all about your sneaky plan. Did you come alone? When did you arrive? And who picked you up? How was the flight?"

She chuckled and kissed my jaw, rubbing her cheek against mine. "Well, the reason you were sent to camp with Sam was not to let you call me. That was the time when I was traveling."

"Sam was in on it too?" My voice came out unreasonably high-pitched.

No wonder he kept finding new things to do every time we got some network and I wanted to call Meera.

She continued, "And Akira and your parents came to pick me up."

I didn't even realize I stood on top of the bed, looking down at her in shock. "My parents were in on it too?"

Meera sprawled naked on her back and let out a loud chuckle. "Yes. You have no idea how nervous I was to meet your mom. I was coming off a thirty-two-hour flight, I looked like a mess, and there she was hugging me."

"Thirty-two-hour flight? It doesn't take that long. What airline did you take?"

She glared at me. And oh, I missed those too. I jumped on her and smacked a deep kiss on her lips. "Well, just because I used your money doesn't mean I wasn't going to look for the cheapest flight. I didn't mind the travel time at the discount I got."

This woman. I moved my now-hard cock against her because of course I got hard the moment she threw her glare at me, and said, "First, it's your money now, and you can use it for whatever you want. And second, our flight back will be a one-stop flight."

She gasped when I moved, but she nodded. "Okay."

I kept moving slowly and said, "How long do you plan to stay here?"

With a gasp when I moved over the right spot, she said, "I've taken a leave for two weeks."

"Fuck, yes. I'm gonna show you so many great places."

"Luke," Meera whimpered.

"Yes, darling?"

"Get the condoms first."

"Oh fuck, yes. Wait."

I climbed off her and opened the nightstand. Empty. My stomach dropped. But then, it clicked for me. Naked, I rushed to one of my packed bags.

Behind me, Meera giggled. "Your butt is so cute. It jiggles when you run."

I turned my head to look at her, all the while fumbling through the pockets of the bag, because I knew I packed a box in here. I wanted to be prepared the moment I met Meera.

"Yours will jiggle too when I fuck you."

She moaned and cupped herself. "Hurry."

And I nearly spilled myself again. Right there.

After digging around for what felt like forever, I finally found it and opened the box. Quickly, I got on the bed, between her thighs, and opened a pack. Slowly, I rolled it down my cock, Meera watching me with hungry eyes.

I dropped on my arm above her, and slowly, slowly pushed the tip in. She was soaked, and I slipped farther in. The tightness, her heat, the pressure enveloped me, and all I wanted was to be buried deep inside her for hours. Pleasure danced behind my eyes, and Meera moved her hips, taking me deeper.

I pulled her legs tighter around me and pushed. Meera moaned and clung to me like her life depended on it.

And soon, our bodies were one, gliding, pushing, fucking, *loving*. Our mouths collided as we tried to kiss, our tongues met and played, our hands clutched and squeezed. I pumped into her faster, needing to be deeper inside her, dying to claim her back and remind myself that she was in my arms.

With every pump of my hips, she moaned louder.

I chanted her name, pressed my lips against her neck, and sucked where her neck met her shoulder.

She screamed my name, and her teeth bit into my shoulder.

She was so fucking wet her juices slid down my balls and made a squelching sound every time I pushed inside her. "Look how wet you are, Meera. You're soaking my balls."

She whimpered at my words, her pussy clenching around me.

I buried my face near her ear and pushed myself deeper and stopped there, not moving, and said, "You're going to drench the sheets, aren't you, baby?"

She arched off the bed and dug her heels into my ass, trying to get me moving. "Move! Please, move, Luke."

I pushed my tongue in her mouth and started moving like a man possessed, needing to taste her moans, gulp in every breath she took as she rode her pleasure.

My body took over all my senses, and my control snapped. My hips started to jerk as pleasure shot down my spine, and I thrust harder and faster. And with broken whimpers in my mouth, Meera came, clutching my hair, squeezing my cock so tight I followed right behind her, my orgasm roaring through my body, my voice hoarse from calling her name.

Sated, drenched in sweat and soaked in love, we slept in each other's arms after two hundred and fifty-nine days.

29

Song: *Taarif Karoon Kya Uski*
- *Mohammed Rafi*

Meera

An unbearable pressure from my bladder roused me from my sleep, and I found myself enveloped in a warmth that I'd so achingly missed for months. Luke's hot chest against my back, his arm circling my waist, his leg thrown over mine, felt like a cocoon I never wanted to leave. But when Luke moved his leg up over my hip, the pressure increased.

Slowly, so as not to wake him up, I moved his arm from my waist and got out of his grip. I pulled the mess of my hair in a top knot and rubbed the sleep out of my eyes.

With quiet steps, I made my way to the attached washroom. After finishing my business, I washed my hands and stared at myself in the mirror. My lips were swollen from all the kissing we'd been doing since yesterday afternoon.

I wore Luke's T-shirt and his boxers that almost reached my

knees. It was the following morning, and we'd only left his room in the late evening to eat the dinner Sam and Akira had put in the fridge for us.

After dinner and a quick shower together, we'd gone back to his bed, reuniting our bodies, talking about everything and nothing. I saw toothpaste in a holder on the sink. I squeezed some on my finger and brushed my teeth. We'd have to go to Akira's old apartment to get all my stuff. Till then, this would have to do.

Once freshened up, I got out of the washroom to find Luke still fast asleep. I had no intention of waking him up, but I couldn't stay in the room anymore. My stomach rumbled in hunger. With quiet steps, I walked out of the bedroom and quietly shut the door behind me.

I walked down the small hallway that led to an open space that consisted of the living room, kitchen, and dining room. The moment I stepped into the living room, two faces turned toward me at the same time. Akira's face widened into a big smile, while Sam's lips turned up a little, and he gave me a polite nod.

They sat close together on the sofa, Akira's legs sprawled over Sam's, his one hand resting on her leg while his other held a mug.

With a mischievous glint in her eyes, Akira said, "I'd ask you how the reunion went, but you look happy and satisfied to me."

Heat rushed through my cheeks, and I could barely meet her eyes. Thankfully, Sam didn't respond to Akira's teasing and went back to sipping his coffee.

"Akira," I moaned. "You're crazy."

"Yep," Sam piped up from beside her, all the while drinking his coffee.

She laughed and nudged her elbow into his ribs. He glared at her, but his eyes turned warm when he looked at her. He lightly pulled her hair, and she pressed a quick kiss to his lips. I averted my eyes and looked toward the kitchen.

My stomach growled again, and Akira snorted. She got up and walked toward the kitchen. "I'll make some chai for us. There are donuts on the breakfast table, and I also have some Indian snacks to go with the chai," she said in Gujarati.

"I'll help you make the chai," I said, following her into the kitchen on the other side of the breakfast bar. We could see Sam drinking coffee and surfing on his phone from the kitchen.

"I'm so happy you're here, Meera. It's so good to spend time with someone from back home."

How did Akira do it? Live so far away from her family back home. And she had a huge family of fourteen people. To leave that support, that constant presence of family around you, and live in a new country all alone? It couldn't have been easy.

"That reminds me. Your mom sent a few snacks and a bag full of clothes and accessories with me."

She laughed in exasperation. "I told her I didn't need anything."

"As if Aunty would listen."

Once the chai was ready, we carried the Indian snacks and chai to the dining table. At that moment, soft footsteps padded down the corridor, and Luke appeared in the living room. His hair was mussed, lips pouty, eyes slightly tense in worry.

Without meeting Sam's or Akira's eyes, he came to the table, tugged me to his chest, clinging to me for five whole seconds, and placed a kiss on my head. Softly, he murmured, "You weren't there when I woke up."

I caressed his jaw, his scruff prickling my hand. "I didn't want to wake you."

He moved his finger near my temple, smoothing my hair. "I thought you were a dream."

Oh, my heart. I imagined how I would've felt to wake up

without him, and a sudden panic gripped my chest. "I'm so sorry. Next time, I'll wake you up or get back in bed with you."

His lips stretched into his wide, warm smile that always melted me. "It will just take some time for my mind to register that you're actually here."

A loud cough jerked us apart. Akira looked at us with heart eyes, her hands clutched under her chin, her lips stretched wide in a teasing smile. "I just had to warn you guys before you started making out right here."

Luke straightened from where he was bent over me and gave Akira a smile, his face lit up in happiness. He walked closer to her and pulled her in a hug. "I don't think I can ever thank you enough for this lovely gift. You are officially my favorite person in the world."

Just to tease him, I coughed loudly. From above Akira's shoulder, Luke quickly shook his head and said, "You don't count, baby," and blew me a kiss.

At that, Sam coughed loudly, to which Luke said, "You definitely count. Friend for years, and Akira still beat you in the friendship department."

Akira pulled off the hug and did a victory dance, mocking Sam. Sam immediately got up from the couch and ran toward Akira.

They ran around the living room, Akira shrieking and apologizing.

Luke turned to me and said, "I'll freshen up and be right back."

I raised my cup of chai. "I'll be right here."

Quickly, he kissed my head and jogged toward his room.

Soon, Akira sat across from me with her chai while Sam fumbled with the coffee machine. The aroma of coffee was so strong I could barely smell my chai. Sam returned with two cups and the coffee pot in his hand at the same time Luke rushed out of his room.

Luke kissed my cheek— right in front of Sam and Akira— making me embarrassed as hell. He chuckled and brushed his thumb across my cheek.

"Luke, are you ready to discuss our plan?" Sam asked, pulling us out of the momentary haze of connection.

For a second, Luke looked as confused as Akira and me. Then you could see it all clicked and he said, "Yes. Yes. Of course."

He poured himself a cup of coffee, and added a pack of sugar. "What're you guys talking about?" Akira asked, her eyebrows scrunched up in confusion.

Luke put one of his arms on the back of my chair, lightly brushing his fingers along my shoulder, as he said, "Sam and I were talking about my future plans, how I planned to work as well as stay with Meera."

Guilt had me looking down into my half-empty cup of chai. A light tug at my hair had me looking at Luke. "Meera, you don't have to feel guilty. One way or another, we have to figure out our plans, right? Hear me out, and then let me know your thoughts. Okay?"

When I nodded, he continued, "So, as I was saying, the possibility of Meera moving to America is zero since there is no way that the US would grant a green card or any visa that would let Hari and Meera's mom be with us. The only option is for me to move to India."

Akira nodded, and I looked at Luke with a hundred questions on the tip of my tongue. He shook his head at me to let him finish and said, "Now, I know what you're thinking. I did my master's, so how do I plan to work? There is absolutely no scope for an architect in the village. What about Wilson and White Constructions? So, Sam and I wondered if I could work on preparing the designs, drawings, and construction documents from India while Sam and you, Akira, could handle the client meetings and on-site construction. And of course, you guys will join in the design process since you would have more clarity about the site. This way, I can work for our company while living with Meera."

Akira turned to Sam with an open mouth, pride clear in her eyes. "You helped him plan that, didn't you?"

Sam straightened his glasses, and said, "Of course. He was just going to up and leave the country and go with the flow. No thoughts whatsoever for our company."

Luke grumbled, "I was obviously going to think about the future once I'd been back with Meera for a few days."

He turned to me and said, "I promise."

I smiled and nodded.

"What do you think?" Luke asked, holding himself tight.

Akira clapped and, with a big smile on her face, said, "I love it."

I cleared my throat, and everyone looked at me. Guess this was as good a time to put my idea on the table. "I too was waiting for later to discuss future plans. But since we're already discussing..." I looked at Luke and continued. "Maa told me that she's finally ready to sell our farm. I didn't want to take any major step without talking to you or without you being by my side, so I've continued to pay the loan. But I was hoping that maybe, if you wish, we could move to the city. I was thinking of Ahmedabad."

Akira shrieked at that. She was from Ahmedabad, and her entire family was there. I smiled at her right as Sam told Akira, "Sweetheart, let her finish."

She shrugged in apology, and I looked back at Luke, trying to gauge his reaction. "And I was wondering, that is if you want to, and if you think it's best for you, you can open an architecture office in Ahmedabad. Like an Indian branch of Wilson and White Construction. I mean, this is just an idea..."

I found hot lips that smelled of rich coffee pressed against mine. And I couldn't help but taste more. But too soon, they moved away, and my eyes opened to Luke's big, grinning face. "You, Meera, are a genius."

"Not really. If you'd known I was okay selling our farm, you'd have the same idea too."

He shook his head, and said, "Whatever the case, I do like this idea. There could be a lot better scope for an architecture company in the city."

Akira piped in, "Not *could be,* Luke. Ahmedabad is developing rapidly, and people are getting more interested in hiring professional architects than ever. We will surely find many clients to work with. And we can have an entire workforce that prepares construction documents and designs in India. That would save us a lot of money. Even if you pay a very good salary to employees you hire in India, it would still be significantly cheaper than what you'd pay an employee in the US."

Sam looked at Akira as if she was the biggest piece of the most delicious cake and he was ready to dig in.

Akira turned to Sam. "What do you say, Sam?"

"I say you keep talking business strategy in the bedroom too."

And before any of us could say anything, Sam dragged Akira into the other hallway leading to their bedroom. A loud thud of a door closing echoed in the hallway, and Luke said, "Well, since that's decided, what shall we do now?"

A loud moan came from the hallway, and both of us jumped out of our chairs. "Certainly get out of here for a while."

Luke nodded. "Excellent idea. I'll show you my campus."

Warmth bloomed in my stomach. Before I could tell him how much I loved him, another moan rang off the hallway, and Luke threw a sweater at me, clutched my hand, and dragged me out the door.

≈

Luke

That evening, I took Meera to visit One Vanderbilt Avenue, one of the best rooftop views to visit in New York City. The view at the top opened to the Empire State Building at the front and center. It was magnificent.

What was even more magnificent was the view of my girl in my fucking sweater and a tight pair of jeans with a coat on top. I'd almost stumbled when I'd seen her wear that. But right now, with a hundred mirrors around us, the bright light from the glass facade raining down on her, and the view of the NYC skyline in the background, I couldn't look elsewhere. She was my whole world.

Her eyes were wide, looking everywhere, taking it all in. The place was a tourist spot, so it was crowded as hell, but not enough to deter her wonder at everything. I clutched her hand and led us closer to the glass wall. Her hand tightened around me, and she pulled me back, her eyes wide. "Luke. Stay back. We're too high up."

I stopped where we were, a few feet away from the glass wall, where we couldn't see the street below, and turned to her. "Are you afraid of heights?"

She shrugged, her eyes moving between me and the view beyond. "I've never been this high. So...um...I don't know."

I stepped closer to her and pressed a kiss on her forehead. Her gaze quickly darted around, probably at the PDA, but then she blushed. Softly, I asked, "Would you like to try? I won't release your hand."

She looked at the view again and, after a second, nodded.

I quickly pressed my lips to her forehead again and led us closer. Her hand was like a vise in mine.

But the moment we reached the glass, she gasped. She touched the glass wall and peered down. Her eyes were wide in wonder, and when she looked at me with the biggest smile, my heart soared.

I couldn't stop it. I bent down and captured her smile with my lips, tasting her wonder on my tongue.

I was so far gone for this girl, it wasn't even funny.

We walked around the observatory, checking out various exciting displays in different corners. We got a different view of the city as we walked around the place. I pointed at the famous landmarks — Central Park, One World Trade Center, Chrysler Building, Times Square, and many more.

After a while, we found a glass corner overlooking the approaching sunset, and we sat with her between my legs, her back to my chest. Her head rested against my shoulder while I played with her fingers. Tourists surrounded us, but they were all just a blur to me. Meera was my only focus.

She was quiet in my arms, so she took me by surprise when she asked, "How would you ever leave all of this, this beautiful, big world, and not resent me in the future?"

My arms tightened around her, and I looked down at her face. She looked at where our fingers were joined, refusing to meet my eyes. How could she still not know?

I kissed her hair. "Look at me, baby."

Her chest moved in a sigh, and she turned her eyes to mine.

This time, I kissed her nose. "The only one I would ever resent is myself if I didn't follow you to the ends of this earth. This city would be, as it was for the last two hundred and sixty days I lived in it without you, a glaring reminder of how achingly empty my life was before you. *You* are the one who brings joy and love for the places I visit and the work I do. Without you, nothing else matters."

Her eyes glistened with unshed tears, and this time, she captured my words on her lips. "I will love you every day, every hour, every minute, every second of my life. I'll love you so hard that you'll never regret coming home to me. You're never, ever getting rid of me now."

My nose tingled, my eyes were blurry, and my lips were stretched into the widest smile I ever had as I brushed a soft kiss on her lips. "Now you're getting it."

She brushed a stray tear off my cheek with her thumb, sucked it in her mouth, and turned around to the devastating view of the sun setting in the Hudson River, the Empire State Building encased in golden-orange light.

We didn't leave the observatory till the sky was dark. The entire city was lit up in its golden yellow lights, the billboards at Times Square illuminated the entire block, and the entire observatory was awash with a colorful light show.

We walked back home, hand in hand in the city, *my* city, as I pointed at my favorite buildings, places I'd visited during my architecture school, and restaurants I'd loved. I shared all my memories with her.

When we got home, she stripped us bare of all our clothing and kissed me everywhere she could. I laid her on her back and kissed her neck, sucking her dark brown nipples till she arched off the bed and wrapped her leg around my waist. I moved lower and lower, tasting her along the way until I reached her hips.

I brushed my stubble against her inner thigh, and she whimpered, her legs closing on instinct.

"Open your legs for me, darling." I kissed the top of her thigh and ran my nose where her thigh met her mound.

She moaned my name and opened her legs, her hands clutching the sheets around her.

"That's my girl. Look at you." I lowered my head and finally, after two hundred and sixty days, tasted my girl.

Her taste, her smell, her wetness coated my tongue, and a bolt of pleasure rocked through my body. My cock throbbed and jerked as I took another taste of her. Her thighs tightened around my head and pushed me deeper, and my cock was already leaking.

Fuck, this would be over fast.

Slowly, I pushed my fingers inside her, and she clenched around them. "More, Luke. Please, more."

"Fuck, darling. Come on my fingers. I want to feel you on my fingers and taste you on my tongue."

She cried out as I lowered my head and lost myself in bringing her to the edge.

Her hips started to move faster, her feet dug into my back, and the moment I sucked on her clit, her back arched off the bed, and she shattered on my fingers.

I was so close my cock throbbed against the bed. If I just thrust twice against the bed, I was gonna blow.

Before I could do just that, Meera sat up and had me on my back in a blink. She straddled my legs and said, "Now, your turn. Teach me how to do that to you."

And I'd gone to heaven.

"I'm very close, baby. You might just have to breathe on my cock right now."

She laughed, and my cock jerked. "Fuck, Meera. Don't laugh."

She looked down at my very hard, very erect cock, and grazed her finger against the length. She'd seen and given me a few hand jobs when we were in India, but we never got around to her sucking me off.

"You're sure?" I asked.

And she glared at me. My cock hardened at that, and she appeared shocked. I raised my eyebrows. "Told you I love it when you glare at me."

She shook her head with a smile and lowered her head so her lips were a hairsbreadth away from my tip.

My hips moved, trying to get closer to her mouth. "Open your mouth and give it a lick, baby."

Her breath touched me before her tongue. And my body buzzed with a jolt of electric pleasure as her tongue licked my entire length. Before I could tell her what to do next, her mouth closed around my tip, and my brain short-circuited.

"Fuck, Meera! Perfect. God."

My words were a jumbled mess as I tried not to come, as I tried desperately to hold off and savor her mouth for just a few more seconds.

I quickly leaned on my elbows to watch her take my cock in her mouth for the first time. "Suck me, baby."

The moment I saw her lips wrapped around my cock, her cheeks hollowing out as she gave me a long, hard suck, pain and pleasure coiled in my belly and raced down my spine, and my back arched into mind-numbing pleasure as I came in her mouth. In hindsight, I should've warned her, but my mind-to-mouth connection had been severed.

And my gorgeous girl swallowed every single drop.

I wiped away the little bit of my cum near her lips with my thumb and slowly pushed my thumb into her mouth. "You okay?"

Her eyes were dazed with pleasure as she sucked the cum off my thumb, and a smile played on her lips, as she said, "You taste disgusting."

I snorted. I pulled her on top of me and winked at her. "You don't taste like a chocolate milkshake either."

She chuckled, and I cupped her head and dove into her mouth, tasting myself on her tongue.

THE NEXT DAY, we reached my parents' house around noon. Mom had insisted we stay for the whole day, so here we were. Meera had gone shopping with Akira just for this occasion. She got a beautiful white wrap-around dress that hugged her curves just right. The moment she'd walked out of the bathroom wearing that dress, my mind had completely blanked out.

And I had made us very, very, very late to my parents' house as I showed her *how much* I loved her in that dress and how I would get her all the dresses in the world.

We now sat in my parents' living room. Mom and Dad had gone all out for Meera's welcome. The house was sparkling, fresh flowers adorned the different corners of the house, and so many pretty pastries were arranged in that British-style three-tiered glass set.

On one hand, it made me so fucking happy to see my parents make all the effort to welcome Meera into our home, but on the other hand, I could feel Meera getting overwhelmed.

Mom took a bite of her pastry and looked at Meera. "So Meera, honey, how are you finding New York?"

Meera cleared her throat and put the pastry she was holding back on her plate. "It's beautiful, Aun—Olivia. Luke took me to One Vanderbilt Avenue Observatory the other day, and I must say, I could sit there for hours."

I gently placed my arm around Meera. "You guys need to visit, Mom. It's really amazing."

Mom shook her head with a smile. "You know how I hate the city, honey. So much chaos. It freaks me out. I can't release your father's hand for a second."

Dad chimed in at that, mischief shining in his eyes. "That seems like a good reason for us to go, Livvy."

Mom blushed, and Dad gave me a wink.

Meera, too, had a small smile on her lips.

We chatted for a while about Meera's life in India, our trips to the stepwells and forts and palaces, and everything we saw there. Later, Dad wanted me to look at a few clients' proposals and projects he was considering bidding on.

I told Meera I'd be back in no time, and Mom waved us off.

30

Song: *Chhu Kar Mere Man Ko*
  - Kishore Kumar

Meera

L uke left me alone with his mom. I watched him go until he climbed the stairs and disappeared from my sight. My heart pounded so hard I was afraid Olivia could hear it.

I looked at her and smiled. What did I even talk to her about? We were so, so different. I knew Luke was rich, but this looked *really* rich to me.

Their house was in a gated community, made of stone walls, fancy wood textures, and large glass windows. I guess that's what you would expect from a family of architects. Even the interior was opulent but cozy.

It wasn't cold, but soft gray couches with lots of colorful pillows were laid out around a large wooden coffee table. A large portrait of a young girl, definitely Luke's sister, hung over the chimney. It looked like a shrine.

Plants and flower vases were everywhere, and so many different decorative items and souvenirs hung on walls and were arranged on shelves.

It all left me speechless. How would Luke's parents ever understand or accept Luke leaving all of this behind and starting fresh with me? He had everything here.

My eyes met Olivia, and she placed her plate in her lap and gave me a small smile. "Meera, honey, are you okay with Luke moving to India with you?"

Shouldn't I be asking this question to her? My shock must've been apparent on my face because Olivia continued. "Luke has always been a sweet and gentle soul. He's never asked for much from us, never had a crazy, rebellious phase. Especially after my angel, my Lucy's passing, he simply stopped asking for things."

She looked down at her hands. "Or maybe we just stopped seeing when he was asking for things."

She looked at me then. "We haven't been the best of parents, honey. Especially when we really needed to be."

I had to interrupt her there. "I'm sure you did the best you could. I know how crippling it can be to deal with soul-crushing guilt and regrets and pain."

Olivia's eyes glistened with tears. "I...I wouldn't wish that pain on my worst enemies."

She slowly stood from her seat on the other side of the couch and sat beside me. She smiled with tears in her eyes. "It steals your will to live. To move on and face another day without them in it. But Luke, my darling boy, he brought us back to life. Even though James and I didn't know how to live without our firstborn, Luke was always there. He always wanted us to smile. And laugh. And wanted us to love him. And when we couldn't love him enough, he loved us more. He slept between us at night. He always told us his god-awful jokes."

I couldn't help but smile at imagining a younger version of

Luke. And I couldn't help but feel sad for him. "Did it help you?" I asked.

Olivia smiled and shook her head. "Not quite at those moments. But one day, I had gone to James's office to give him lunch. Sam and Luke had joined their dads at the office that day. And I overheard Luke ask Sam how he made his parents love him. It absolutely crushed me. That was the last day I let myself, my life, and my guilt destroy me and my family. I'd failed one child. I couldn't fail another one of my precious babies."

Tears rolled down her cheeks.

My eyes were blurry as I held her hand. "You did not fail either of your children. You're simply human. And life sometimes takes our loved ones away before we're prepared. All we can do is love them with everything we have for as long as we get to have them."

She squeezed my hand and nodded. "And will you? Love my Luke?"

Tears ran down my cheeks, and I nodded. "I already do."

"Good. Good. I'm glad, Meera. Because, believe me, Luke does too. My boy has always loved hard. There have never been conditions to his love. Only acceptance. He never accused us of being lousy parents. He just kept waiting for us to get better. He loved us through all our pain and healing. And all I want is for him to find someone who will love him with all their heart."

I nodded. "I do. Luke is the brightest star in my darkest nights. He laughs, and my world comes alive. He looks at me, and my mind quiets down. My life was nothing but a never-ending cycle of pain and regret. And one day, this wonderful man comes along, making silly jokes, always trying to make me laugh, and he made my days more bearable. His light, his love, his smiles. I can't live without them in my life. I'm sorry, Olivia. But I'm keeping him forever."

She chuckled and sniffed. "Nothing makes me happier, honey, than knowing he gets loved by you."

Hearing those words lifted this invisible weight from my chest. Olivia and I weren't that different after all. Her pains, her guilt, her regrets, the life she'd been dealt, all shaped her to be the mother, the wife that she was today. Her country, her luxurious life, the color of her skin, her profession, nothing mattered to me when the connection I shared with her was of pain and loss. And Luke, our salvation.

"C'mon, let's get some dinner prepared. These men eat like beasts."

I chuckled, and we made our way to the kitchen, where Olivia regaled me with stories of Luke and made me fall in love with him again and again and again.

When Luke and James came downstairs, they noticed our swollen eyes and instantly went on high alert emotional support mode. We put dinner aside and jumped directly to dessert. Luke made us all laugh in a matter of a few minutes, and I saw his love for his family and his forgiveness for the past shining through.

As I looked at him laugh at something his dad said, his eyes shining with tears of mirth, his arm around my shoulder, the occasional brush of his hand on my thigh, I silently thanked Akira for pushing me to come to the States.

Soon, we would leave for India, and I promised myself to love him so much that he never felt unloved again. To love him so much that he never regretted leaving his world for me. To love him so much that he never regretted loving me.

31

Song: Pal Pal Dil Ke Paas
  - Kishore Kumar

Luke

The pasta sauce bubbled in the pan, and I had a big bowl of boiled pasta in the strainer.

Hari was about to sprinkle the red chili pepper flakes as I clutched his little arm. "No, no, Little Hari. We need to wait a little."

He pouted and asked slowly, thinking about his words, "How many minutes?"

I patted his cheek in praise, and said, "Five more minutes."

He nodded and sat on the kitchen counter, legs swinging, clutching the little container of the chili flakes.

Meera and I got back to Meera's home three days ago. And for the past three days, Hari hadn't left my side. And to my utmost surprise, Meera's mom had given me a very traditional welcome, moving a plate full of candle, turmeric, rice, and other red powder in a circle in front of my face. Meera had told me that parents gave such welcome to their son-in-law. And like the good future son-in-law that I was, and with the training that Akira had given Sam last year, I touched her feet for blessings and completely stole her heart.

Meera's eyebrows rose sky-high when I looked at her.

"Hari!" Meera shouted from the living room. Her voice, and Hari's startled gasp, brought me back to the boiling pasta sauce. Hari shouted something back in Gujarati, and Meera shouted back something in Gujarati even louder, which caused Hari to look at me expectantly, as if I understood what was going on.

I raised my eyebrows in question. "Su thayu?" I asked *what happened* in Gujarati. I'd decided to start learning the language too, and I'd started to grasp some phrases.

Now that I'd asked him the question, I realized he didn't know enough English to tell me what had happened, so he just looked toward the kitchen door and back at me.

Right then, Meera walked into the kitchen, smiling, and said something that had Hari turning to look at the kitchen entrance once again.

And in walked Abhi, Akira's younger brother.

"Hey, Luke," Abhi said and ruffled Hari's hair.

"That's what you were shouting at each other about?" I asked Meera.

She chuckled and nodded. "I told him to come outside, but he refused because he had to put the chili flakes in the pasta. I asked him to tell you to hurry up."

Ah. I looked at Hari and said, "Let's go, buddy. Start sprinkling."

With a serious frown of concentration, Hari got to it. With every three sprinkles, he looked at me, asking if he should continue, and every time, I nodded. After what felt like ten times of him asking, I told him it was enough.

"So, Abhi, when is Aakar coming?" asked Meera.

Abhi looked at his watch and said, "He went to drop

Mummy at home. He should be here soon. How many people are coming?"

Today was the day. The day when Meera paid off her loan to Baldev. She thought it was better to have as many witnesses as possible when she handed over such a large sum. And thankfully, she agreed to use the money I had left her. Today was also the day I decided to cook a little thank-you dinner for every one of Meera's friends who were there for her when I wasn't. We made some calls, and people started to show.

Abhi being the first. As the youngest of the elders, his job was to stay upstairs with Hari. Since Baldev could arrive any minute, I got some pasta on a plate for Hari and sent him and Abhi upstairs. He was happy to stay upstairs in the air-conditioned room, playing on their iPads. And yes, I got Hari an iPad, despite hearing all about its disadvantages from Meera. The smile on the little man's face was worth it all.

Soon, Surbhi arrived. And a half an hour later, Meera's best friend, Kriti, came rushing through the door. "Am I late?"

And well, to say she was a little overdressed would be an understatement. While Meera deliberately dressed in her most unflattering clothes, Kriti dressed in bright pink traditional wear with huge earrings that touched her neck, bangles, and perfectly applied makeup.

"Am I?" she asked again, this time louder.

And I realized that every one of us was stunned into silence.

Meera shook her head, and said, "Uh. No. Baldev hasn't arrived yet."

"Thank God." After looking at all of us still staring at her, she said, "What are you guys looking at? Maa roped me into a sudden meeting with a boy. Apparently, they were going to be in the village just for today."

She huffed and walked into the kitchen. Meera and I looked at each other, but she just shrugged her shoulders and led me into the kitchen too. We found Kriti tasting the pasta in a small bowl.

"How did the meeting go?" asked Meera.

Kriti swallowed the pasta, and with a frown on her face, muttered, "Actually, not bad."

She didn't look too happy about that.

"Is that a bad thing?" Surbhi asked.

Kriti turned to Surbhi and said, "I don't think so. It's just...it's kinda easier when things don't go well in these meetings. It's an easy no. Now, if the guy is interested, we'll have to talk again, and then deal with all the questions and rushing from the parents."

While Meera, Surbhi, and Kriti talked, I spread the garlic butter on the bread. Once the deal with Baldev was done, I'd just have to toast the bread before lunch.

Not even ten minutes passed when the doorbell rang again. Meera said, "That must be Aakar. Let's go to the living room. Baldev must be arriving soon."

In my periphery, Kriti was frowning severely. Before following Meera to the living room, I raised my eyebrows in question to Kriti. She shook her head and smiled at me. All of us stepped into the living room, and right then, Aakar turned to look at me with a smile on his face. The smile morphed into shock when his gaze landed behind me.

"You?" he said, his face turned slightly red, and he looked around all of us.

"You know Meera?" asked Kriti, a shocked noise escaping her throat.

Aakar, once again, looked at all of us, who were blatantly watching them, and moved toward Kriti. Not that it helped in the small living room full of people. "Um, yeah, family friends," he said. "How do you know Meera?"

"She's my best friend."

He stepped closer to her, and slowly, I made my way to

Meera, who stood gaping at the two. She didn't even notice me, so I nudged her with my elbow. Startled, she looked toward me and relaxed, then raised her eyebrows and indicated to Aakar and Kriti, who were talking in low murmurs.

"Guess he's the one she met in her arranged marriage meeting, huh?"

Meera nodded, and before I could say anything, Meera got a call.

She talked to someone and then turned to all of us. "Baldev's on the way here."

Aakar straightened, and so did the rest of us.

Meera lifted the mattress of the double bed in the living room and pulled out a big pouch that held the loan money. She turned to all of us and asked, "Ready, everyone? Luke, Aakar, and I will meet with Baldev, and you guys will stand on the porch. Just so he knows that everyone saw us exchange the money."

Once everyone nodded, all of us moved out on the porch. The three of us stepped down once the car entered the main gate. And for the first time, I came face-to-face with the man who had been Meera's nightmare. A red haze of anger had my hand clenching into a fist. Only Meera's soft touch pulled me back from the edge of landing a punch on his mouth.

The only thing that gave me some sort of satisfaction was the confusion on his face.

Baldev moved his gaze over Meera, and I instantly stepped in front of her. Meera's tight hold on my shirt at the back stopped me from moving any farther.

Sensing the tension, Aakar said, "Remember me?"

Ego had Baldev walking toward us with a cocky swagger that I looked forward to crushing.

He met Meera's eyes from behind me, and said, "You keeping bodyguards now? I didn't know I scared you."

Meera stepped forward, and it took everything in me not to

pull her behind me. "You don't scare me. You disgust me."

"You—" Baldev sneered.

Before he could talk further, Meera extended the money toward him. "Here. Everything that my father owed you. With interest."

Silence. Shock. Anger. All the emotions flashed behind Baldev's eyes. "You... How...?"

"That is none of your concern," I said to him, my jaw clenched tight in anger.

He looked at me, top to bottom, disgust and mockery in his gaze. Without responding to me, he looked at Meera and asked something that had Aakar stepping forward.

But before any of us could do anything, Meera flew toward Baldev and punched him in the nose. Quickly, I had her in my arms, away from Baldev, while Aakar stood between us, bellowing at him. Baldev said something, and even Aakar slapped him across the face. Baldev pushed Aakar in challenge.

What the fuck was going on?

"Leave me, Luke!" she screamed, her hands stretching into claws toward him. "I'm going to kill him."

"Settle down! I want to punch him, but I can't if I'm holding you back," I shouted at her.

That had her calming a little. She stopped fighting and said, "Put me down. And you better punch him harder than I did."

"Tell me what he said that had you go off like that," I demanded, needing to know how hard to punch that motherfucker.

Meera's cheeks darkened, and she looked away from me, her jaw clenched. "He...he implied I sold myself for the money."

That. Motherfucker.

Quickly, I let her go and ran to where Baldev and Aakar pushed at each other, mouthing off in their language. I pulled Baldev away from Aakar by the back of his shirt, turned him to me, and punched him in the nose. I felt the crunch in my knuckles, and Baldev landed on his back.

I bent over him, and said slowly, enunciating every word, "How dare you talk to Meera like that, you rotten, fucking piece of shit? Take your money and leave. And if I *ever* see you around this house, in this lane, I will destroy you. I have the money and resources to make your life miserable. Get out before I break your jaw."

Fuck it.

I decked his jaw again before Aakar pulled me back.

Baldev scrambled back on his ass and took a glance at Meera. I rushed him, making him whimper. "Do not look at her. You understand?"

He joined his hands and nodded.

"Get out. Now."

And he ran to his car.

Five seconds later, his car tore through the main gate.

The next thing I knew, Meera and I sat on the couch, holding ice wrapped in a cotton handkerchief over our knuckles. Everyone else had dispersed to various tasks. Aakar, Kriti, and Surbhi were in the kitchen, heating lunch and preparing garlic bread.

Meera looked at me with just as much pride in her eyes as I looked at her. "You have never looked sexier. Truly a goddess," I said, still thinking about her punch.

She laughed and placed her head on my shoulder. "I wish he had just accepted the money and left. His cruelty and anger just proved that he got sick pleasure at bullying weaker people."

I kissed her on her head and asked, "How do you feel?"

She didn't say anything for a while. "I guess it hasn't sunk in that I don't owe anything to anybody. Everything that I earn, I'll be able to keep."

She looked at me and asked, "Isn't that amazing?"

This woman. The things that she found herself grateful for, the things so many of us took for granted. Everything she wished to have in life, I'd give my all to bring her that. I kissed her once again on her forehead and was about to say something when Surbhi walked out of the kitchen, a small smile playing on her lips.

"What're you smiling about?" Meera asked, her hand lightly patting ice to her knuckles.

Surbhi brought a plastic chair closer to the couch and shook her head. "Those two, Aakar and Kriti, something's happening there. I felt like a third wheel even when they weren't talking to each other."

Meera's eyes shone in excitement. "Really?"

Before she could get more excited and start dreaming about scenarios, I murmured, "Not our business."

She waved me off. "I can think about whatever I want. I won't interfere."

She might've noticed it was just her, me, and Surbhi in the living room because she got serious and turned to Surbhi. "Surbhi didi, I wanted to talk to you about something."

Surbhi frowned but nodded. "Sure. What is it?"

Meera looked at me, and when I nodded in encouragement, she said in English, for my sake, "So, soon, all of us are moving to the city. And we were wondering if you would like to use this house and the farmland for all the widows and children who have nowhere to go."

Surbhi gasped, and her eyes shone with tears. She clutched Meera's hands and said, "But don't you want to sell it? Or, I don't know, keep it for when you want to come back?"

Meera smiled and shook her head. "To be honest, Maa is finally ready to let go of the place. But Luke convinced me to keep it. We decided to ask you. If you want, and if you think it would be easier to make our house and the land a community place, all of us can work on it. Luke had some ideas too."

When Surbhi turned to me, I said, "We have a few options for using the land. We can either start using it as a farm again, and since most of the women already help out on the farms, they know what they're doing. And if farming is not a financially viable solution, we can build a center here that has rooms for people, workshops to teach new skills to ladies, and a space where they feel at home. Meera and I can also work together on charity funds in the city. We can also extend financial help to farmers."

Meera chipped in, her voice shaking with tears. "I don't ever want other farmer families to feel helpless. It crushes your soul. And if we can use our land, where I lost my father, to give back and help other farmers, I know nothing would make him happier."

"Oh, Meera," Surbhi said and hugged Meera, tears flowing from both of their eyes.

I turned to find Aakar and Kriti standing at the living room door, watching Meera and Surbhi. Kriti came over and talked to them, making them laugh.

Once they settled, Surbhi turned to me and said, "I don't know how we came to be so lucky. Thank you, Luke. And I know those two words could never be enough. But I'm just... Thank you so much."

"Of course. It's an honor," I said and ran into the kitchen before my emotions got the better of me.

I saw that Aakar and Kriti had gotten all the food ready. I carried the pasta pot in the living room, and called out, "Let's eat, shall we?"

Quickly, everyone rose. Meera went out to the porch to call her mom inside. Ever since Baldev left, she had stayed outside, claiming she needed a few moments. When I went to see what was taking them so long, I found mother and daughter hugging and crying in each other's arms.

And I watched as, for the first time, they felt freedom.

32

Song: *Mere Samne Wali Khidki Mein*
  - Kishore Kumar

Meera

Late at night, after everyone had left and Hari and Maa had gone to sleep, I climbed up the stairs to the second floor. Standing against the parapet of the terrace, I found Luke. He was staring up at the stars, wearing his soft gray sweatpants and a white T-shirt, looking like an angel dropped into my life to change my entire world. To make it better. Brighter. Happier.

Not that I wouldn't have ever been happy without him. I would've been. I believe Maa would have moved on and let me sell the farm at some point. We would have paid off the loan by selling it, and my salary from teaching would've been enough. But would I have found love? Would I have yearned to move to a city and dreamed of more for myself? Hopefully, I'd never have to find answers to those questions.

I stepped onto the terrace and placed the jug of water on

the small table. Luke turned at the movement and gave me a warm smile. He reached his hand toward me, and when I placed my hand in his, he pulled me in his arms. We stood together, his arms around my waist, looking at the brilliant moon and the sea of stars shining in the midnight blue sky.

Luke pressed soft kisses along my neck, the sensation of his lips, the depth of his love, setting me on fire. My neck arched, asking for more. His hands clutched my waist tighter, his body pressed against mine, stoking the rising heat between us.

"Meera," Luke's gruff whisper of my name sent shivers down my spine.

"Luke," I moaned. He kept kissing me. Slower. Neck to shoulder.

"Talk to me. Today's been a long day."

I clutched his hands and nodded. "It was. It's like a huge weight has lifted from my shoulders. I feel so light I could fly. For years, I imagined, I dreamed of what it would feel like to pay off all my loan. And today was that day. And it felt so much better, so much lighter than I'd ever dreamed."

He kissed me again. I didn't need any words. Just his arms around me were everything.

"C'mon," he said, leading me to our cots he'd pushed together.

Since returning from America, we'd been sleeping on the terrace. However, there was a new addition tonight. He'd brought out the cassette player from the bedroom.

"Oh, I totally forgot to bring it out," I said.

We got on the bed, Luke's arm under my head and a soft blanket over us. "I haven't. Sleeping here, under the starlight, wrapped around you, this was the only thing missing. This is what brought us closer."

It was astounding how the same music, same songs, meant something different to us.

He must've seen something on my face because he asked, "What is it?"

"Ever since I started listening to music after my father passed, it has always been an escape. That momentary period when I forgot about the real world and all the disasters in it, and just enjoyed some peace. I had hardened myself so much. Those emotional songs were the only outlet for my emotions, my tears. And here you are, seeing it as a beautiful moment that brought us together, as much a part of us as these skies and the stars and the moon and our nights together. I guess I just wanted to thank you for making music, and the cassette player, a source of happiness for me."

He looked at me, the intensity in his eyes, the silence of his emotions, all making me look away. His rough breath and a soft kiss on my shoulder had me turning back to him.

"You're going to kill me with your words someday."

And I couldn't help but chuckle at that.

He pulled me into his arms, and I said, "Wait. Let me put the cassette in the player."

He released me, caressing my back as I reached for my cassette pouch. "What are you playing me today?"

I looked for the cassette I had in mind, and said, "Well, with you making music happy for me, I'll play a happy song."

He playfully bit my shoulder and lay on his back, smiling at the dark sky. "Yes, those are my favorite. Especially the one that gets you yodeling."

I laughed, remembering the first time I'd yodeled in front of him. It had also been the first time I'd laughed so much in a long time. "This one's a little more romantic. It reminds me of the time when I was starting to fall for you, and when we had just started listening to music together."

"Now you have me beyond excited," he said, turning to face me.

I found the cassette, popped it in the player, pressed play, and quickly snuggled myself in Luke's arms. His hand went into my curls, and he started playing with them.

The playful tune began with all sorts of funny sounds. My feet instantly started tapping, and Luke jumped out of our bed.

At my raised eyebrows, he pulled me up. "Dance with me, darling. Listen to these beats. You can't help but want to move."

And I wholeheartedly agreed.

I placed my hand in his, and he pulled me closer to him, his hand spread across my back, causing a million butterflies to take flight in my stomach.

I murmured the translation of the song, as the legendary singer Kishore Kumar started singing the song "Mere Samne Wali Khidki Mein."

> "In the window across from me
> Lives a piece of moon
> The only problem is
> That it stays somewhat detached from me."

Luke twirled me as he shook his head at the detached part. The melody had us swaying as the cool breeze of the summer night blew our hair.

> "Ever since I've seen them,
> I've forgotten to light the lamps
> I'm sitting here clutching my heart,
> I've forgotten to come or go anywhere
> Now constantly in my eyes
> I see that playful face."

I playfully flick Luke's nose. With every line that I sang and meant with my whole heart, he pulled me closer to him. The

words affected him as much as they did me. He twirled me
again and kissed me.

> "The rains came and went
> The clouds thundered and rained down
> But for one glimpse of them
> I was parched, O God of beauty.
> When will the thirst of my eyes quench
> Is all I worry day and night."

And there was no stopping Luke after that. His eyes shone
with passion and maybe even relief. That I, too, counted every
day and night, waiting to see a glimpse of his face. He clutched
my hair and raised my head to press a soft kiss against mine. I
pressed deeper, and with a loud groan, he picked me up.
Bringing me closer. Diving into my mouth. He quickly laid us
on the bed and covered me with his body. Every inch of me
touched every inch of him.

His touch burned through my clothes, and the desire
swirling in his gaze had my heart beating faster, and all I could
do was beg him to come closer. Take me higher, like only he
could.

And he did.

We moved slow; we moved fast. Under the thin blanket,
with the wind racing across our naked skin, Luke clutched me
closer to him. He moved so he was on his back, and I leaned
over him. He looked up at me with hooded, passionate eyes
that screamed his burning need for me.

His hips, his hardness, brushed along my center, and it took
me higher. The song of the night, the melodies from the player,
added music to our love.

Because that was what we were doing.

Making love.

For the first time, I was loving Luke unshackled from all the burdens of life. For the first time, I was flying. With Luke by my side, with Luke inside me, higher and faster. And when we exploded with pleasure, for the first time, I was ready.

Ready to love Luke. Forever.

Ready to love life. And all the adventures it would bring me.

Ready to be *me*. Unshackled. Loved. Happy.

EPILOGUE

Song: Dekha Ek Khwab
  - Lata Mangeshkar, Kishore Kumar, Amitabh Bachchan

Luke

Six months later
Meera was going to kill me. I was late. Really late. For the ninth day in a row. I quietly stepped inside our four-bedroom house in Ahmedabad. The first floor had just one night lamp on. The light in Meera's mom's bedroom was off, too.

In my defense, setting up the Indian branch for Wilson and White was no easy feat. It had taken me an entire month just to find an office space in the city. Some were in an awful building, some didn't have proper light and ventilation, and some were just too small.

The next few months were spent designing the office space, researching and hiring the contractors for the work, and then constantly monitoring every little detail. During that time, Meera decorated and arranged our house, and had already secured a teaching job in the same school we got Hari admitted to. Hari was beyond excited to be in the same class as one of Akira's cousins.

And Meera's mom was excited to live within walking distance of Akira's family.

Now, most days, she hung out with Akira's mom and aunts and grandmother, their conversation and company always leaving her happier.

Quietly, I placed the car key in the bowl above the shoe rack and climbed the stairs. The second floor had two rooms. Meera and I were in the primary bedroom, and Hari slept in the room across from us.

A faint light could be seen from under the door to his room. He was eleven and like my little brother. I knocked and, after three seconds, opened the door.

"Meera didi was angry," he said in English. Ever since we'd decided to move to the city, he's been serious about learning English. And we've been practicing.

I flinched at the update. "Was she really *really* mad?"

He had his iPad on his lap and looked about ready to sleep. But he laughed at my nervousness and said, "A big vein came on her forehead. And every time she looked at the clock, she did this."

He then proceeded to impersonate Meera shaking her head in disappointment.

"That bad, huh?"

He nodded. "We miss you at dinner."

Hari's words had the power to bring me to my knees. I sat at the foot of his bed and clutched his leg. "From tomorrow, I'll leave my office at six."

"Promise?" he asked, hope and relief in his voice.

"Promise. You done with all your homework?"

He nodded and said, "It was so easy. Meera didi checked it too. She said I can watch *Lord of the Rings*. With subtitles."

"That's great, buddy. But don't stay up too late. You gotta wake up before me."

He nodded, and after a kiss on his head, I left his room, silently closing the door behind me.

Just to come face-to-face with my very angry, very disappointed wife.

Yes. We had a court marriage three months ago. My parents came, and Meera's mom, Hari, and Kriti. We wanted to start living as a family as soon as possible. We planned to have a ceremony in the US once things were more settled and Meera's documentation and visa issues were sorted.

But right now, she looked at me like she wanted to eat me, and not in a good way.

"I love you," I said, bringing out the puppy dog eyes.

Her eyes softened, only for a second, but she quickly gathered herself, rolled back her shoulders, and said, "Be downstairs after your shower. I'll reheat the food."

She was about to pass by me to go downstairs, but I clutched her hand and asked in a low murmur, "You wanna join me?"

The glare that came my way was enough to *throw* me in the shower.

I freshened up as quickly as I could, pulled out the one thing that could help me from my bag, and went downstairs.

Delicious aromas of spices and onions wafted through our dining and kitchen area. The warm hanging light over the dining table was turned on, and Meera sat adjacent to where she'd placed the food.

Instead of sitting on the chair, I got down on my knees where Meera sat. Her eyes melted, and her body swayed, but her fists were clenched tight on the table. She really wanted to hold on to her anger. She was justified in her anger, too. I had told her I wouldn't stay late, but I really got into the work that Sam had sent me, and instead of breaking my stride and continuing it at home, I decided to finish it.

I held her hand that was on her lap and pressed a kiss on her knuckles. "I'm so sorry, baby."

Before she scolded me, I brought out the red rose I held behind my back. "A rose for my queen. I know I disappointed you. And it kills me that I did. But I promised Hari, *promised* him, that I would always leave work at six."

Her eyebrows rose in disbelief. "You promised him?"

I nodded quickly.

She plucked the rose from my hand and smelled the flower. "It's pretty," she mumbled, her eyes now warm like honey.

"How I missed you," I said and moved closer for a kiss.

She glared and clutched the front of my T-shirt in both her hands. "And whose fault is that?"

"Mine. My brain lost its way. Only a crazy person would choose to work when they had the most beautiful person with the best kisses in the world waiting for them at home."

"I knew I hadn't married a crazy person."

Then I kissed her. She pulled me closer and deepened the kiss. My hands moved under her T-shirt, caressing her waist and her back. Her spine arched, asking for more.

At that moment, my stomach gave a loud rumble.

Meera chuckled, her laugh grazing my lips, and my arousal kicked up a notch.

She pulled back from the kiss, though, and pointedly looked at the plate of food. "First food, then the other thing."

I nodded and quickly polished off the three paneer parathas with yogurt. Ever since we'd started living in Ahmedabad, and with nothing holding Meera back, she'd found a new pleasure in cooking, and I'd found a new pleasure in eating all that mouth-watering food.

I needed to contact Aakar and ask for his gym details because it would be too easy to let my body go with the amount of ghee and milk and sugar and cheese and paneer and potato in every new recipe my beautiful wife, my other half, the love of my life, came up with.

I was washing the utensils in the kitchen when Meera came up beside me and with one hand caressing my butt, said, "I got an interesting mail today."

I wiggled my butt and turned my lower body so she knew what she did to me, and asked, "Oh yeah?"

She moved her hand away with a wink and raised a red and golden envelope to my face. I rinsed my soapy hands as she tugged a red card out of the envelope.

"Is that a wedding invite?" I asked.

And it suddenly struck me. "No way!"

Meera laughed, knowing that I'd guessed it. She nodded and read the invitation aloud.

"Mr. Saurabh Pandya and Mrs. Reshma Pandya request your gracious presence on the occasion of the wedding of their daughter, Kriti Pandya, with Aakar Mishra, son of Mr. Pravin Mishra and Mrs. Shilpa Mishra, Saturday, the twenty-seventh of February."

"Holy shit, that's so soon."

"Right? I'm so excited. Kriti and I will be back in the same city again, living so close to each other."

"I hope she gets a job in the same school as you."

Meera did a little shimmying dance that made my hardening dick twitch. "Wouldn't that be just the best thing ever?"

"Second to only our lovemaking," I teased, trying to lead her into her sexy mood.

She all but snorted. "I don't even remember what that's like."

And my jaw dropped. She looked at her nails, at the fan, at the clean countertop. Everywhere but me while I tried not to choke.

"Meera," I gasped in mock outrage.

"What? It's been a while."

As she talked, I washed up all the remaining vessels and put them in the drying rack.

Quickly, I dried my hands with the towel and stepped closer to her.

With my finger, I lifted her chin so her eyes met mine. Her eyes still twinkled with amusement, but her lids lowered, telling me she too was aroused.

Moving closer so she felt the entire length of my cock, I murmured, "Missed me, did ya, baby? You are so going to taste *the best thing ever*, take *the best thing* ever, feel *the best thing ever*. So hard. So deep. So good. Any time you hear the words 'the best thing ever,' only one thing will come to your mind."

Her body shook with every word, and with her grip tight on my T-shirt, she whispered, "Less talking, more showing."

With that green light, I hefted her over my shoulder as I raced upstairs, only pausing to shut off all the lights and check all the locks.

Then I showed her *the best thing ever*, all the while knowing in the depth of my soul that *she* was the best thing that had ever happened in my life. Living with her, loving her, being her husband, and watching her reach new heights and achieve her dreams was the greatest joy of my life.

The End

GLOSSARY

Bataka poha: Bataka Poha made with flattened rice with tempered onions and potatoes along with curry leaves, flavored with basic spices, peanuts, sesame seeds, fresh cilantro with just right amount of sweetness and tanginess

Beta/Beti: child

Bhai: a term used to refer to an older brother

Dal: Dal is an Indian dish made from pulses such as chickpeas or lentils.

Didi: a term used to refer to an elder sister

Dhokla: A food, visually similar to cake and compositionally made from a batter of gram flour (from chickpeas), cooked by steaming, and typically eaten in India.

Dupatta: The dupattā, also called chunni, chunari and chundari, is a long shawl-like scarf traditionally worn by women in the Indian subcontinent to cover the head and shoulders.The dupatta is currently used most commonly as part of the women's shalwar kameez outfit, and worn over the kurta and the gharara.

Khandvi: Khandvi is a savory snack in Maharashtrian cuisine as well as in Gujarati cuisine of India. It consists of yellowish, tightly rolled bite-sized pieces and is primarily made of gram flour and yogurt.

Kurti: A kurti is a long-sleeved, collar-less tunic worn by women throughout Southeast Asia.

Sabzi: Sabzi, or subji, is an Indian term that defines simply a "vegetable dish.

Salwar-Kameez: The salwar kameez is a traditional outfit worn by Punjabi women. It comprises a pair of trousers known as the salwar and a tunic called the kameez. Traditionally, the salwar trousers are tailored to be long and loose-fitting with narrow hems above the ankles that are stitched to look like cuffs.

Roti: A type of flat, round South Asian bread

Rupees: 1 USD= 83.20 Indian Rupees

Patli-Velan: Rolling board and Rolling pin

AUTHOR'S NOTE

Dear readers, thank you so much for reading Luv Under Starlight.

According to "Accidental Deaths & Suicides I India 2021" report, a total of 10,881 persons involved in farming sector (consisting of 5,318 farmers/cultivators and 5,563 agricultural laborers) have committed suicides during 2021, accounting for 6.6% of total suicides victims (1,64,033) in the country.

I wanted to write a story that sheds light to the suffering of farmers in India. But more so, I wanted to write a story about the people left behind. I wanted to write a story about a family not only grieving the loss of a family member, but also dealing with insurmountable debt and other hardships. I wanted to write about women thrown into taking charge of their life, daughters growing up too soon and making sacrifices for their family and building a community and a safe space for themselves.

Having said that, I also didn't want to get too lost in the even more grim realities of the suffering of the farmers and their families. I deliberately chose to focus on romance and admit that I've taken many creative liberties to give a fairy-tale story to

Meera and Luke. I love romance. I love *love*. I hope you felt Luke and Meera's love and their connection. I hope this story brought you more joy than tears.

I hope I did justice to these incredible strong characters like Meera and Surbhi. If I offended anyone by my portrayal of any of my characters or storylines, I sincerely do apologize.

ACKNOWLEDGMENTS

This book wouldn't have happened without the support of so many incredible people.

I would like to thank my alpha readers – Afsha, Pallavi and Kruti. You guys gave me the push and the motivation I needed to finish writing the first draft. You guys have read the most number of revisions and rewrites and I couldn't be more grateful to you guys.

Julia, thank you for reading my book and giving me the invaluable suggestions to improve my book.

I would also like to thank three wonderful people who agreed to beta read my book – Anna P, Marianne and Andrea Gonzalez. Your commentaries, your suggestions, your critique helped me shape my book into what it is today. You guys are true romance readers, and your knowledge and thoughtfulness have truly elevated my book.

Thank you to all my bookstagram friends who have always supported me and stuck by me throughout my bookstagramd days and into my author days. Your support and encouragement means the world to me.

Thank you to my new booktok friends who have given me a chance and who continue to support me.

Thank you to every one of my wonderful readers who gave my books a chance, who messaged me and emailed me that you loved it, and who are helping me spread the word about it. Thank you from the bottom of my heart. I love you.

Thank you to my family for being so cool about me writing

romance books and showering me with all your love and blessings. I thank you even more for NOT reading my books.

And last and the most important, thank you to my husband, who's never once stopped believing in me, whose constant support is the reason that I've been able to write and publish books. I love you the most. Thank you for being the cutest and the coolest.

ABOUT THE AUTHOR

N.M. Patel is a passionate author who writes romance novels inspired by her love of Bollywood movies. Her books are filled with humor, steam, and plenty of love, featuring strong heroines and swoon-worthy heroes. Get ready to be transported into a world of desi culture, unforgettable characters, and a romantic escape that will leave you feeling warm and fuzzy inside.

You can find N.M. Patel on social media:
Sign up for her Newsletter for bonus content, monthly giveaways, writing tips, and more: https://dashboard.mailerlite.com/form...
Instagram: @nmpatelauthor
Tiktok: @nmpatelauthor

Made in the USA
Las Vegas, NV
05 December 2023

82152550R00213